THE
KINGDOM'S
RECKONING

ALSO BY NEENA LASKOWSKI

OF FIRE AND LIES

The Heir's Bargain: Fynn's Story (prequel)

The King's Weapon, book 1

The Crown's Shadow, book 2

The Throne's Undoing, book 3

The Kingdom's Reckoning, book 4

OTHER BOOKS

Between Blades and Vows

THE KINGDOM'S RECKONING

NEENA LASKOWSKI

OF FIRE AND LIES

BOOK FOUR

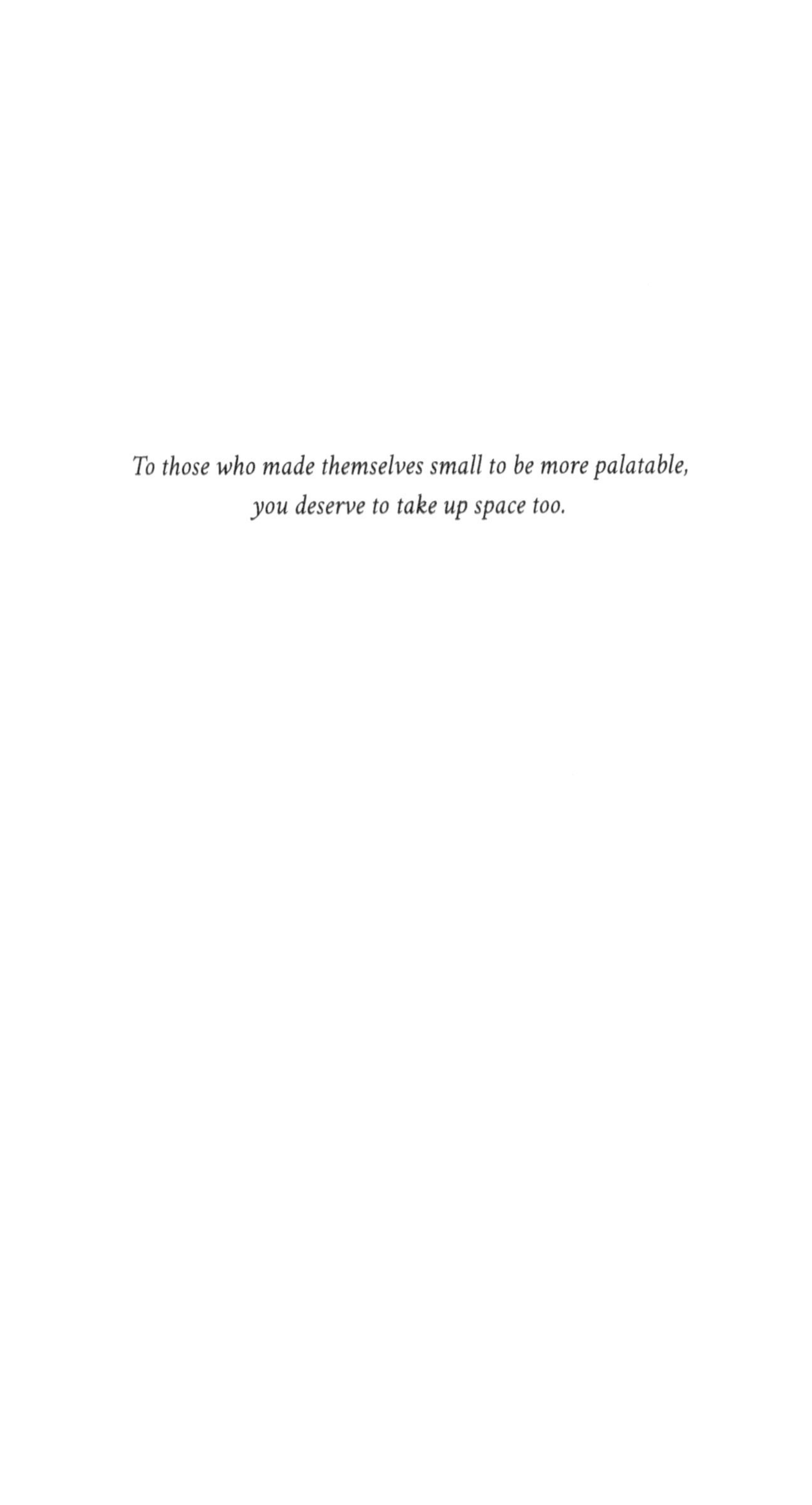

To those who made themselves small to be more palatable,
you deserve to take up space too.

THE SEVEN KINGDOMS OF VANERIA
THE MIST
THE WHISPERING SPRINGS
PONTIA
THE RED SEA
BORGAN
TWIN
THE THREE LADIES
TETRIA
THE QUEEN'S CROW

THE GLACIERS
RIVER OF ICE
RAGOLO
THE FROZEN LAKE
THE NORTHERN SEA
KADIA
LUCIAN R.
ALDERIAN MTNS
HIGH R.
TROJIAN MTNS
ZIA
LAKE OF TEARS
ARDENTOL

CONTENT WARNINGS

The Kingdom's Reckoning includes elements that may not be suitable for all readers, such as references to alcohol consumption, explicit content, mature language, violence, gore, manipulation, on-page death, and assault. If any of these topics are harmful to you, please proceed with care.

PRONUNCIATION GUIDE

Please note: these are fictional characters and places. The following pronunciations are simply the way the author pronounces them. However, if you, the reader, have a different way of pronouncing the names, please do so.

<u>*People*</u>

Cetia - *ket-EE-uh*

Domitius - *do-mi-TEE-us*

Esmeray - *es-mer-ay*

Euralys - *ur-el-ees*

Fynn - *fin*

Graeson - *grey-sin*

Danisinia - *dan-i-sin-EE-uh*

Dronias - *dro-NEE-us*

Kalisandre - *kal-ih-SAN-dra*

Kolen - KOL-en

Laurince - *lore-INS*

Lothian - loth-EE-in

Lundril - *LOON-dril*

Lysanthia - *lis-an-THI-uh*
Medenia - *muh-deen-EE-uh*
Myra - *MY-ra*
Mynhos - *myn-OS*
Rian - *RYE-in*
Sebastian - *sa-BASH-tin*
Sylvia - *sil-VEE-uh*
Terin - *TARE-rin*
Troia - *TROY-uh*

<u>Gods:</u>
Barinthian - bar-in-THI-an
Misanthia - *mis-an-THI-uh*
Nerva - *nur-VUH*
Pontanius - *pon-TAN-EE-us*
Ryla - *RYE-la*
Sabina - *sa-BEE-na*
Tanzia - *tan-ZEE-uh*

<u>Kingdoms:</u>
Ardentol - *ARE-den-tall*
Borgania - *bor-GAN-EE-uh*
Frenzia - *Frenz-EE-uh*
Kadia - *Cade-EE-uh*
Pontia - *Pont-EE-uh*
Ragolo - *ra-GOL-o*
Tetria - *te-TRI-uh*

PROLOGUE
KAGE

Kage ran his fingertips across the thousands of glass vials littering the shelves of the frigid storage room. The collection had grown into something quite outstanding, something beyond what he initially dreamed up decades ago. He paused at a section where a thick layer of dust had collected. He swiped a finger across the glass, wiping away the dust particles.

Most people feared anger. They ran from it, hid from it. They stuffed it down, tried to ignore it, and waited for it to fade away. To an extent, Kage understood their fear. More often than not, anger and rage were untamable beasts that could wrap their tendrils around your throat and choke you if you weren't careful. The king of Ardentol, however, was not afraid of his anger. He did not ignore it. He did not will it away or pretend that it would disappear on its own. Instead, he embraced it. He let it fester within him and build and build and build until he needed it most. Until he could use it to its full potential.

He hadn't always been this way, of course. Kage could vaguely recall a time in his life when he was like the rest of the world—when he, too, would run away from someone's anger and hide from his own. Those years, thankfully, were lost to time, and Kage Domitius was not in the business of going backward.

He plucked a vial from the shelf and spun the glass tube between his thumb and index finger. The liquid sloshed against the sides of the glass and splashed onto the bottom of the cork, soaking it.

While Kage hadn't anticipated the two prisoners escaping, he always had a plan in case things didn't go according to schedule. He hadn't gotten this far without creating contingency plans, after all.

"Sir," the captain of the King's Guard called from the entrance to the storage room. "She's ready."

Kage grabbed a second vial and handed both tubes to the young healer standing nearby. "Prepare the table. This should only take a moment."

With blood from the most recent transformation soiling his apron, Dr. Stone eyed the two vials warily as he took them. "Are you sure you wish to go through with this, Your Highness? Once we start, we cannot stop."

Kage tilted his head to the side.

When Dr. Thorne was training the young healer, Kage had done his best to stay as far away from him as possible. With Thorne's death, Kage no longer had a choice in the matter. The young man lacked the same quiet resolve the former healer had adopted in Kage's presence. Instead, Dr. Stone preferred to ask questions, to dig deep into the weeds of the experiments and the obstacles that they had faced over the years.

Kage stepped forward, and his nostrils flared at the iron coating Stone's apron. "Do not question my decisions, Dr. Stone."

The healer quickly bowed. "Of course, Your Majesty."

Huffing, Kage strolled past the healer and said to the captain, "Let's go, Lundril."

The door swung shut behind them. With the captain a step behind him, Kage made his way through the damp hallways beneath the castle. When he reached the secluded cell, Kage halted.

"Open the door."

Lundril slipped the key into the lock and twisted it, the mechanism clicking. As he opened the door, the hinges creaked. Torchlight spilled inside the small room, illuminating the prisoner within.

The seer lifted her head, the chain around her neck screeching as she moved. Leaning her head against the wall, Lysanthia squinted, her eyes adjusting to the sudden flood of light. "Is it time already?" she croaked.

Kage ignored the seer's question and stepped inside, his gaze sweeping across the four bare walls. The cell reeked, and his nose scrunched in disgust. "After all this time, I have to ask, do you enjoy being in this cell? Have the chains become a source of comfort?"

Lysanthia stared at him, her light gray eyes ghostly. Her thin, pale skin was even ghastlier.

"Not in a talkative mood today?"

"Ask what you seek, Kage," she said.

He sighed. There was usually more bite to the seer. Kage typically looked forward to their conversations. Lysanthia was one of the few people who ever dared challenge him. Even as the chains wore into her wrists and weighed her body down over the decades, she somehow maintained her spite. It was perplexing. Admirable, even.

He supposed he did have a schedule to keep. "You can see the future. You already know what I wish to know."

"There are many things I know, and many paths yet to be written," she answered as if bored.

"Do you ever grow sick of the riddles?" he asked, curious.

She cocked her head, and her greasy black hair fell to the side. "Not even in the slightest," she said with a saccharine smile.

There she was.

"It did not have to come to this, you know," Kage said.

It was a shame, really. She had been useful to him over the years. Some things weren't meant to last, though. He had learned that a long time ago.

"Are you afraid of death, Kage?" Lysanthia asked.

"I should be asking you that," he said, motioning for Lundril to come forward. The captain slid his sword from its sheath, and the steel blade gleamed in the torchlight.

"I have known my death was coming for decades," she said. "Once the tapestry has been woven, the future is sealed. But your future is still in the works, the stitches yet to be sewn. Because of this, I have seen your death many times. I have seen you die of old age, by fire, by blade." Her pale gray eyes roamed over him, observing him as she spoke.

Kage gave her nothing, though. He remained rigid, cold, indifferent.

Lysanthia continued, "The saddest instance, though, is the first. For when you are lying in your bed and time has finally strangled the life from you, I see the loneliness of a life that could have had so much love."

Kage tossed back an amused laugh. Here the seer was again, prattling about love. He did not care about such frivolous matters. Not anymore. Not when the power of the world was nearly in the palm of his hand. He snapped his fingers.

Lundril snatched Lysanthia by the chains hanging from her neck. She nearly toppled over, her feeble frame too weak to stay upright.

"You seek power to fill the void she caused," Lysanthia said, peering up at Kage through the greasy strands of hair that fell in front of her face. "You can take the stolen powers, you can create your monsters. But at the end of the day, no matter what you do, the void will never be filled."

Kage scoffed. "I do not wish to fill a void."

"Ah, that's right. You only wish for power." A smile split her face in two, revealing yellowed teeth. Her gray irises, once dull, now flared with amusement. "But your power will never compare to that of a god."

The muscles in his jaw ticked.

Catching the movement, Lysanthia smirked. "Do you wish to command Kalisandre again?"

Kage smoothed out a wrinkle on his suit jacket. "Soon, I will no longer need her."

"But she would make it easier. She is the key to your plans, the key to commanding the armies, is she not?"

He poked the inside of his cheek with his tongue. While he had built his army without Kalisandre, losing her required him to readjust certain aspects of his plans. He was making do, though.

"If you spare me, you could gain all that you wish and beyond."

He huffed. He had been right all along despite her claims. The seer did fear death. If she didn't, she would not have been bargaining with him today. "Why would I bother sparing you? Your use has run its course."

"Have I strayed you wrong yet?"

Lundril looked at him for the order, but the seer's question made Kage hesitate.

Kage thought the answer was simple, but when he considered it, everything she had told him, every direction he had led her in, had only gotten him closer to achieving his goals. The experiments had proven successful, his army had grown in strength and numbers, the war was starting, and his allies were falling in line.

"If you spare me, Kalisandre will try to save me for the one she loves. She will propose a trade: her for me. If you take it, you could have the power of the gods at your fingertips. The world will go up in flames because of you."

As if in response, the torchlight flickered in the reflection of Lundril's sword.

Kalisandre's emotions were always her weak point. Even as a child, she cared too much, too easily. When the handmaiden had stripped her of her emotions, Kalisandre had truly shined.

A smile stretched across Kage's lips.

Perhaps her weakness could be his advantage.

PART ONE

IGNITING THE FLAME

CHAPTER 1
KALLIE

Patience was a virtue that Kallie no longer possessed. Although if she was being honest with herself, she had never truly been a patient person.

When Kallie looked out the window, darkness still cloaked the sky, but she could see the ominous shades melting into soft purple hues. She leaned forward, her hip pressing against the wall and elbows digging into the windowsill. Her head rested heavily in her palm, her fingers tapping along the side of her cheekbone. Repeatedly, anxiously.

Dawn would arrive soon, which meant several hours had already passed since Domitius' declaration of war. When the messenger had read the letter aloud, haphazard plans were shouted, demands were spewed and ignored, insults were spat from every corner. Even though Kallie knew this was coming—by the gods, they all did— hearing the declaration chilled her to her bones and made her question everything she had been doing for the past few months.

Since Graeson and the others had saved her from marrying Rian and had torn her mind apart, Kallie had been too focused on putting back together the broken pieces of her soul that she had barely stopped to think about the consequences that were bound to come. Her ignorance had made her believe she was safe from Domitius' wrath. She had let herself *hope*. But hope, she was quickly learning, was a mirage, a false pretense meant to trick its victims into believing a sense of security before the Fates snatched it and crumbled it to ash in their palms.

Yet even with the time that had passed, the weeks of recovery, the weeks of unweaving the web of lies, Kallie still felt incomplete. Like a piece of pottery forced back together, where anything poured inside of it slipped through the imperfect seams.

After living with Domitius for almost eighteen years, Kallie was well aware of the type of man he was. Had she truly thought he would stop trying to take control of Vaneria? He had told her a war would come. He had warned her that the seven kingdoms would need to make a choice. That they would either be forced to stand with him or would fall before him. Kallie had never imagined that *she* would be the reason, though.

Even now, thousands of miles away, she was still the king's weapon. A device for him to use however he saw fit, a reason to start a frivolous war. She should have stormed back to Ardentol the second she woke up and ruined any chances he had of achieving his goal.

But she had no army, no troops to her name. She had no crown or authority.

Her nails dug into her cheek, the bite of pain sharp and bright. A tree-covered field stretched outside her window, and her eyes followed it before the field dipped beyond the horizon toward the city. A light breeze swept by, rustling the leaves in the nearby trees and stinging her eyes. Her vision blurred, a film of water rising to the surface and gathering on her lash-line. Blinking, she felt her lashes brush against her cheeks, wet and cold.

She wished she could blame the pain or the wind for the tears, but that would only be another lie she told to make herself feel better. Domitius would never stop. No matter what obstacle he came across, he always had an alternative plan.

Kallie pressed her palms against her temples, her nails scraping against her scalp.

Her thoughts went to the people in the castle, the lives that would be or already were irrevocably changed forever.

She thought of Medenia and Ophelia and how their hands interlocked after hearing the king's declaration of war. Blanched knuckles, wide eyes, ghostly faces. How their quivering gazes revealed the fears they didn't dare voice.

She thought of Emmett and Sylvia, who had left Pontia not only to save someone whom they didn't know but the very person who had destroyed their homes.

She thought of the Tetrian warriors clutching the hilts of their blades as they tipped their heads to the top branches of the towering oak tree sitting at the back of the dais. Their lips forming silent prayers to the gods.

She thought of Terin, who would now have to speak on behalf of an entire kingdom while simultaneously handling Esmeray's order for their return to Pontia.

But most of all, Kallie thought of Dani. How her anger and frustration seeped into every step she had taken in the throne room as she paced. How deep grooves creased her forehead as she silently assessed the strategies and outcomes. How she absentmindedly swept her hand across her swollen belly that could no longer be hidden beneath a loose blouse.

Kallie swiped at a tear that escaped, flicking it away before it could slide down her cheek.

Graeson had accidentally let it slip to Kallie that Dani was pregnant on the way back from the springs. And just as it had when he told her, Kallie's heart ached for Fynn, Dani, and their unborn child.

Even though the general was surrounded by friends, Kallie wondered if Dani felt alone. If she felt the pending weight of the world pressing down on her shoulders from the need to give the child a safe place to grow up.

Could a child truly flourish in a world soaked in darkness, a world plagued with endless conflict and greed? Kallie wasn't sure.

Outside, shadows lingered on the ground, sticking to the trees and pavement as if it refused to leave even as the sky bled into lighter hues.

Kallie tried to force back the tears, but they spilled down her cheeks, anyway. With her hand, she silenced her sobs as best she could.

She pushed away from the window, and a glint of silver sparkled in the faint moonlight, giving her pause. As if pulled by it, Kallie padded over to the desk, her bare feet lightly tapping against the cold oak floors. She ran her hand across the back of the chair, the wood rough beneath her palms. As her gaze trailed over the gem-encrusted hilt that glittered in the moonlight, Domitius' voice rose in the back of her mind and threatened to pull her down.

Your emotions will be your downfall.

He had said those words to her countless times, but Kallie refused to cower from her emotions any longer. Tears were not a sign of weakness. Her emotions were not a flaw. Kallie picked up the blade Myra had gifted her years ago and ran her thumb across the words scrawled on the polished metal.

You are the holder of your own fate.

A pang of grief soaked her bones. The dagger was one of two possessions Kallie still could claim as hers.

Although Kallie did not miss being under Domitius' control by any means, she yearned for part of the girl she was back then. The one who did not second-guess her actions. The one who did not let others speak on her behalf. The girl who did not question her purpose.

When the letter had arrived, Kallie had stood silent in the throne room, allowing the others to control the conversation. She should have spoken up. At the very least, she should have demanded that Cetia allow her to attend the meeting. Instead, she had stayed silent out of fear and cowardice.

Not only did Kallie fear the unknown, but she feared herself too. Despite Domitius' claws having been ripped from her mind, Kallie still did not trust herself.

But a decision hadn't been made yet, had it?

There was still time.

Kallie slid the sheath over the blade and stuffed the dagger behind the waistband of her skirt, tucking it beneath her blouse. She slipped on a pair of flats and strolled toward the door with quiet, light footsteps. Turning the doorknob, she peered through the crack. When she found no guard outside her door, she pushed it open but came to an abrupt halt when she heard a soft snore. Her gaze fell upon the man slouched against the wall, head hanging down. Raven-black hair fell over features softened only in sleep.

Graeson slept soundlessly beside her door, his chest rising and falling at a steady rhythm. His fingers twitched in his lap, but he did not stir otherwise. Her gaze shifted to his soft lips, which were slightly parted.

Their conversation before they had parted ways outside the throne room came rushing back to her.

"I'm here if you need anything," Graeson had told her.

She vaguely recalled him shifting on his feet as if he wanted to comfort her but didn't know how. She could see the words on his lips, the plea for her to come back to his room, that she shouldn't be alone. And maybe he had asked her, but the fog in her mind had been too thick to make sense of his words at the time.

She desperately wanted to be the type of person who could lean on him.

Or maybe that's simply what Graeson wanted. He wanted to be her savior. He wanted what they had shared earlier that night to have changed things. And it did, but not in the way Graeson wanted it to.

Kallie could no longer say she did not care for Graeson, but her feelings for him didn't matter. Love and war did not mix. Love and war were a recipe for disaster and heartbreak.

Dragging her attention from Graeson's sleeping form, she scanned the hallway and listened for the sound of guards patrolling the halls.

When only silence greeted her, Kallie closed the door behind her as quietly as she could and quickly padded down the hall, her mind set. Whether or not she was mad at Myra, Kallie couldn't ignore the ancient words etched into the blade that stared back at her with such intensity. Kallie was the holder of her own fate, and she would be damned if she let someone else decide the course of her life again.

CHAPTER 2
KALLIE

A SINGLE GUARD STOOD ON DUTY OUTSIDE THE PRISON. UPON SEEING Kallie, the woman immediately straightened and fisted the small throwing knife she had been previously spinning.

With the dagger pressing against her back, Kallie held up her hands. "I only wish to speak with one of them."

The guard snorted, her posture relaxing and amusement tipping up the corner of her lip. "Be my guest," she said, ushering Kallie forward before spinning the blade again.

Kallie's brows shot up her forehead, surprised the guard didn't argue further.

Fearing the guard might change her mind, Kallie thanked her and hurried down the steps. But as she descended the stairs, Kallie wondered if there was a reason for the guard's easy compliance. Kallie quickly brushed the concern off, though. She had come here for a reason, and she wouldn't turn back now.

A couple of fading sconces hung at each end of the prison. She counted eight cells on each side. She wondered if this was simply a temporary holding place for prisoners. She had visited the castle's dungeon in Ardentol many times, and it was at least five times the size of this one.

Kallie shuffled down the aisle, her head swiveling back and forth as she looked inside each cell. The closest cells were empty, but she halted at the second set, her breath catching.

Were her eyes playing tricks on her? It wasn't humanly possible. There was no way—

"If you're worried about us breaking out," a tired voice said, which Kallie quickly recognized belonging to the captain of Rian's guard, "don't bother. I already tried. It's impossible—except for whoever or *whatever* broke apart those bars."

Indentations marked the bars, grooves that she bet would perfectly match Graeson's fingers. Hands that had touched her with such tenderness, such longing that it was hard to fathom they could cause this sort of destruction. Kallie had heard rumblings about Graeson escaping a cell after they had first arrived. She hadn't given the rumors much heed, but seeing the curved bars with her own eyes sent a chill down her spine. She thought she had seen every side of Graeson, but she was beginning to think she had merely scratched the surface.

A normal person would have been afraid. A normal person would have been concerned. But Kallie had never once felt in danger in Graeson's presence. Instead, Kallie could only think about how scared he must have been in that moment. Had he trembled later that night like he had when she found him in the woods?

Kallie shook the thoughts away. Now was not the time.

Refocusing on her reason for coming here, she forced her feet forward, but she didn't make it far.

Laurince slammed his fist against the bars of his cell the moment Kallie came into view. "What are you doing here?" he demanded, rising to his feet.

Kallie held up her hands in acquiescence. "I didn't come here to fight with you. I came here only for answers."

"We've already been questioned," he spat, the veins on the sides of his neck quickly becoming more predominant. "Or do they still doubt our intentions and have finally decided to use their little pet to see if we're lying?"

"What are you—" Kallie choked on her words.

He *knew*. He knew what Kallie could do, which could only mean one thing: Myra told them.

Laurince smirked, the twitch of his mouth anything but kind. "You don't feel so righteous now that we know your little parlor trick, huh?"

"Laurince."

Kallie went rigid at the sound of the Rian's hollow voice.

None of this was going as planned. She had thought that they would all be asleep, that she would be in and out. But the captain and Rian were proving that was easier said than done.

"Rian, she—"

"Is not worth your time," Rian said, cutting off Laurince.

Rian's words shouldn't have hurt her, yet they were a punch to her gut. Kallie peered into the cell across from the sneering captain. Rian sat against the wall at the back of the cell. His wine-red hair was longer and more unkempt than when they were in Frenzia together. His shirt was covered in grime, and the collar was wrinkled and worn around his neck. His brown skin was dull in the shadows of the cell.

Rian was the man she was supposed to make fall in love with her, the man whose crown she was supposed to steal. He had the right to be angry with her.

While Kallie might not have been locked inside a cell for the past few months, she knew what losing control felt like. She knew what it felt like to watch one's world fall apart in the palm of one's hand, unable to stop it from crumbling, no matter how hard one tried to keep it together.

Kallie exhaled a soft apology.

Rian didn't move.

Maybe he hadn't heard her? She cleared her throat and stepped closer. "Rian, I—"

"I heard you," Rian snapped.

"Oh," Kallie mumbled, the apology thick in her throat. She shifted on her feet, uncomfortable.

"Is that it, then?" Rian asked, head still hanging low.

Kallie blinked. "Pardon?"

Rian lifted his head, and Kallie barely stopped herself from retreating when his eyes locked onto hers. The nearby sconce cast dark, heavy shadows beneath his eyes. Even before today, there had been a sadness that lingered in the green hues from the grief of his father's death. While Kallie may not have recognized it months ago, there had once been a molecule of hope flickering in the sea of green. Now, there wasn't a single drop, and its absence surprisingly gutted her.

"Is that why you are here? To apologize?" Rian clarified, his tone colder than she had ever heard it. He didn't just hate her; he *loathed* her.

"I—" Kallie spun her mother's ring around her finger, the metal threatening to carve into her skin. Apologizing wasn't the initial reason for the visit, but she couldn't say that to him. Rian deserved an apology, and maybe she should have considered his anger before coming here tonight.

It was too late now, though.

Pressing his palms against his knees, Rian stood. He strolled forward, every step filled with malice. "What exactly are you apologizing for, Kalisandre?" He didn't give her a chance to respond, though, and barreled forward. "Let me see if I can help jog your memory. Are you apologizing for lying to me about the reason for our engagement? Are you apologizing for pretending to have an interest in me when you were just using me for my crown and army?"

"Rian, I—"

But Rian wasn't done. He tore her apart, word by word. "Or perhaps for cutting off our engagement and destroying my kingdom's sacred temple in the process?"

"I didn't mean—I didn't know about the attack!" Kallie sputtered. It was as if she was being doused with buckets of water. She struggled to find the correct words—the words that would make it right—for none existed.

"No?" Rian released a bitter laugh. Shadows danced across his face as he stepped closer to the bars. "Or maybe you're apologizing for my brother stealing my throne because of the mess *you* created?"

Each remark stung worse than the last. Sweat pooled at the back of Kallie's neck as she held her breath. From the corner of her eye, she saw movement from the fourth set of cells.

"Or are you apologizing for manipulating me every second we were together?"

There were no words to explain everything she had done. Everything that came to mind felt like an excuse.

"Oh, my apologies, *love*. Was that harsh of me?" Rian asked, blinking down at her, his lashes brushing the tips of his brown cheeks.

"Not harsh enough if you ask me," Laurince interjected, leaning against the bars.

Hands shaking at her sides, Kallie took a jilted step away from the two cells. "I want to fix things."

Kallie winced when the men laughed.

"*Fix* things? Everything you touch turns to shit." Laurince slid down the wall and sat on the floor with a shake of his head, his arms falling lazily over his knees.

"I know," Kallie admitted, forcing herself to continue. "I know that this is my fault. I didn't come here to deny that."

"You shouldn't have bothered to come at all," Rian said.

This was going absolutely terribly. Maybe she was cursed. Maybe she had angered the gods or the Fates.

Still, she refused to back down.

"Rian, I know my word no longer holds any weight, but I am deeply sorry for lying to you, for betraying you, for all of it. But—"

"Of course there's a fucking but," Laurince spat.

Kallie ignored the captain and continued. "As much as I wish I could, I cannot change the past. All I can do is hope to make the future better."

"And war is your solution?" Rian asked, his features painfully contorted.

Lifting her chin, Kallie clenched her fists at her sides to steady them. "That is why I'm here: to stop it," she said with as much conviction as she could gather.

"Ha! You and what army, Princess?" Laurince hissed.

Shaking his head, Rian returned to the back of his cell and plopped on the ground. "You're too late, Kalisandre."

Kallie bit the inside of her cheek, the pain pinching. She had to believe there was still time to fix this. Because if there wasn't, everyone's sacrifices would have been for naught.

"War was always going to come," Kallie said, voice quiet yet steady. "Our absence—our supposed abduction—is simply the reasoning Domitius has gone with. But there is something else that has been bothering me since the three of you showed up."

"Which is?" Rian asked.

Kallie glanced at the bent bars of the destroyed cell before returning her attention to Rian. "How did you do it? How did you escape?"

Rubbing his bruised wrists, Rian glanced at Laurince.

"We fought our way out," Laurince explained, his head slumped back against the wall. "We almost didn't make it. We *shouldn't* have made it, but by the graces of the gods, we weren't followed."

"You didn't find that strange?" Kallie asked, her hands falling from the iron bars.

The captain shrugged. "At the time, I was too busy making sure none of us died. I was injured. I—it was hard enough to keep going as it was. While the thought crossed my mind, I didn't dare question it since I was barely hanging on myself. We needed a blessing, and we got one."

"So you mean to tell me that Domitius didn't send *anyone* after you?" Kallie asked, the question painted in doubt.

Laurince's lips parted and shut, unable to find an answer.

"Why would he bother if he was planning on declaring war?" Rian asked.

Even if that was the reason, something still wasn't sitting right.

"He could have declared war at any point. I was here," Kallie stated. "He didn't need to involve you. So while I'm not surprised he's declared war, I am surprised he waited this long and let us all go. According to Graeson and the others, he let them take me the day of our wedding. But if there's one thing I know about Domitius, it's that he doesn't do things without reason. So what's changed? Why didn't he declare war earlier? Why did he wait? Why did he let you go unscathed?"

The sound of chains scraping against the cement floor called Kallie's attention to the last occupied cell, the true reason she had come here. Myra leaned against the bars, listening to the conversation. Her blonde hair hung down her back in thick, limp strands, its normal sheen dull. The hem of her wrinkled skirt was torn, the fabric stained with dirt and grime from traveling.

Kallie forced her feet forward because, as long as Kallie could remember, Myra was always there, listening, watching, observing. "Earlier, you said Domitius' plans were twofold. What else is he doing?"

Myra's face paled. She wiped the palms of her hands down the sides of her skirt. "He's been performing tests on people with abilities. I think he…I think he seeks to acquire them for himself."

Sweat coated Kallie's palms as Myra's words settled in her stomach.

That can't be true, Kallie thought.

Had that been his goal the entire time? Was that why he wanted *her*? To steal Kallie's ability? If Domitius acquired it, he would be unstoppable.

"Was he successful?" she asked, fear coating every syllable.

Myra's gaze fell to the ground. When she spoke, a slight tremble rang through her voice. "I can only assume he was. I never…I never saw what happened to the victims."

"What victims?" Kallie asked, needing to know the truth yet fearing it all the same.

"Pontians," Myra answered quietly. "He—he's been collecting them."

"*Collecting* them?" Outrage filled Kallie's voice, her previous intention to stay calm long forgotten.

Myra nodded, expression haunted.

"That—" Kallie shook her head, taking a step back. Her back hit the bars of Laurince's cell, and she jumped, startled. "There's no way that's true," she whispered.

There was very little that Domitius could do that would surprise her. So it wasn't his cruelty that shocked Kallie, rather that he had most likely done it under the same roof as her. How had Kallie never noticed? How had—

Her lungs dropped to the bottom of her stomach.

How many times had Domitius left the castle for some mysterious excursion? How many times had he returned with some stranger and requested Kallie's assistance in forcing them to speak the truth when the king interrogated them?

Kallie had never stayed around to witness the interrogations. Domitius had never allowed her to, only asked Kallie to use her gift before sending her away. Was it possible the individuals had been Pontians? That they were the ones he had been collecting? Had she been helping Domitius even more than she initially thought?

Her legs trembled, on the verge of buckling. She was going to be sick. How many times was she going to discover the hidden truths behind her actions? How many times would she be forced to face the fact that she was a monster? The very reason for Vaneria's ultimate demise?

"What did he do to them?" Kallie asked, her heart pounding in her eardrums.

Myra's gaze grew distant, as if she was somewhere else, as if a ghost of her past was haunting her. She shook her head as if to rid herself of the resurfacing memories. "Like I told Queen Cetia, he has been turning some of them into the creatures Rian called drakonises."

"But Nyrri isn't human," Kallie said, certain of at least this.

"If Nyrri was one of the earlier experiments, Sebastian probably wasn't testing his experiments on humans yet. Things have… developed," Myra said, rubbing the back of her neck with her palm.

"Are they all Pontians?" Kallie asked. She wondered how many people were undergoing the transformation. What horrors were they facing right now? How many people were there who were still suffering?

"No," Myra said with a shake of her head. She glanced at Rian and Laurince, her brows drawing tight and something unidentifiable passing between the three of them. "He tried to transform His Majesty as well."

Kallie looked at Rian, whose face was masked in shadows as he sat at the back of his cell.

"If we hadn't—" Myra choked on her words.

Kallie could only guess what Myra was about to say. If they hadn't escaped when they had, Rian might not have been sitting in that cell.

Myra cleared her throat. "Domitius told me that his true goal was to give the giftless the same abilities."

"He can't do that. That goes against the ways of the gods." But the moment Kallie spoke the words aloud, she knew better than to doubt Domitius. If this was his goal the entire time, then nothing would stop him from achieving it, not even the gods.

Swallowing the rising fear threatening to drown her, Kallie forced herself to voice the question she feared the most: "How? How is he doing it?"

"It was supposed to be you," Myra whispered, her fingers curling into the cotton fabric of her wrinkled skirts. Her back hit the wall, and her voice trembled when she spoke. "You were supposed to be the one to force them into obeying. But when you hadn't come back, he had to find another way. The healer said the victims needed to be willing to receive the serum or else they wouldn't take to the transformations. I—" Myra's bottom lip wobbled, and she bit it as tears slipped free. Instead of swatting them away, Myra let them fall down the contours of her pale face. Slowly, as if the weight of the tears hanging on her lashes was too heavy to bear, she lifted her glossy gaze to meet Kallie's. The gold flecks within her hazel eyes glistened with water. "You were supposed to be the one, but you weren't there. I had no choice. I had to—"

"You always have a choice," Kallie snapped. She pulled the dagger out, unsheathing it.

Myra choked on a gasp, the whites of her eyes widening. Laurince shouted at Kallie, his arms popping through the spaces between the bars, but Kallie dodged them.

She held the dagger up to Myra's face. "*You* are the holder of your own fate," Kallie spat, flashing the words etched into the metal blade so Myra could see them. "*You* had these very words etched on here, not me."

Myra would not blame Kallie for this. People could blame Kallie for anything else, but not this. Not these experiments. What Myra had done to aid Domitius in his pursuits was not Kallie's doing.

"You don't understand. He—he had my brother."

Kallie flinched. "Your *brother*? You don't have a brother."

"I do," Myra said. But then quieter, she corrected herself, "I did."

Kallie didn't understand. She had known Myra for over nine years. She had spent nearly every day with her until a few months ago. If Myra had a brother, Kallie would have known. Right?

But as she stared at the woman, whom Kallie had once believed to be her best friend, Kallie no longer knew who she was looking at.

"You never…you never told me," Kallie whispered.

"I didn't know if he was alive. I didn't—" Myra rubbed the heel of her palm across her chest. "I didn't want to jeopardize his life if he was still alive. Domitius…he used him as a bargaining chip. He kept him hidden away, always promising I would get to see Mynhos if I just did this *one* thing. But his list never ended."

Myra's voice was thick and haunted, and then Kallie realized what Myra had said: she *had* a brother.

A pang of loss struck Kallie in her chest. Once, she would have reached out and offered Myra comfort, but now…

Now, Kallie didn't know what to do.

"Frenzia was supposed to be the end. I was supposed to be

released once..." Myra's voice trailed off, but Kallie heard the unspoken words: once Kallie married Rian.

"There's a lot you didn't know back then," Myra said, pushing through the heavy silence that had formed. "But it doesn't excuse what I did. I know I have betrayed you, and I know I may never regain your trust. But..."

Kallie's sea-storm eyes locked onto Myra's and remained there as the two women stared at each other in silence. They had both made irreparable mistakes, but Kallie was realizing it wasn't that simple. They were both at fault for so many wrongs that had come to pass over the years. But more than that, they were both victims. They had both been led to believe many lies. Both of their actions were at the root of the coming war that neither of them wished to take part in. Yet they would each have to play a part in it if they wished to take down the king.

While forgiveness was not something Kallie was prepared to offer, there was a sort of understanding that passed between the two women.

Myra gripped the iron bars that separated them, her fingers flexing over the metal. "He needs to be stopped."

"He will be," Kallie promised.

"You know, that's all fine and dandy, but how do you expect to stop him?" Laurince demanded from his cell, annoyance hanging on every syllable. "You have no military."

Kallie's gaze flitted across the floor as though the answer was written there. She had come here for an answer, for a solution. Instead, she found only more questions. Then Myra spoke up.

"There's something else I have to tell you."

CHAPTER 3
GRAESON

Graeson was burning from the inside. He jerked, but chains held him down, bolting him to the ground. The metal pinched his skin, the manacles too tight around his wrists and ankles. He yanked his arm back, but it only made him scream out in pain as his shoulder popped out of its socket. He collapsed onto the ground as the fire within overwhelmed him.

"Make it stop!" he shouted into the void. But no matter how loudly he yelled or how much he screamed, the pain didn't relent.

He tried to calm his mind; he tried to think of anything else. But he couldn't. All he could focus on was the heat that was overtaking him. All he could feel was the flames licking at his bones and crawling its way up his body, the heat increasing with every passing moment.

Graeson could find no reprieve, no salvation from the ravenous heat that tore through his chest and up his limbs and neck. Sweat coated his forehead and dripped from his raven-black hair. He exhaled, and the released air burned his lungs as if he had inhaled smoke.

A breeze brushed his skin, but it did little to soothe the pain from the scorching heat. Instead, the temperature of the flames only grew hotter.

"Give in," a low voice whispered.

Graeson lifted his head, searching for the source of the voice. All around him, shadows danced, but he couldn't make out the form. He tried to call out, but his throat burned, the pain too great.

"What are you waiting for?" the voice asked. "Why do you insist on walking among mortals when you should be above them?"

A shadow slithered across the ground, spreading and melting over the stone.

"It's almost time," the shadow hissed.

Graeson tried to focus on the shifting shadow, but his vision blurred. He coughed, and smoke filled his lungs. The fire was no longer contained inside his body. But he was now *on* fire. As the flames crawled over him, drowning him, Graeson saw the shadow blink at him.

GRAESON JOLTED FORWARD, his fingers digging into the thin blanket. His skin was slick with sweat, drenching the sheets and pillow. He tried to take a deep breath but nearly choked when he smelled the faint aroma of charcoal and smoke.

The nightmare had returned.

CHAPTER 4
KALLIE

SEVERAL SHARP YELPS FILLED THE COUNCIL ROOM AS KALLIE BURST through the doors. Chairs screeched against the wooden floor. Before Kallie could even take more than two steps inside, hands wrapped around her wrists. Her body sprang back, and her head jerked forward. Strands of chestnut hair slipped free from her bun and tickled her skin. Through the pieces of hair, Kallie spotted every face turn toward her, eyes wide and mouths agape.

When Kallie had decided to crash the council meeting, she had intended to walk through the doors with her head held high, her hair perfectly tucked into a low bun, and her dress unwrinkled. Not looking like some unhinged person.

One stubborn piece of hair brushed the tips of her eyelashes. She blew it away, but it fell down and danced in front of her eyes again as if to say, *I told you this was a stupid plan.* But what else was she supposed to do when the guards had denied her entry? Turn around?

With a sneer, Kallie yanked one arm, trying to rip it free from the guard's grasp. The woman tightened her hold.

"Have you always been one for the dramatics, Kalisandre?" Cetia asked, sitting in a wingback chair at the head of the table. The Queen was one of the few individuals who appeared unfazed by the disturbance. Maybe even amused. Not a single drop of tea had spilled over the edge of the porcelain cup in her hand.

"Ever since she was a child," Terin answered, calling Kallie's attention to the opposite end of the table where the Pontian prince leaned back in his chair. Her brother scratched his jawline in a poor attempt to hide his amusement. "Some things never change, it seems."

Ignoring the brief flash of nostalgia for a life she did not remember, Kallie ripped her arm free from the guard's hold at last. "I apologize for the disruption, Your Majesty," she said, forcing her voice to sound even. "The guards refused to open the doors when I had asked nicely."

"*Nicely?*" the guard to her left retorted. "You demanded and threatened to chop off our heads.

Kallie rolled her eyes. "Now that's a bit dramatic, don't you think? I said your hair, not your heads."

She had been as nice as the circumstances had allowed. At least she hadn't manipulated them.

"Your Majesty, we're happy to escort Princess Kalisandre out," the other guard said.

Cetia flicked her hand, her sharp black nails slicing through the air. "No need. She may stay."

Kallie brushed her hair away from her face, not bothering to hide her satisfied smirk when the guards reluctantly released her. The two women bowed to the queen before departing.

"I was wondering if you were going to show up before we started or if you would make us wait. Come. Sit." Cetia gestured toward the surrounding chairs.

Medenia, who sat on Cetia's right, smiled brightly at Kallie when their gazes met. The princess' ink-black hair was twisted into a single braid draped over her shoulder. She wore a simple but elegant sage-green dress layered with a black leather corset that was embroidered with beautiful beadwork. Myra would have been in awe of its artistry.

The fleeting thought took Kallie by surprise, but she shoved it down along with the mess of emotions accompanying it.

Scanning the rest of the table, she searched for an open chair. Around the enormous table sat nearly a dozen strangers. Kallie tried not to let the less-than warm welcome of the Tetrians creep under her skin.

"You can sit here," Terin suggested, offering the seat to his left. His white-collared shirt was cleanly pressed, but the purple hue beneath his eyes gave him a rather disheveled appearance.

With a tight smile, Kallie strutted forward but stumbled at the sight of Dani. Her brown hair had been twisted into a loose bun atop her head. A few stray curls framed her face, drawing attention to her hazel eyes, the deep green hues prominent in the light seeping in through the large windows. But it was the curl of Dani's lip, her raised brow, and her arms folded across her chest that had Kallie pausing.

The general snorted and looked away.

Doing her best to squash the rising embarrassment, Kallie took the seat across from Dani. For years, she had wanted to have a seat at the table. She would not let a small misstep ruin this moment.

"I am surprised you arrived before Graeson, and especially without him," Cetia said, tapping her nails along the table.

Kallie grimaced. "He's with Nyrri. I told him I was going to meet him, but…" She shrugged, but the guilt made the movement stiffer than she had intended.

"How long do you think it'll take him to realize you tricked him?" Ellie asked, her gaze sweeping across the table as she leaned forward. Like the rest of the warriors, Ellie was clad in an all-black ensemble. "Shall we place bets?"

"Oh! Yes!" Medenia interjected with a raised hand and a wide smile. She tapped her rosy cheek with a long nail and pursed her lips before declaring her guess with a finite nod. "I give him an hour."

With a laugh, Ellie flipped her paper-white hair over her shoulder. "An *hour*? The man can barely go ten minutes without knowing where she is," the warrior said, pointing at Kallie and causing her face to redden. "If she doesn't show up, he'll—"

"Can we please return to the matter at hand?" Dani interrupted, massaging her temples with two fingers. "There's a war that will be knocking on our doorsteps any day now, yet you two wish to place bets about whether Graeson can keep his—"

Cetia cleared her throat, and Dani mumbled an apology.

Cetia took a long sip of tea before setting it down. "As you are all aware, late last night, the guards in the east found and brought three individuals here, including the king of Frenzia. Shortly after their arrival, a letter arrived from Domitius declaring war."

To the council, Cetia relayed the information Rian and the others had revealed to them, from Sebastian abducting Rian after the wedding to the beasts Domitius and Sebastian were creating. All the while, Kallie patiently waited, her hands folded in her lap and her back stick-straight as she observed the room and everyone's reactions to the news. Those who were not present last night and had not heard about the experiments were horrified, their faces paling and eyes widening.

The council members had all seen Nyrri roaming about the gardens over the past few months, but until then, they only had their assumptions about how the drakonis came to be. With this new information, the weight of Sebastian's actions sat heavily in the room. Nyrri was only among the first of the drakonises to exist.

Based on what Myra had revealed last night, Kallie feared what was to come if Sebastian and Domitius were now experimenting on humans too. While she wanted to hope that Nyrri's temperament was not an anomaly, the sick twisting of her gut suggested otherwise.

"Do we think King Rian had anything to do with the declaration?" an unfamiliar councilwoman asked when Cetia finished.

"While I think it is a strange coincidence, I do not believe that the three individuals have come here with ill-intent," Cetia said. "Are you in agreement, Kalisandre?"

Kallie's eyes widened at the direct question. "Your Majesty?"

"Do you believe King Rian and his two companions are working with Domitius? After all, you visited the prisoners last night, did you not?"

Kallie's face flushed bright red. In her periphery, she saw Dani raising her brows in suspicion.

With her mouth drawn in a flat line, Kallie nodded. "I did visit them, Your Majesty, and based on our conversation, no, I do not."

Dani scoffed and leaned back in her chair. "Why should we believe you? You were on the other side of this war not long ago."

Terin dropped his face into his palm. "Not this again," he mumbled. He made to face Dani, but when his lips parted, Kallie placed a hand atop his.

This was her fight, not his.

"You can distrust me all you want, but I am not lying. We are on the same side here."

"*We?*" Dani sneered. "Don't tell me your friend took a page from your book and gave you some sob story to make you believe her?"

"Myra didn't need to," Kallie said, forcing her voice to remain calm. Anger would do her no good here. She addressed the entire room. "Acting as my handmaiden, Myra has been by Domitius' side for years. She has been a part of conversations that even I was not privy to when I was under his control. The bottom line is she has information we need. It would be unwise to dismiss that."

"Such as?" Cetia asked, her interest piqued.

Kallie relaxed her shoulders. This was why she had come here. To make a stand, to end this. She couldn't do that without giving everyone all the information. "Domitius has been abducting Pontians and stealing their blood in order to recreate the gifts the gods have given them."

"Th-that's not possible," Dani breathed out, horror flooding her features and dulling her warm complexion.

Terin grabbed Kallie's wrist. "Are you sure?" he asked, his deep brown eyes darting across her face, searching for another possibility.

Kallie nodded. "I'm sure."

Terin's gaze fell to the table, unfocused and defeated.

"Why didn't the handmaiden say as much last night then?" Dani demanded, eyes narrowing. "*If* this is true, why didn't she tell us when she had the chance? Why did she admit it only to you?"

"If you recall, the conversation was cut short when the letter arrived and some people had some choice words to say," Kallie said, glaring at Dani.

Dani's expression hardened. When the letter had arrived, Dani had demanded immediate action. Those present had proceeded to talk over one another, their words and demands blending together and becoming incomprehensible. With a slam of her cane against the dais, the Queen had silenced them all, demanding everyone return to their beds and ending the conversation for the night.

"According to Myra, this has been Domitius' ultimate goal the entire time: to give powers to the giftless."

The center of Terin's forehead creased as his brows drew

together. "Domitius did say something to Graeson on the day of your wedding. I had thought nothing of it then, but…"

"What did he say?" Kallie asked when his words trailed off. The beat of her heart was a thunderous roar as she considered the possibilities. Fear welled up inside her, and she struggled to get ahold of it.

"He said something about being a collector of useful things and that Graeson would be a valuable piece in his collection." Terin held his head between his hands as if it was too heavy to hold up on its own. "I-I didn't even…I hadn't known what he had meant, but if what you say is true, then…"

Terin and Kallie exchanged worried glances, their thoughts no doubt aligning. If Domitius got his hands on Graeson, neither of them wanted to think about the fatal consequences that would come about. But even Domitius, who had trained Kallie and was a force to be reckoned with, wouldn't have been a match for Graeson. Kallie knew that like she knew the back of her hand, and yet…

"Prepare the warriors, Cetia," an older woman said, calling Kallie's attention back to the present.

"Grandmother is right," Medenia said.

Grandmother?

Kallie's mouth fell open as she gawked at the woman, realizing who she was. Loralaine Perseianes was one of Tetria's first queens when Vaneria separated into seven kingdoms. Kallie had read so many stories about her—stories Domitius had failed to keep away from her. Loralaine was among the first Tetrians who had stepped onto the battlefield and one of the last to leave it. Her aim was one of the deadliest of her generation, not only in Tetria but all of Vaneria. She was legendary. Loralaine's hair was now as white as salt, her skin thin and nearly translucent, the small blue veins beneath predominant. The Great War had happened one hundred years ago, which meant that Loralaine must have been—

"Don't do the math," Terin whispered in her ear as if hearing her thoughts. "It will give you a headache."

Kallie's cheeks reddened, and she snapped her jaw shut.

"When we agreed to attend the royal wedding," Medenia said, forcing Kallie's attention away from the former queen, "we put ourselves at risk of being in the middle of whatever came after. We must lie in the bed we made."

"Spoken like a true queen," Loralaine said with pride.

Medenia beamed at her grandmother's appraisal, but it was short-lived.

"You are not a queen yet, Medenia. If war can be avoided, we must consider it," Cetia said.

"A war has already been declared, Mo—" Medenia cleared her throat, noticing Cetia's fingers flexing around the emerald orb atop her cane. "Your Majesty."

"We can still end it before it begins," Cetia said.

"Domitius' plan is set into motion. Words will not stop it," Medenia argued.

"But *her* words could."

Every head turned toward Kallie, and she tried not to shrink back into her chair at their renewed interest in her.

"I—" But Kallie didn't get much farther than that before Dani interrupted.

"She has no power. She is no queen."

Cetia hummed. "She may not be a queen, and in normal circumstances, her word would barely hold any power because of her title."

"Which at this point is questionable," Dani mumbled.

"Dani," Terin chided.

"What? She's not Domitius' daughter."

"But she is my sister." Terin's gaze connected with Kallie's. His expression was soft and serene and too painful to bear. "She is and always has been the Princess of Pontia."

"I do not...I have no right," Kallie whispered, unable to accept the title.

Dani muttered an agreement.

Cetia waved her hand dismissively, as if to bat away the conversation. "Her title—or lack thereof—is of no importance to me. Titles are only a small part of who we are, and these are not normal circumstances. *You* are not normal, Kalisandre. Your word is power."

Kallie pushed her back into the chair, her heart beating even faster. This was not the plan Kallie had come to discuss. Yet her gift stirred in her stomach as if begging her to reach for it. It buzzed inside her, thrumming in her veins, eagerly and excitedly. But beneath the excitement and the golden haze that often accompanied her power, a darkness hummed. It stirred in the darkest corners of her, ominous and daunting.

"My ability is a curse. It is the reason we are here today. It is the reason..." Kallie's words trailed off as thoughts of Fynn surfaced. Tears sprang to her eyes, but she blinked them away when she made the mistake of glancing at Dani, whose hand had fallen to her stomach. "To command someone is to bend their will to my own. It is a violation of the vilest kind. I made a promise to myself I would never use it again."

Cetia wove her hands together beneath her chin. "You are correct. The gift you bear, the one that the gods have given you, should not be taken lightly. For years, you have been forced to do unspeakable things, to use your words to betray and to kill. But right now, Kalisandre, you have the power to do good. You have the power to end this war before any blood has been shed."

"I-I've never manipulated Domitius. I—" Kallie choked on her words. She twisted her mother's gold ring around her finger. "I don't know if I can."

"You do not know if it is possible because you think he cannot be manipulated *or* because you do not know if you can betray him?"

There was no judgment in the Queen's expression, only curiosity, yet Kallie could sense the ridicule from the others around her. The mistrust and suspicion. She didn't need to have Myra's ability to notice the way the council members' eyes narrowed or the way the ones closest to her shifted away.

Even Ellie looked at Kallie with a questioning gaze, as if trying to see if Cetia's work had failed somehow. As far as Kallie knew, it hadn't, yet she hesitated all the same.

"I hold no loyalty to Domitius," Kallie clarified, forcing some of the strength back into her voice.

"Yet you hesitate," Cetia stated.

Despite the lack of criticism in the Queen's voice, heat crept up Kallie's neck. Kallie wanted to deny Cetia's claim. She wanted to be as strong as the two queens sitting at the table. But who was she kidding? Kallie was not one of them. She was never meant to rule or be a queen.

Her eyes slid to the others in the room—to Medenia and Ophelia, to Ellie, to Terin and Dani, and to the strangers who surrounded her. Kallie came here to prevent those she cared about from getting hurt. She came here because she finally wanted to take hold of her fate. Why, then, was she trembling?

"You are riddled with fear, child," Loralaine said.

Kallie blinked. She tried to speak, but she could not form the words, her mouth too dry.

The former queen nodded. "Good. You should be."

"Loralaine," Cetia called out.

Loralaine held up a hand. "No, I will not lie to the girl. You were not alive during the last war. Were you, daughter?"

Cetia pursed her lips, the first visible sign of her frustration.

Loralaine leaned forward, and the guard beside her shifted, as if expecting the woman to break if she moved too fast. But when the former queen spoke, there was no questioning the power that remained within her bones.

"My memory might be frail, and when it comes to the war, some things are foggy at best. But I recall many things. I recall the bloodbaths that soaked the earth, the violence that ran through the streets, the innocents who suffered.

"War is not for the faint of heart. War is brutal and cruel. The battle forces us to turn into the worst versions of ourselves in order to survive. We have to block out our emotions. To keep on fighting, we must become shells of ourselves to deal with the death that surrounds us. We're told that fear will cripple us, that it will only get us killed. But the truth is, fear reminds us we are human.

"So you should be afraid, Kalisandre. Kage Domitius is not a man you should go running toward without some semblance of fear and wariness within you." Loralaine paused, inhaling a deep breath, and it seemed everyone around her did the same, concern restricting the flow of oxygen as if this was the most she had spoken in a while. "But what will get you killed—and what might get us all killed—is if you fear yourself. Do not cower from who you are or who you may become because of the gift inside you. Only you have the power to control it."

Loralaine's words weaved their way into Kallie's mind and reached the deepest parts of her soul—the insecurities and doubts, the shame and self-hatred. Loralaine was right; Kallie was afraid of her gift. She could not recall a single time when she had used her gift for a purpose other than promoting Domitius' goals. It was not *her* gift, but his prize. Something he had taken from her and molded. Even when it called out to her now, Kallie shirked back, afraid of what would happen, of what twisted horrors she would enact.

Loralaine might have believed Kallie was the one in control of it, but in truth, it controlled her.

Beneath the table, a hand landed atop hers. Terin gave her a weak smile. "No one can make you do anything, Kallie. It is your choice what you do."

Her choice.

She wondered if she really had a choice, though. If she said no, what would those in the room do? Would they prepare for a war? Didn't she want to stop Domitius and prevent further catastrophe and death? Wasn't that the whole point of her being here?

If she did what they were suggesting, she wouldn't need an army. No one else would have to get hurt.

A honeyed warmth filled her veins as her gift danced in her core, eagerly waiting as if it knew the answer before even Kallie did.

"Fine," Kallie gritted out, her nails biting into the flesh of her palms. "I'll do it. I'll manipulate him."

Loralaine grinned, and that small twitch alone did something to Kallie. Loralaine didn't know Kallie. She shouldn't have had any faith in her at all, and maybe she didn't. Either way, a terrified yet fervent energy zipped through Kallie's bloodstream. Yet before the feeling could fill her entire body, a voice ripped through the room like a thunderous crack.

"You will *not* use her as a weapon."

CHAPTER 5
GRAESON

Graeson stormed through the doors, and the paintings on the walls shuddered. "You will not use her as a weapon. We are not *him*," he seethed, chest heaving as he scanned the room.

His best friends, the woman he loved, and the council of a foreign kingdom all stared back at him, aghast. Graeson should have known something was amiss the minute Kalisandre had been late. She was never late when it came to spending time with Nyrri. When the bell tolled, he ran as fast as he could, hoping he wasn't too late.

Once he had reached the council room, Loralaine's regal voice seeped through the cracks of the closed doors, halting Graeson in his pursuit. The former queen spoke of bloodshed and battles, of fear and death. Then, when he heard Terin speak to Kallie and heard her response, fear wrapped around Graeson's throat like a python, strangling him tighter and tighter with every word that passed. He burst through the room, his feet propelling him. He would not lose her. Not again.

"Ha!" Ellie shouted, calling Graeson's attention momentarily. "I told you!"

Medenia groaned and sunk into her chair. A crystal bracelet slid across the table, and Ellie snatched it, smiling victoriously.

Graeson barely gave their exchange a second thought before glaring at the prince. Terin knew the type of person his sister was, knew the guilt she harbored. Kalisandre would never see sacrificing her safety as a choice but a necessity. If there was something she could do to right her wrongs, she would do it—no matter the danger it put her in.

"Gray, you have to understand," Terin begged, standing from his chair. He held up his hands, and Graeson nearly laughed. As if *that* would stop him.

Terin pressed onward. "We do not ask this of Kallie lightly. We all know how powerful her gift is. If this war happens, it will touch every inch of the seven kingdoms. Domitius will not stop until he gains control over everything and everyone."

They mean to use her, to sacrifice her, the god within hissed.

Filled with white hot rage from both him and the god, Graeson prowled forward, his lip curling into a sneer. He sensed the tension of the guards behind him, their anxiety palpable. The warriors around the table slipped their hands beneath the table, and the soft scratch of leather pierced his ears as they reached for their weapons. His attention, however, was solely on Kalisandre.

She didn't deserve to bear the weight of this war. She just escaped Domitius' grasp. If she went back to him…

"Kalisandre," Graeson pleaded, "you do not have to do it. They can't make you."

At last, she met his gaze, and a sea of emotions swam through the array of blue hues that held him hostage. "No one is making me do anything," she said. "This is my choice. If I can stop this war by manipulating Domitius, I will do it."

Graeson's eyes bounced across Kalisandre's face, but all he found were the walls he had thought were finally crumbling. Instead, they were fortified once more, stronger and thicker than before. She was pushing him out, pushing him away.

A part of him cracked. He couldn't lose her; he wouldn't.

Graeson didn't care if she accepted the bond or not. Because if she listened to the others, if she actually tried to manipulate Domitius, he feared what the king would do to her. Not because Kalisandre could not handle herself, but because Domitius was always several steps ahead. He had already tried to destroy her mind. Would he destroy her soul next?

Every muscle twitched as he struggled to contain himself. This was what she wanted, though. How could he deny her that choice? It was simple: he couldn't.

"What's the plan then?" he demanded. If he couldn't stop her, he would at least make sure they weren't sending her on a fool's errand.

"There is no plan, is there?" Graeson asked when he was met with silence. "Were you going to send her straight into the bull's den, let her see if she could survive with no support and no way home? What if she were to get caught?"

"If you only gave us a moment," Terin interjected, "we would—"

Graeson's anger burned bright. "Why am I surprised? Whenever it comes to her life and well-being, none of you stop to think about the consequences." He narrowed his gaze at every person in the room, letting them see his anger, letting them feel his brewing wrath. "You didn't stop to think when you took her and ripped her mind apart. You didn't think about the consequences then, so why would you now?"

Terin flinched, guilt forcing him back into his seat.

"She turned out fine, didn't she?" Ellie retorted, folding her arms over her chest.

He looked to Medenia, his last hope, but she averted her gaze, her eyes dropping to her bare wrist.

Graeson couldn't believe them. While he shouldn't have been entirely surprised, he would have thought the time they spent with Kalisandre would have changed their opinion of her, made them see her worth. He had thought Ellie and Medenia had befriended her, yet both defended this path? Did neither woman see the problem with it? The moment Domitius got his hands on Kalisandre, he would kill her. She was a loose end, a risk he would not let go again.

"This is different!" Graeson yelled, hoping they would hear him. "It's Domitius. We would be fools to run in there haphazardly."

"Who said anything about *we?*" Kalisandre shot back. She pointed at her chest. "I started this war; I will end it."

Normally, Kalisandre's stubbornness was one of the qualities he admired most about her. But did she not value her life at all? Did she truly wish to throw it all away?

"He's dangerous," Graeson said, digging his fingers through his hair.

"I know that! By the gods, I know that better than most, Graeson. But what choice do I have?"

Fear consumed him as he thought of Kalisandre risking her life, unprepared and outmaneuvered. He didn't want to take her choice away; he never did. But he couldn't willingly let her throw her life away either. There had to be another way. He could—

"As much as I hate to say it, Graeson might have a point. You haven't even used your ability since you've been here, have you?" Medenia inquired.

Graeson sighed in relief. *Finally,* he thought. Someone understood.

Kalisandre tipped her chin up, determined. "I will find a way."

"You won't even get close to him. You won't be able—"

A fist slammed against the table, cutting him off. "You do not get to tell her what she can or cannot do, Graeson!"

He snapped his head in Dani's direction. "Are you afraid that if I talk some sense into her, she won't go along with whatever mad plan you are creating?"

He looked at the Queen next. She sat silently at the head of the table, her chin resting atop her hands as if this was some performance at a dinner. "She is not a weapon you get to use," he repeated.

A hand gripped Graeson's arm. Despite the anger boiling over, the gentle but firm touch forced him to drag his gaze away from Cetia. Kalisandre stood before him, her brilliant blue eyes staring up at him, pleading and breaking his heart simultaneously.

"I have always been a weapon," she said. "It's what I was raised to be, but at least this time it's my choice for how I am to be used."

Her eyes glazed over. Quickly, Kalisandre blinked away the tears before anyone could notice them. But Graeson had. He had noticed them right away.

She was afraid, and he loathed it. He hated that they had put her in this position and made her believe she needed to be a martyr.

"Kal—"

Kalisandre shook her head, cutting him off. Her eyes welled up with tears, and she fought them off as much as she could. "I will not let people continue to sacrifice themselves for me."

He heard the words she didn't say aloud: *I am not worth their sacrifice.*

To him, though, she was worth every sacrifice, every risk. But him saying that would not change her mind. Still, he wondered if Kalisandre knew how much she was loved—and not the sort of infatuation two young lovers shared. One that came purely from the heart, from a place of care. Did she recognize that sort of love when it was present? Because if she could, how did she not know she was worth every sacrifice? That she deserved to be protected, too?

Lately, it seemed she feared love more than anything else, as if she felt she was unworthy of it. That might have been one reason she denied accepting the soul bond. It was probably in part why she still struggled to get close to Terin, despite her brother's attempts. She had even kept up her walls with Medenia, whom she had found an easy kinship with after the first few weeks.

However, there were times when she had let her walls down—in the forest when Graeson had almost lost himself, or when he had found her in the bathtub after Dani had yelled at her. Or when she would lie on the grass beside Nyrri as they watched the clouds drift by the towering spires of the castle. Graeson savored those moments as if they would be his last.

He wanted to show her what true love felt like, what genuine friendship was.

He understood then how the soul bond must have complicated things. It made their relationship muddy, something the fates had decided rather than something they nurtured. A relationship wasn't something that was bought or created because of the blood two people shared. Friendships grew. It blossomed as two people became closer and discovered their true selves. It flourished when two people finally allowed themselves to be vulnerable. Graeson wanted to show Kalisandre what that felt like more than anything else. But how could he if she went down this path?

He wished he could read her mind like Fynn could. As their gazes remained locked, a million thoughts must have been racing across her mind. But before Graeson could even identify one, Kalisandre looked past him.

"I'll manipulate him, but on one condition," she said.

"Go on," Cetia said.

"We make a trade."

"A *trade?*" Dani asked, incredulous. "What could Domitius have that he would willingly give up?"

Kalisandre's gaze flicked back to Graeson, and a chill ran down his spine, drawing his brows together. He took a step backward as if sensing the oncoming pain, yet there was no way he could prepare for what was to come. Kalisandre's lips moved, but all his senses seemed to stop working.

He wasn't sure if the room had gone completely silent or not, for all he could hear was his heartbeat in his lungs. He grabbed onto the nearest item—a person, a chair, the wall, he didn't know or care—because the two words that finally struck him in the chest nearly toppled him over.

"Your mother."

CHAPTER 6
GRAESON

"My mother is dead." Graeson retreated a step and stumbled over the fallen chair.

Kalisandre knew this. Why would she mess with him? Why—

She grabbed his hands, her touch sending warmth into his body. But no matter how tightly she squeezed, his large hands were limp in hers. He shook his head, unable and unwilling to hear the truth.

"No, she's not."

Sweat coated Graeson's skin, and his breathing became labored. His chest rose and fell at such a rapid pace that his knees threatened to buckle. He vaguely felt his body make contact with a chair as someone pushed him down onto it. Words were said, but he couldn't hear past the ringing in his ears.

Kalisandre's lips moved. Was she talking to him? She looked at someone in the room. A small vein popped in her forehead as she spewed a demand.

A flash of movement.

The sound of boots pounding on the ground.

Hands were on him, grabbing him, touching his shoulder and arm, coaxing him. Yet Graeson remained frozen. The only thing grounding him, the only thing he could focus on were the two sea-blue eyes staring back at him.

His mother was alive?

His mother was *alive.*

"How? Where?" The questions were no more than rough grunts.

"She'll tell you everything she knows," Kalisandre whispered, squeezing his hands.

"*She?*" Graeson asked, confused.

"Myra."

A RATTLING of metal rang in the halls, and Graeson nearly tumbled over as he hurried to stand, the sudden movement making him dizzy.

A hand landed on his back. Although he did not turn to confirm who it was, he welcomed Kalisandre's touch, intrinsically knowing it belonged to her.

Guards led the handmaiden and the two men who had accompanied her to Tetria into the council room.

"You saw my mother?" Graeson demanded, the words tumbling out of his mouth.

Myra flinched, her soft hazel eyes widening. There wasn't time for niceties, though. He needed answers, and he needed them now.

"I-I didn't know she was your mother. Not at first," Myra said, voice shaking. "I only realized the connection when we were escaping. I had only seen your mother once before that—when we had first returned from Frenzia. The king was outraged that Kallie had escaped, and he blamed your mother, believing she had lied to him." She swept her gaze across the room, taking note of the queen and the council hanging on every word. Her throat dipped.

"Apparently, she had been providing Domitius with glimpses of the future to guide him in his pursuits."

Outrage propelled Graeson. His weight pressed against the table that separated him from the handmaiden, his palms burning into the surface. "Do you mean to suggest that my mother has been working for Domitius?"

Kalisandre wrapped her hand around his arm, beckoning him to calm down, to hear the handmaiden out. "If Lysanthia was a prisoner, I'm not sure she had a choice, Graeson."

He looked at Kalisandre then, and his expression softened marginally.

"She probably did what she had to do to survive," she said gently.

Her words settled in his mind. His mother had not died when he was a mere child. She was a prisoner—had been a prisoner for nearly two decades.

"Domitius has a way of getting what he wants—several of us here know that fact all too well," the king of Frenzia said, his nostrils flaring.

A low rumble came from the god inside Graeson. Rian may have been the man who was previously engaged to Kalisandre, but Graeson had no energy to fight him or yell at him. In truth, he pitied the worn king. Chains adorned his wrists, and fatigue soaked his expression and body.

"While Lysanthia may have been providing glimpses of the future for King Domitius, she was definitely not on his side," Myra said, calling Graeson's attention back to her. "When I first saw her, she wasn't afraid to show how delighted she was that the wedding had gone up in flames. It was admirable. The way she wasn't afraid to speak out against him. Despite being chained, she did not fear him. Not in the slightest."

Terin squeezed Graeson's left shoulder. "My mother always said Lysanthia was a fighter."

At the prince's remark, a glimmer of pride prickled in Graeson's chest, but it was short-lived. The darkness returned in an instant. "Yet you still left her," he spat, narrowing his gaze at the handmaiden.

Myra wrapped her arms around her torso and swallowed her excuse.

He scoffed in disgust.

The man beside Myra—Laurince, Graeson recalled—stepped forward, the chains around his ankles clanging. "Do not blame her. I was the one who told Myra we had to leave. We only had a small window of time to get out."

Graeson slammed his fist against the table, the tea cups rattling across the surface. "You left her with him!" His knuckles bit into the grain of the wood, and he could have sworn he heard the wood splinter from the pressure.

"I tried to convince her to come," Myra explained, her voice wobbling. "Sh-she refused."

"You should have forced her then!" Graeson shouted, his fury reddening the corners of his vision.

"She was chained to a fucking wall!" Laurince shouted.

The Tetrian warriors inched closer, but the captain pressed on, a vein protruding beneath the red scar on his neck

"We had no key, no way of getting her out. We barely made it out alive as it was. How do you expect us to have freed her?"

"You should have tried! You should have broken the chains—anything! If she was one of your parents, you would have done anything to free them."

Laurince scoffed. "*She* told us to leave her!"

Like a frayed rope hanging on its last thread, Graeson snapped. He stormed forward, grabbing the captain by his collar and yanking him—

He froze, time coming to a stop as something foreign slithered over his skin.

CHAPTER 7
MYRA

LAURINCE AND GRAESON'S ANGER WHIPPED AROUND THE SPACE, lashing out angrily. Their rage drenched the council room and seeped into every surface. It soaked into the grain of the floorboards, saturated the plush floral rug, and stained the glass windows. As their emotions slithered across Myra's limbs, she couldn't help herself. It was instinctual. She grabbed onto those threads—

Graeson's iron-tipped gaze snapped to her in an instant. The gray hue of his irises shifted from pewter to liquid mercury.

Flinching, Myra released the threads. But she wasn't quick enough. Graeson's fury was so bright it bled into her soul and poured down the string, hot to the touch, burning her from the inside out. When she peered down at her trembling hands, she could have sworn her skin was pinker than it had been seconds before.

"You overstep, handmaiden," Graeson growled, his ire dripping and snaking around her neck.

"I—I didn't mean—" She gulped, the rock in her throat nearly impossible to swallow.

She hadn't intended to mess with Graeson's emotions. She didn't want to give anyone any more reason to hate her—they already had plenty. But it was second nature to soothe and calm. To deescalate a situation.

"*This* is why we cannot trust them," Graeson said, releasing Laurince and shoving him away. The captain's back hit the wall with a smack. Graeson's anger continued to ripple off him as he retreated.

"Can you blame the girl?" Queen Cetia asked.

Graeson's lips curled, a snarl forming that was so inhuman it sent goosebumps running up Myra's arms. "She has no boundaries."

"Your anger has no boundaries. Now sit," Cetia ordered.

Graeson's nose twitched, but he fell back into his chair. He ran a hand down his face and squeezed the bridge of his nose. "If she is dead," Graeson whispered, "know there will be nowhere to hide."

Myra sent a silent prayer to the gods, begging for even an ounce of mercy. She did not wish for Lysanthia to die. She had tried to convince Lysanthia to come. But trying wasn't enough she realized.

"I'd like to see you try."

Myra went rigid at Laurince's threat.

With his hand hovering over his face and casting dark shadows across his features, Graeson cocked a brow at the captain. "What was that, pretty boy?"

"She's not dead," Myra quickly said before Laurince could respond. She might not have been able to deescalate the situation by altering Graeson's emotions, but she could at least distract him from Laurince's blatant inability *not* to provoke him.

The moment Graeson turned his attention back to her, though, Myra regretted interfering.

"How would you know? You're no longer there, now are you?"

Waves of hatred crashed into her at Graeson's words. Grappling for space to breathe, Myra struggled to stay afloat. Her mother had always told her to look for a friendly face when the sea of emotions began to flood her system. As a child, the rush of emotions had been so overwhelming it nearly paralyzed her. Her throat would seize up, her hands would shake, and her legs would crumble beneath her. But as she scanned the faces at the table, only strangers and the best friend whom she betrayed stared back.

Something brushed against her side.

Blinking, she looked down to see Laurince's knuckles beside her hip. She dragged her gaze up to meet his, and the captain offered her a reassuring smile. Without thinking, she mentally reached for him. Anger and hatred still spewed from him, but beneath those rancid emotions, she felt something else—something kind, something bright. Even though it might have seemed like she was alone, she wasn't. Not really.

She took a deep, albeit shaky, breath before finally answering Graeson. "Because she told us."

Graeson crossed his arms, the muscles straining against the cotton fabric. He mumbled something unintelligible, but she didn't dare ask him to repeat himself.

Instead, Myra latched onto Laurince's emotions and pushed forward. "I believe she wanted to stay because she knew something about the future that we are not privy to."

"Did Lysanthia happen to tell you this future?" Dani pressed, tapping her foot beneath the table.

Myra tried to recall the seer's exact words, but recalling that night left a bitter taste in her mouth and a pang of sorrow pinched at the back of her eyes. Still, she had to try.

"She said…she said that she could do more if she stayed. That if things follow fate's path, we would see each other again."

"Then that settles it," Kallie said, straightening. "We offer the trade: Graeson's mother for me."

Myra balked. *That* was Kallie's plan? To sacrifice herself in exchange for the seer?

"No," Graeson said gruffly, his fist curling atop the table. "We will find another way. We will not lose you again."

"Gray—" Kallie began, but Cetia cut her off.

"Graeson is right," the Queen said, demanding the attention of the entire room. "This plan has been made in haste and without a careful analysis of all the pieces at play. As Medenia has pointed out, Kalisandre has not used her ability since she has been here. But not only that, the seer has clearly seen something that could very well be in our favor. If we act imprudently, we may only make matters worse."

Kallie's frustration wafted off her, hitting Myra in the stomach. Myra sensed a disagreement coming, but Kallie sat back in her chair, defeat washing over her. Graeson's entire body sagged in relief, as did Myra's.

While her relationship with Kallie was still strained, Myra did not want Kallie to sacrifice herself. Domitius was too smart. He would see through whatever plan they came up with.

Rian shifted, the chains rattling as he took a step forward. "And what of the matter of our unjust imprisonment?"

Myra held back a groan.

First Laurince, and now the king? Did neither of them wish to leave this room alive?

"*Unjust?*" the white-haired Tetrian—Ellie, Myra recalled—said with a cocked brow. "You snuck into our queendom like thieves in the night and proceeded to make demands the moment you arrived here."

"*Demands?*" Rian hissed. "All we asked for was asylum."

Ellie huffed and flicked her hand in the air. "You are still alive, are you not?"

Myra's gaze darted between the two. She had the urge to step in, to prevent the dispute from worsening. But what good had that done when she had interfered with Laurince and Graeson's argument?

"*That* is your basis for refuge?" Rian implored, eyes wide. "What kind of hosts are you?"

"The kind that cannot help but see the coincidence in your arrival and Domitius' declaration!"

"Enough," Cetia demanded.

Ellie sunk back in her chair, although not before glaring at Rian.

"That matter is already settled," Cetia said, continuing. "Tetria has always been a safe place for those in need, and it will continue to be one as we head into this war. Due to the current situation, we will grant you asylum. The three of you will no longer be viewed as prisoners. Your rooms have already been prepared. However, for the protection of Tetria and those who reside here, my guards will keep a close eye on you during your stay."

Myra's shoulders sunk in relief, but she seemed to be the only one. Rian continued to glare at Ellie as the Tetrian offered him a saccharine smile. Meanwhile, remnants of anger still drifted off Laurince in waves. At least neither of them were vocalizing their contempt.

"With that out of the way," Cetia said, "let us move on to the matter that needs to be addressed with haste. As most of you are aware, Queen Esmeray has requested that the Pontians return to their home on the grounds of treason."

Myra's eyes widened. She looked at the Pontians, but where she expected to find a semblance of fear wafting from them, she only found annoyance.

"Doesn't the declaration change things?" Kallie asked.

Cetia tapped her long black nails along the table. "I cannot say. Esmeray is in her right to demand her people's return."

Dani shifted, leaning her elbow on the table and resting her chin atop it. "Esmeray is as stubborn as all three of her children," she said, eyeing Kallie and Terin.

The pair pursed their lips, a disagreement forming. However, neither one had the chance to refute the claim before Dani continued.

"Esmeray will still want us to return home, and we should. While I do not believe she will deem us traitors, we need to be ready for the coming war. My soldiers need to be ready."

Terin opened his mouth, but Dani held up a hand. "Do not even say it," she said through her teeth.

"You don't even know what I was going to say," Terin argued.

"That if a war is coming, I shouldn't be leading the charge because of my *condition*."

Terin rubbed his neck. "I—I wouldn't have said it like that, but..."

"I'm *pregnant*, Terin, not sick," Dani said, rolling her eyes. "I can still lead."

Myra's mouth fell open. On instinct, she looked to Kallie for confirmation, and Kallie immediately met her gaze. For a moment, it was as if they were back in Ardentol, overhearing gossip. But unlike those times, a crash of grief smacked into Myra rather than surprise or joy.

"I never said you couldn't," Terin stated. "I'm only trying to look out for you."

Dani hummed in disbelief. "The point is, it is in all of our best interests to return to Pontia."

WHEN THE MEETING was over and the people filed out of the room, Myra had fully expected to hear the clang of the chains, despite the Queen's reassurance that they were no longer prisoners. Myra had been a prisoner for so long that feeling safe was a strange sensation. Even when she was on the run with Rian and Laurince, paranoia weighed her down and made her steps heavy. While some of that anxiety still existed, there was also an ounce of relief for once.

Around her, conversations stirred to life from those leaving the meeting. Their voices were merely noise in her ears, though, her wayward thoughts consuming her. Myra wasn't sure where she was going, but she knew she needed to keep moving. Everyone seemed to have something to do, somewhere to go, something to prepare for. The Pontians were already making arrangements for their return to Pontia. While Domitius had claimed Myra's parents were from Pontia, Myra did not think Kallie or the others would want her to join them.

Even Rian, who the others had persuaded not to return to his kingdom yet, seemed to have a sense of purpose.

Myra chewed on the tip of her thumbnail as she walked down the hall aimlessly, her thoughts wandering beyond the castle's wall. Someone called out, but Myra kept walking, her feet continuing forward. Whoever it was did not need her.

For nearly a decade, Domitius had dictated her life. Who was she now that she wasn't Kallie's handmaiden? Now that she was no longer a servant to the king?

"Myra, hold on a moment."

Muscle memory took over, and she spun around, folding into a curtsy.

"What are you doing?"

Myra peeked through the chunk of blonde hair that had fallen in her face. Laurince was hurrying toward her, amusement wrinkling the corners of his eyes. Her gaze trailed lower, and her breath caught in her throat. Did he...did he have a dimple?

"Uhm..." Myra stood, the movement more rigid than she would have liked. She smoothed out the fabric of her skirt, needing something to do. "A habit, I suppose." She peered down the hall. "Shouldn't you be with His Majesty?"

"There are plenty of guards around," Laurince said with a shrug. "And I'm afraid I cannot help Rian right now. He's spatting back and forth with that white-haired woman—Ellie, I think? You saw them in there. I'm not getting anywhere near that." He chuckled as he shifted his weight to his other foot.

"Is there something I can help you with then?" Myra asked.

The captain rubbed a hand over the scar that had finally scabbed over. "I was going to ask if you wanted to get some fresh air. After being stuck in that cell, I thought it would be good to—"

Myra's eyes widened.

Laurince cut himself off, and a flurry of embarrassment rushed off him. He waved his hands frantically. "I didn't mean—if you don't want to—"

"I—" Myra swallowed. It was as if a dozen rocks sat on her tongue. Sweat dampened the back of her neck as she glanced between Laurince and the space behind him.

"What's wrong?" Looking over his shoulder, Laurince did a double take.

Graeson was barreling toward them, his emotions unreadable.

"What do you want?" Laurince demanded, stepping in front of Myra as though to shield her.

Myra peeked around him.

Graeson raked a hand through his ink-black hair. The light seeping in from the windows caught on his scar, illuminating it. Instead of answering Laurince, he addressed her, "I only wanted to ask you a couple of questions."

Laurince side-stepped, blocking her from Graeson's view. "Haven't you asked enough? Ever since we came here, we've been interrogated. Can't you—"

"It's fine, Laurince," Myra said, stepping around him. "What did you wish to ask me?"

Laurince mumbled something under his breath, but it was too quiet for her to hear. His posture remained stiff beside her.

Graeson stuffed his hands deep into the pockets of his trousers. But as if second-guessing the movement, he removed one hand and rubbed his neck. It was Myra's first time seeing him uneasy.

Curious, Myra cautiously reached out. At first, she struggled to find the invisible thread, for it was so thin that she nearly missed it. But, once she did, she felt a nervous energy buzzing across the string of emotions that poured from him. She quickly let go before she was tempted to dig further into his emotions. After seeing how he had reacted the first time, Myra was not willing to experience his wrath again.

"I—" Graeson looked out the window, hesitating. "How was she?"

At Graeson's question, Laurince marginally relaxed beside Myra.

"Your friends were right," Myra said with a soft smile. "Your mother is a fighter and hasn't stopped fighting."

"But," Graeson tugged at the ends of his hair, "how did she look?"

A lump formed in Myra's throat as sadness filled Graeson's pained gaze. She did not wish to tell him that Lysanthia was nearly skin and bone, that her hair had hung limp around her face, that her cheeks were sunken, and her skin nearly translucent. He didn't need to hear that. Graeson had not been shy about expressing his anger toward them during the meeting, but pain and anger had a way of blinding people. Myra had no desire to make him feel worse.

"She's alive."

"I see," Graeson said, tone hollow, understanding the truth behind the statement.

Silence filled the space between them, and the three of them stood there awkwardly.

Then Myra gasped, straightening as she recalled something else Lysanthia had said before they had left. "She did have a message for you, though."

"She did?" Graeson asked, hopeful.

"She said to tell you not to fear your true self. That you"—Myra wrung her hands together, struggling to remember the seer's exact words—"you have to embrace it."

Graeson looked around the hall at the people who still lingered outside the council room. He took a small step closer. "Are you sure that's what she said?"

Myra nodded. She was positive.

"Why didn't you tell me sooner?"

Myra flinched, realizing her mistake. "I—I didn't mean to—"

Laurince stepped in between them and pressed a hand against Graeson's chest, preventing him from coming any closer. "It's been a long day—actually, a long fucking few months. Lay off."

Graeson glanced down at Laurince's hand, his nose twitching. The two men nearly stood toe-to-toe, almost matching in both height and stature. With one movement, Graeson swiped it away as if the caption was no more than a fly. To Laurince's credit, he didn't shrink back and instead held his ground.

"Do you know what she meant?" Myra asked, ignoring the overwhelming stench of masculinity.

Graeson's attention snapped to her, and something she couldn't pinpoint flashed across his face. He retreated one step, then another.

"It's not important," he said before storming off in the opposite direction, his hands curled into tight fists.

"Did I—did I say something wrong?" Myra asked, staring blankly at Graeson's back before he disappeared down an adjoining hall.

Laurince was silent beside her, and she couldn't blame him.

Graeson was an anomaly she didn't think anyone fully understood. But there was something there, something she had spotted before he had spun around. She only hoped that whatever it was, whatever he had to embrace, he would be able to do it before it was too late.

CHAPTER 8
GRAESON

When Graeson tilted his head up, the sun streamed through the foliage, and cracks of light fell upon the ground in broken, golden fragments. The leaves above rustled as the birds zipped around the branches and fled toward the sky.

Graeson's throat was torn, scratched raw from the anguish that had poured out of him. He collapsed on the ground, his pain and sorrow too great to bear. On his hands and knees, he dug his fingers into the ground, and dirt piled beneath his nail beds. His breaths were short and labored. No matter how much he tried, he couldn't inhale a full breath, the oxygen cutting off before it reached his lungs.

As a breeze swept through the woods, the wind barely kissed his cheeks as if it, too, was afraid of the beast that had created such a disturbance in the forest. Still, the little wind that dared to get close was cool enough for him to notice that his cheeks were damp.

His mother was alive, and he had gone his entire life without knowing.

Not even a year ago, Graeson had been in Ardentol, inside the very castle she was being held captive. Graeson hadn't even known. He hadn't—

"I did not take my son for a crier," Barinthian's voice broke through the trees like a wave crashing against the shore.

Graeson squeezed his eyes shut, willing the tears to disappear. They were not for the god, and Barinthian, father or not, did not deserve to see them.

The god chuckled, the sound stirring up the fallen auburn leaves that covered the forest floor. "At least you're not denying your heritage," Barinthian said when Graeson didn't respond.

Graeson scanned the area even though it was useless. The god never showed himself, instead opting to hide within the shadows. The smell of mildew and decaying leaves filled his nostrils. Other than the sound of quivering leaves, silence enveloped the space. Even the critters had gone quiet.

"What do you want?" Graeson demanded.

"What I have always wanted: for you to become the god you were born to be." Barinthian's voice sent a chill skittering across Graeson's back. And although Graeson could feel Barinthian's eyes on him, the god was still nowhere to be found.

"Did you know?"

Barinthian sighed, clearly annoyed by Graeson's diversion. "Know what?"

Graeson pushed himself off the ground. His limbs shook, and the muscles in his back strained as if his wrath flooded his bloodstream. "That my mother was alive."

"Oh, *that*," Barinthian said as if they were merely discussing the color of the sky. "Yes."

"*Yes?*" Graeson twisted toward Barinthian's voice, but the direction from which it came kept shifting as if it flew on the wind itself. "And you didn't bother to tell me?"

Light laughter wrapped around Graeson like a noose.

"Why would I when I knew the result would be this?"

Graeson's hands flexed at his sides. "Do not act as if you care about my suffering."

"Oh, no. It's actually quite the opposite, son." The god's words brushed Graeson's neck as though he stood right behind him. "You need to suffer. You need to feel this pain. Without it, you will never become who you are meant to be."

Graeson's skin itched as though the god within begged to be released. But if he lost control now, he would only be giving Barinthian what he wanted.

Momentarily, Graeson wondered who would have been worse to have had as a father: Domitius or Barinthian. While Graeson had interacted with Domitius very little, he knew the king was not an overly affectionate man. At least Domitius pretended he cared. Although Graeson wasn't that sure that was any better. While Kalisandre might not have wanted to admit it, she had cared for the king once. Graeson wouldn't blame her if part of her still did. Love and family were complicated. Even when they hurt the ones they loved, many still found themselves loving them. It didn't matter if Domitius didn't share her blood; part of her would always care for him in some shape or form. And that's what made Domitius even worse than an unfeeling god.

Graeson never wondered about Barinthian's true intentions. He had always known his father was a spiteful, egotistical god who thrived on the sufferings of others. There were no surprises with Barinthian.

When he was a child, there might have been a time when Graeson yearned for his father's love. Growing up, he would see King Markus interacting with the twins, throwing them in the air with a bright, proud smile. While Esmeray and Markus had always treated Graeson like a son, their love for him was different. He could feel the difference when one of them would talk to their peers and boast about their children's accomplishments.

Once, Graeson had overhead Markus praising Fynn's ability to read minds to the captain of his guard. "He's only just gotten a grasp of his ability," Markus had said, "but mark my words, my son is going to change the world one day." It was the pure adoration in the way Markus had said the phrase, *my son*, that had struck Graeson.

When Barinthian first visited Graeson, there was no adoration in his tone, no sense of pride or appraisal when he spoke to his son. Instead, Barinthian had treated Graeson as if he was merely an amusement, as if he was something to be studied, something that had not proven its worth yet.

Some things never changed, he supposed.

Graeson cracked his neck, a strange sensation crawling over his skin. "And what is that, exactly?"

Bright silver orbs peeked through the trunks of the trees, and his skin felt like it was on fire.

"You were born to tear this world apart, to burn it to the ground. You were born to be the kingdom's reckoning."

CHAPTER 9
KALLIE

During the days that followed the meeting, Kallie made herself scarce, finding it hard to face the others. Their lack of faith in her had shaken her. While she understood their initial mistrust in her, she had hoped they would have learned to trust her by now. Although she supposed she hadn't given them a reason to believe she could handle coming face-to-face with Domitius alone.

Maybe Cetia was right. Maybe Kallie was too much of a risk.

Riddled with shame, she avoided public meals and gatherings as best she could, finding any reason to hide away in her room or in the gardens with Nyrri. It was only a matter of time, though, before one of them came knocking.

She had expected it to be Graeson but was surprised, and a little relieved, it was Terin who found her sneaking outside after breakfast. Now, the two siblings strolled through the royal garden, both speaking very little.

Perhaps Terin needed the quiet just as much as she did.

When they had first arrived in Tetria, the garden had been full of life. But once autumn crept in, the vibrant colors had since dulled as if a film covered the land. It was as though the world itself was reminding Kallie there was no stopping time, no matter how many times she asked the gods to do so.

As she walked beside Terin in silence, Kallie's attention strayed toward the forest beyond the stone gate encircling the garden. A flash of black mixed among the white tree branches. It came and went in the blink of an eye, but Kallie recognized the drakonis' silhouette easily. Graeson must have taken Nyrri out to the woods to continue her training. Although the exercise was good for Nyrri, Kallie longed for the drakonis' presence. She had grown attached to the animal.

"Where will Nyrri go?" Kallie asked. She had only heard whispers of the arrangements Terin and Cetia were making for their return, but she had yet to hear what would happen to Nyrri.

"Medenia has volunteered to take care of her," Terin said, looking out toward the woods as Nyrri's form appeared before disappearing again.

"Graeson is fine with that?" Kallie knew how much Graeson cared for Nyrri and couldn't imagine him wanting to leave her behind.

"While her wing has healed, Nyrri is still somewhat skittish when it comes to flying. Medenia was able to convince Gray to let Nyrri stay until she gets over the fear."

Though saddened, Kallie nodded. She'd hoped for the drakonis' company during their trip, despite the complications Nyrri's presence would have likely caused. Terin had informed Esmeray about the drakonis' existence, but seeing the creature was an entirely different experience.

"Are you nervous about returning home?" Terin asked, peering at her.

Home. Pontia was not her home. By now, Kallie had spent more time in Tetria than she had in Pontia. Either way, *nervous* didn't begin to cover her feelings.

"I—" The clang of metal erupted in the distance, cutting Kallie off. "What is that?" she asked, following the sound of swords clashing together.

As they peered around a tall set of hedges, Kallie found Dani and Ellie sparring. With sweat dripping down their brows, the two women swung at each other. Their swords crashed together with a rancorous clang that rang sharply in Kallie's ears. On the sidelines, Sylvia cheered Ellie on with a hunger only one's subordinate could muster.

"God's breath." Terin groaned and brushed a hand through his brown curls. "The healer told her she needed to rest."

Cursing, Dani gritted her teeth and dug her heel into the ground, creating a divot in the earth.

"I don't know if the word *rest* is even in Dani's vocabulary," Kallie mused as they joined Sylvia.

"Definitely not," Sylvia said.

"I will rest when the war is over," Dani shouted as she blocked Ellie's next jab.

Each woman moved with an elegance that rivaled the other. Dani fought as if she was playing a game of chess, carefully analyzing and identifying her opponent's next move before it was made. Meanwhile, Ellie swung and blocked as if she was performing some intricate dance. Although their techniques differed, they were both skilled.

With a swift kick, Dani knocked Ellie onto her ass. Dani peered down at her and smirked. Dani held out her hand, but before Ellie could grab it, Terin was there. He snatched Ellie's hand and helped her up onto her feet.

"Gods, you're insufferable," Dani said, resting her hand on her hip.

Kallie chuckled. "At least we can agree on one thing."

To Kallie's surprise, Dani didn't roll her eyes at the comment.

Terin ignored both of them. Although he meant well, Kallie had witnessed how he quickly turned into the overbearing brother when it came to Dani's safety.

Ellie rubbed the dirt off her trousers. "Did Medenia find you?"

"No, why?" Terin asked.

She tossed her hand in the air with a careless wave. "She said something about needing to speak to you."

"Did she say about what?"

Ellie cocked her hip out, her hand resting atop it. "Do I look like her messenger?"

Dani held up her sword, inspecting the blade. "Kind of."

Kallie laughed alongside Sylvia, but Kallie quickly wiped the amusement from her face when Dani glared at her. This, of course, only made Sylvia laugh harder. Maybe Kallie had let her hope get the best of her.

"I didn't ask you," Ellie grumbled before turning to Terin with a small shrug. "Whatever it was, I think it was important."

Terin's gaze met Kallie's, a silent question passing between them.

Before Kallie could respond, Dani held out her sword, hilt out. "Here. You should train too. Your footwork is still sloppy."

Kallie blinked at the hilt.

"I don't know if that's a good idea," Terin said, hesitant to let Kallie join in. Even Sylvia looked skeptical, clearly remembering when Kallie and Dani had sparred last. But Dani wasn't trying to fight. Instead, she was offering Kallie her place.

Kallie eyed the sword. Throwing herself back into her training would be good for her. She grabbed the offered sword before Dani could change her mind and stab her with it instead.

"Go talk to Medenia," Kallie told Terin. "Dani is right."

"I'm often right," Dani said with a scowl. "Don't act too surprised, Princess."

Kallie held back an eye-roll and adjusted her grip. The leather wrapping was warm to the touch.

"Princely duty calls," Ellie said, shooing him away with a flick of her hand.

"Very well," Terin said, though his hesitation was still apparent.

Kallie offered him a small smile in reassurance.

He shook his head but took his leave, muttering something unintelligible about needing more sleep before they left for Pontia.

Kallie shifted her weight. Although she preferred her dagger, the sword was well-balanced and fit nicely in her hand. The hilt wasn't too big or uncomfortable, unlike the longswords she had occasionally wielded in Ardentol.

"He means well," Ellie said as she raised her weapon.

"I know he does," Dani said, approaching Kallie, who stiffened immediately. Shaking her head in disappointment, Dani shoved Kallie's foot back with her boot. "There."

Kallie's brows raised in surprise at the correction.

Dani crossed her arms. "Terin believes it's his responsibility to protect me, but I know what my body can and cannot do."

"Have you tried telling him that?" Sylvia asked, twisting their ginger hair into a bun.

"Of course, but his skull is as thick as Fynn's was, apparently."

Kallie had no time to wallow in the rising guilt and grief before Ellie swung. When Kallie dodged, her balance wavered, and she stumbled.

"Keep your weight even," Dani instructed.

Before Kallie could get her bearings, Ellie struck again. Her sword sliced through the air, and Kallie narrowly missed it.

"Come on, Princess," Ellie taunted.

Kallie rolled her neck and focused. When Ellie swung next, Kallie was prepared. She dodged the attack smoothly. She tried to retaliate, but Ellie was too swift. This fight, fake or not, would not be easy. Kallie and Ellie continued sparring while Dani and Sylvia discussed their plans for the Pontian troops once they returned. Occasionally, Dani would shout out various instructions and pointers, and Kallie took each one, grateful for the advice.

In the warriors' presence, Kallie felt like a novice despite her training. She had been trained not only by Domitius but by some of the best guards in Ardentol. But despite their accomplishments and accolades, none of the men had taken her stature into account, not like Dani was. Kallie understood then how Dani had risen in the ranks so effortlessly. She wasn't just good at fighting, but excelled at instructing and leading. So Kallie latched on to every piece of advice like it was a raft.

Once both women were keeled over and gasping, they finally put the swords down and opted to enjoy the warm weather before the cool autumn night swept in. As they sat in the garden, Kallie brushed a hand across the grass. The blades tickled her calloused palm. She licked her lips and could taste the salt from how hard Dani had pushed her. She craved a good bath and was about to leave to fulfill that craving when Dani spoke.

"How serious were you the other day?" she asked, spinning a fallen leaf between her fingers by the stem.

Kallie's brows knitted together. "Pardon?"

Dani released the leaf and let it fall to the ground. "About offering yourself to Domitius in exchange for Graeson's mother."

Kallie dug her fingers into the ground, crushing the grass beneath her palm. "Does it matter? The council voted against it."

"Based on what I heard," Sylvia said, "Graeson vetoed it. Terin and the Queen simply said it was risky."

"I don't really see the difference. Their message was clear either way," Kallie stated.

Dani pursed her lips as she watched the clouds. "I think they're misguided."

"I do too," Ellie said casually, as if they were discussing their least favorite meal rather than disagreeing with the Queen of Tetria.

Sylvia hummed in agreement.

Kallie simply stared blankly at them all. "If you all feel that way, why didn't you speak up earlier?"

Ellie snorted. "Have you already forgotten how upset Graeson was simply at the *idea* of you marching over to Domitius?"

"I saw him storm off into the forest after the meeting. He was *not* happy," Sylvia said.

Kallie grimaced, the regret bitter on her tongue. By the time she had left the council meeting, Graeson was already gone. Although she wanted to go after him, she had thought better of it, not wanting to blur the line between them even more. But maybe she should have. Maybe he needed her...

"And," Dani added, pulling Kallie back from her thoughts, "I needed time to think it through. Cetia was right. The plan was made in haste, but that doesn't mean it was a bad idea."

"I thought you said we needed to return to Pontia?" Kallie asked, confused.

"Both can be true."

Kallie narrowed her gaze. "Why are you bringing this up now?"

Dani leaned back on her palms. "Because I do not wish for more blood to be spilled if there's a way to prevent it."

"I thought you didn't trust me."

"Here's how I see it." Dani held up a finger. "You're either successful and stop the war before it's even started." Another finger joined the first. "Or you fail, and Domitius kills you for trying to best him." She flicked her hand dismissively, as if it was a matter of which dress to wear to a ball, not a matter of life or death, of saving everyone or dooming Vaneria.

"Dani," Ellie chastised.

"I'm not going to lie to her just because it is the nice thing to do,"

Dani said, unfazed. Then, directing her full attention to Kallie, she said, "Am I still angry at you? Yes, and I probably always will be. But Graeson had a point when he said that many people have sacrificed a lot to rescue you from Domitius' grasp. Those sacrifices will be for naught if we let this war go on. Trading you for Lysanthia might be our only chance at squashing this war before more are hurt."

It was as if Dani had taken the words right out of Kallie's mouth. Ever since the meeting, Kallie couldn't stop thinking the council had made the wrong decision. She would rather risk her life than let war strike Vaneria. Graeson might have viewed it the opposite way, but what was the point of any of it if war befell them? If Domitius won?

Dani stretched out her legs in front of her and ran a hand over her stomach. "Do you think you can manipulate him?"

Kallie chewed on her bottom lip as she thought back to when she would try to bend Domitius' will as a child.

"I—I've tried before," Kallie admitted, wiping her palm on her trousers. "But that was years ago, before I had truly gotten a grasp of my ability."

"What happened when you did?" Dani asked.

Kallie rubbed the back of her neck, trying and failing to work the kink out of it. "I couldn't," she said, defeated. There was no point in bending the truth. She had failed every time.

Sylvia leaned forward. "Because you weren't strong enough?"

Kallie winced as if she had been slapped. But it was true. Kallie hadn't been strong enough. Although she now knew that wasn't the only problem back then.

"I think Myra's influence also played a part. Whenever I tried to command him, I would always feel like I was betraying him. But now that she no longer has a hold on me..." her words trailed off.

"Do you think you can now?" Ellie prompted.

Kallie folded her legs under her and considered it. "I think so."

"You *think*, or you know?" Dani asked, twisting her wedding band around her finger. "The difference is important."

Kallie's gaze fell to her lap. She didn't know if she had an answer to Dani's question. She felt no attachment to Domitius, only rage and hurt. But was there any point in even contemplating this plan?

"Graeson will never agree to do this," Kallie said.

"Does he speak for you now, princess?" Ellie asked, brows arched.

"No, but—"

"But nothing," Dani said.

It was then that Kallie remembered Dani had defended her right to choose her path during the meeting. Was Dani's reasoning simply because she did not care about the dangers Kallie would face and would rather let her take the risk? That should have been a warning signal, yet it didn't prevent Kallie from considering it. This was what she wanted. To choose, to fight. To do *something* right for a change.

"He doesn't need to know," Ellie added.

Kallie blew a stray piece of hair away from her face. "He'll find out. I can't just sneak out of this castle without his notice while he boards the boat to Pontia."

The others exchanged glances, an unspoken conversation passing between them that Kallie wasn't privy to. And Kallie didn't know what she was more surprised by: that they had clearly discussed this already, that they wished to hide it from Graeson, or that Dani had not insulted her once.

A rueful smile rose on Ellie's face. "That's exactly what we were thinking."

"Well, with one slight modification," Dani corrected.

"Which is?" Kallie asked.

"I'm going with you," Ellie said, straightening.

"What? Why?" Kallie demanded. "The whole point is to prevent anyone else from getting hurt. I can't promise your safety if you go with me."

Ellie cocked a brow as if the answer was obvious. "No offense, but I'm not sure your directional skills will even get you out of Tetria. You were passed out the entire time on the way here, so it's best if you have someone who knows the way through the swamps."

"Plus, in case you need backup, Ellie is a good person to have around," Dani added, and the sincerity with which she spoke almost made it seem like she cared—at least marginally.

Ellie pressed a hand to her heart. "You flatter me, Danisinia."

Dani shoved Ellie with her foot, and Ellie barked out a laugh.

"I'm her best friend, you know," Ellie said, leaning toward Sylvia.

"Only in your dreams," Sylvia said with a playful eye-roll.

The corner of Kallie's lip ticked up, but the smile didn't stretch any further. She ran a finger over the amethyst stone on her mother's ring. She had made a promise to Graeson that they would be honest with each other. If she didn't get on that boat, he would be furious. But Lysanthia deserved a chance at freedom. *He* deserved to get to know his mother.

It was a risky move, but a move Kallie needed to make. Too many people had suffered because of her. If she had the chance to save the others and stop this war before it even began, she had to take it. If she didn't, what would that say about her?

She did not wish to be the enemy anymore.

"Will you tell Terin?" Kallie asked.

"In order to get Graeson on that boat, I think we will have to," Dani said. "He can help sway Gray to let you go. If anyone can convince him to do that, it's Terin."

Kallie nodded, but something about her expression must have given her inner turmoil away because Ellie nudged her with her boot.

"This is for the best," she reassured.

"I know," Kallie said solemnly. Still, she couldn't shake the eerie feeling that was coursing through her veins.

"I know it's none of my business," Dani said, shifting as though uncomfortable, "but have your feelings changed about the soul bond?"

Kallie blinked at the sudden change in topic. "I—I haven't really had time to think about it."

Dani nodded, but there was something else there that she wasn't saying.

"What is it?" Kallie pressed.

Dani drew light circles across her stomach. "He'll hate me for saying it..."

"But?" Kallie prodded, nausea rising in her stomach.

"Tell her," Sylvia said, squeezing Dani's wrist.

Dani took a deep breath. "No matter how this ends—whether you're successful or a war comes—you two can never be together. Your paths..." Dani paused, her gaze bouncing across Kallie's face as if she was unsure what to say—or really how much to say. "Lysanthia had several visions of the two of you."

Kallie didn't understand what Dani was saying. She was lying. This was just another way to push her away, to encourage her to leave.

"This is really unnecessary," Kallie said, a sick twisting forming in her gut. "I already said I would go."

Ellie and Sylvia both refused to meet Kallie's gaze, their attention focused on the sky as if something interesting floated in the clouds. Not even a bird flew in their vicinity, though.

"No, you don't understand." Dani wiped her hand across her face. "I'm not telling you this to convince you to do anything. I'm telling you this because I care about him. Graeson is one of my oldest friends. I can't..." She shook her head, her hazel eyes wet. "I don't want to see him get hurt, so I'm telling you the truth because he won't."

"Why didn't he tell me?" Kallie asked, still leery.

Dani released a heavy sigh. "Because in most of the visions Lysanthia had of you, you two do not end up together."

"Most?"

"All but one," Dani explained, holding up a single finger. "As the odd optimist and hopeless romantic that he is, Graeson takes that single chance as a sign of hope. But you and I both know where the future is headed, that chance might have already slipped away. When Gray finds out you left, he will want to come after you because he is determined to hold on to that thin strand of hope. We hope he will be too late if he does. But if he's not," Dani said, her fingers tracing her wedding ring, "don't make him believe in some fairytale ending. Don't make him convince you otherwise."

"He won't," Kallie said. She might not have changed her feelings about the soul bond, but she did not want to hurt Graeson.

Dani reached over and grabbed Kallie's ankle. Her hold was firm yet gentle as she stared at Kallie with sad hazel eyes. "The soul bond is special, but when it's gone, it destroys you in more ways than you can count." Her expression darkened, but it wasn't with anger. Rather, it was something harder, something deeper, something only someone familiar with loss could understand. "This will feel like a betrayal, but my hope is that you see that the Fates have already made this choice for you—as painful as that might be. Better that *both* of you realize it now before you accept the bond and it's too late."

CHAPTER 10
MYRA

As Myra wandered the halls, she hesitated when she reached the open doors of the library. In Ardentol, Myra had never been allowed inside the library unless Kallie had sent her there to fetch a book from the librarian. But more often than not, Kallie had preferred to go, finding solitude in the quiet. Sometimes, although rarely because of the paranoia of being caught, Myra would sneak inside, pretending to look for a book for the princess.

When Myra peered inside now, she expected someone to reprimand her for even looking at the books that were held within the glorious room. To her surprise, no shouts came.

She glanced around, but none of the nearby guards moved. Was it a trick?

She ventured closer, placing her feet just before the entrance. She gripped the door frame with her hand, yet the guards remained unfazed.

Myra stepped inside the library, her steps light as if the floor would crumble beneath her for even daring to enter. When she crossed the threshold, the floor did not quake, insults were not spat at her, and questioning gazes were not directed at her. She dropped her shoulders in shocked relief, the tension she hadn't known she was harboring dispersing.

The warm, woody scent of old books and ink scrawled across pages welcomed her. Similar to the rest of the castle, beautiful stained glass decorated the exterior walls. With the library facing the east, the sun's rays spilled into the room, casting an array of broken rainbows across the glossy pine floors. She wondered how the room would look in the early morning hours as the sun rose, how the glass would be affected by the vibrant pink and orange hues.

When she spotted the librarian, Myra jolted backward and folded into a quick bow. "My apologies, my lady."

The stranger, who had been watering a group of plants, paused. She cocked her head to the side, and her long, slick black hair fell to the side, brushing her hip. "Do you often apologize for silly things?"

Straightening at the woman's light laughter, Myra blinked. "Pardon?"

"Have you done something to insult me personally?"

"I—" Myra bit her lip and shook her head, suddenly feeling rather ridiculous. "I do not believe so, but if I have, I do—"

"Don't say it," the woman said, setting the can down and holding out a hand.

Myra chewed on her lip, unsure what to do or say. The only words that sat on her tongue were another apology, which would no doubt upset the librarian even more.

"Ah, you're the newcomer, right? Her Majesty has informed us you may roam the castle. You are more than welcome to peruse the library while you are here. Knowledge should be shared, not hoarded—no matter one's status," the librarian explained, bringing Myra back to the present. She held out her hand and smiled warmly at Myra. "Please, come in."

With a wobbly smile, Myra bent into a small curtsy. "Thank you, miss…"

"Magnolia," the woman said. Then quickly added, "*just* Magnolia. If you're going to be in Tetria for a while, you should know that most of us don't go around calling each other lords and ladies."

"Really? How else do you show respect to those with titles?"

"A title does not always warrant respect. Wouldn't you agree?"

Shame immediately heated Myra's cheeks. She was fully aware that people like Domitius and Sebastian didn't deserve to be held above others simply because of their status. Still, the habit had been ingrained in her for so many years that it was harder to break than she had imagined.

Myra made to venture deeper into the library, but before she made it much farther, she turned back to Magnolia. "Are there any books that are off-limits?"

"Off-limits?" Magnolia asked, as if she had never heard the words.

"Any books that are only for the royal family?" Myra clarified.

"Oh." Magnolia chuckled and waved her hand in the air. "No. You can peruse or borrow anything you see. While Princess Medenia often forgets to return the books she borrows, we don't separate the royal family's books from the public."

Myra nodded and headed off, leaving the librarian with the plants. As she searched the shelves, she wondered what a normal life was like in a kingdom that shared knowledge so freely, one where books were not kept away based on a person's status. Perhaps instead of inquiring whether there was a need for more handmaidens, she could ask about a position in the library. Spending her mornings with a cup of hot tea surrounded by old books before the rest of the castle awoke seemed like a rather splendid way to spend her life.

She surveyed the various colored spines sitting on the shelves and soon found herself being pulled to one section of the library. The sun streamed in through the windows, illuminating the leather-bound books. Her gaze trailed over the various titles, such as *The Creature of the Red Sea*, *Dragons: Gone but not Forgotten*, *Legendary Creatures: An Anthology*, and *The Beasts of Vaneria*. Myra began plucking various books from the shelves, an idea forming in her mind. She might have been useless with a sword, but she was apt at gathering information. And that too was important when fighting a war.

HOURS LATER, a messy stack of books covered the table Myra had claimed. A majority of the books contained only a few sentences pertaining to dragons, if any information at all. One went into great detail about their appearance and how their pearlescent scales helped protect the beasts from unwarranted attacks. Another had theorized that the creatures had gone extinct because hunters were killing them and taking the dragons' scales to form impenetrable armor. Myra's stomach had twisted with nausea more than once when she read that particular text.

Set on finding something useful to help fight against the drakonises, Myra returned to the shelves again and again.

As she ran a finger over the leather spines, the hiss of exchanged whispers tickled her ears. Turning toward the noise, she found Rian and Laurince hurrying past the library with their heads tilted towards each other. She recalled Kallie mentioning the king's interest in dragons. Maybe he would be interested in helping her.

She made to call out to the two men but stopped, not wanting to disturb the other patrons who were quietly reading. Instead, she snatched the book she had been eyeing from the shelf and hurried toward the doors. When she spotted Magnolia, though, Myra skidded to a stop.

"I'll be back to clean up the stack of books, but can I borrow this?"

"Of course," Magnolia said with a wave. "Borrow as many as you'd like. I'm sure you'll return them quicker than Her Highness. And don't worry about the other books. I'll take care of them later."

Myra gnawed on her lip as she glanced back at the table in the far corner. "Are you sure? I'll be back. I can—"

"Are you still looking through them?" Magnolia interrupted.

Myra pursed her lips. There was nothing in those tomes worth looking at again. "No," she said, disheartened.

"Then go. If you have any chance of catching up to those two handsome men who just passed, you better hurry."

Myra's cheeks reddened. "Oh, I'm not—I wasn't—"

With a knowing smile, Magnolia winked and returned her attention to the books she was organizing, ending the conversation.

When she was in Frenzia, the staff members were constantly giggling and gossiping about Rian's good looks. Myra couldn't deny that the king was handsome. Laurince was attractive, too— objectively speaking.

She bit the inside of her cheek and swiftly ducked out of the library before she could give the thought any more attention.

When Myra came to a fork in the hall, she halted, hesitating.

A gust of wind followed by the sharp click of a latch had her turning down the corridor to the left. When she reached a set of beautiful, ornate doors, she pushed them open and strolled outside. Myra stood on her tiptoes and scanned the garden, searching for the men.

With a sigh, she sank back on her heels. But just as she was about to turn around and head inside, she spotted Rian's signature wine-red hair peeking over a series of tall bushes. Quickly, Myra weaved her way toward the pair, her steps light atop the cobblestone path. When she rounded the bend, though, Myra halted in her tracks as fear wrapped around her. The book she was holding slipped from her hands and smacked the ground. She vaguely felt Rian and Laurince's attention turn to her, but she couldn't move. Her feet were cemented to the ground, her entire body going rigid as blood-red eyes snapped to her.

The unfamiliar creature's nostrils flared. Its leg muscles contracted as the creature stood at its full height. Black webbed wings flared out from either side.

Myra's breathing shortened as she was transported to the throne room in Ardentol. Feathered wings weighed down with blood consumed her vision as the ghost of her brother's agonizing screams filled her ears. Her legs trembled, and she grappled for something to keep her upright. She was going to fall. She was going to—

Her body jerked to a stop as wide, dark brown eyes replaced the ruby ones. Lashes brushed across cool, light brown cheeks. Laurince's lips were moving, but she couldn't hear a word he was saying. She blinked—once, twice, three times—yet the creature remained.

Laurince's hold tightened, and he shook her gently. "Myra?"

She leaned to her left, looking past him. Her brows drew together. Was the beast…was it *rolling* its eyes at her?

"Hey," Laurince said, calling her attention back to him. "Nyrri won't hurt you."

"Unless she deems you to be a threat, then all bets are off," Rian said a few feet away.

"Don't listen to him," Laurince said, flicking a rude gesture in Rian's direction. "You're safe," he promised with a soft smile, though the stretch of his mouth seemed forced. "Plus, I reckon you would struggle to hurt a fly."

"Is it…is she…" Myra stammered, unable to find the words as she looked between Laurince and the creature.

"A drakonis?"

Myra hummed in response, and the captain nodded.

"She looks different from…" Myra gulped. Images of her brother surfaced again: Mynhos flying across the room, the skin of his back scarlet, the pitch-black wings protruding from the raw skin between his shoulder blades.

"Breathe," Laurince commanded softly.

Myra inhaled a slow breath. Once, twice. Until the nerve-endings finally settled and her brain recognized she was not in immediate danger. Mynhos was dead. He was no longer in pain, no longer Domitius' pawn.

Once Myra calmed down, Rian said, "I believe Nyrri was one of the first successful experiments Sebastian conducted before he and Domitius had partnered and started experimenting on humans." The king's warm brown complexion turned a shade of green. He had been too close to being another victim, to becoming the same monster Mynhos had been turned into.

Several yards away, the drakonis settled back down and began licking her paws, from which ivory talons gleamed in the sunlight. Myra's gaze slipped over the animal's form, over the fur coating her legs, the small spikes adorning her tail, and the delicate wings tucked against her sides.

"She's kind of…" Myra hesitated.

"Beautiful?" Rian suggested, staring at the creature with a look of awe.

Myra nodded, though it wasn't the first word she would have used to describe Nyrri. The drakonis was terrifying, but she was also a sight to behold. It was strange thinking that something beautiful came from the atrocious experiments Sebastian had conducted.

"I think you dropped this," Laurince said, holding out the book.

"Oh, thank you," Myra mumbled. She took the book from the captain. Their fingers accidentally brushed, and Laurince quickly took a step back, stuffing his hands into his front pockets. Myra's cheeks reddened.

"Doing some light reading?" Rian jested, pointing to the large tome.

Myra turned her attention away from the captain, thankful for the question.

"I was actually researching dragons to see if I could find anything noteworthy in the library's collection in case it was useful. I recall Kallie mentioning you enjoyed researching, Your Majesty. Would you be interested in joining me?"

Rian and Laurince exchanged glances.

Myra hugged the book tighter to her chest, the pressure a much-needed comfort in the awkwardness. Before the obvious rejection could come, Myra quickly back-stepped. "It's fine if you can't or do not wish to. I don't even know whether the research will help. But I figured I wasn't doing anything else and wanted to help. I'm sure you both have better things to do than spend your days in the library with me."

Laurince sighed. "Myra—"

"No, really. Time alone would do me some good, I think. Don't you? My whole life I've been under Domitius' rule. Some alone time could be beneficial. It could help me get my bearings, help me figure out what I want to do next. It was a silly thing to—"

One of them said something, but she didn't hear him.

Realizing she was rambling, Myra grimaced. "I'm sorry. What was that?"

Laurince nudged Rian in the side, but Rian stared at the captain, dumbfounded.

"It wasn't silly," Laurince said, clearing his throat. "It's a good idea. Right, Rian?"

"Sure, but—"

Laurince threw his arm around Rian's shoulders, tugging him against him. "We have nothing better to do."

Rian, hunched over, side-eyed the captain. "Do you even read?"

Laurince jabbed the king in the side again. "Of course I fucking read. I'm not an absolute buffoon."

"At least you know you're a partial one."

Laurince shoved Rian away, causing him to stumble over his feet. But before the king could hit the ground, Nyrri was there, nudging him upright with her snout. And for once, Myra's laughter wasn't forced. Not even a little.

CHAPTER II
KALLIE

KALLIE HAD GOTTEN GOOD AT GOODBYES QUICKLY.

Well, perhaps she hadn't become good at *saying* goodbye, for that would have required her to say the word. In reality, she hadn't uttered it once, her mouth refusing to form the syllables. But when Medenia pulled Kallie into an embrace the moment she arrived, Kallie didn't pull away.

"Don't be so surprised," Medenia whispered as she threatened to crush Kallie's ribcage.

"Surprised? I'm not—"

Medenia gently slapped Kallie on the back. "You hug as if you are made of ice," the princess said before releasing Kallie. Medenia's ink-soaked hair was twisted into a thick plait that wrapped around her crown. Thin wisps floated around her porcelain face. Taking a small step back, she folded a stray strand behind her ear and gave Kallie a sad, knowing smile.

Kallie wrapped her arms around herself and shrugged. "I'm just not used to physical affection," she admitted. Kallie wasn't even sure when the last time someone had hugged her, let alone someone she could call a friend.

"Or having friends, it seems," Medenia added.

"That too," Kallie mumbled.

"You have many friends, Kallie. Many people who care about you. Just look around the room," she said, squeezing Kallie's arm.

As if to prove Medenia's point, Ophelia inched closer, placing her hand on the small of the princess' back. The warrior wore slick leather pants that were only marginally more formal than her normal uniform. Her blouse was made of a pretty silk fabric that draped over her curves as if spun by the wind and dipped in a bucket of rose petals.

Beyond the two women, people crowded the room, several finding their seats before the dinner started. More people than Kallie had expected were in attendance. Initially, Kallie had assumed they were there either by order of the Queen or to see the others off. But before Medenia had arrived, the first people to swarm Kallie were the healers who had spent day-and-night taking care of her during those first couple of weeks.

While Kallie wasn't quite friends with all those gathered in the dining hall, there was a sense of connectedness. Yet, as she continued to scan the faces, a heaviness pressed down on her shoulders, forming a knot at the base of her neck. Kallie might not have known everyone's names, but she did care about them. She cared about their survival and the lives they had yet to live.

Pinching her eyes shut, Kallie inhaled a deep breath. The subtle floral notes of Medenia's perfume filled her senses and grounded her. She allowed herself one second of panic before she squashed it. She placed her hand atop Medenia's. "Thank you, Medenia, for everything."

The princess chuckled. "For everything? All I did was offer you kindness."

"You have shown me kindness when I was undeserving."

Medenia tilted her head, confusion drawing her dark brows

together. "You are a living being, are you not? Everyone—every person, every animal, every living thing—deserves to be treated with benevolence. We are all on this world together, and if we cannot offer each other that, then we are no better than those we fight against. Kindness costs us nothing, yet has the power to save many." Medenia squeezed Kallie's arm, her smile turning sad as she did. "Anyway, it is I who should thank you."

Kallie's eyes widened. "*Me?*"

"I am beyond grateful for your friendship, Kalisandre." Medenia smiled and dropped her hands. "Now, I have some choice words to say to Ellie about a bet before she tries hiding from me." Medenia spun on her heel, the silk fabric of the bottom of her dress flying around her ankles.

Ophelia gave Kallie a quick nod. "Be safe," she whispered before following Medenia.

Kallie wrapped an arm around her stomach, suddenly feeling more alone than she had previously.

Across the room, she spotted Graeson talking to Emmett. She might have been alone, but she did not wish to attract Graeson's attention. Ducking her head, Kallie weaved her way through the crowd. She only had to get through the next few hours and then—

Kallie crashed into someone. She hurried to steady them before they both fell over.

"I'm so sorry, I—" They both started before snapping their mouths shut as they faced one another.

Sweet, wide hazel eyes blinked back at Kallie. Long eyelashes fluttered across pale, freckled cheeks.

"Sorry," Myra mumbled, taking a step back.

"Myra?" Laurince called out, stepping to one side of Myra as Rian stopped to the other. "Is everything all right?"

"Oh, yes, we—*I* just ran into her. I didn't mean—"

"You do not need to apologize, not for that," Rian said,

interrupting Myra. "She ran into you. She should have been paying better attention."

Myra seemed to want to say something, but she held her tongue.

"We should find our seats," the captain said to Myra. "The Queen should be making her address any minute now."

Rian nodded in agreement, his gaze skating over Kallie.

Wrapping her shawl tighter around her shoulders, Kallie sidestepped around them, but a dainty hand grabbed her wrist.

"Kallie, wait."

Kallie's attention fell to Myra's hand, and Myra quickly let go.

Myra looked over her shoulder at the two men and waved them off. Rian and Laurince retreated only a few steps.

"Sorry, I just—" Myra clasped her hands together and began cracking her knuckles. Old habits died hard for everyone, it seemed. "How are you?"

"How *am* I?" Kallie repeated, aghast at the feeble attempt at conversation

Myra's lips parted. "I didn't mean it that way. It was a silly question. Things are rather bleak right now, aren't they? I only meant...I..." She blew a strand of hair from her face with an unsettled huff. "Well, to be honest, I'm not sure what I meant. This is all so..."

"Awkward?" Kallie suggested, voice thick.

Myra nodded, mouth drawn flat.

Had Myra truly expected them to return to their old ways? To be easy friends again? When it came to their friendship, Kallie no longer knew what had been real and what had been a facade.

Kallie's gaze slipped to Rian. She supposed she wasn't the only one who likely felt that way.

"Are you going to be all right with them?"

"Huh?" Myra asked, brows knitting together.

Kallie didn't know what had prompted her to ask and was just as shocked by the question as Myra was. She didn't know where it came from or why she was asking. She didn't even know why she cared. This was the same woman who had lied to her, yet Kallie still wanted to ensure Myra would be safe and taken care of.

Kallie nodded her head in Rian and Laurince's direction, and Myra followed Kallie's gaze.

"Oh, yes. They've only been kind to me," Myra said.

"Good. That's good," Kallie said. "The Queen can also be blunt, but she will ensure you are cared for as well here. Medenia will too. If you're looking for something to do, she can..." Her words trailed off.

"You're sounding like me," Myra mused. When Kallie quirked a brow in confusion, Myra clarified, "The rambling."

Kallie straightened, suddenly self-conscious. "Oh."

The corner of Myra's lips twitched, but the flicker of movement was brief. "Do you...do you think you'll join in the fight when the war comes?"

Kallie hoped it wouldn't come to that, but she did not trust Myra enough to tell her the truth. So instead, Kallie lifted her chin and said the closest thing to the truth she could. "He raised me to be a weapon, so it's about time I strike back."

"Don't underestimate him, Kals," Myra said, the old nickname slipping off her tongue as if by accident.

Kallie, surprisingly, didn't jerk away from it. "I won't."

"I suppose this is goodbye then, huh?"

"I suppose so," Kallie said, a strange spout of grief forming in her throat for the lost friendship.

"You were my first friend, Kals," Myra said, blinking away a glimmer of tears that coated her hazel eyes.

"You were mine too, Mys."

THE LOUD CHATTER of those attending the farewell dinner inside the castle was a mere hum in the garden. It was only noise to Kallie's ears as she stared at the blanket of stars outside. Among the brilliant specks of light, the moon was only a sliver of its true form, and the night sky was ominous without its full glow illuminating the land. As an autumn breeze swept in, the silk dress the handmaidens had set out for her did little to block the cold air from nipping at her skin. She pulled the cashmere scarf around her shoulders tighter.

She could take the cold a little longer. It was better than being inside. Kallie had sat at a table overflowing with food and drinks, pushing around the chopped up lamb and roasted vegetables, for as long as she could. Every time Graeson looked her way, she found some excuse to turn away. The moment Cetia had finished her toast, Kallie had excused herself, not caring if it made her a coward. She had intended to go to the washroom but found herself wandering outside instead.

At least ten minutes had passed since she left, but her reprieve was finally ending. Boots clapped against the stone path behind her, and her shoulders dropped. Realizing it wasn't Graeson by an instinct she had no hope of understanding, she was both relieved and disappointed. Both feelings sat uncomfortably in the pit of her stomach.

"I wish we weren't saying goodbye again," Terin said, stepping beside her.

Kallie hugged herself a little tighter and dragged her attention away from the sky. "I take it Dani told you?"

With pursed lips, Terin nodded solemnly. "I don't suppose there is any convincing you otherwise, is there?"

Kallie shook her head. It was during silent moments like these that Kallie wished the gods had granted her Myra's or Fynn's ability rather than her own. Although she could have asked Terin how he felt, Kallie opted not to. Some things, she supposed, weren't meant to be uncovered.

The cool air swept through Terin's brown waves that hung past his ear. Instead of saying what she wanted, she simply said, "You need a haircut."

He cocked an eyebrow. "Is this your way of saying goodbye? Because if so, there's some room for improvement there."

Kallie gave a half-hearted shrug. "I've never really liked goodbyes."

He gave her a half-smile. "Then let us not call this goodbye."

"Terin," Kallie protested, not wanting to give him a false sense of hope. While she tried to believe she would succeed at manipulating the king, she did not know what would happen after. If she could beat Domitius at his own game, would she go to Pontia? Would she return to Ardentol? Would she find a cabin in the woods and live the rest of her days in solitude? Kallie had no idea, and she couldn't afford to think about the answer to those questions. Not yet.

Thankfully, Terin didn't push the subject. He tugged on a section of hair, his brows shooting up his forehead as he tried to look at the ends. "I suppose I do need a haircut, don't I?"

The corner of Kallie's mouth ticked up. "Only if you want one."

"Maybe when I return home, I will. I think I'll enjoy having the wind fly through my hair on the ship." Terin shook his head, making his hair appear even more unruly.

Kallie laughed, but the sound was hollow and died as quickly as it came. "It gets in the way more than you think," she admitted. Although she wasn't sure if she was talking about hair anymore.

He shrugged and kicked a small pebble on the ground, sending it skittering across the pathway. At first, the pebble headed straight down the path. Then it hit a lip in the stone and shot out to the right, disappearing into a rosebush.

"He's going to be furious when he finds out," Terin said.

Kallie chewed on her bottom lip, worry rubbing it raw. "I know."

"He'll go after you."

Kallie tilted her head toward the stars. "The hope is that we will be long gone before he can reach us."

"Tonight then?"

"Once everyone heads to bed." She already had her clothes laid out and her bag packed. She did not wish to stay any longer than she had to.

Ellie had received Domitius' response earlier that morning. To their surprise, he had agreed to each of their terms. They would meet in Borgania, in neutral territory. No armies. Of course, neither Dani nor Kallie believed he would come alone. He would at least bring a squadron with him. But when Ellie suggested they bring a group of warriors just in case, both Kallie and Dani had rejected the suggestion. The fewer people involved, the better.

Kallie was no longer the king's pet. He wouldn't be able to control her. She could handle him.

A chill from the breeze crept up her bare arms, leaving a trail of goosebumps. She grabbed the ends of the shawl and pulled the fabric tighter, but the cashmere fabric did little to protect her from the cold.

Terin stepped closer, shielding her from the wind. "Have you even talked to him since the council meeting?"

He didn't need to specify who; Kallie already knew.

She shook her head. "It's for the best if I don't."

"Is it?"

It was the same question she had been asking herself for the past several days. She kept returning to the night she had spent with Graeson. Sometimes, in the middle of the night, when the nightmares edged the corners of her mind, she yearned to go to him. He was the one person who could make her forget, the one person who didn't make her feel bad about being who she was. But she refused to use him.

While Kallie didn't regret seeking him out before, she wondered if it would have been easier now if she hadn't. Even though Kallie hadn't accepted the bond, which to her understanding was required for it to snap into place, Graeson was already in too deep. He needed to understand that Kallie would never—*could* never accept it.

When she had discovered they were soul bonds, she vehemently opposed it, refusing to tie herself to another individual the first second she gained some semblance of freedom after being the king's puppet. But now, her reasoning was even greater than that.

For his entire life, Graeson believed his mother to be dead. Kallie was all too familiar with the complicated emotions that came with discovering a monumental truth such as that. While Kallie wasn't sure if she would get a chance to mend the strained relationship with her mother because of the divide that separated them, Graeson deserved one. And Kallie would do whatever it took to give him that chance, even if it meant sacrificing whatever they could have been together to do it.

Dani's warning was clear: accepting the bond would only damn them. If Kallie failed and Domitius killed her, it would destroy Graeson. She had seen the aftermath of the others locking him up when Cetia was undoing the web of lies woven into Kallie's mind. With Graeson's power and the rage of a god within him, who knew what havoc would ensue if the worst happened?

She cared about Graeson too much. She cared about him more than she even wanted to admit. They would never become soul bonds because she had to protect him. She had to protect *everyone*.

"Take care of him, all right?" she croaked, voice wet with the remorse she failed to swallow.

"Kallie," Terin begged, "please don't think like that."

"I have to. I'm not sure—" She choked on the words.

Terin grabbed her wrist tenderly and squeezed it. "I have faith in you."

Unable to hold his gaze for a second longer, Kallie ripped her hand from his and looked back at the castle. A warm glow hummed in the windows. People walked past, the dinner portion of the evening having ended.

"You should get back in there."

Sadness dimmed her brother's brown eyes. "You should too."

"I will."

They both knew it was a lie, but she had to give him credit for not pointing it out.

Understanding he couldn't convince her to change her mind, Terin started to walk away, but paused. His foot hovered in the air as though he wanted to step closer. In the end, though, he only leaned back on his heels.

"No matter what happens, I will always be here for you, sister."

CHAPTER 12
KALLIE

Slipping out of the dining hall, Kallie made her way toward the stairs. For once, she was thankful she didn't have too many belongings. Fewer things to gather, less baggage to hold her down.

As Kallie took the first step up the staircase, a large, calloused hand wrapped around her wrist, sending a spike of heat soaring through her arm.

"A word?"

Eyes squeezed shut, Kallie silently cursed herself for not having left sooner.

Slowly and reluctantly, she turned around. Graeson immediately released her wrist. Yet, even though his hand was gone, the warmth of his touch lingered, searing into her. Briefly, she hoped it would remain on her skin forever, a permanent mark. Then, immediately, she hoped it would evaporate into thin air, never to appear again.

Graeson stuffed his hands into his pockets. "You have been avoiding me ever since the council meeting." His mouth formed a small pout, the curve making his lips look even softer than she already knew they were.

She tried not to think about it.

She had been trying not to think about a lot of things lately.

Graeson leaned his weight onto his heels, nodding in understanding. "So it is intentional, then."

"I just…" Her tongue became leaden in her mouth, heavy and unmovable. She did not wish to lie to him, but she also couldn't tell him the truth. She shifted on her feet, struggling to find the words. She released a heavy exhale. "I have a lot on my mind."

"You can talk to me, you know."

"I know," she mumbled, avoiding his concerned stare. If she looked too closely at him, if she let those gray eyes draw her in like the moon pulled the tide, she would be done for.

Silence fell between them, and she wondered if Graeson could sense its weight too. The quiet had never been uncomfortable between them before, so it was strange how heavy it bore on her shoulders now. Was this because of the soul bond? Did it intensify her guilt? Could it do that even though she hadn't accepted it?

"Kalisandre, I—" Graeson swallowed the rest of the statement as his gaze dipped to her hands.

Her gaze followed his, landing on her fingers. She stood twisting the ring round and round.

Gingerly, he grabbed her hand, his touch delicate and barely there. He swiped his finger over the ring. "I need to tell you something."

The hair on the back of her neck stood upright at those words. She went to speak, to prevent him from saying whatever it was, but he was quicker than she was.

"This ring wasn't your mother's."

Kallie took a step back, her hand falling from his. "Yes, it was. It—"

Her mouth slammed shut as she looked at him. His expression was contorted with pain. He was telling the truth. Kallie gripped the railing as her legs threatened to give out.

When Graeson spoke, his voice shook. "There are two parts to the bond. The first is when both parties recognize the bond exists between each other and accept it. The second..." He hesitated, his gaze once again falling to the ring. "The second involves fortifying the bond. Once a pair recognizes the bond, often the next step is to exchange a set of—"

Kallie was already shaking her head and retreating further up the stairs. Her heel hit the back of the step, and she tightened her grip on the railing to stop herself from falling.

"—special rings made from a rare material off the coast of Pontia. The loved ones of the pair, typically the parents, are the ones who gather the metal from the coast and forge the rings together. It's a symbol of the two families, the two lines becoming one. That ring—"

"Stop," Kallie blurted, holding up her hand. She gaped at the amethyst stone in the middle of her ring staring back at her. She quickly dropped her hand and squeezed her eyes shut. "*Stop.*"

But Graeson didn't stop. He kept going.

"I should have told you the first time I saw you wearing it, but I didn't—I *couldn't.* Our mothers made that ring together, just like they made this one," he said, twisting one of the more worn rings around his finger. "The metal is imbued with some of Pontanius' magic, strengthening the bonds. It is a tradition that the parents forge them."

Graeson looked down at the ring that sparkled in the light of the candles adorning the hallway. "When I saw that you still had it the first time I saw you, I was shocked. I had thought it would have been taken from you when Domitius had stolen you from us."

Kallie's gaze fell to the ring. Her deep blue eyes widened, and her chest rose as she inhaled sharply.

"Are you saying..." She swallowed, her words getting stuck in her throat. "Are you saying that we're already..." She couldn't say the words aloud. She had thought she had a choice. She had thought—

"No, no," Graeson stammered, taking a cautious step toward her.

Kallie stepped backward.

He ran his hands through his hair as if to stop himself from reaching out to her. "We're not...we haven't cemented the bond. You can still deny it if you wish. I just...I wanted you to know the truth about the ring, just in case..."

Her breathing became shaky. It shouldn't have mattered. It shouldn't have changed anything. Yet it felt as if someone had thrust their hand in her chest and was clutching her heart, threatening to crush it.

"While your mother and father both had a part in creating this ring, it has always been yours, Kalisandre. I know you haven't made a choice," Graeson added, "and I want you to take the time to make it. But what I don't want is for you to push me away. I can already feel you doing it. I can already feel..." Graeson squeezed his eyes shut, and a million emotions rushed across his features.

Kallie told her body to move, to flee. She tried to turn around to escape before he opened his eyes. But the moment she lifted her foot, it was too late. His silver eyes were on her, locking her in place.

"Are we going to pretend that the other night never happened?"

She folded her hands behind her back and steeled her expression as she ran a finger across the stone. She thought of Dani's words, her warning. Kallie couldn't explain how much that night meant to her. Not now. She tugged on the ring, pulling it free. "That night was a mistake."

"A mistake?"

Kallie fisted the ring in her hand, the stone digging into her flesh. "It should never have happened. I warned you nothing would change, and if you think something has, then you only have yourself to blame."

Her heart cracked at the lie, the shattered pieces crumbling and falling to the bottom of her stomach. She had to do it, though. She needed to push him away. The more time she spent with Graeson, the more likely she was to accept the bond. But accepting it would only cause Graeson more pain.

So, despite not wanting to, she met his gaze. He needed to believe her. He needed to let her walk away.

"This isn't some fairytale, Graeson."

He took a step closer, determination burning brightly in those silver-moon eyes that dared her to let him in. "You say nothing has changed, but you and I both know that couldn't be further from the truth. Look around you, Kalisandre. So much has changed already."

She saw the slight changes everywhere she went. During the day, the hallways were filled with an influx of warriors, and the gardens were filled with squadrons training. Hushed and worried conversations flitted about the castle from the staff. Fear had spread fast.

"While things have changed, nothing has changed between us. I need you to believe that," Kallie said, silently begging him to believe her. To make breaking his heart easier.

Graeson grabbed the end of the railing, his fingers flexing over it as if he yearned to eliminate the distance between them.

Why couldn't he see that the space between them was the only way he would survive?

"I know that returning to Pontia isn't what you wanted to do," he said, " and I know you blame yourself for the turn of events. If you told me right now that you didn't want to get on that ship, I would stay with you. I would fight with you."

By the gods, a part of Kallie wanted that more than anything. But she couldn't be who she needed to be with him trailing her and protecting her. She needed to destroy his hope. Even if it broke her to do so.

"I will follow you to the end of the world. If you just gave me a chance, I'd prove—"

"There is *nothing* for you to prove, Graeson," Kallie snapped, unable to take the pain any longer. "You have done enough."

"But it's still not good enough, is it?" He rubbed his fist against his chest as if his heart was breaking. "Why does it feel like I'm losing you again?"

Pain flashed across his face, and Kallie wanted nothing more than to wipe it away. But she couldn't. If she truly cared about him, she couldn't risk it. So, instead, she drove the knife even deeper into his heart.

Kallie grabbed his hand and opened his palm. She placed the ring in the middle of it and folded his fingers over the band. "You cannot lose me when you never had me, Graeson."

Tears stung the back of Kallie's eyes, but before Graeson could see them, she spun on her heels.

"Kalisandre, please."

Biting back the tears, she forced her voice to sound steady. "Do not make this any harder than it already is, Graeson. All I do is hurt people. I do not wish to hurt you, too."

"And yet you are all the same," Graeson whispered at her back.

Even though every bone in her body told her to return to him, Kallie didn't let herself turn around. She hurried up the stairs, hoping that breaking his heart would be the thing that saved him.

CHAPTER 13

KALLIE

Despite the layers Kallie wore, the crisp night air nipped at her cheeks and reddened the tip of her nose.

"Are you sure you want to do this?" Ellie asked, leading two horses over by the reins.

"Yes," Kallie said, wiping the moisture from her face with her sleeve before grabbing one of the reins.

"Very well," Ellie said, turning away and mounting her horse.

As Kallie took in the horse before her, she shoved her old fear down. Right now, there was no time to hesitate, no time to fall into the nightmares. She shoved her foot into the stirrup and hoisted herself up onto the horse's back. She shifted atop the saddle and clicked her heels against the horse's side. Kallie kept her attention on the shadows ahead and refused to look back despite the ache in her chest.

CHAPTER 14
GRAESON

STANDING AT THE EDGE OF THE DOCK, GRAESON STARED AT THE SMALL ripples in the water as small orange and red fish swam beneath the surface. Every time one jumped out of the water or popped its head up, the sun's rays caught on their pearlescent scales. The red and orange hues turned golden as if tiny fires illuminated the water's surface. A few fish dove beneath the small riverboat that bobbed up and down, waiting for its passengers, their bags already stored.

The bitter taste of goodbyes twisted in the wind around him. Most of the Tetrians had already said their farewells during the dinner the night before, so only a few people were gathered on the dock.

He could only imagine the stress Kalisandre was feeling. She hadn't been to Pontia since Fynn had passed. Seeing the village would surely be hard for her. But while Graeson wanted to be there for her, she made it clear last night that wasn't his place. He understood she did not wish to accept the soul bond, but he still cared for her. Was being friends truly off the table?

You have done enough.

Even now, he could hear the frustration vibrating in her throat when she had said those words. He had messed up. Without meaning to, he had pushed her too far, and because of that, he might have ruined everything.

He promised he would give her the space she wanted. Even if it hurt him to do so. Even if every instinct told him she needed someone to lean on, someone to watch over her. But maybe he wasn't that person. Maybe he couldn't be.

Graeson saw Terin's reflection appear beside his in the water. Terin slapped him on the shoulder. "Ready?"

Graeson grunted, turning away from the river.

He wished he could say he was excited or even relieved to return home, but he wasn't. Not even in the slightest. His mother was still in a cell, locked up and at Domitius' mercy. Every step he took felt like a betrayal. How could he leave her? How could he not storm into Ardentol and rip the castle apart until he found her? Until he saved her?

He looked out toward those gathered on the dock. Despite the fresh heartache, Kalisandre was the first person he searched for. His brows knitted with concern when he still didn't spot her in the crowd.

"Kalisandre still isn't here."

"Oh," Terin said, scratching the back of his neck. "Someone said she was running late."

Graeson poked the inside of his cheek with his tongue. "Has she...has she talked to you?"

"About?"

Graeson shrugged. "Anything, really. She's been avoiding me, and I'm sure she's nervous about returning to Pontia."

"She has not been avoiding you," Terin argued.

Graeson's jaw popped. "Yes, she has."

Terin snorted, but the sound was slightly forced. "You're reading into things too much."

Graeson arched a brow. Was Terin that oblivious? "She admitted it last night."

"Oh." The tips of Terin's ears poking through his dark brown hair burned pink. "I—I'm sure she has a good reason. She has a lot—"

"—on her mind," Graeson said, speaking over Terin and eyeing him quizzically. "I know. Are you sure you haven't talked to her because that's the same thing she told me?"

"It's not that hard to figure out. She's still working through everything—and there's a lot to work through."

Graeson sensed the god studying the prince with a leeriness that twisted his insides into knots.

Something's wrong, the god whispered, his voice slithering around his mind.

Graeson narrowed his gaze. "Terin," he said, his hand twitching.

"Hmm?" The prince didn't look him in the eye.

Before he knew what he was doing, Graeson snatched Terin by the collar. "Where is she?"

"What do you mean?" he stammered, eyes wide.

A deep growl hummed in his throat, and Graeson tightened his grip. The fabric in his hand wrinkled, the cotton fibers stretching, pulling. Straining. Someone called out to Graeson as the attention of the crowd was drawn toward them, but Graeson didn't pay them any attention. Not as red seeped into the corners of his vision and the god bristled.

"Sh-she—" Frantically, Terin looked all around him, everywhere except at Graeson.

He was hiding something.

"Gray," Dani warned, "let him go."

Graeson's anger rose to his eardrums. Every other sound turned into a monotonous hum as he lifted the prince up onto his toes. "Not until he tells me where the fuck she is," he growled.

"I don't know!" his friend shouted.

Lie, the god roared. *He's lying.*

"I am not lying. I-I don't know where she is. She—" Terin gulped, his eyes darting to the others.

The bars of the mental cage rattled, the metal creaking, heating. Smoke filled Graeson's lungs as the god tried to break free.

"She *left,* Graeson." Dani's words came at him like an arrow piercing him in the chest.

Graeson's vision quaked. The nerves in his fingers went numb. Pain spiked along his spine.

In an instant, Terin fell to the ground, his knees smacking against the planks. The prince nearly tipped over the dock, but he narrowly caught himself, curling his hands around the edge of the wooden planks.

Every inch of Graeson's body felt like it was burning from the inside out.

"What do you mean, she *left?*" Graeson demanded, his control slipping.

"She ran away," Dani said.

"Do you really blame her?" Emmett mumbled near the boat. "You're frightening the shit out of me right now." He took a step back and waved a finger at Graeson. "Your eyes are doing that weird glowing thing."

"They do do that, don't they?" Sylvia asked, hands propped on their hips and head cocked.

"Shut up!" Graeson yelled, the rumble of his voice shaking the very platform they stood on. Every bone, every muscle vibrated with rage as the people in front of him gawked at him with fear in their eyes. The only people foolish enough not to avert their gazes were his friends. But right now, he wasn't sure if he could call Dani and Terin that.

"If someone doesn't tell me right now where Kalisandre is, I'll—"

"You'll what? Hmm?" Dani challenged, inching closer.

"Don't, Dani," Terin warned.

"No. I want to hear this. What are you going to do, Gray? Because I don't think Kallie will take too kindly to an outburst. Did you stop and think that perhaps *you* were the reason she left? That maybe she left because you can barely control yourself?" She tilted her head to the side, eyeing him.

Under her scrutiny, the god pushed at the barriers of his cell. *Do not listen to them. They preach only lies, only falsities.*

Yet Graeson couldn't help but wonder if there was some truth to Dani's claim. Kalisandre might have comforted him when he had nearly lost control that day in the woods, but maybe she had finally gained some clarity. Maybe she finally saw the monster he was, the danger he was.

Barnithian's voice swept across him, spinning around him. *You were born to tear this world apart, to burn it to the ground.*

Dani smirked. "It gets worse and worse every day, doesn't it? You're hanging on by a thread. I can see it; we *all* see it. I bet Kallie sees it too. So let her go." She was toe-to-toe with him now, and the god peeled back his lips, snarling. "Life isn't some fairytale, Graeson. You have always known that there was only a small chance that the two of you would be together in the end."

Graeson bit down, his jaw cracking.

"You pretend as if love conquers all, but it doesn't. Some things you cannot change. Some things have already been decided by fate, and the sooner you realize that, the easier it's going to be. You're not some hero who can save everyone. If you try, even more people are going to die."

As Dani went on, a warning bell rang in his ears. Something Dani had said swirled in the back of his mind. What had Kalisandre told him last night?

This isn't some fairytale, Graeson

Their phrasing was too similar, nearly exact. There was no way it was a coincidence.

The bars of the cell bent back, and the god slipped an arm through the gap.

When Graeson spoke, his words were clipped. "What the fuck did you say to her, Danisinia?"

"I said what had to be said. I said what *you* were too afraid to admit to her."

Movement behind Dani caught Graeson's attention. Medenia twisted her hands together, and a look of sorrow drenched her expression. His gaze slipped to the people around her.

The witchling, the god hissed. *She's not here.*

Ellie would not have missed sending them off. She gave Graeson so much crap when she didn't receive a proper goodbye the last time they visited Tetria.

"Medenia, where is Ellie?" Graeson asked, his temperature rising.

"Where she needs to be," the princess stated, her lips set in a firm line.

Graeson took a step back, slamming his eyes shut. The betrayal of his closest friends hit deep in his core. He shouldn't have been surprised. After all, they had gone behind his back to rifle through Kalisandre's mind, so why wouldn't they keep this away from him too?

"Please," he begged, his worst fears rising, "just tell me she didn't go to him. That she's not planning on doing something reckless."

Silence answered him.

With his heartbeat pulsating in his throat, he opened his eyes. Hanging on to the last dredge of his control, he looked at each one of them. "When did she leave?"

Terin released a heavy sigh, defeat dragging his shoulders down. "Last night."

Graeson cursed and stormed forward.

Emmett immediately retreated several steps, hands up. "If it's any consolation, I have no fucking clue what's going on," he whispered.

Sylvia scoffed. "And for a good reason."

Graeson ignored them both. He snatched his bag from the canoe, but Terin reached for it at the same time.

"Have faith in her, Gray." Terin tugged the strap, forcing Graeson to halt.

"He will kill her!" Graeson ripped the bag from his best friend's fingers.

"She's stronger than you give her credit for."

"I know she's strong, but Domitius cannot be bested. Not like this. He will suspect something is amiss the moment he sees her. This isn't—" Graeson stumbled over his words. "This isn't fair."

Terin sidestepped in front of him and blocked his path. "She wants to do this, so let her. It's what she would want."

"No, it's what she thinks she deserves," Graeson corrected. "There's a difference, and if you can't see that, I pity those you will rule over one day."

Terin's jaw fell open, but Graeson didn't stop to see if he would pick it up off the ground. He shoved his way through the crowd. Kalisandre already had a half-day's head start. He had to move.

"Graeson, where are you going?" Medenia asked, following him.

"To find Kalisandre and be some ignorant hero, apparently," Graeson shouted back.

"Heroes sacrifice themselves. But if you try to stop her, you'll only be the villain in her story," Dani yelled after him.

Graeson didn't stop.

The history books could call him whatever the historians wanted. If there was a story to write about, that meant at least one of them would survive this. And he would be damned if Kalisandre simply became a martyr.

CHAPTER 15
KALLIE

Silence was a constant companion as Kallie and Ellie traveled through the swamps of Tetria. The horses made their way slowly, finding the least treacherous path and weaving between the cypress trees with ease.

Ellie had advised Kallie to let the horse lead while in the queendom, but Kallie had not seen the advice for the warning that it was. Now, she regretted not having listened to it more closely.

The moment Kallie had tried to sway her horse one way, Winter released a disgruntled whinny in protest. Kallie should have listened at that point, but she hadn't. Instead, she was too determined to put as much distance between them and Graeson before he inevitably came running. She hadn't realized her mistake until Winter reared, her front hooves pawing the air. And by then, it was too late. Kallie rolled off Winter's back and landed in the muck with a splat.

It took over three tries and two near face plants before she could get her feet out of the thick mud.

Ellie had snickered behind a hand, her bemused expression saying what she dared not to speak aloud: *I told you so.*

Nearly an hour later, Kallie's pants were still wet.

"How are you doing back there?" Ellie asked, failing to hide her grin when she looked back at Kallie.

While Kallie had done her best to wipe off the mud, clumps of it remained stuck in her hair. When she turned her neck, she felt the dried muck cracking, and it sent a shiver down her spine. She feared even an hour's soak wouldn't rid her skin of the stench of rotten eggs.

"Could be better," Kallie grumbled, adjusting her positioning. Every time she shifted on the saddle, the damp fabric of her trousers clung to her skin. "This really isn't helping my fear of horses, though."

Ellie snorted. "Graeson mentioned that silly fear of yours once."

Kallie grimaced at the mention of Graeson, but she was thankful Ellie didn't question it and instead turned around.

"Do you think your fear is because of Domitius?" Ellie asked, curious.

Everyone had always thought Kallie's fear of horses was irrational, a strange phobia that had appeared out of nowhere. But now that Kallie knew that the recurring nightmare of a horse dragging her away was actually a memory, the phobia made sense.

Kallie lifted a shoulder haphazardly. "Most likely."

"You're holding your own better than I expected," Ellie remarked thoughtfully.

Kallie supposed she was.

Still, while she may have been managing her fear, she did not enjoy it by any means. Everything hurt. The arches of her feet ached from the stirrups, her hips screamed in agony from sitting astride the horse for so long, and even the vertebrae in her spine protested every bump. The rough rope of the reins had reopened the calluses from sword fighting that had finally healed. Still, despite the discomfort and ounce of mistrust between her and Winter, Kallie didn't tremble with trepidation.

Mulling the realization over, she said, "I suppose I have you to thank for that."

"Me? What for?"

"You assisted the queen that night. If it wasn't for the two of you—"

Ellie pulled at her reins, and Kallie swallowed the rest of her explanation as she braced for impact. Thankfully, Winter's reactions were quicker than Kallie's, and the horse stopped in time to prevent a full-on collision.

"You give us too much credit," Ellie said. "While the queen is powerful and I've learned a great deal from her, we are not miracle workers. We simply opened the pathways. You did all the work after that."

"I don't understand," Kallie stammered.

Ellie tightened her slick-back ponytail and draped her snow-white hair over her shoulder. "You were the one who cut the cord. You were the one who ripped apart the handmaiden's work. It was *your* will that persevered. Give yourself more credit, Kalisandre. You freed yourself; no one else did."

Could that be true? Kallie had assumed that it was Cetia and Ellie's work that had vanquished Myra's manipulations. Was it possible that she had done more than she thought to break the hold?

Kallie's eyes widened as she thought of something else. "Did you…were you able to see what was happening?"

Ellie shook her head. "It doesn't work like that. We read and react to one's aura, the pressure and strain on the body." She grimaced and wrinkled her nose. "Although…"

"What? What is it?" Kallie demanded, nervous.

"While we were not privy to what was going on inside your mind, we could hear you when you spoke."

The tips of Kallie's ears flamed red. "Wh-what did I say? What did you hear?"

Ellie's mouth twitched. "I tried not to listen too much. You were kind of whiny, to be honest."

Kallie's jaw fell open. "*Whiny?* Do you know how painful that was?"

Ellie barked out a laugh, and Kallie narrowed her gaze.

"You're messing with me, aren't you?"

"A little," Ellie admitted, amusement wrinkling the corners of her eyes.

Kallie tossed her head back in frustration.

"Sorry, but you're so gullible right now. I couldn't help it," Ellie said.

As if that made up for it.

Ellie released a heavy sigh, and when she spoke, her tone grew serious once more. "Kalisandre, the mind is a powerful thing. Although you harbor much darkness, if you let yourself, you could be even stronger than you think possible."

Kallie blinked at the sky. Her eyes stung from the wind and the sour aroma—or at least that's what she told herself. If only it was that easy to believe in her strength. She might have been freed from Domitius, but she still had plenty of work to do before she could fix the broken pieces inside her.

"We are often the ones who get in our own way of achieving greatness," Ellie added after a moment. Then, with a quick snap of the reins, she trotted down the makeshift path.

With no direction from Kallie, Winter followed.

As the birds flitted from one tree to another, the warrior's words repeated over and over again in Kallie's mind. Kallie knew there was some truth to them, but she didn't know if she was capable of getting out of her way. Because even though she may have broken

Myra's hold on her, Kallie could still hear Domitius' voice in the back of her head.

She wondered if she would be strong enough when she faced him or if this was all a waste of time.

CHAPTER 16

GRAESON

"Where are all the fucking horses?"

Bengi, Ophelia's little brother and the only stable hand around, blinked at Graeson, his face rapidly paling. To his credit, though, Bengi didn't take a step back. Even with quivering hands, the young boy squared his shoulders. He was the spitting image of his sister in that moment, her fierce stubbornness and all.

"They're not here, sir," Bengi said, voice trembling only a little as he rushed to follow Graeson into the stable.

"Where are they?" Graeson opened each stall he passed, slamming each door when he found only hay.

"They're out."

The stall gate ricocheted off the latch.

Graeson's jaw cracked as he bit down. "All *one hundred* of them?"

Bengi nodded. Then he tilted his head and peered up at the roof, squinting. "Wait, no. That's not right."

Graeson sighed with relief and leaned against a post. He could still make it. He could still get to her in time. "Thank the—"

"There are one hundred and *nineteen* horses, actually."

Graeson's hand curled into a tight fist, his short nails carving crescent moons into his palm. His knuckles cracked. "Where could one hundred and nineteen horses be, Bengi?"

Bengi blinked as if it was obvious. "My sister and the others took them out for training."

"And they didn't think to leave any behind in case of an emergency?"

Bengi shrugged nonchalantly. "I'm sorry, sir, but I am not privy to those decisions. They came, they mounted, and they left."

"When?" Graeson demanded, the syllable rough in his throat.

"Pardon?"

Graeson bit down on his tongue, trying to maintain his composure—the little he had left, anyway. "*When* did they leave?"

"Early this morning, sir. They're not expected to be back until after dinner. I don't think any of the horses will be in shape for another journey until tomorrow. I heard Ophelia talking about running them hard to—"

Graeson slammed his fist against the post. The horseshoes hanging on it rattled, threatening to fall.

"Where's the nearest stable?"

"About six miles west," Bengi said, picking up a broom that had fallen.

Graeson groaned and spun around.

That was in the opposite direction Kalisandre had likely gone. By the time he found the stable, he would be even further behind than he already was. He pressed his hands against his temples, cursing the gods as he stared at the sky outside the stable.

There is a way, the god within whispered.

In the distance, a roar filled the air. Graeson's hands fell.

Then, before he knew it, he was running.

"Come on, Nyrri," Graeson pleaded. He lifted the leather saddle and dangled it as if he could somehow trick the drakonis into thinking it was a treat. "It's not going to hurt you."

Nyrri blew out a puff of air and rolled onto her back as she sprawled out on the crisp grass. She pawed at the air as a butterfly flew by, her claws nearly slicing the insect's wings.

"There are plenty of butterflies in the sky. You can chase as many as you want—birds too." Graeson inched closer. "Just let me—"

She released a whine and rolled over in the opposite direction, tucking her paws beneath her stomach.

Graeson groaned. "Oh, don't be like that."

Nyrri huffed and tipped up her chin in disdain.

You are wasting time, the god hissed.

Graeson held back his retort and focused his attention on Nyrri.

"I didn't want to leave you, all right? I begged them to take you with us, but Medenia said there wasn't any room on the boat."

Nyrri glared at him, and her ruby-red eyes turned into slits.

"That's not what I meant, and you know it," Graeson said.

He couldn't believe he was arguing with an animal right now, but Nyrri was his last hope. She was faster than the horses, which still had yet to return. Her landing may have needed some work, but her wings were fully healed. She was strong enough. She had soared through the sky countless times now.

Graeson groaned, and the large saddle knocked into the backs of his knees. Medenia and Graeson had worked with the royal saddler to create the leather seat over the past few weeks, but they had yet to put it on Nyrri. Every time they tried, she threw a fit. Once Nyrri had even knocked the princess into a rosebush, the thorns ripping through her silk dress. Ophelia nearly combusted when she saw the minor scratches marking the princess' arms and back.

Graeson scratched his chin. "Honestly, I think Medenia said that because she wanted to keep you for herself. But don't you want to see something new? Something other than this godsforsaken garden?"

Nyrri continued swatting at the butterfly that circled her as if he wasn't even there. As if she was perfectly content to be surrounded by butterflies and decaying flowers.

This is a waste of time, the god complained, his patience dwindling. *To have wings yet refuse to fly—such a pity.*

Graeson may have been a demi-god, but he couldn't force Nyrri to fly.

The saddle hit the ground with a sad thump. Graeson plopped down beside it. He propped his elbows on his knees and rested his chin on his interlocked hands. "You know, I expected more from you. Do you remember when you saved us? We would have been dead if it wasn't for you. You didn't have to stop, but you did."

Gods, what was he doing? Talking to animals wasn't anything new to him, per se. They might not have been able to talk back, but Graeson still believed they could understand him. If nothing else, they could understand emotions: love and fear, hate and sorrow. But he had never had to convince his horse Calamity to do anything. She loved riding—anytime, anywhere. Still, as foolish as it might have seemed trying to convince Nyrri to put a saddle on, he persisted.

"I know you have a good heart, Nyrri. The *best* heart." He was laying it on thick, but desperate times called for drastic measures. "Kalisandre needs us right now."

Nyrri's paw stopped in the air, her talons withdrawing an inch. An ember of hope ignited in his chest.

He kept going. "Kalisandre is out there, and she needs us. She needs *you.*"

Nyrri rolled over, her limbs spread out like a starfish across the grass

Graeson raised a brow as he carefully brought his hand close to the saddle. "You promise you won't try to bite my hand off this time?"

Nyrri set her chin on the ground with a defeated huff.

Smiling in relief, Graeson snatched the saddle and hurried over before she changed her mind. To his relief, Nyrri didn't back away, only sneered at the saddle, a sharp, yellow canine peeking beneath her top lip. She closed her eyes and sulked as Graeson strapped it on her.

The saddle was beautifully crafted, made of a similar black leather the Tetrians used for their sheaths and uniforms. Along the edges, the maker had sewn brilliant purple, green, and opaque crystals into the material—Medenia's idea, of course. Graeson had to admire the craftsmanship, for in the sun, the crystals sparkled brilliantly, like stars in the night sky.

Snapping the last latch shut, Graeson patted Nyrri on the back. "See? That wasn't so hard. Now was it?"

Nyrri wiggled as if she was trying to shake off the new accessory. When the saddle didn't budge, her head fell. Disappointed, she huffed out a heavy exhale.

"It's only temporary," he promised.

She blew smoke out her nose before reluctantly crouching and lowering her back for Graeson.

Once mounted, he shifted, grabbed the pommel, and leaned forward. He tapped Nyrri on her neck like he would Calamity. "Let's go get our girl."

Nyrri released a roar as if in agreement, and Graeson barely had time to reestablish his grip before she sprinted across the open field. Her paws smacked the ground and kicked up plumes of dirt. When she spread her wings out parallel to the ground, Graeson flattened his body against her back. Then she jumped.

Nyrri flapped her wings, fiercely beating the air. As they soared up the side of the castle, Graeson could hear nothing but the racing wind roaring in his ears. The wind pushed his hair back. He squinted against the force of it, trying to maintain a visual on the path ahead.

He peered behind him, and he could have sworn the saddle shifted an inch.

Do you seek to kill us? the god roared, his fingers wrapping around the cage of his cell as he gritted his teeth.

This was your idea, he snapped back, gripping the pommel tighter.

The god exhaled a low rumble that hummed through his veins.

He supposed it didn't matter whose idea it was, not as Nyrri scaled the castle and pivoted around the spire. He sank deeper into the saddle, his body pressing flat against the drakonis' back as she climbed higher and higher. Air zipped past his ears, a numbing drum.

Unable to help himself, Graeson peeked at the ground once more. Dozens of tiny individuals scattered across the property, stopping and pointing at them in horror.

You are an embarrassment, the god hissed.

I do not care, Graeson gritted back.

As he held onto the pommel, his knuckles blanched, the thin skin drained of its normal warmth. He did not care if he looked like a coward or an embarrassment. For Kalisandre, he would do anything.

He only hoped he would make it to her in one piece.

CHAPTER 17
MYRA

"Is that...?" Laurince's words trailed off as he held his hand up to block the sun.

Beside Myra, Rian scoffed as he too stared at the drakonis scaling the castle. "It couldn't be. He wouldn't be that idiotic."

A small grin ticked at the corner of Myra's mouth. "He most certainly would."

Graeson was no more than a blip on Nyrri's back as he molded his form to hers to keep from falling off. His black hair and leather ensemble melted into the scales lining the drakonis' spine.

When Myra had talked to Kallie last night, she had instantly suspected Kallie was up to something. Kallie always was. So when word spread that the princess was missing this morning, Myra knew it was only a matter of time before Graeson went after her. She sent a quick prayer to the gods. Graeson needed all the luck he could get.

"He's a better man than I am," Rian said.

Laurince snorted and crossed his arms. "I'm not so sure about that."

Involuntarily, Myra's attention flicked to the captain's muscles straining against the cotton fabric. She swallowed hard and quickly forced her attention back to Rian as she silently sent another prayer to the gods, this one for purely selfish reasons.

"I don't know if I would have the courage," Rian said.

"*That's* courage?" Laurince asked, striking the sky as he pointed to the small figure. "You just said it was idiotic!"

Myra muffled her laughter with her hand.

"Of course it is. But if that doesn't prove he cares about her, what would?"

Laurince's gaze narrowed, and his nose twitched. "Are you still in love with her?"

Rian's face twisted, and a wave of muddied feelings washed over Myra.

"I don't know if I ever was *in* love with her," Rian said. "I cared for her—as much as one could in such a short timeframe. But to say I was in love with her would be taking it a step too far. Don't you think?"

Myra pursed her lips and shrugged as Nyrri headed toward the clouds. "I don't know. I don't think there is a schedule that love abides to. With the right person at the right time, it could happen in the blink of an eye." Realizing she had said the answer aloud, she ripped her gaze from the flying pair. Her two companions stared at her, dumbfounded.

"You really are something, aren't you?" Laurince asked, perplexed.

Myra wasn't sure if it was a compliment or not, but she decided to believe it was one. She knew she loved easily. She had always been a hopeless romantic, one who often chose the wrong man. Armen, her last love interest who had introduced himself to her under a different name, had been a spy for the Pontians and disappeared the moment he and Myra had arrived in Pontia. Many people would have sworn off love after that, but Myra was a glutton for punishment. As she stood there, she couldn't help but hope that one day someone would love her enough to fly after her.

If the war didn't kill me first.

The thought rushed over her like a bucket of ice-water. She blinked away the fantasies and wiped the sweat from her palms on her thighs.

"Did you know she was going to run?" Rian asked her.

"Run?"

Rian nodded. "That's what she's doing, right? Running away?"

"Kallie wouldn't run. Not this time." Myra was certain of it. If she knew Kallie, the princess would be running straight toward King Domitius.

"Then where is she—" Rian gasped. "She wouldn't."

Myra didn't bother voicing a response. Whether Rian and Laurince harbored ill-feelings towards Kallie or not, they all were there when she had suggested a trade.

Rian looked at Laurince, eyes wide. A silent conversation passed between them, but before Myra could analyze it further, Laurince brushed his hand through his hair and said, "Come on. Let's get back to it."

Myra tipped her head back and groaned.

"Arms up, feet apart," the captain instructed.

"This is useless, you know," Myra whined, her body already protesting. They had been practicing positions and movements for over an hour. She hadn't even picked up a training sword, yet her body screamed when she bent her knees, her thighs aching. She would be even sorer come morning.

"The ability to defend yourself is not useless," Laurince argued. "Now, come on. Just like we practiced."

Pouting, Myra grumbled and shifted into the stance Laurince had made her learn when they were on the run.

"If I have to spend hours reading, you can spend an hour training," Laurince said.

She glanced at Rian, who had returned to his own training. "I know you said research was not his strong suit, but maybe arithmetic is actually the captain's weak point. It's already been an hour."

Rian snorted, the longsword nearly slipping from his hand as he struck the training dummy.

"I'm more than happy to call it a day if you can run through the movements without falling flat on your ass," Laurince challenged, tucking his hands beneath his crossed arms.

"Fine." Myra shook out her arms and began.

Three movements in and she was already flat on her back.

"That rock wasn't there a second ago! You sabotaged me."

Laurince stood over her, his head blocking the sun and casting a shadow across her. His dark hair fell around his face in a halo. "I didn't have to sabotage you. You're the one who let a pebble bring you down," he said, holding out a small rock.

"That's not a pebble," she mumbled.

Laurince arched a brow, and Myra's gaze flicked to the dimple that appeared at the corner of his amused grin.

"Let's try that again, shall we?"

CHAPTER 18
KALLIE

THE GROUND QUAKED, AND THE HORSES REARED. KALLIE FLATTENED herself against her horse's back. A couple seconds later, Winter's hooves pounded the ground, the jolt so violent it vibrated across the vertebrae running down Kallie's spine.

With labored breathing and shaking hands, Kallie looked at Ellie. The same fear that undoubtedly shone in Kallie's eyes was reflected in Ellie's own wide, dilated pupils.

That was not a natural quake. She would recognize the sound of the Frenzian explosives anywhere. Even though they were likely miles away, Kallie could almost taste the metallic tang and acrid bite of smoke.

"We can't," Ellie said, righting herself. Wisps of white hair floated around her face.

"We have to," Kallie pleaded, her hands flexing over the reins.

They hadn't left Tetria yet. These were Ellie's people, Medenia's people. If civilians were in danger, they couldn't abandon them.

"We don't even know what we're up against. What if it's Domitius' army? What if he lied? We can't—"

"If people are in danger," Kallie interrupted, knuckles blanching, "we need to find out. We need to help them. That's the whole point, isn't it?"

Ellie's mouth formed a flat line. She twisted the reins around one of her hands, and the rope dug into her skin.

Kallie broke eye contact, her attention turning toward the woods. Her power thrummed inside her core. She bit her bottom lip, debating.

"Fine," Ellie gritted out at last.

Kallie sunk into the saddle, thankful she didn't have to persuade Ellie or abandon her.

With a tug on the reins, Ellie steered her horse toward the blast. "But whatever happens, you stay by me, got it?"

Kallie nodded. Then they were off, riding toward the dark smoke billowing in the sky.

FLAMES CONSUMED THE SMALL VILLAGE, untamable and enraged, as they whipped across the crumbling roofs. The black smoke swallowed the blue sky. Kallie coughed and pounded her fist against her chest, the smoke still thick and rough, even hundreds of yards away.

On the outskirts of the village, where the ash was only a sprinkling of snow, the survivors huddled together. Parents cradled their children as they watched their homes crumble to rubble. The flickering flames shone in their horrified eyes as they cowered together, unable to stop the catastrophe from spreading. The fire was too far gone.

Ellie and Kallie jumped off their horses. Kallie held her arm against her mouth as they ran to the crowd.

"What happened?" Ellie asked, her gaze darting across the blazing sight.

The closest villager, a small, stout woman, swiped her ash-covered curls away from her face and smeared soot across her brown cheek. "It all happened so fast," she said through the tears running down her face. "I—I don't even understand what I saw."

Wood splintered. The woman choked on a cry as the roof came crashing down, and the small house flattened from its weight.

"They came from the skies," a man said, pulling the trembling woman against his chest. They shared the same golden brown eyes. He must have been her son.

"The skies? What are you—"

Kallie sucked in a sharp inhale, and Ellie's gaze smacked into hers.

The war had already started. They were too late.

CHAPTER 19
KALLIE

THEY HAD ONLY STAYED WITH THE VILLAGERS FOR A FEW HOURS, helping where they could and providing comfort where they couldn't. Ellie had told the Tetrians to go to the castle, to tell Queen Cetia what had happened, what they had seen in exchange for shelter, food, and protection. Most of the survivors were too shocked to understand or parse what had happened. The attackers didn't stay long, only flew over the village to drop the explosives that had set the village aflame before darting back east. A few of the villagers had even spotted the Frenzian crest on the assailants' breastplates. From what Kallie and Ellie could gather, the creatures that had attacked the village were the new humanoid experiments Myra had mentioned. Humans bearing large wings—Kallie hadn't believed it when Myra told her, and she struggled to believe it now. Yet, the evidence was right there.

As Kallie stared at the aftermath of the destruction, she debated returning to the castle. With the war already having begun, what was the point of continuing down this path? Domitius had already started attacking. They needed to gather troops.

"There's still time," Ellie had said when she had seen the doubt creeping into Kallie's eyes. "You can still end this before more people get hurt."

Kallie was no longer sure, though. How many more people would die before then? How many more attacks would befall innocent civilians?

But as she took in the sight of the Tetrians rallying around each other, neighbors wrapping wounds, mothers squeezing their children's faces and wiping away their tears, Kallie knew there was no other choice. She had to continue. She had to reach Domitius. Now more than ever.

So as they made their way through Borgania, Kallie shouldn't have been surprised that Ellie returned to the other urgent matter Kallie had repeatedly ignored.

"You need to practice," Ellie said, folding her arms over her chest. They stood along a river as the horses rested. Birds chirped as they bounced from branch to branch. It was strange to see the forest untouched after witnessing such destruction.

Kallie kicked a rock and sent it bouncing deeper into the woods. "We need to keep moving."

Whenever they stopped, Ellie would ask Kallie to practice manipulating her. While Kallie knew she should use her power, she found every excuse not to. She needed to relieve herself; she needed to sleep; they needed to get going. It didn't matter what the excuse was; she found one.

At first, Ellie didn't push her too much. While Ellie hadn't admitted it, Kallie had suspected the warrior could hear Kallie's mind spinning with worry—worry over the friends they left behind, worry over the path ahead, worry that Graeson would find them before they reached Domitius. But as the hours and days slipped by, Ellie's patience grew thin. And with the situation advancing and becoming more emergent, it was practically nonexistent.

Kallie snatched her bag from the ground.

"What are you going to do when you face Domitius and your gift fails you?" Ellie pressed, stepping into Kallie's space. The stench of old smoke smacked Kallie in the face. Despite the distance they had put between themselves and the burning village, the aroma still lingered on their clothes and in their hair.

"It won't." The lie was ash on her tongue, but she didn't have the strength to face it right now. They needed to keep moving.

"But how do you know?" Ellie snapped. "Dani warned me what happens when someone doesn't use their power for an extended period, Kallie. This isn't healthy. You need to use it."

"My emotions are fine!"

Ellie quirked a brow.

Kallie groaned. "*This*—my anger, my frustration—has nothing to do with not using my power. It has everything to do with what we just saw! The war is already here, Ellie, yet what are we doing? What is *everyone* doing? Wasting time." Kallie took a deep breath, closing her eyes as she steadied her breathing.

She was in control.

She was in control.

She was—

"You don't have to do anything crazy. All you need to do is have me pick up a stick or something," Ellie said.

Kallie put her hand on her hip, her knuckles digging into the sharp bone. "What would be the point of that, hmm?"

"At least then you would know you can still access your power!" Ellie shouted, making the birds in the nearby trees flee from the branches.

Kallie's gift stirred in the pit of her core, eagerly awaiting her to use it, to pull from it. It twisted inside of her, teasing, taunting. It was second nature. She grabbed onto it, coaxing it. All it took was one touch, one thought, and it was soaring through her bloodstream, pouring down her fingertips. It was honey and sweet and—

Kallie released it in an instant, tossing it away. "Accessing it isn't the problem." She spun on her heel and stormed toward Winter.

"Then what is?" Ellie shouted at her back.

Kallie mounted the horse. "We've wasted enough time. Let's move."

Ellie groaned but got on her horse without another word.

I'm in control. I am not him.

KALLIE AWOKE to the sound of rushing water. Her eyes sprang open, expecting to be drenched by a storm. But when she looked up, all she saw were white fluffy clouds and an ice-blue sky. She went to push herself up, and her hands sank into the soil—no, not soil, *sand.*

Kallie gasped and forced herself into a sitting position. Her gaze immediately flicked to the large boulder sitting at the edge of the lake. Her heart dropped to the bottom of her stomach as she recognized the Whispering Springs.

"He's not here."

Kallie spun around, and sand flew into her mouth from the movement. "*Terin?*"

Her brother leaned against a tree at the edge of the beach. "Hi, Kals," he said with a weak smile.

Her attention flicked to his hair. The long waves were gone. "You cut your hair," she said, standing up.

He brushed a hand across his head. "It was time."

Kallie brushed the debris from her hands and looked around, confused. There was only one other time she had been here in this dream-state when Fynn wasn't. "If Fynn isn't here, why am I?"

"It was the easiest way to reach you. I wanted to let you know we arrived in Pontia."

"And?" Kallie asked, her heart pounding in her chest. Was something wrong? Was someone hurt?

"*And* mother is outraged, to say the least," Terin said as he approached, his hands stuffed deep into his pockets.

"Has she deemed you all traitors?"

Terin scoffed and flicked his hand dismissively. "No. That's not why she's outraged. Apparently, she was bluffing, knowing the threat would get us back home quicker. I should have listened to Dani when she said she was."

At Dani's name, concern flooded Kallie's body like a tidal wave. She hated sea-travel on a normal day, and she couldn't imagine how the journey went for Dani while carrying. "How is Dani?"

"Her mother and the healers are currently suffocating her, but she's doing well. Her mother is beside herself that Dani wants to leave already." A half-grin appeared on her brother's face as if recalling something amusing. "Dani keeps trying to sneak away to join the council meetings to help figure out our plan of attack. Movement is slow on that front."

Kallie nodded in understanding. Then she recalled something else he had said. "Wait, if Esmeray isn't mad that you all came to the mainland, then why is she?"

Terin's mouth flattened into a thin line, and a knowing look passed across his face.

Kallie pointed at herself. "You can't mean that she's mad at *me*?"

Terin scratched his head. "She's mad at me too, if it's any consolation."

"Why is she mad at you? You did nothing wrong."

"For letting you go after Domitius. She doesn't trust him, and she's worried he will try to trick you."

She squeezed her hands into tight fists. "I can handle myself."

"I know. But she also knows who Domitius is. They have history."

"History?" Kallie asked, blinking.

Terin nodded. "She refuses to give any details about it, but she's worried about you." Terin reached out a hand, but Kallie took a step back.

"I won't turn around, Terin. I can't."

Her brother sighed. "I know that, but Mother at least wanted me to try."

"Is that why you came?"

"Not the only reason," he said, shifting on his feet. His brows bunched together. "I also wanted to make sure you were all right."

Kallie rubbed a hand across her neck. "I'm fine."

His gaze flicked to her hand. A small patch of pale skin wrapped around her bare finger. "And is Graeson…?"

She dropped her hand and covered it with the other. "He hasn't caught up yet."

Nodding, Terin stuffed his hands in his pockets. "Will you promise me something?"

"What?" Kallie asked hesitantly.

He took a step toward her but didn't reach out. "If things go south and you see a way out, take it."

Kallie swallowed the lump in her throat as the world faded around them. The sun dimmed as if its flames were dying. The sky lost its vibrancy, the shade turning into a muted blue hue.

"Promise me, Kals," her brother pleaded, fear spilling from his eyes. "Promise me we will get to be a family again."

Tears sprang to her eyes, and she bit her bottom lip. She couldn't promise Terin something she knew might be impossible to keep.

But before she could even try to lie, the dream slipped from her fingertips like raindrops falling into her palm.

CHAPTER 20
GRAESON

For most of his life, Graeson had believed he would die at the end of a blade. The past few days, however, were making him question that theory.

After only a few days of traveling, Graeson had lost count of how many times he had almost died by flight. The first day of flying had consisted of a series of near-death experiences. He didn't know which was worse: taking off or landing. Every time Nyrri launched into the air, Graeson was thrown back. His knuckles would turn stark white as he held onto the pommel with a deadly grip. Even when he pressed his body flat against Nyrri's back, the strength of the wind and the pull of gravity threatened to send him falling to his death.

As they flew over the cypress trees, the air, which had previously nipped at Graeson's fingers, turned thick and suffocating. Graeson yearned to be back on the ground, but he had to keep going.

You cannot lose me when you never had me.

The last words Kalisandre said to him rang in his mind on an endless loop. They twisted together like an infection, and once it was in his bloodstream, he couldn't shake them.

Was he making a mistake? Kalisandre would undoubtedly be furious with him when he finally caught up with them.

But then Graeson imagined Domitius driving his blade through her heart.

Graeson would find another way to save his mother, even if that meant flying to Ardentol himself. He squeezed his thighs against Nyrri's back and tugged on the reins. At the signal, Nyrri dove, nose first, spiraling toward the trees. Graeson's hips lifted, pulling away from the saddle, and he tightened his hold. With every ten feet, he could feel his weight shifting more and more, his life flashing before his eyes as he held on. His muscles strained, and his stomach jumped into his throat.

Nyrri weaved through the trees, her wings rigid as she pivoted and dodged the long branches that threatened to rip them from the sky. The ground barreled toward them.

The moment he thought he was done for, when he thought his luck had run out, Nyrri straightened and landed with a crash. The drakonis' heels dug into the earth. Dirt and leaves flew into the air in a plume of smoke and debris.

When they finally came to a teeth-clattering stop, Graeson's limbs were nearly locked in place. Somehow he unlatched himself from the saddle and rolled off the drakonis' back. Hitting the ground, he rotated onto his stomach and pressed his palms into the dirt. He pushed himself up on shaking arms and retched.

He finally understood why Kallie despised sea-travel.

What an embarrassment, the god hissed. *A god who can't even handle the skies.*

At the god's insult, Graeson gritted his teeth. His fingers curled into the dirt, breaking the hard earth. As he hovered over his bile for the third time that week, he wondered if he had made a drastic mistake in thinking taking Nyrri would be faster than a horse. They had to have been traveling faster than the horses were. But right then, he didn't know if speed was in his favor. They still had to check the ground every so often because of the foliage covering the landscape. He didn't want to risk losing Kallie and Ellie simply because he had passed them.

Beside him, Nyrri growled, the noise deep and low.

Graeson tensed. Slowly, he peered through his hair. A small group of people stared back, their faces drained of color. Their expressions varied from horror to fear to disgust.

Graeson pushed himself into a crouch and wiped his mouth with his sleeve. "You would throw up too if you barreled through the sky."

One man held out a dagger, his hand trembling. "Stay back."

The god chuckled. Graeson almost did too until he scanned the group. His attention fell to a little girl holding her father's leg. Her small blue eyes darted between Graeson and Nyrri, whose growl was a low hum as the drakonis crouched into a defensive position.

Graeson pushed to his feet despite his body's protest and held up his hands. "I do not wish any of you harm."

The man with the dagger took a step forward, signaling for the others to move behind him. "I said, stay back!"

Freezing, Graeson eyed the strangers. Their clothes were covered in soot, and ash was smeared across their faces and necks. He sniffed and smelled a faint trace of smoke wafting from them.

"What happened?" he demanded, fear spiking through him. Kallie had to have gone this way. Was she hurt?

"Are—are you one of them?" the girl's father asked.

"One of *who*?" Graeson asked, confused.

"Don't play dumb!" the man wielding the weapon shouted.

"Whoever you think I am, you are gravely mistaken," Graeson said.

Inside, the god snarled. Graeson did his best to keep him contained, but he was exhausted, his energy depleted from the long day of traveling. The Borganian border was only a few more hours away, and he wanted to reach it before nightfall. With every minute that passed, the sun sank lower and lower. Shadows were already spreading across the terrain. While Nyrri didn't have a problem seeing in the dark, Graeson would have a hard time identifying anyone through the trees. Their window of opportunity was closing in, and both of them knew it.

"Who attacked you?" Graeson asked when no one moved.

"Like you don't know," the man spat.

Another member of the group stepped forward. "They wore the Frenzian crest," an older woman said. "They came from the skies."

"The *skies?*" Graeson asked, unsure if he had heard her correctly.

The woman nodded. "Some of them looked like the same species as…" She eyed Nyrri, whose lips pulled back into a snarl. "So you can see our hesitation to believe you."

Graeson's entire body went rigid. The war had begun. Had they found Kalisandre? Had she already tried to—

"Jewels!"

Graeson's attention snapped to the little girl who stumbled forward. The father tried to grab her by the wrist, but she slipped from his grasp.

The girl, Jewels, cocked her head at Graeson, eyes wide and unblinking. "You won't save her."

Graeson's heart skipped a beat at the girl's words. Even the god was on high alert. "W-who?"

She blinked up at him, and the hue of her eyes brightened, melting into the same shade as the sky. Goosebumps ran down Graeson's neck as she stared at him.

"The one you're after. You won't save her," she said.

Graeson's gaze snapped to the father. "What is she talking about?"

"I-I don't know," the father said, snatching Jewels from the ground and eyeing those around him. "Sometimes she says things she doesn't mean."

Graeson's brows drew together as his attention flicked from the man to his daughter. A strange thought popped into his head.

It wasn't possible. She couldn't be a seer. Unless...

"She's just a child," the father pleaded as he cradled his daughter in his arms. Tucking her head against his chest, he whispered something into her ear. But Jewels continued to stare at Graeson, sadness curling her brows inward.

Leave, the god roared. *Now!*

Graeson didn't have time to convince the strangers he was not a threat. The child, whether a seer or not, was not his enemy. Not by any means.

"Come on," he said to Nyrri.

The drakonis released a tired sigh but lowered her back. After spending this much time together, he knew to interpret that as a soft yes. He hoisted himself back into the saddle.

The strangers stared at him as they huddled closer together, fear dripping from their countenances.

Nyrri released a quiet whine.

He patted her on the back. "We'll find them."

But as Nyrri took off for the skies once more, Graeson wasn't sure if he was trying to convince Nyrri or himself.

CHAPTER 21
MYRA

THE PRECARIOUS STACKS OF BOOKS WOBBLED ON THE TABLE. MYRA pursed her lips to hide the blooming smile. She flipped to the next page. Through strands of blonde hair, she peered at the captain sitting on the other side of the table. "You're doing it again."

"Doing what?" Laurince asked.

"The—"

But that was as far as Myra got before the tower of books collapsed.

Someone cleared their throat, and Myra looked over her shoulder at the older man sitting at a nearby table. He glared at them and pushed his thick, round-framed glasses up the bridge of his nose with a shove.

A loud bang sounded, and the table jolted once more, sending a few more books falling.

Myra turned to find the captain rushing out of his seat.

Apologizing to the man, Laurince knelt on the ground and began picking up the texts. "I—I'm sorry. I didn't even realize I was doing it."

The captain had been bouncing his knee nonstop since he sat

down with Myra and Rian. If it wasn't his knee, he was tapping his finger on one of the leather-bound books. Every *thump-thump* was a reminder of the time ticking by, the time spent reading books that had thus far proven useless.

Yet, despite the creeping doubt, a small grin poked at the corner of Myra's mouth at Laurince's bewildered expression. They might have found nothing particularly useful yet, but Myra could not say she regretted the time spent in the library with the captain and the king.

She joined Laurince on the floor. She ran her hand over one book, the old leather curling at the corners. "It's all right. These ones were useless anyway." She meant for the words to come out light and playful. But when Laurince's expression turned solemn, she knew she had failed.

"Myra," Laurince said, drawing out her name, "don't give up yet. There's bound to be something." He held up a book and smiled, amused. "Get it, *bound*?"

Her brows scaled her forward.

"*Bound* like a book is bound?" He lowered the book, his smile faltering. He swiped a hand through his hair. His recent haircut had gotten rid of the slight wave in his hair. A piece hung in front of his face, and he shoved it away and shrugged. "I suppose it wasn't that funny."

Myra shook herself out of her stupor. "No, it was. I'm just..."

"Worried?"

Among other things, she thought.

Laurince offered her a sad smile. "I'm sure Graeson has caught up with them by now. They should be back any day now."

"No, Kallie's too stubborn. Once her mind is made up, there's no changing it." Her gaze fell on the books still scattered on the ground. Some had landed face-down and open. Several pages were now bent and folded over. She should offer Magnolia her services in the morning to pay for the damages.

A calloused hand landed on hers. "She's going to be all right," Laurince said.

Myra's tongue went dry. "I—"

"What happened here?"

Myra ripped her hand from Laurince's and stood, her hip bumping into the table. "Nothing," she blurted as Laurince said, "I accidentally knocked them over."

Rian glanced at Myra, a question flashing across his features. Before she could explain the lie, Rian turned to Laurince and chuckled. "You really hate reading, don't you?"

Myra's shoulders sagged in relief.

"I don't hate reading."

Both Rian and Myra raised an eyebrow at that. They both had caught the captain falling asleep on numerous occasions when they were supposed to be researching.

The captain rolled his eyes. "I just don't love reading *these* texts."

Rian pointed over his shoulder at a series of shelves. "I found some children's books earlier. Want one of those instead? One had a dragon on it and tons of illustrations. Very few words."

Laurince shoved Rian in the shoulder. "The words aren't the problem, *Your Highness*," he said, the title a playful hiss. He bent down and grabbed the rest of the books. He placed them on the table and leaned against it, tapping his fingers on the cover. "I am getting peckish, though," he mumbled.

Myra sighed, a sense of hopelessness replacing the previous embarrassment. "We should probably give this a rest today anyway."

"We can return tomorrow if you want?"

Myra couldn't tell if the offer was out of pity or sympathy. Either way, she forced a smile on her face and nodded. Although the smile she wore didn't reach her eyes. Not even a little as the doubt crept in and created a home inside her chest.

MYRA NEVER CONSIDERED herself to be skilled in premonition. The gods, while often cruel, had spared her by not granting her the ability to see the future. Yet somehow the doubt that had followed her from the library to the dining hall that night seemed to nag at her. She struggled to eat the meal in front of her and pushed the roasted potatoes around her plate aimlessly.

The dining hall was full of staff and its inhabitants, but the head table was barer than usual. Both the queen and the princess were absent, along with several others.

Every whisper, every footstep had her looking over her shoulder. Something was wrong. She could feel it twisting around the wide-open space, latching onto the walls, and crawling toward the ceiling like ivy.

"Rian?"

At the sound of Medenia's voice, Myra snapped her head up from her barely touched plate.

Still in her training leathers, the princess strolled toward them. Wisps of hair floated around her, and her braid was nearly falling apart. Ophelia walked beside Medenia and wore a similar set of leathers. When they reached the end of the table, apprehension dripped from the pair like a leaky roof.

"Hmm?" Rian hummed over a mouthful of veal.

"Can I talk to you, please?" The princess tilted her head toward the hallway.

"Now?"

Medenia nodded, mouth drawn flat.

"Very well," Rian said, standing. Laurince followed suit.

Medenia cocked a brow. "I only asked for the king's presence."

"If I go, he goes," Rian stated.

Medenia pursed her lips, her gaze flicking between the two men. But as if deciding it wasn't worth the argument, she conceded. Without another word, the four of them filtered out of the room.

As Myra sat at the table alone, the nausea only worsened. She didn't know how long she had sat there. With each minute that went by, her mind spiraled further. Had Medenia heard something? Had Kallie already met with Domitius? The possibilities worsened with every passing minute.

Soon, the clatter of dishes stirred her from her thoughts. Blinking, she looked around her and found the room almost empty. Nearby, a few staff members were clearing the dishes. Her gaze turned to the two empty seats across from her, the plates still half-full. Clearing the stiffness from her throat, Myra stood, grabbing her plate. She began stacking the other two as well when a staff member stopped her.

"I got it," the man said, offering her a polite smile.

Myra awkwardly set down the stack of plates and left the table.

Exiting the dining hall, she strolled through the hallways, her steps heavy as she made her way toward her room. She passed several staff members and warriors scurrying across the castle, their heads tilted together and their whispers a hiss in the air. In their wake, thick anxiety trailed after them.

Myra turned a corner and nearly yelped when she almost ran head-first into the librarian.

Eyes wide, Magnolia reached for the wall to steady herself. "Apologies, Myra. I should have been paying closer attention."

"No, no. I should have," Myra said with a soft smile. The curve of her lips twisted into a frown, though, as Magnolia tried to maneuver past her. She spun around, following her. "Is something going on?"

Magnolia halted. "You haven't heard?"

"Heard what?"

"A borderland village was attacked."

"*Attacked*? By whom?" Myra asked, though she had a feeling she already knew the answer.

"Ardentol and Frenzia. The village was burned to the ground. The survivors are on their way here. The entire staff has been asked to pitch in to help prepare the castle for them."

Myra shifted on her feet. The start of a rash began to break out across her neck. "Is there…is there anything I can do?"

Magnolia shook her head. "No, but thank you. The best thing you can do right now is get some rest." She chewed her bottom lip, and fear spread across her countenance. "I…I fear this is only the beginning."

CHAPTER 22
KALLIE

Beyond the trees, thick, ominous clouds rolled above them. A storm was coming, and the last thing Kallie wanted was to be caught in it.

Wrinkling her nose, she asked, "Are you sure we can't stay at an inn?"

"We've already passed the Borganian border," Ellie said, untying her bag from the grommet on the saddle. "If word has spread that Domitius is looking for you and Rian, then we need to stay away from anyone who might recognize you."

Kallie snorted. "I am not that recognizable."

"Shall we recount the number of times you have been paraded around in the past year alone?" Ellie threw her bag a few feet away from her and dug her fists into her hips. "First at that ostentatious ceremony in Ardentol, then during the week-long wedding extravaganza. Nearly half of Vaneria was invited to your wedding. Next to Rian's, your face is one of the most recognizable faces in the seven kingdoms."

Kallie squeezed the bridge of her nose and groaned. She longed for a warm bed and a blazing hearth at her feet. She scanned the terrain. Only dirt, decaying vegetation, and various unfamiliar trees surrounded them. She eyed a small bush. That had to be more comfortable than lying on the ground. It was somewhat pillow-shaped.

A pillow likely crawling with spiders and other insects.

Gods, she was losing her mind.

"So, no inns?"

Ellie tossed her hands up with a frustrated humph. "How daft are—"

Kallie's smile broke.

Ellie narrowed her eyes. "I hate you, you know."

Kallie chuckled. "So that's the real reason you're forcing me to sleep on the ground when a storm is coming." She grabbed her bag from Winter's saddle. There had to have been something inside it she could use to shield herself once it started pouring.

"The trees will provide substantial coverage. And if your hair gets wet, so be it." Ellie flicked her ponytail behind her. "I don't remember you being this annoying the last time we traveled together."

Kallie frowned. "I was unconscious almost the entire time."

Ellie snapped her fingers. "Ah, that's right. You were much more tolerable that way. How long do you think it would take to send a messenger bird to Terin and see if he can join us? Or do you think he can work his magic through that dream state of his?"

The two women laughed. But when their gazes connected and reality returned, their joviality swiftly fell to the wind.

Ellie looked up at the sun and sighed. "I'll get a fire going. We still have some daylight and some time before the rain comes in. Might as well use it."

THE TINY REMNANTS of their meager meal burned in the middle of the coals. Today's pickings were slim, but they made do. A rumble of thunder shuddered through the trees. The storm had held off during dinner, but it seemed their luck was soon to dry up.

Kallie held her hands near the dying fire, soaking up as much warmth as she could before they would have to extinguish it. The nights were already cold as it was. The storm would only make it worse.

A bed of coals lay beneath the three logs that were leaning against one another. They glowed in the fire, steadily changing from red to yellow to white and back again. Soon, the coals would start crackling and embers would fly out, threatening to land on them.

"Will you at least—"

"No," Kallie interrupted before Ellie could ask her to use her ability again.

"You don't even know what I was going to ask," Ellie argued.

Kallie peered across the white smoke twisting in the space between them.

The warrior sat on the other side of the fire in nearly the same position as Kallie. Ellie's hands hovered over the small flames, her pale nose tipped pink. Although unlike Kallie, Ellie's wide, black eyes reeked of false innocence.

Kallie cocked a brow. "You mean you *weren't* going to ask me to manipulate you for the hundredth time?"

"Actually, no. I wasn't." Tucking her legs closer to her body, Ellie wrapped her arms around them and rested her chin on her knees. "So I'll take that apology now."

Kallie snorted. "As if I believe that."

"Aren't you curious about what I was going to ask instead?"

"No, not really."

It couldn't have been anything good. Whenever Ellie asked

questions, it made Kallie think. And right now, thinking was dangerous. Her mind kept wandering to the village. Were the people all right? Had they reached the castle yet? Had Domitius and Sebastian sent more of their cronies to Tetria? And what of Pontia? Had Terin and the others made any progress gathering the army?

Kallie rubbed the heels of her palms against her eye sockets. "Fine, what is it?"

"Why *won't* you manipulate me?"

Kallie's lips parted, then closed, her tongue becoming heavy in her mouth. "I already told you," she mumbled.

"No, you didn't. You've denied my request one hundred times, but you haven't told me why once." Ellie stoked the fire with a long stick and shrugged. "While you don't owe me an explanation, I am curious."

Beneath the thick cloak, Kallie rubbed her arms, her hands running across the scattering of goosebumps that poked through the fabric of her blouse. Every time Ellie had asked Kallie to use her power, her power sang, beckoning her to pull its threads, to twist and tug at them. A few times, Kallie had nearly relented to its call but had dropped the thread of golden honey before it was too late.

"Whenever I have manipulated people in the past, it always gave me a rush," Kallie admitted quietly. "I felt unstoppable. I could make anyone do or say anything I wanted. I could bend someone's very will to my own. If I wanted them to jump, they would. If I wanted them to crawl on their knees before me, they would do so without hesitation. If I told them to take their life…" Kallie swallowed, letting her words trail off. Ellie could figure out the rest.

She didn't dare look at Ellie, afraid of what she would see. Kallie had done many things she was ashamed of, many things she had never spoken aloud before. All the memories, the assignments, and the punishments sat heavily on her chest. It was as if a brick sat on her ribcage, making it harder and harder to breathe as the regrets pressed against the bones.

"Who am I to take someone's will away?" Kallie asked, voice raw. "I am no god."

"But the gods did grant you that power, did they not?" Ellie asked without an ounce of criticism tainting her voice. "It is because of them that any of you even have these abilities. Do you not believe that maybe they entrusted you with it for a reason?"

Kallie's nails dug into her arms. "What reason could that be? All I have ever done is cause those I care about harm."

"Is that really true though?" Ellie asked.

Kallie didn't bother to respond. They all knew what she did, the lives she had cost.

"Terin told me about the day your brother died," Ellie said after a moment.

Kallie bit her tongue, and tears sprang to her eyes. The flames before her transformed, transporting her to the Pontian village set ablaze by Sebastian and his soldiers. She could hear Dani's cries as she knelt on the shore, hear the plunk of Fynn's body as it hit the water. How many months would have to pass for the memory to fade?

She wondered if it ever would.

"If I hadn't been born with this ability, none of that would have happened," Kallie said, voice trembling.

"I can't say whether that is true. However, what I do know is that more people would have died if you *hadn't* used your gift. Terin told me what you did when you followed Sebastian to the safe room. He told me how you were the reason he, your mother, and so many others made it out alive."

Terin was only trying to see the silver lining. It wasn't that simple. Nothing ever was.

"Sebastian and his men were searching for *me*," Kallie explained, her throat burning and her vision blurring.

"But when you revealed yourself, they didn't leave right away. The guards were going to kill them, weren't they?"

A tear slipped down Kallie's cheek. She looked up, but the wilting foliage covered the dark sky. Not a single star slipped through the brown, dying leaves and the tenebrous clouds.

A raindrop smacked Kallie on the forehead. The storm had finally arrived.

Rain pelted the leaves above. The foliage was so thick that only a few droplets slipped through and fell to the ground.

Kallie wiped the raindrop away.

A hand gripped her knee. She didn't know when Ellie had moved, but now Ellie was sitting beside her, and Kallie found herself leaning into the woman's embrace.

"You manipulated Sebastian that night. You *saved* them."

"But I couldn't save Fynn. Not when it mattered."

The patter of the storm was a soothing drum, loud enough to block out the sound of Kallie's thumping heart. Loud enough to cover her soft cries.

Ellie held her tighter. "You may never forgive yourself for that night and many others, Kallie. You may even think that your gift is a curse. However, remember why we're here today. You have the chance to stop this war, and that is a gift in itself. But if you don't—"

A loud crack ripped through the trees, and Kallie jumped.

"What was that?" She sat up and wiped her cheeks with her palms.

"It was just thunder—"

Another sound cut Ellie off. The noise was almost feral, human yet not.

"That wasn't thunder," Kallie mumbled. "Unless thunder now growls."

Ellie was already on her feet, a weapon in each hand. Kallie did the same and unsheathed her dagger. The warrior tilted her head and pointed in one direction, then another.

With a single nod, Kallie crept toward the trees on the right. She sank into the shadows, praying that her fears were for nothing while knowing that was wishful thinking.

CHAPTER 23
KALLIE

KALLIE TIGHTENED HER GRIP ON THE DAGGER'S HILT AS SHE SNAKED her way through the forest. For the first time that night, she was thankful for the rain as it covered the sound of her footsteps. When she came upon a large branch, she stopped in her tracks and took a slow breath to steady her racing heart. Fear pounded against her chest, and sweat pooled at her nape. She scanned the trees, searching.

Then, she heard it—a low growl quickly followed by rattling branches. But this time, it was directly above her.

On trembling legs, she forced herself to look up.

Twisted high in the branches was a large form bathed in shadows, blocking the moon's light. She squinted at the blob, trying to identify it, but she couldn't make out a single—

The wood splintered, a crack ripped through the forest, and a horrendous screech came from the form. Kallie stumbled backward, and her heel caught on a wet log. She hit the ground with a teeth-clattering whack, and the air left her lungs. She choked on a gasp and scrambled back on all fours, her legs refusing to stand as the sky fell. Leaves, branches, twigs, and the shadowed form rained down. A mangled roar filled the forest as Kallie's back hit a tree trunk. A gust of wind smacked into her chest, forcing her eyes shut as the ground shook.

A few seconds passed, and a harrowing whine sounded.

Hesitantly, Kallie cracked open an eye and peered through the dust plume. She stifled her cough as she inhaled a puff of dirt. Swatting away the debris, she spotted the ball of shadows beneath a pile of broken branches and swallowed her scream.

She should run.

She should flee.

She should do *anything* other than stare.

Yet Kallie couldn't get herself to move. Her feet were locked to the ground.

Something akin to a groan spilled from the heap, and Kallie's lungs dropped to her stomach. The sound was not animalistic, but human. That couldn't have been right, though. What kind of human was—

The heap moved, and something shiny and black caught in the moonlight.

Was that a…was that a *wing?*

Shit. Shit.

Where was her dagger? She scanned the area, searching for it.

Two feet away, steel sparkled in the sliver of moonlight that spilled onto the ground. Without hesitation, Kallie dove for it, snatching it. The hilt was slick from the rain, and she tightened her grip around it.

They'd come. The drakonises. Domitius' army. They were here. They had found her.

The wing moved, and red orbs popped open. Kallie's jaw dropped. She recognized that snout, that lopsided tilt of the drakonis' mouth.

"*Nyrri?* What are you—"

A black leather saddle with brilliant stones that sparkled in the moonlight caught her eye. One of the straps was broken, its edges frayed.

Kallie sprinted forward.

Her knees smacked onto the ground. Ignoring the spike of pain vibrating up her bones, she frantically lifted and pushed the drakonis, searching, searching, searching.

She was wrong. She had to be.

Graeson wouldn't have risked flying here. He wouldn't have been so impudent as to do something so stupid as that.

Her movements became frantic; her breathing labored. Tears stung the backs of her eyes as she failed to move Nyrri, her body too slick from the rain. Was Nyrri wounded, too?

"Nyrri, you need to move. I can't—I can't lift you," Kallie cried out.

The drakonis released a short whine and lifted her wing that was tucked against her body. The dim light of the moon caught on raven-black hair.

Graeson.

Kallie scurried over to the other side, nearly trampling Nyrri to get to him. Her knees slid across the wet ground. Her hand trembled as she reached out. This was all her fault. She knew he would follow. If she had just gotten on that stupid boat, this wouldn't have happened.

He had to be alive. He had to be. She would know if he was dead. The bond—

Kallie hadn't accepted the bond, though. Was that even how the soul bond worked? Would she have known if he was dead if she had?

Her vision blurred, and her throat seized up.

Nyrri uncurled herself around Graeson, revealing his limp form.

Mud was smeared on his face. His shirt was soaked and stained, but Kallie couldn't make out the color in the dark.

"Graeson?" she called out, her voice hoarse.

He didn't move, didn't even flinch.

Behind her, Nyrri released a sad, high-pitched whine as the drakonis nudged him with her snout.

Swallowing the sharp lump in her throat, Kallie brushed his damp hair from his face, the moonlight catching on his scar. He had to be fine.

Rain poured through the foliage above, drenching them. Her teeth rattled, but she barely even felt the cold nipping at her skin. "Gray, wake up. Please—"

A muffled groan slipped from Graeson's lips, though his eyes remained shut, his brows pinched with pain.

"Thank the gods." She fell forward and dug her hands into his hair. When she realized he might have hurt his head from the fall, she softened her touch. Her gaze darted across his body, looking for any sign of a wound.

Graeson mumbled something, but the words were unintelligible.

"W-what was that?" She inched closer.

He took in a short, raspy breath. "I said"—he coughed, the sound as rough as sandpaper—"you never need to beg me, remember?"

Kallie's jaw fell open as she jerked back and stared down at him, aghast. This was no time for jokes or quips, yet there he was. And although he smirked at her, a glimmer of pain twitched at the corner of his lips. If he could joke, she could let some of her anger slip free.

"You imbecile! Why would you *fly* here?" Kallie shook her head, her thoughts a mess and her questions coming out one after another. "What happened? Are you hurt?"

He slowly cracked open his eyes and wrapped his hand around her wrist. "I'm fine, little mouse."

Kallie's attention fell to where he touched her. She held his shirt with a white-knuckled grip. She tried to peel her hand away, but Graeson slipped his fingers between hers, holding her hand against his chest.

"I-I wasn't sure if I was going to find you," he whispered, staring up at her.

She chewed on her bottom lip. She had always admired the moon's glow, its ethereal beauty. But as she looked into Graeson's eyes, she realized the moon was no match for the shade staring back at her. Threads of brilliant silver spun around his irises, the shade as sharp and clear as a fresh blade and even brighter than a full moon.

Then, right before she got lost in them, she remembered what she was supposed to be doing, *where* she was heading.

Kallie leaned back on her heels, putting space between her and Graeson. "You shouldn't have come," she said, forcing her voice to sound as cold as possible.

Graeson coming after her was inevitable. No matter what lies the others tried to weave, he would always come after her. She knew that. But now that he was in front of her, Kallie's heart was torn in two: one part of her wanted to make sure he was all right, and the other part of her was frustrated that he believed he could storm in here and stop her.

This was her mess to fix. This war was her fault. She had to put an end to it before more people were hurt.

She told Graeson the night she left that nothing had changed. It might have been a lie, but a necessary one. Yet there he was, still chasing her.

Still, as mad as she was, she couldn't deny the feeling that fluttered in her chest from seeing him there, alive. At least, she couldn't deny it to herself anymore.

Water splashed onto his cheek and rolled down his face. She

reached out, her hand hovering in the space between them, inches from touching him.

"I—" Graeson began but cut himself off when branches broke.

Gasping, Kallie spun around. Her grip loosened around her dagger when she spotted Ellie barreling through the trees, weapons in hand and lip curling.

Spotting them, the warrior dug her heels into the muck. "Thank the gods! It's just you." Ellie swiped her hand across her forehead, pushing her hair away from her face. Her hand fell when a huff sounded to Kallie's right. Ellie's eyes widened. "*Nyrri?*"

The drakonis puffed up her chest, sending her wings back and hugging them tightly to her body, as if insulted Ellie hadn't recognized her right away.

"Fuck," Ellie breathed out. "You two sure know how to make an entrance." She peeled her wet hair away from her neck with the tip of her blade. "Although it took you long enough. I thought you would have caught up with us on the first day, Gray. What happened here anyway?" she asked, waving one of her knives in a circle.

Groaning, Graeson dropped his head back onto the ground. "The storm came out of nowhere. We couldn't see. We were flying over when I saw what looked to be a fire. Nyrri's still getting used to carrying me, then add the element of rain and..." Graeson made a small crashing noise.

Nyrri shook out her wings, sending water droplets flying at them. Kallie wiped the water from her cheek.

Graeson huffed. "Look, Nyrri, you overestimated your ability. I'm not going to sugarcoat it."

Nyrri growled in annoyance, her ears folding back in shame.

"It's his fault for dragging you out here," Ellie said, scratching Nyrri beneath her chin. "We had expected him to take a horse, not put you in danger."

Nyrri released a soft humph as if in agreement.

"Wait," Graeson said, eyes bouncing between Kallie and Ellie. "You knew I'd follow?"

Ellie shrugged. "You're rather predictable."

Graeson sat up on his elbows and hissed out.

"Are you hurt?" Kallie asked, hurrying to help him. She scanned him, trying to identify the source of his pain.

Graeson ignored her concern. "Why didn't you tell me you were leaving?"

"Well, I'm going to go…tend to the fire," Ellie said, spinning on her heel.

"The fire is probably—" Kallie's words fell to the wind as Ellie scurried into the woods toward the campsite.

Kallie began to stand, but Graeson tugged on her hand, still expecting an answer.

She released a long exhale. "Can I please check to see if you are hurt before we talk about this?"

"I already told you I'm fine," Graeson said gruffly.

"Then stand up," she demanded, moving away.

Graeson muttered something about avoidance, but Kallie ignored him and folded her hands over her chest, waiting. The moment he leaned forward to push himself up, though, he released a hiss.

Kallie looked at his back and cursed.

A large stick protruded from his lower back. It punctured his shirt, piercing his skin. She grabbed her dagger and cut through the material.

"Hey! I liked this shirt." Graeson tried turning, but Kallie dug her nails into his shoulder.

"Don't move," she ordered. The skin around the stick was red and irritated. Blood dribbled down his back.

"Whatever it is, it's—" Graeson choked on his words the second

Kallie touched the stick. He dug his hands into the ground, his knuckles cracking.

She carefully let go of the stick. "You're not fine."

"Just pull it out," Graeson bit out through clenched teeth.

Kallie hesitated as she stared at his back. "I should go get our first-aid kit."

He pointed to Nyrri. "In the pouch."

Attached to the saddle on Nyrri's back hung a small pouch. Kallie leaned over and unhooked it. Opening it, she pulled out the supplies she needed.

Eyeing the stick, she asked, "Ready?"

Graeson groaned a noncommittal response.

Kallie pressed one hand on his shoulder, stabilizing him. She raised her other hand, and it shook in the air. She swallowed and carefully wrapped her fingers around the stick. "Deep breath, all right?"

Graeson inhaled. When she felt his breath hit its height, she pulled. He spat out a curse and snatched Kallie's hand holding his shoulder.

"Was that intentional?" he bit out.

"Perhaps," she said, tossing the stick away. She began cleaning the wound one-handed. It was a little awkward and would have been much easier and quicker if she had the use of both hands, but she couldn't get herself to ask him to release it. She told herself it was because she didn't wish to make a fuss, but she knew the truth. His touch was holding her together as much as it was him.

"Kal, I—"

She applied the alcohol to the wound, and he snapped his mouth shut.

"It doesn't look like the stick drove in too far. There's probably going to be a nasty scar," Kallie said, analyzing the wound. "We should move to the camp so I can stitch it."

Graeson released a disgruntled groan.

"Can you stand?"

Graeson nodded. Pressing his palms against his knees, he stood awkwardly. He leaned against her; whether on purpose, she didn't know. Either way, she wrapped an arm around his back.

"Come on," Kallie said, beginning to head in the direction Ellie had disappeared.

Graeson caught her hand in his. "Wait."

Kallie grimaced. "We really should stitch it up before it gets infected."

"It'll be fine."

She looked back at him and lifted a brow. He still seemed like he was in pain. His features were twisted, and his complexion was dull and devoid of its usual warmth. Had she missed something?

"What is it? Are you hurt somewhere else—"

"No," he said, interrupting her. "I just...I want to talk to you without Ellie around."

"Graeson," she warned. "I have to do this. Nothing you say will change my mind. She's your mother."

"And you're..." Graeson's words fell off as he looked at her. His hair was soaked, and the strands stuck to his forehead as water dripped down the contours of his face.

She wished he had believed her lie. It would have made this so much easier.

"Dani told me the truth," she admitted.

Tilting his head to the sky, he closed his eyes as the storm persisted with no end in sight. In the moonlight, the exhaustion was plain across his face. She wondered how much sleep he had gotten since leaving Tetria. How long had he been flying before Nyrri had crashed?

"Dani's always butting into things she shouldn't, isn't she?" he said.

Kallie curled a loose strand of hair behind her ear. "I'm glad she told me. I...I get it now."

"You do?"

She sighed and tucked her dagger back into its holster. "You think you can change fate, Graeson, but you can't. Neither of us can."

"I don't believe that. I don't believe our fates are sealed. I don't believe there is nothing we can do, that we have to accept that our chances are slim to none."

"Aren't you tired, though? How many times have you chased after me? How many times have you already fought against fate?"

"And how many times have I beaten it?" Graeson turned toward her, standing on his own. "I'm standing in front of you now, aren't I? I will never grow tired of fighting for you." He brushed a strand of hair behind her ear. The touch was almost nonexistent, yet it sent a wave of energy spiraling down her neck.

Ever since Kallie had arrived in Tetria, she had let herself sink into the shadows. She had lost her purpose. Since she had woken up in the hospital ward, she had felt like she was falling with no end in sight. For weeks, she had been waiting to hit the ground, wondering if she would crash or somehow land on her feet.

While she was still falling, Kallie finally felt herself rotating, turning, preparing to land. She no longer wished to freefall.

Accepting the bond would only hurt him. If the trade went south, if something happened to her...

She couldn't do that to him. She couldn't put him through that.

She refused to return to Tetria and pretend the war wasn't already here. She would never forgive herself if she gave up, if she let Domitius win.

"I cannot be what you want me to be," Kallie whispered.

His brows bunched together, and his eyes flicked back and forth between hers. "Who do you think I want you to be, Kal?"

"You want me to be safe, not reckless. You want me to sit somewhere while those I care about put their lives at risk for me."

"I—" Graeson began, but Kallie cut him off before he could say anything else.

"I'm going to go through with this whether or not you like it," Kallie said, determined. She needed him to understand. She needed him to know why she was breaking his heart—breaking both of theirs. "You may think that I am only doing this because I blame myself for this war, but that is not the entire truth. While my actions are in part to blame, I do not care that my reputation has been tarnished. I'm not doing this because I want people to look at me differently. Nothing I do will rewrite the past. I have come to terms with that. Not only do I need to do this, I *want* to. For the first time in my life, I have a choice, not only to prevent bloodshed, but to use my ability for good.

"Ever since we freed my mind, I've believed my gift to be a curse, that it could only be used for evil. Domitius didn't only infect my emotions, he twisted the way I viewed myself. That is not something that Ellie nor the queen can fix. That is something that I have to do on my own. I need to do this because I need to prove to myself that I am not his weapon. There has to be a reason the gods gave me this ability other than to start a war." She took a deep breath. "And if you can't respect that, then I kindly ask you to leave."

Although she was afraid to see how her words hurt him, she was proud of having spoken her truth. If Graeson could not understand where she was coming from, then that was his fault. And perhaps the very reason the Fates were against them.

But then Graeson did something she did not expect. He smiled. A true, genuine smile.

He grabbed her hands and squeezed them. "Kalisandre, you misunderstand my hesitancy. I'm sorry that you believe I want you to make yourself small. I have *never* wanted that. I have only ever wanted you to have a choice. Domitius has always been several steps ahead of us, so my hesitancy only comes from fear. I do not wish to lose you. And yes, part of that is me being selfish. But if this is what you wish to do, then please, let me be there by your side when you face him."

There was a plea in his eyes, but she realized he meant what he said. He wasn't begging her to turn around. It was something entirely different.

His gaze was locked onto hers, unflinching and undeterred. "Let me see you become the woman I've always known you could be."

CHAPTER 24

MYRA

Myra peered over the top of her book. At the end of the row of bookshelves, Laurince stood with his arms crossed and his foot tapping as he talked to Rian. The survivors' arrival from the eastern border had made him, and everyone else, restless.

The war was here, and they were woefully unprepared.

Every day, messenger birds arrived, delivering news of more attacks, more death. Every day, they trained. Every day, they returned to the library, and every day their patience grew thinner and thinner.

Myra no longer even knew what she was looking for. The words were a puddle in her mind. She had read countless stories about the gods, and one text supported Rian's theory that the gods had come from the stars, but the *how* was beyond vague. Laurince had read another text—if a children's book could have been called such—that featured the child of a mortal and immortal. The child's immortal mother took various shapes, appearing as a bird, a rabbit, and even a bear in the story. Laurince had quickly tossed the book back onto the shelf, rolling his eyes. Days had gone by, and they had yet to find anything useful.

As Myra read the ancient book before her, faint whispers tickled her ears. She fought to ignore the king and captain bickering several feet away, their voices a blurry drone against the musty scent of aged paper. She squinted at the faded ink on the yellowed pages. Myra sighed. Deciphering the faded script was hopeless, like chasing shadows in the dark.

"Come on. Just tell her," Laurince whispered.

"We've been through this," Rian argued.

Myra peeled her attention away from the book as the two men joined her. She looked down at their empty hands.

"Tell me what?" she asked, her brows curling in confusion. They had said they were going to grab more books to sift through, yet they stood empty-handed.

"Nothing," Rian said, waving it off.

Laurince nudged him in the side with his elbow.

"What?" Rian asked, exasperated.

The crease in the middle of Myra's forehead deepened. She slipped a bookmark inside the book and closed it.

"She deserves to know," Laurince urged.

"Laurince," Rian warned.

Myra swallowed, sensing the truth.

The captain pressed his palms on one of the open books, and the paper crunched beneath his hands. "We're going back to Frenzia."

Rian smacked Laurince on the shoulder. "Why don't you say it louder so everyone can hear you, hmm?"

Laurince rolled his eyes as he plopped down in the seat across from Myra.

"Oh," Myra mumbled, folding her hands beneath the table. Her nails dug into her palms, the pain sharp. She knew this was coming, yet she was surprised at how much her heart ached. She shouldn't have been sad. Rian was the king of Frenzia—even if his brother was currently sitting on his throne. His people needed him; Frenzia needed him. Yet, she couldn't deny she had grown accustomed to their company. Their constant bickering had become a strange comfort, one she would miss.

Guilt, sorrow, and a sense of determination wafted off the king and rushed over Myra.

"I cannot abandon Frenzia and leave them to deal with Sebastian," he whispered, leaning his hip against the table. "It's not right. Despite what some might think, I'm still king. My word still means something. It has to."

"When?" she asked, even though she was afraid of the answer.

"Tomorrow," Laurince answered.

Oh was all she could say.

The captain massaged his jaw, but the tension didn't leave his sharp features. "We thought it was best if we left sooner than later. The attacks are becoming more frequent." He swallowed, his throat dipping. "We don't want…we haven't told the others."

"I see." She tried to convince herself the slight burning sensation she was feeling was because of the dry air in the library and no other reason.

"We would have told you sooner, but we—" Laurince pursed his lips and scratched the back of his neck. The collar of his shirt shifted, and the jagged scar peeked beneath the fabric.

"Don't worry. Your secret is safe with me." Myra forced a tight smile onto her face. Looking at the book in her hand, she drew a line down the leather cover. "You should prepare. If…if I find something before you leave, I'll let you know."

She stood, her chair nearly collapsing. She mumbled an apology as Rian saved it from crashing to the ground. Her feet carried her toward the shelves.

The smell of old parchment and dried ink had always been a comfort, yet today it strangled her. Her gaze was unfocused and blurry as she scanned the bookshelves. She chewed on her bottom lip, willing the tears away. She wouldn't cry. There was no reason to cry, yet Myra couldn't help but feel an overwhelming sense of purposelessness.

If she had been strong enough to fight off Domitius' demands, if she had been able to say no, if she had held onto her morals—none of this would have come to fruition.

Was everything Myra touched cursed?

Was everything she did doomed to turn for the worse?

She tightened her grip on the book, pressing it against her chest. Her lungs constricted, her breathing growing shallow.

Perhaps it was better that everyone was leaving her. She didn't want to doom them even more.

She stumbled, her toe catching on air. Panicking, she reached out and grabbed the first thing she could. Books went tumbling. Her hand slammed against the shelf.

"Shoot." She knelt on the ground and began stacking the books.

Footsteps pounded behind her, but she didn't turn.

"Myra, are you—"

"I'm fine," she blurted, cutting Laurince off. "I tripped. Clumsy feet, you know?" Her voice was thick, and she prayed he didn't notice.

When she stood, books piled high in her arms, a hand touched her elbow, helping her up. She muttered thanks and moved away, letting Laurince's hand fall.

One by one, she shelved the books. And although her attention was fixed on the spines, she couldn't read a single title.

"Are you sure you're not hurt?" Laurince asked gently.

Myra nodded.

The captain refused to take the hint, though. He tugged on her elbow, his coarse hand impossibly soft, and beckoned her to face him.

His deep brown eyes stared at her, his thick brows drawn together. "Come with us."

Myra blinked. "I'm sorry?"

Laurince loosened his grip but didn't let go of her, not entirely. "Come with us to Frenzia. What will you do here? How many more books can you read? We have found nothing useful."

"Yet," Myra argued. "There has to be something." She refused to give up.

He cocked a brow at the book in her hand. "Frenzia has books, too. I'm sure Rian would let you read his personal collection—the man has more books about dragons than I think anyone does. If there's an answer in them, I'm sure you would have better luck finding it in his family's library."

Myra shook her head, taking a step back. "No, I'll just get in the way."

"No, you won't," Rian said, appearing behind the captain. He leaned against a bookshelf. "You'll probably keep us on track. Laurince is known for slipping into one too many taverns and making a fool of himself."

Laurince's hand fell from Myra's arm as he scoffed. "I do not!"

"Remember three years ago when we stopped at the pub in Ragolo? You started dancing on the tables."

Laurince shoved Rian. "That's not fair, and you know it. You dared me to do it."

Rian smiled, the corners of his eyes crinkling with amusement. "I would have paid for our drinks even if you hadn't, but you can't deny you enjoyed doing it."

"Whatever," Laurince mumbled, rolling his eyes. He placed an arm on Rian's shoulder, and an ear-to-ear grin spread across his face. "So what's it going to be, Haze?"

"*Haze?*" Myra questioned.

Grinning, Laurince turned to Rian. "Code names are necessary in a coup, wouldn't you agree, Your Highness?"

Rian snorted. "I suppose. But is it really a coup if it's my throne I'm taking back?"

"Semantics," Laurince said, dismissing him. "Either way, the name fits."

"How?" Myra asked, confused about everything that was going on—from the conversation to the captain's sudden awkwardness to the code name.

Laurince scratched the back of his head. "Your eyes are hazel, aren't they?" The question sat between them, and there was a strangeness to it she couldn't quite pinpoint. Before she even had the chance to respond, though, he asked, "So, what's it going to be? Are you coming?"

Myra glanced between them. Was there even a debate? Her life wasn't here. Her life had been in Ardentol, but as of right now and possibly forever, that version of her life was no more. Maybe this was the path she needed to follow.

"Fine," Myra said, a timid smile forming. "I'll come."

"That-a girl," Laurince said with a wink.

Myra's eyes widened. She swiftly faced the shelf again, returning the last few books to their spots. Her control slipped, and she felt her power reaching toward him. A honeyed warmth flooded her system, and something fluttered in her chest. She quickly reined in her gift the moment she realized what she was doing.

"Come on," Rian said.

Walking backward, Laurince called out, "Dawn, Haze."

And for some reason, Myra felt herself blushing again.

CHAPTER 25

GRAESON

"AGAIN," GRAESON ORDERED, ARMS CROSSED.

Kalisandre wiped the sweat from her brow and glared at him.

Graeson only arched a brow in challenge. Inside though, he was screaming. Their relationship—if that's what he could call it—was fragile enough. He did not wish to further divide them, but he refused to let her face Domitius unprepared.

Plus, Kalisandre glaring at him was better than the cold shoulder she had been giving him in Tetria. Any attention she would give, he would gladly take it. His heartbeat was a frantic tattoo against his ribs at the intensity of her gaze, a gaze that felt like both a brand and a balm.

He had yet to bring up the soul bond topic, and he didn't plan to. She needed to focus on the task ahead. Especially since Ellie informed him around the fire that Kalisandre refused to use her gift despite Ellie's protests. When they woke up the next morning, Graeson insisted Kalisandre practice until it was as natural as before.

Graeson understood Kalisandre's fear. By the gods, how many times had he refused to lean into his god-side over the years because of that same trepidation? When the god took over, the hunger for power and death was overwhelming. If he wasn't careful, he could lose sight of his humanity. But Kalisandre was stronger than he was.

"If I keep going, I will have nothing left when I see him," Kalisandre argued, her knuckles digging into her hip.

Whenever they stopped to rest, Kalisandre went to work, commanding Ellie and shaping her will. At first, she trembled when she reached for her power. She had nearly thrown up, her complexion turning green. Now she stood strong, and her commands were confident. Still, sweat slicked her forehead and dampened her hair.

The god within stirred, and Graeson dug his fingers into his biceps.

Was Graeson pushing her too much? Possibly. But it wasn't that she couldn't handle it. She only needed to believe she could.

"She has been successful in manipulating me so far. A break seems warranted," Ellie said, wiping the dirt from her hands.

"Having you catch a rabbit and cook it is hardly anything to cheer about," Graeson said, eyeing the warrior. Ellie was supposed to be on his side.

"Don't forget, she also made me get on Nyrri," Ellie added— rather unhelpfully.

Graeson snorted. "You didn't even fly."

"Whose fault is that?" Ellie whined, pointing at Nyrri, who was currently lying on her back and soaking up the sun.

Graeson struggled to hide his amusement as he recalled Ellie mounting the drakonis. After Ellie chased Nyrri around the clearing they had stopped at, Nyrri had plopped on the ground, refusing to move. Ellie had tried to coax her, promising Nyrri all the rabbits she could desire, but nothing would work. And Kalisandre's laughing probably hadn't helped either—although it did make Graeson smile hearing it.

"Fine," Graeson grumbled, conceding. "Rest."

Kalisandre dropped to the ground and sprawled across the grass, releasing a relieved sigh.

Wiping away his smirk, Graeson crouched beside her and rested his arms over his knees. Her eyes were closed as the sun kissed her pink cheeks. Her chest rose and fell at a steady rhythm. When he leaned forward, his shadow fell over her.

She squinted up at him. "What?"

"You lied," he said, narrowing his gaze slightly.

"About what?"

"You aren't afraid of running out of stamina. After visiting the springs, you practiced on Terin for days. I don't think you've even gotten close to the end of your well." Graeson cocked his head to the side, curious. "Why do you doubt yourself?"

Her shoulders sagged, and her body sank into the ground. "It's nothing," she mumbled, closing her eyes.

By the deep crease that formed between her brows, Graeson knew it was anything but nothing.

His fingers twitched, the desire to reach out to her buzzing at his fingertips. "Whatever it is, you can talk to me. If you're nervous, if you're—"

"I'm fine," Kallie interrupted. "I can handle it."

Graeson pursed his lips. He stared down at her for a second longer, hesitating. In the end, though, he pressed his palms against his thighs and stood, opting to leave her.

Maybe one day Kalisandre would learn to trust someone with the things that haunted her. Even if it wasn't him.

GRAESON CRACKED his neck as the darkness twisted inside him.

The god was eerily silent, but Graeson knew he was watching, observing. Waiting.

He brushed his thumb along the edge of the star. Shifting his stance, he inhaled.

Exhaling, Graeson flew the throwing star at the tree trunk. It struck the tree, and the blade drove deep into the bark.

They had stopped for the night, and he needed something to do before he combusted. He could sense the unrest within himself getting worse and worse as the hours slipped by during their journey. A series of divots were now carved into the trunk, a near mirror of the scars that marked his soul.

"Are we going to talk about it?"

He dug his hand into the bag at his side. When his fingers touched only lint at the bottom of the bag, he ground his teeth together and stalked forward. One by one, he ripped the sharp steel from the bark. The jagged edges scraped the pads of his fingers.

"You will not ignore me, Gray," Ellie demanded.

"I am not ignoring you. I am simply not answering you," Graeson said, plucking another star free from the trunk. As he returned each one to the bag, the metal *tinked* together.

"That is the definition of ignoring someone."

"Go bother someone else, Ellie."

"Why are you being so sour? Is it about the plan?"

Their plan, while not ideal, was fine. *If* Domitius followed the rules. According to the agreement they had made, both parties promised not to bring an army. Graeson, however, didn't trust Domitius within an inch of his life. The king was not foolish; he would bring soldiers with him, hidden or not. When Graeson raised this issue, Ellie waved his concern away, claiming Graeson could handle the army if it came to that.

Graeson might have experienced less than favorable odds

before, but he was not happy about taking that risk. There was too much at stake. If he had thought ahead and asked Sylvia for some of their explosives, then maybe they could have evened the odds.

Kalisandre, on the other hand, wanted bloodshed to be a last resort. She planned to hand herself over to Domitius once Lysanthia was with Graeson. Then, she would manipulate the king and whomever he brought with him.

Graeson trusted Kalisandre would be strong enough to do her part. If on the off chance she failed, they would be there, weapons ready.

It wasn't a perfect plan, but it was all they had. If it meant stopping this war, saving his mother, and freeing Kalisandre from the guilt she carried, then he would do whatever he could to ensure they were successful.

"No," he said, pulling the last star from the tree. He returned to the line he had drawn in the dirt with his boot a few dozen yards away from his target. "Kalisandre is strong enough. She always has been."

"Then what—" Ellie cut herself off and groaned. "If I had known that I was going to be in the middle of a couple's quarrel, then I would have stayed with Medenia and Ophelia."

"There is no couple's quarrel."

"Oh, really? Then what do you wish to call it? A couple's spat?" Ellie asked. "Can't you two make up and kiss already—or whatever it is that couples do?"

Graeson snorted. "I do not think she would appreciate that."

"Why not?"

"First, we are not a couple," Graeson clarified. "Second, before you snuck off in the middle of the night, she made it very clear she did not wish to be one ever."

"Aren't you two soul bonds?"

Graeson grabbed a star and spun it between his fingers. He rubbed the flat part of the star with his thumb. "Yes."

"Then does that not make you a couple?"

He tilted his head back. "No."

Ellie waved her hand flippantly. "Then apologize for whatever you did and profess your love to her."

Graeson eyed the tree. He took several steps back, then aimed. The jagged point drove straight into the bark and wobbled. It landed right in the center of the carvings.

"I already did."

"And what? She ignored you?" Ellie asked.

He cleared his throat. "She bandaged me up and then refused to talk about it."

Ellie grew silent, and for a second, Graeson thought she had left. But when he looked over his shoulder, she was still standing there, mouth agape.

A breeze swept through the forest, rustling the leaves. Somewhere nearby, a critter sprinted behind the brush, twigs snapping in its wake.

"I'm sorry. I'm having a hard time understanding. You might have broken me. You apologized for…"

"For making her believe I didn't have faith in her," Graeson finished.

"And she wrapped the wound you received after you made the dumb decision to *fly* across the kingdoms to help her?"

The god peered out of his cell, silently observing.

He shifted on his feet. "To be fair, my original plan was to convince her to return."

"You came to your senses, though," Ellie said.

Graeson shrugged. "I suppose."

She massaged her temples with two fingers. "So, what's the problem again?"

Graeson tilted his head back and sighed. "She asked for space, so I am giving it to her."

"She asked for space?"

Graeson nodded. "That's what she said, more or less, before she left."

Ellie snorted. "Have you seen the way that woman looks at you?" she asked, hands propped on her hips. "Anytime I brought you up, she grimaced. She's clearly in love with you; she's just afraid to admit it."

He stared blankly at Ellie. She was wrong. Kallie wasn't in love with him.

"We're trying to stop a war, Gray."

"I know!" he shouted, losing his patience. He did not wish to be a distraction. He rubbed his hands across his face. Then, quieter and calmer this time, he said, "I know. This is bigger than her and me. There's no room for anything else."

"By the gods, Gray," Ellie said, shaking her head, disappointment dragging the corners of her lips down. "You are an even bigger fool than I thought you were if you believe any of that."

CHAPTER 26
KALLIE

Ellie was wrong. Kallie wasn't in love with Graeson. She couldn't be.

With Ellie's words spinning in her mind, Kallie quietly pushed away from the tree she had been hiding behind and returned to the horses and Nyrri. She hadn't meant to eavesdrop on Graeson and Ellie's conversation. She had ventured over to ask them if they should pick up her training again, but then she had heard bits of their conversation.

Kalisandre is strong enough. She always has been.

It was those words and the sincerity with which Graeson spoke that had made her pause initially. She hadn't known how much she needed to hear someone say them, to have someone believe in her ability, believe in *her*, wholly and completely.

She stroked Nyrri's nose.

"Ready?"

Kallie jumped at Graeson's voice and spun around. "For what?"

"To get going," he said, tipping his head in the direction they had been heading. When he looked at her for a moment longer, his brows knitted with concern. "Unless you need to rest longer?"

"No," Kallie blurted. "I'm fine. All good."

He studied her quizzically. "Are you all right?"

She grabbed her finger, about to twist the ring around it. But when she touched bare skin, she quickly dropped her hand and stuffed it in her pocket. "Yes, of course. Just…" Kallie looked at the sky. "We're losing daylight. We should go."

She darted toward Winter, but she could feel his eyes on her back as she mounted.

She didn't love him.

She couldn't.

CHAPTER 27
MYRA

"Look! There's an inn up ahead," Rian said, pointing toward a quaint building in between the cypress trees. "We should take the chance to sleep in a bed while we can. Once we cross the border, the chances of being recognized will increase tenfold."

Myra looked at the captain. They had been riding since dawn, and dusk was coming in faster than any of them would have liked. After trudging through the swamps, a good night's rest sounded too good to pass up.

"I suppose you have a point," Laurince said, albeit reluctantly. "Although, it's not our fault you stick out like a brick in a pile of sticks. Maybe you should sleep outside in a tree, and we'll get rooms for ourselves."

"Ha! If I have to sleep outside, you do too," Rian said, jumping off his horse.

Laurince followed, his boots slamming against the ground. He mumbled something unintelligible and pulled Rian's hood further down his head, covering his deep auburn hair. Rian swatted at the captain's hand, and Myra rolled her eyes. The two men continued to bicker as they handed their horses to the stable hand.

She almost regretted accompanying them. The last time they had traveled together, none of them had been too eager to converse, their minds weighed by the horrors they had barely escaped in Ardentol. It seemed that was no longer the case. Laurince and Rian bickered like an old married couple, neither agreeing with anything the other said unless it was about food or sleep. And even those topics often resulted in a long-winded debate.

"Let's just see if they have a room, all right?" Myra asked.

Rian looked over his shoulder at her, his green eyes hopeful. "Can we also see if they have something to eat?"

Laurince's stomach growled. "That's actually not a bad idea."

When they turned to Myra, waiting for an answer, she sighed. Sometimes, Myra couldn't believe these two men held such prestigious titles.

"Very well."

They both gave her wide grins. Laurince yanked the door open.

Inside, the warmth of a burning hearth wrapped around Myra's frigid limbs, dispersing the creeping night's chill. Notes of fresh bread, cinnamon, and thyme sprinkled the air and instantly had her mouth salivating. A large chandelier hung from the wooden ceiling, casting a warm light upon the tables topped with flickering candles.

But it was neither the warmth nor the comforting scent of baked goods that made Myra's entire body sag in relief. For the first time in a long time, there wasn't a single feeling of hostility, rage, or fear. The emotions swirling in the tavern were light and playful. The brightly colored threads brushed her cheeks like a gentle caress. The only dredge of paranoia she sensed came from the two men beside her, and even their anxiety had dwindled by several degrees since entering. It was as if a spell had been cast over the building that forced merriment upon its patrons. Whatever it was, it had the three of them bee-lining to the innkeeper at the bar, their steps perkier than they had been only seconds before.

The innkeeper was a tall, thin woman. Her blonde hair was tied in a knot that sat on top of her head. Small curls framed her face, the ends bleeding into a black tint as if she had dipped the bottom half of her hair in a bucket of ink. When she faced them, the strands of multicolored crystals dangling from her ear clattered harmoniously.

Wiping her palms on the front of her beige apron, the woman smiled at Rian. "How can I help you, handsome?"

With a cocky smirk, Rian rolled up his sleeves and leaned on the bar, his gaze momentarily lowering to where a large selenite pendulum necklace rested on the woman's collarbone. "That depends. Are you on the menu by chance?"

The woman laughed. Throwing the towel she held over her shoulder, she grabbed a loose string hanging lazily between her breasts and twisted the slim fabric around her index finger.

Laurince pressed a hand against Myra's back. "Come on," he said, nodding toward the tables. "Let's grab a table while he sorts out the rooms."

Myra nodded, not caring to see Rian carelessly flirt his way into a room.

Laurince patted Rian on the back and winked at the woman. "In case he forgets to ask, we'd like two rooms, please."

Before the innkeeper could respond, Laurince ushered Myra forward, letting her lead the way. She wove between the tables, offering the other patrons polite smiles as she passed. The inn must have been a popular location, for most of the tables were already occupied. Women and men chatted and laughed as they drank from mugs while a lanky man played a mandolin in the corner. The mandolin player suddenly changed songs, and cheers erupted across the tavern, the tune apparently a crowd favorite. Several people got up from their seats, their feet smacking against the wood at a lively beat as they danced closer to the mandolinist.

Unable to help herself, Myra reached for the threads of the patrons, latching onto their joy as if it would be the last time she would come across it. Instantly, her smile grew wider and her steps lighter.

"Apologies, my lady," a man said when he bumped into Myra. "I didn't see ya there."

"Perhaps you should look where you're going," Laurince said gruffly behind Myra.

"It's quite all right," Myra said, smiling meekly and silently apologizing for her companion's rude behavior. The sooner they sat, the quicker they could eat and go to sleep, both of which were much needed if the captain's attitude was any indication.

The stranger looked down at her and tipped his hat. He headed toward a table across the room where a small group was laughing.

Myra felt the light press of a hand on the small of her back. As Laurince leaned down, his breath kissed the side of her neck. She stiffened.

"Over there," he said over the music, his deep voice sending a ripple of goosebumps over her skin, "to the right."

In the corner, a table with four chairs sat against the back wall. Myra made her way toward it. Although, her steps were more rigid than before as her focus kept returning to the warmth on her back.

When they reached the table, Laurince pulled out a chair with his free hand, and the legs scratched the rickety floorboards. He gestured to it, and Myra sat, her back suddenly cold once he removed his hand. Laurince plopped down in the seat across from her. Tossing his arm across the back of his chair, he scanned the crowd.

"You should be more careful," he said after a moment without looking at her.

"Pardon?" Myra asked. What did he expect? Someone to charge

at them in the middle of the tavern? How barbaric did he think people were?

He turned toward her. "You nearly got knocked over. What if the man had pulled a knife on you? What would you have done? Smiled and thanked him?"

Myra's mouth fell open. "A *knife*? We're in a public place. You have to be joking."

His expression remained flat.

Apparently, not.

"I never joke about safety," he said.

"Oh? And what about our friend over there, hmm?" Myra asked, avoiding saying the king's name in case someone nearby heard her. She may have been clumsy, but she wasn't ignorant. "Shouldn't you be focusing on *his* safety?"

"I am," Laurince stated, matter-of-factly.

Myra leaned back in her chair. "Really? How? You're on the other side of the room."

"I can see him just fine from here," he said, flicking his hand dismissively. "And he's armed. You're not, despite my efforts to change that."

Shaking her head in disbelief, she looked over her shoulder.

Rian still stood at the bar, chatting with the innkeeper. The woman was now leaning her elbows on the bar, mimicking Rian's position. Rian twirled one of her ink-dipped curls around his finger, and Myra could faintly make out a blush coloring the innkeeper's cheeks.

"What if *she* pulls out a knife on him?" Myra asked.

"Honestly, if she does, good for her. That'll mean she hasn't fallen for his sad-boy eyes."

Myra snorted. "His *what*?"

"Oh, come on," Laurince said, rolling his eyes. "You've seen them."

"I don't think I have."

Laurince sighed and leaned one arm against the table's edge. Myra's attention caught on his bicep for a second before he waved his hand in a circular motion in front of his face. "You know, he has that face—that look-how-sad-I-am-won't-you-fix-me look. Everyone falls for it."

Affronted, Myra sat up straighter. "Not me."

Laurince arched a brow. "If you say so, Haze."

Warmth spread to her cheeks, and of course Laurince quickly noticed. He slapped his hand on the table. "See? I knew it!"

She could feel the red hue deepen, but she kept her lips sealed. Because if she denied it, he would have known that the blush wasn't a result of Rian's supposed "sad-boy eyes" but the nickname the captain used so freely with her. And she really did *not* want to admit that.

"Anyway, I think you've strayed from the point," Laurince said, leaning back in his chair so the front legs lifted off the ground. "People will take advantage of your kindness. You need to be careful." The chair legs smacked the floorboards. With one last cursory glance her way, he faced the crowd again, his posture becoming rigid once more.

Myra tapped her fingers on the side of her chair as she observed him. "You know, he said you were more fun at taverns, yet so far all I've seen you do is get your feathers ruffled by a drunk stranger and pout."

"I am not pouting," he said, tucking his hands beneath his arms.

Cocking a brow, Myra hummed.

Laurince scoffed and unfolded his arms.

"I think you're just jealous," she said with a smirk.

"*Jealous?*" Laurince asked, eyes widening. "What do I have to be jealous about?"

"He's flirting with some stranger while you're stuck over here babysitting me."

His lips parted, but he shook his head as if deciding against his original response. "Let the man flirt. After his engagement went up in flames, he deserves some kind of romance, even if it's fleeting." He flicked his hand, but she could taste the bitterness on his tongue.

Myra pursed her lips.

"Unless," Laurince began, leaning forward with a knowing smirk, "you wish he was flirting with *you* instead?"

"*Me?*" If anything, Myra was jealous of how carefree Rian was, how simple and nonchalant the two were flirting with one another. Myra only wished she had an ounce of the innkeeper's confidence. Of course, she admitted none of that and instead said, "I'm nothing but a handmaiden."

"You *were* a handmaiden," he corrected.

Myra shifted uncomfortably. She was still getting used to that. Beyond traveling with Laurince and Rian, she still wasn't sure what she wanted to do. It was hard to think about her future when a war was upon them.

As if sensing her tension, Laurince said with a mischievous glint in his eyes, "I've honestly found that I prefer handmaidens over the ladies in the court." He wrinkled his nose. "They're a little too *stuffy* for my liking."

Myra's stomach twisted at the captain's words. But before she could stew in it for too long, Laurince added, "Plus, sorry to disappoint, but I only dance on tables when I've had one too many pints of ale."

A pitcher slammed onto the table. Myra and Laurince both jumped back as liquid sloshed over the rim and spilled onto the table.

"Would spiced mead do the trick?" Rian asked with a wide grin and a red smudge on his cheek.

CHAPTER 28
MYRA

Myra burst into raw, unfiltered laughter as Rian tried to pull Laurince up to force him to dance. Laurince glared at her, and she slapped her hand over her mouth to muffle her laughter.

"Come on, Cap'n," Rian said, stumbling on his feet and acting very *un*-kingly. "You know you want to."

"I really don't," Laurince argued. Although Myra could see the shadow of his dimple at the corner of his mouth. "Perhaps you should go to bed. Are you tired? *I'm* tired."

Rian yawned, and his grip on Laurince slipped. "I suppose I am a little"—he stumbled—"tired."

Laurince clapped his hands triumphantly. "Let's all go to bed then." He reached for the king, but Rian swatted Laurince's hand away.

With an unsteady finger, Rian pointed at Myra and Laurince. "No, no. You two should stay. Have some fun. You're both always so..." The king waved his hand around as if searching for the right word. Suddenly, he clutched his hand as if snatching the word from the air. "*Uptight.*"

Myra's mouth fell open. She didn't know whether she should be insulted or simply laugh.

"That's quite enough," Laurince said, ushering Rian away from the table. "I think it's time to go to bed."

"When did you become Mr. No-fun, huh?" Rian challenged, poking the captain in his chest.

"I am fun," Laurince retorted, batting Rian's hand away with a small pout.

"Prove it." Rian tipped up his chin. "I'll go to bed if you stay here and prove to Mys that you can actually be a good time."

At the mention of her name, Myra straightened in her seat.

The captain scoffed. "You're being ridiculous."

"No, *you* are. Right, Mys?"

"Uhm…" Myra glanced between the two men. Had someone added more logs to the hearth? Suddenly her shirt felt a little too thick, her collar a little too tight.

As if seeing the debate in her gaze, Laurince shook his head slightly.

Her stomach flipped. And perhaps it was the mead or whatever magic was in the tavern, but instead of agreeing with Laurince wholeheartedly like she should have, she said, "I suppose you're not wrong."

"See!" Rian shouted and slapped his hand against his thigh.

Myra took a sip of mead, hiding her amused grin.

Groaning, Laurince hung his head and pressed a hand to his chest as he leaned heavily against the back of his chair. "You wound me, Haze."

Rian slapped Laurince on the back. "Now, I'm going to stop at the bar and head to bed. Fifth room on the left. Don't be too early," Rian said with a wink before taking off.

Myra's gaze trailed after him. "Are you sure he'll be fine?" she asked when Rian was far enough away.

Laurince grabbed the back of his chair and leaned his weight against it. Myra's attention dropped to his arms. He had rolled up his sleeves, revealing a few veins crawling up his forearms. She quickly glanced away and took another sip of mead. The liquid warmed her throat, but it did little to cool the feeling blooming in her core.

"Would you believe me if I said he's an even better fighter when he's drunk?" Laurince asked.

Myra snorted. "Absolutely not."

"Well, it's true. He took down five men the night I danced on the tables." A small smile graced his face at the memory.

"You're lying."

"Nope," Laurince said, his lips smacking together and making a small popping sound. He slumped back down into the seat. He tapped his fingers on the table as he turned his gaze to the crowd.

After a moment, Myra mumbled, "I am not uptight."

Laurince squinted, tilting his head in thought. "You are a little. But I certainly am not."

With a scoff, she rolled her eyes. "A rock is still a stone, you know. Just because I might prefer staying inside doesn't mean you're not uptight too."

Laurince smirked. "Dig the knife deeper, why don't you?"

Myra chuckled, and Laurince's faint grin widened, turning into a full-fledged smile. Her stomach fluttered at the sight of his dimple.

She dropped her gaze to the cup and twisted it in her hands.

Laurince leaned back in the chair and rocked it back onto its two back legs. Drumming his fingers on the edge of the table, he looked around the tavern. It was early enough that a decent number of people were still dancing, the music not yet having slowed.

Laurince was probably right. Rian would be fine. They were still on Tetrian soil. The people here didn't seem to be fazed by the attacks that were plaguing the seven kingdoms. They were safe. For now. For tonight.

Slowly, Myra let the music soften her concerns. Soon, she was swaying to the rhythm.

"Well," Laurince said, the front feet of his chair slamming down as he reached for the pitcher, "might as well not waste this, right?"

She eyed the pitcher. Her neck was already warming, and the tips of her ears were buzzing. Yet she pushed her cup forward, anyway. Laurince poured the mead, dividing the rest evenly and filling their cups to the brim.

He raised his mug. "To being *un*-uptight."

Myra's hand halted an inch from his. "That's not a word."

"Just cheers me, Haze. We know I hate reading."

Laughing, Myra clinked her mug against his and drank. She might have taken an extra sip for good measure.

When she set her cup down, she ran her fingers along the side of the mug as she looked out toward the strangers. She admired the way the people moved with such unabashed joy and reckless abandon. They danced without a care in the world. She wished she could have a single moment in her life when that could have been her, too. For her entire life, she had been riddled with guilt or paranoia. She wondered what it was like to let go.

Resting her chin atop her propped-up hand, she sighed. She must have done so louder than she had intended, though, because Laurince heard her and pushed himself from the table.

"Let's go."

Myra stared at his outstretched hand. A pang of sadness twisted in her throat. Leaving might have been the smartest choice, but she wasn't ready. She wanted to relish everyone else's joy a little longer. She scraped her teeth across her bottom lip and debated how she could convince him to leave without her.

He wiggled his fingers. "Are you going to leave a man hanging, or are you going to dance with me?"

"*Dance* with you?"

Laurince shrugged nonchalantly. "Might as well, right? You're not a very good liar. If Rian remembers to ask you tomorrow, you'll give me away if we go to bed before I at least make a fool of myself once." He gave her a rueful smile. "When was the last time you experienced your own joy and not someone else's?"

Myra's breath hitched. As if on its own accord, her hand rose and slipped into his.

Laurince tugged her up to her feet before she could second-guess herself. The air whisked through her hair, sending the blonde strands whipping around her. Then he was pulling her behind him, heading closer to the musician, where a small crowd danced. The song was an upbeat tune. But as Laurince spun her around, making her face him, the song melted into something else, something slower, more intimate. The people around them coupled up, hands meeting, fingers entwining, chests pressing together, hips swaying.

No, no, no.

Myra took a step back, her hand uncurling from the captain's.

"I said we'd dance, didn't I?" Laurince asked, a brow cocked.

"But this is…" Myra glanced around. She couldn't dance to *this.* Not with him.

"Do you doubt my dancing skills that much?" Laurince quipped.

Flashes of the captain moving around the dance floor during the week of Kallie and Rian's failed-wedding surfaced. Laurince had been one of several men who had taken part in the traditional Frenzian dance, so Myra had witnessed just how well he could move. She recalled how his suit hugged his frame, perfectly molding to the muscles that lay beneath the fabric. The image made her a little dizzy.

Or was that the alcohol?

Definitely the alcohol.

"I would never," Myra said, forcing her voice to sound light and playful, though she wasn't sure she successfully hid how nervous she was.

He pulled her closer. "Don't worry, Haze, I'll be a perfect gentleman." His voice, low and husky, sent a ripple down her spine. "Place this hand here," he said, guiding one of her hands onto his shoulder, "and hold my hand with this one."

"I've danced before," Myra mumbled, suddenly feeling the need to defend herself.

His free hand slipped to her waist, his gentle touch searing through the fabric of her blouse. He wiggled his fingers, tapping his pinky against her hip. "Your hips say otherwise, Haze. They are as stiff as a board." He leaned closer, his breath brushing the tip of her ear. "What was that you said about not being uptight again?"

Is he flirting?

Myra must have been misconstruing his tone. The temptation to reach out and see what emotions danced along the thread was strong, but she hesitated. His emotions were his own. She refused to violate them. She let the thread slip between her fingers like water, the emotions drifting away before she could grasp them.

Laurince chuckled and moved his hand higher up her back. He guided her forward, swiftly falling into a simple box step. As they danced, a comfortable amount of space remained between them, yet the faint traces of cinnamon from the spiced mead and pine consumed her senses. Gods, she could drown in it—

"There you go," he said, interrupting her wayward thoughts as she fell into step with him.

A shy grin twitched at her lips from the praise. When she realized she was staring up at him, she instantly dropped her gaze to his chest. But that was even worse. The cotton fabric stretched across his chest, bringing attention to his pectoral muscles. She had a strange desire to lay her head there. A desire to hear his beating heart. Was it beating as fast as hers?

She stumbled over her feet and stepped on Laurince's boot. "Sorry," she mumbled, face flushed.

"Just follow my lead, Haze," he whispered, not missing a beat. As if it were only the two of them.

"Where did you learn to dance?" she asked, hoping talking would distract her. She may have danced before, but never like this. Never with someone who was actually skilled at it. Most of the guards she had been acquainted with in Ardentol were too serious to dance, even behind closed doors.

Laurince's gaze slipped over the crowd before falling back to her. "Rian made me take classes with him. It was one of his conditions if I ever wanted to be the captain of his guard."

"Why? Does it help you wield a sword?"

"The lessons did teach me to be more fluid with my movements, but I think he wanted to embarrass me more than anything. He thought I'd be horrible at it." He chuckled, the memory softening his features. "And at the time, I had a crush on the instructor's daughter, who often attended the lessons."

"Oh, how cruel!" Myra said, feeling sympathy for young Laurince. She could imagine him being a lanky boy, his current stature not quite built yet, flailing around the dance floor as he tried to impress the girl. "You must have gotten better. You don't seem too bad to me."

Laurince wore a cocky grin and said, "I never said I was bad at dancing, Haze. I'm actually quite a bit better than he is. He loathed me for it, too."

"I bet he did," Myra mused, her grin unstoppable.

His smirk turned devious, as if there was a secret hiding beneath it. He inched closer, his breath brushing her ear as he said, "I'm better at a lot of things than him, believe it or not."

Heat blossomed in the pit of her stomach. What was he doing? The question plagued her, yet she found herself leaning into whatever it was.

"Oh? Like what?" she asked, her voice thick as she leaned back. Her gaze caught on that godsforsaken dimple.

He cocked a brow. "Wouldn't you like to know?"

His hand disappeared from her back, and he stepped back, spinning her around. Her hair floated around her, twisting around her neck. As the sweet melody continued and she felt the warmth of the nearby fire on her skin, she let herself relax.

She let herself smile.

She let herself experience her own joy.

MYRA MIGHT HAVE BEEN drunker than she had planned. Her footsteps were light but clumsy as she headed up the stairs. Her toe caught on the lip of a step, and she nearly fell. If it wasn't for Laurince, she would have. Because there he was, a hand on her elbow and another on her waist, steadying her.

"Woah there. Perhaps that last drink was a mistake."

Myra waved a hand dismissively at him. "I'm perfectly fine." Once she reached the top landing, she spun around on her heel and placed her hands on her hips, triumphant. "See? Made it up in one piece."

"You should be very proud of yourself," Laurince said with a cheeky smile. "You made it up an entire flight of stairs."

Narrowing her eyes, Myra leaned forward, pointing a finger at him. "Are you *mocking* me?"

Laurince fell into a comical mirror of her posture with one hand on his hip, knees slightly bent. He lightly poked her in the shoulder, throwing her off balance, and her back bumped into the wall. A picture rattled behind her.

"Oh, my apologies," she said, patting the picture.

"Did you just *apologize* to the wall?"

"What? Of course not," Myra said, astounded that he would even suggest such a thing. She looked over her shoulder and pointed to the couple in the gilded frame. "I apologized to Maurice and Lily."

"Maurice and Lily?"

"Mhm," she hummed with a curt nod.

When she realized what she had said, embarrassment reddened her complexion. Before she could utter some feeble explanation, Laurince did something she never would have expected from the esteemed captain.

He bowed, dramatically rolling his hand with a pompous flourish with his back parallel to the floor. "My apologies, Maurice and Lily, for I, too, am at fault for rattling you."

Laughter burst free, and before she could stop herself, a small snort escaped. Myra slapped her hand across her mouth, muffling the sound.

The corners of Laurince's eyes crinkled as his smile widened.

A nearby door creaked open, and someone poked their head out, rubbing the sleep from their eyes. A tattoo of a dragon crawled up his neck. "Do you mind? Some of us are trying to sleep."

"Apologies, good sir," Laurince said, bowing dramatically again, forcing Myra to look away and stifle her laughter. "The lady and I were simply passing by."

The man's lip curled. "Do so quieter, why don't you?" He slammed the door shut with a disgruntled groan.

Myra mouthed an apology at the door. And when she looked at Laurince, he was struggling to contain his amusement. Laurince grabbed her hand, pulling her away, before they nearly combusted and the stranger came out of the room to chastise them again.

As they quickly padded down the hall—as quietly as possible for two drunk people—he asked, "Which room did Rian say he and I were in?"

Myra cleared her throat, the laughter finally fading. "The fifth door on the left."

Laurince looked back and counted the doors. "Ah," he said, finding it. "I'll ask him which room is yours. Just wait here, all right?"

Myra nodded, and Laurince cracked open the door. He peeked inside as if checking to see if the innkeeper had stayed longer than expected. She must not have been because he dipped inside, leaving the door cracked behind him.

As she stared after him, the hall spun around her. Myra leaned against the wall. Pressing her palms flat against the floral wallpaper, she steadied herself, letting the buzz of the alcohol wear off as she waited. A yawn poured from her mouth. She shut her eyes as a wave of exhaustion came over her.

As she hummed a song she had heard earlier, eager dreams knocked at the edges of her mind. She wanted to fall into them, to let the strong arms that awaited her carry her away. She imagined gentle hands slipping up her waist, higher and higher.

Heat bloomed in her core, and she pressed her thighs together. Her hand brushed her hip, skating over her curves.

Hinges creaked, and she ripped her hand away, folding it behind her back. She blinked, the fog slow to fade.

Laurince slipped out of the room, and the lit sconces in the hall kissed his sharp line. He reached up and scratched the back of his head. The fabric shifted around his arm, morphing to his muscles.

Gods, he was attractive.

She held back a gasp and released her bottom lip, realizing she wasn't dreaming. She prayed she hadn't said that aloud.

Thankfully, she must not have.

"Slight problem," he said with a grimace.

"What is it?"

"He got only one room."

"Are you sure? Should we go check with—"

Laurince was already shaking his head. "Apparently, there was only one room available."

"Oh," Myra said, shifting on her feet. "Are there at least two beds?"

Laurince nodded.

"That's good at least."

He chuckled nervously, warmth flooding his cheeks. "There's one other issue." He pushed the door open and ushered her inside.

She cautiously stepped into the room, unsure of what to expect or how to prepare herself. A crack of moonlight seeped in through the drawn curtains, a dim glow spilling across the space. One bed was completely empty. Then her gaze landed on the second. Rian was lying across the bed diagonally, his limbs spread out like a starfish. There was no way two grown men were going to sleep comfortably with one of them taking up the entirety of it.

"I've tried moving him, but…" Laurince whispered behind her as he shut the door. The lock clicked into place with a thunderous finality.

It was as if a bucket of ice-cold water had been thrown over her, sobering her up immediately. Her heartbeat was in her throat. Her palms grew slick with sweat.

"He sleeps like a log. He barely responded to me when I asked about the rooms. But I'll sleep on the floor. It's not a problem."

And maybe it was because of the mead or because Myra was a foolish woman who wanted to pretend she was confident for a night, the offer slipped free before she could think of the consequences. "No, no. Sleep in the bed. It's big enough."

Although as she looked at it, she wasn't sure that was true when she considered Laurince's build.

"That's really unnecessary. I don't mind," Laurince said.

He was giving her an out, and she could have easily taken it. She could have let him do the chivalrous thing. But it was too late to change her mind. She had already offered.

Swallowing, she gathered the courage that was attempting to abandon her. "Absolutely not. Like Rian said, who knows when we'll be sleeping in a bed again?" Myra was already moving toward her small bag.

"I was really looking forward to that," he said, scratching his chest. "If you really don't mind…"

"I insist," she said, rifling through her belongings. Her hair cascaded around her face, hiding the rising blush. She grabbed her nightgown, which, if she was being honest, was a little shorter than she would have liked when sharing a bed with someone. But it was the only option she had.

She looked over her shoulder at him. "Do you mind?"

"About sharing?"

Myra held up the flimsy nightgown.

"Oh, of course." He spun around, facing the door.

Myra made quick work of changing. Once done, her bare legs felt extra bare. She debated throwing on her trousers but opted against it, hating the idea of sleeping in dirty clothes. She turned around, intending to get into the bed before Laurince saw her, but she stopped dead in her tracks. Her mouth fell open. Laurince was pulling his shirt over his head, and the muscles in his back rippled as he moved. His shirt landed on the ground with a soft thump. And when she heard the quiet metal clasp of his belt, she gulped. Goosebumps spread across her arms. The belt landed on his shirt, but he stopped there.

Myra didn't know if her shoulders sagged in relief or disappointment.

A loud snore startled her, and she swiftly padded over to the bed and slipped beneath the sheets. She turned toward the wall and squeezed her eyes shut, trying and failing to get the image of Laurince shirtless out of her mind. She was afraid it would haunt her dreams for the rest of her life. Was it too late for her to sleep on the floor?

The bed dipped from the captain's weight, and a chilly breeze hit her ankles as Laurince found his way under the covers. He shifted, his shoulder brushing hers. She inhaled sharply.

"Sorry," she mumbled, scooting over.

Gods, she would never fall asleep. If she moved even an inch, she would touch bare skin.

"Stop doing that," Laurince whispered.

She froze. "Huh?"

"Stop apologizing for things that are not your fault," he whispered. "*I* bumped into *you*, not the other way around."

"Oh," she said. Her lips parted, but she snapped them shut.

"You almost did it again, didn't you?"

"No," she said, drawing out the syllable.

"Liar," he said, shifting again. When he spoke next, his voice sounded farther away, as if he had turned away from her. "You don't owe the world an apology for existing, Haze."

Myra didn't respond. She didn't know how to. She hadn't known how much she needed someone to say that to her. Hearing those words settled some of the noise in her head that had been a constant companion for as long as she could remember.

With a deep breath, she sank into the mattress. And whether it was because of the mead, Laurince's words, or his presence, Myra slept soundlessly for the first time in a long time.

CHAPTER 29
KALLIE

F*IRE ERUPTED BEHIND* K*ALLIE AND CAST AN EERIE LIGHT ON THE FIGURE* *before her. The flames twirled across the iron helmet, painting swirls of gold and scarlet shades over the metal. Smoke billowed from the bull's nose. Domitius tightened his grip on the reins, his leather glove stretching over his knuckles. The massive black stallion beneath him smacked its right hoof against the ground, sending up a plume of dust. Domitius kicked the side of his heel against the horse's ribcage, and the horse bolted forward.*

This time, though, Kallie was ready.

When Domitius reached down and snatched her by the arm, tossing her onto his lap, she twisted around, blade in hand. She raised her arm. But as she stared up at him, her hand trembled.

Domitius bellowed, the menacing laughter echoing beneath his full-face helmet. He snatched the dagger from her hand and struck—

K*ALLIE'S EYES SPRANG OPEN.* Sweat coated her limbs, and her entire body trembled as she lay on the cold ground.

"Kal?" Graeson's voice wrapped around her like a blanket,

warm and comforting. She wanted to hug the sound and stay encased inside it. His hand rested on her ankle. "Are you all right?"

She rolled over and found him sitting by a pile of cold coals from a fire that had long since extinguished.

"Bad dream," she muttered, rubbing the sleep from her eyes as she propped herself onto her elbows. She should go back to sleep, and she most certainly should not get up and—

The thin blanket slipped off her. In her next breath, she was moving toward Graeson as if an invisible tether pulled her toward him. As she sat down, his gaze never left her, his brows knitting together and a protest frozen on his lips.

Kallie had thought the night terrors were in her past, but as she crept closer to coming face-to-face with Domitius, that was no longer the case. She would have preferred Terin infiltrating her dreams than returning to the nightmares that always seemed to chase her.

"For a while, the nightmares had stopped. But the closer we get..." Kallie's words fell to the wind. Kallie glanced over at Ellie. The thin blanket was pulled over Ellie's mouth, leaving only the upper half of her face exposed to the elements. She was still fast asleep.

"Is there anything I can do?" Graeson asked quietly, as if afraid to ask.

Her heart twisted from knowing her actions had made him fearful of offering his help.

"You should sleep," she whispered, knocking her knee into his. She didn't know why she had done it. She didn't even know why she had come over. Still, as seconds passed, his closeness seemed to dull some of the previous uneasiness that had been soaking her limbs.

"As should you," he said, returning the gesture.

Her lip twitched but stopped short of a full smile. "I'm serious, Gray."

"I promise I'll go to sleep soon, all right?" he said. But she could see the lie resting between his pinched brows. "Go to sleep for a little longer. I'll wake Ellie in an hour or two. "

"I'm already up. I might as well take watch."

Still, Graeson didn't move. Instead, he returned his gaze to the dead fire. "Do you want to talk about it?"

She shook her head, knowing he was referring to the nightmare. "Not really."

Her attention dropped to her hand. The patch of skin where her ring had once sat was less pale after the days of travel, the tan-line fading. Yet its absence still felt strange. She pressed her palms against the dirt and looked up.

Graeson quickly looked away. He brushed his fingers through his hair, and Kallie tracked the movement. She couldn't help but marvel at the man sitting beside her. The man who—despite Kallie constantly pushing him away and lying about her own feelings— stayed, who always came after her. Who wanted to see her take ownership of her life.

"Perhaps, the next time you wake up from a nightmare," Graeson said, calling her attention back to their conversation, "try rewriting the ending."

"What do you mean?"

Graeson pointed to his head. "It helps rewire the brain. Your mother told me that once when I used to get them a lot."

"You suffered from night terrors?"

He shrugged as if the answer was inconsequential, but it did matter. A lot mattered, especially when it came to Graeson. His past, his present, his future. She wanted to know what haunted him.

"I suppose you don't want to talk about it either, then?" Kallie asked, throwing his question back at him.

"It's not that I don't want to, but..." His silver eyes fell on her. There was a weight to them that had Kallie dropping her gaze and rolling her shoulders back.

"Does it work?" Kallie asked. "The rewriting or whatever?"

Graeson was silent for a moment as he stared out toward the shadows shifting in the forest when the leaves rustled in the wind. "Sometimes. But sometimes I don't bother, wanting the reminder of what could happen instead."

"What do you mean?"

He hung his arms over his propped-up knees. "Sometimes, we need the darkness to appreciate the happy moments—the *good* moments. My nightmares remind me what I'm fighting for, what I'm trying to accomplish. They remind me to continue working to be better."

Unsure how to respond at first, Kallie was silent. What Graeson said made sense, but there was also something sad about it. Her nightmares only ever left her shaken and terrified. But maybe there was something to be said about conquering that fear, about using it to one's advantage.

She scooted closer. "Here," she said, tossing the blanket that was wrapped around her over his farthest shoulder.

He caught the blanket and started unwrapping it. "You really don't need to do that. You should—"

"Stop telling me what I should and shouldn't do, Gray," she interrupted.

He frowned, regret coating his countenance immediately.

A small smile appeared on her face, and she nudged him with her shoulder. "Just take the blanket."

"If you insist." He slipped the blanket back over his shoulders.

When she felt the blanket tug, she scooted closer. Their thighs and shoulders were pressed against each other. Even through her clothes, she could feel how cold he was. She didn't understand how he wasn't shivering.

"Thank you," he said.

Kallie simply nodded.

Although she should have been putting space between Graeson and herself, in case the plan didn't go accordingly when she met with Domitius, she found it harder and harder to do. She enjoyed Graeson's closeness. His proximity settled something inside her. Maybe it was the result of the soul bond, yet that felt too simple—even though being soul bonds was anything but simple.

She wondered how their lives would have been different if Domitius had never taken her. It was something she had thought about often since she had learned the truth about her past. Would Esmeray have told her that Lysanthia had a vision of them being soul bonds when she was a child? Or would her mother have let Kallie find out on her own? Would she have followed Graeson around like a lost puppy as a child? Would she have been one of those teenagers who tried to shake off her feelings and appear aloof? Or would they have already been happily married?

That life seemed so simple, so uncomplicated. Kallie couldn't imagine it. Although she certainly tried as she dozed off.

At some point, her head fell against Graeson's shoulder. Minutes or hours later, her eyes fluttered open. She tried to sit upright and move away, but her head was too heavy. The fog of sleep beckoned her to return, to fall back into its warm embrace.

"Go lay down," Graeson whispered as though he could feel her trying to fight the exhaustion.

Kallie mumbled a disagreement yet found herself moving. But for once, she wasn't moving away from him. She drifted onto his lap, propping her arm beneath her head and resting it on his thigh.

Instead of persuading her to move, though, he pulled the blanket tightly around her.

Kallie turned flat on her back and nestled against him. He draped his arm over her, its weight comforting. When she opened her eyes, Graeson was looking off into the woods again, the same twisted expression drawing his brows together. She wanted to console him and say it would be fine, but she couldn't find it in her heart to promise something she couldn't. She was no seer. Instead, she said the one true thing she could.

"For what it's worth, I'm glad you found us."

Graeson looked down at her with wide eyes, either surprised that she was still awake or that she had said those words at all. But it was true; Kallie was glad. She found comfort in knowing he was with her. Not because she needed his protection, but because he reminded her who she was, who she could be.

"I will always find you, Kalisandre." He gave her a small smile, but sadness swirled across the sea of silver. "You should know that by now."

He turned away, focusing his attention once more on the surrounding forest.

In that moment, Kallie wanted to take back what she had said to him the night she had left. She wanted to wipe the despair from his gaze. Yet she remained silent.

She took a slow breath and stared at the stars peeking through the leaves. Since they had left Tetria, Kallie often wondered about Rian's theory that ancient dragons created the stars by burning holes into the blanket separating the mortal and immortal realms. She wondered whether the story had any merit or if it was just another myth told to lull children to sleep. In the grand scheme of things, she supposed it didn't matter. The dragons were extinct, and the gods barely showed themselves these days. Still, Kallie couldn't help but wonder if it could work in reverse. If the legendary beasts could create holes to other worlds—if other worlds even existed.

Her eyes danced across the constellations, and she spotted

Sabina's constellation easily. Was there war and political strife in the immortal world?

Kallie wanted to believe that the gods were better than humans. After all, that's what the stories alluded to—that the gods were superior, higher beings who were stronger and wiser than mortals. But if that was the case, then why did they come to the mortal world in the first place? Were they so bored with their immortality that they needed to mess with the affairs of humans?

Graeson swiped his thumb across the blanket, calling her attention to him once more. She curled into him and closed her eyes, her thoughts spinning.

It would have been so much easier, Kallie thought, if the gods hadn't come here at all. If they hadn't, the powers Kallie and the others possessed would never have existed. Then maybe Domitius wouldn't have taken her from her home and started a war.

Then again, she supposed Graeson wouldn't have existed either, and she wasn't so sure she wanted to live in a world without him.

CHAPTER 30
MYRA

Myra burrowed deeper into the blankets. The comforter sucked her in, as if wrapping her in a snug hug. The pillow was stiffer than she remembered, and she nuzzled against it, trying to make it more comfortable. She inhaled, and notes of cinnamon and pine enveloped her. Her fingers curled into the fabric, and the blanket tightened around her—

Her eyes shot open, her entire body stiffening.

She wasn't lying on a pillow but Laurince's chest.

In her sleep, she had grabbed the blanket and dragged it closer to her, leaving Laurince's chest bare. From his muscular pectorals to his sculpted abdominals, every inch was perfectly toned. Unable to stop herself, she glanced down.

A squeal of horror nearly slipped from her lips.

The blankets were twisted around Laurince's legs, and one of her legs was thrown high over his. Her nightdress had risen dangerously high and kissed the tops of her thighs.

Embarrassment heated her skin.

She had been cold during the night. That's all. That was the only plausible explanation for their entangled bodies.

Slowly, she uncurled her fingers from the blanket. She tried to untwist her limbs from his, but he squeezed her closer to his chest. Myra's eyes threatened to pop out of her head as she stifled a gasp.

Laurince mumbled something unintelligible under his breath as sleep held onto him with a deathly grip.

By the gods.

Maybe Myra would be lucky, and a storm would roll in and lightning would strike—

She grimaced. That would only make him wake up faster.

She had to get out of the bed. *Now.*

Myra peeled Laurince's hand off her. She crawled out of bed, doing her best not to disturb him. It was bad enough that one of them knew their limbs had been entangled, but both of them? That would be a nightmare—

An amused snort sounded behind her.

She snapped her head toward the window.

Rian was lounging in a green barrel chair. One leg was folded over the other as he leaned back in the seat, an arm lazily draped over the chair's arm. Rian took a long sip from a mug. "Did I mention he's a cuddler?"

Myra tugged on her nightgown. "We never talk about this, got it?"

He lowered his mug, revealing a devilish smirk.

"Talk about what?"

Myra stiffened at Laurince's groggy voice. She silently cursed herself when her cheeks burned redder. How was his voice making her skin flush? It was too early and much too bright for this nonsense.

"Oh, nothing," Rian answered in a singsong tone, his mischievous grin widening.

"Do I have drool on my face or something?" Laurince asked.

Myra looked back and immediately regretted the decision.

Propped up on one arm, Laurince wiped his chin and then scratched his chest. Myra's attention snagged on his collarbone, and she immediately caught herself. Feeling much too exposed, she snatched her bag in search of something to throw on herself.

A flash of silver sparkled as the sun hit the contents of her bag. She rolled her eyes at the small blade, though a small grin poked at her cheek. Moving it aside, she grabbed the first pair of trousers she could find.

"We should get going," she said, shoving her feet into the pants, one after the other, as she fought the fabric of her nightgown.

"What about food?" Rian asked, not bothering to hide his amusement in his tone.

"We can get something on the way out. The longer we wait, the more daylight we waste. The last time we made this journey, you couldn't stop stressing the importance of using the daylight to our advantage. Right, Laurince?" she asked, fully aware she was rambling. She quickly swapped her dress for a simple blouse.

"Uhm, right," Laurince said, rubbing the sleep from his eyes with his fist.

The chair creaked as Rian stood. "I'll go see about snagging us a couple of loaves and leave you two to—"

"I'll join you." Myra threw her bag over her shoulder.

"That's really unnecessary," Rian said, but Myra was already ushering him out of the room.

THE DOOR CLICKED SHUT behind them, and Myra hurried down the hall, determined to put as much distance between herself and Laurince. She needed to shake off the embarrassment before she could safely see him again.

"Is he a bad snuggler? Is that why you're fleeing the scene? Did he drool on you, but you don't have the heart to tell him?" Rian whispered at her back, trailing only a foot or so behind her. "You know, if the two of you wanted the room, I could have found—"

Myra whipped around, and Rian had to catch himself before he barreled straight into her and sent them both tumbling down the stairs.

"There is no 'us.' Got it?" she snapped, her fists digging into her hips.

Rian smirked. "That's not what it looked like this morning."

"It didn't *look* like anything. We wouldn't have been..." Myra hesitated, struggling to find the right words.

"Entangled?" Rian suggested, wiggling his brows.

Myra groaned. "In the same bed if it hadn't been because of you!" She poked him in the chest. "When we returned, you were sprawled across the entire bed."

He rolled his eyes. "We both know he and I were never going to fit in the same bed, anyway."

"You could have at least told us we were all sharing a room!"

Rian lifted his shoulder with a smug look. "It was more fun this way."

"More *fun*? You are preposterous!"

"That's a funny way to say genius," he said, punctuating it with a wink.

"How does *that* make you a genius?" she asked, pointing back to their room.

Rian cocked a brow. "Why do you think he invited you to come with us?"

"Because he felt bad for me," Myra answered, though the words didn't sit right on her tongue.

"If you truly think that's the reason, then you haven't been paying attention," Rian said, moving past her and heading down the stairs.

Myra bounded after him. "What other reason is there?"

Reaching the bottom of the steps, Rian looked over his shoulder and grinned. "Think about it, Haze."

But the way Rian said her nickname differed from the captain. Casual and platonic, and certainly not in a way that sent her heart thundering.

Myra's eyes widened.

But then she recalled the captain teasing her about Rian, and she shook her head, dismissing the thought.

"No, you're wrong. He thinks I have feelings for you."

Rian laughed and grabbed her shoulder. "Everyone has feelings for me, Mys."

"*I* don't." She tipped up her chin and tossed off his hand.

"Oh, trust me, I know." He leaned toward her and whispered, "But don't worry, it'll be our little secret." He playfully flicked her chin with his thumb before turning toward the counter and flagging down the innkeeper.

Begrudgingly, Myra followed him. As she stood at the bar, her brows furrowed as a strange sensation tickled the back of her neck. Before she could identify the source, a smooth, low voice from behind startled her.

"What will be your little secret?" Laurince asked, leaning against the bar beside her.

Myra's heart flew into her lungs, rendering her speechless. She hadn't even heard him come down the steps. How much of their conversation had he heard?

She looked back-and-forth between Laurince and Rian. "Uhm… uh…"

Laurince raised a brow, waiting for an answer. The captain's suspicion slithered its way over her limbs. Something bitter twisted with it.

"It wouldn't be a secret if we told you, now would it?" Rian asked, leaning forward.

A deep wrinkle formed in the middle of Laurince's forehead as he narrowed his gaze at them.

Myra's gaze flicked to his chest. The laces near his collar were loose, and his sleeves were rolled up to his elbow.

"I think...I think I need some air." Myra pushed away from the bar and scurried out of the tavern before either gentleman could voice their dissent.

The brisk morning air bit her cheeks as she stepped outside. Hurried footsteps followed her.

Myra sighed. "You didn't need to follow me—"

But Myra didn't get to finish her rebuttal before a gag was lodged into her mouth, silencing her. The person twisted Myra's arms behind her back. Her shoulder made a sickening *pop* as it was forced out of its socket.

Tears sprang to her eyes, and she tried to scream out for Laurince, for anyone. But it was no use. The gag muffled her cries for help. She jerked around, trying to free her hands from her captor's grip. As she twisted, she spotted a sinister grin and a tattoo of a dragon scaling up the man's neck. Then, an intense pain spiked the back of her head, and her vision flashed white, the inn disappearing.

CHAPTER 31
KALLIE

"WHAT IF DOMITIUS DOESN'T SHOW UP?" ELLIE ASKED AS SHE SAT ON A low-hanging branch of a maple tree. With one leg dangling from her perch, she inspected her weapons, turning them this way and that. She had woven her stark white hair into a simple plait, and thin strands framed her face.

Kallie looked toward the forest at the opposite end of the great plain that stretched in front of them. A crisp breeze rolled in, sending the leaves tumbling. There was no other movement between the trees on the other side of the plain, though, and a nauseating knot twisted in Kallie's stomach. Still, she said, "He's going to come."

"How do you know?" Ellie asked, doubtful.

"Because I know him." Kallie pressed her palms flat on the ground, and blades of dry grass weaved between her fingers, scratching her skin.

Within the surrounding ten-foot square radius, Graeson's constant pacing had flattened the meadow, digging a small trench into the ground.

They had arrived at the agreed-upon time: an hour past high noon. But now the sun was setting behind them. Golden hues painted the field resting between them and the opposing forest. Myra would have thought the view was worthy of a painting to be hung in a grand hall. Kallie, however, saw it for what it was: one last moment of peace before she would come face-to-face with the man who had destroyed her life.

She shouldn't have been surprised Domitius was late. How many times had he made her sit in his office waiting for his verdict? Waiting for her punishment after she failed a mission or failed to increase her power? Kallie had always hated the anticipation that came with sitting in his office alone, never knowing when the door would swing open. The resulting anxiety was a plague, always finding its way to infiltrate her bloodstream and twist her thoughts into a tangled mess. It was a tactic, one Domitius used freely.

And Kallie was falling for it even now, allowing the passing of time, the inevitable doom, to crawl under her skin and set her nerves on fire. It made her question whether she was ready.

Kallie rested the back of her head against the tree trunk. "I should have listened to you sooner."

Above her, Ellie sighed. "Of all times, you admit that *now*? When I don't even get to enjoy telling you I told you so?"

Chewing the inside of her cheek, Kallie shrugged. She should have listened to Ellie from the beginning. Instead, she had let her pride get in the way.

"Hey," Graeson said, calling her attention to him. "None of that."

"It's true, though," Kallie mumbled as he crouched in front of her.

With a finger, he tipped her chin up, forcing her gaze to meet his. "No, it's not. Even without showing his face, Domitius is messing with you, twisting your thoughts. Do not let him win; do not let him have that power over you." His thumb lightly brushed across her jawline. "Got it?"

Kallie gulped but nodded.

He wove his fingers into her hair, cupping the back of her head, his touch soft yet unyielding. Wrong yet impossibly right. "You are not a weapon, Kalisandre. He does not have power over you; only you do." His moon-gray eyes bounced across her face. "Repeat it, Kal."

Her mouth had gone dry, though, and Kallie struggled to repeat the words.

"Louder, little mouse," Graeson insisted.

Kallie tried to focus on the warmth of his palms, the light pressure at the back of her head. But as she looked at him, everything she wanted taunted her within Graeson's storm-gray eyes. She could see the life that she could have had with him. She could hear the moments of laughter that might never come to be, the moments of joy and love. She saw open skies and smiles. She saw a world that was theirs to roam without fear or terror. But the one thing that was missing from those scenes that flooded her mind was his mother.

When Kallie had believed her mother was dead, she would have done anything to spin back time and save her. She would have done anything to have at least one conversation with her, one moment that was just theirs. Now was Graeson's chance to have that, and Kallie would do anything to ensure he got it.

She rolled her hands into fists. "He doesn't have power over me; only I do."

Speaking the words aloud was like a ship crashing against an unexpected plot of land. A sudden jolt forward. But instead of falling over, Kallie felt sturdier than she had moments before.

As if seeing the words sink in, Graeson leaned closer. His forehead touched hers as his shoulders dropped. "No matter what happens," he whispered, "do not forget that. Do not forget that we are here with you. You have the power, but you are not alone. Not anymore."

Kallie closed her eyes and leaned into him, leaned into his words and the knowledge that Graeson was right. She wasn't weak. She wasn't powerless. But more importantly, she wasn't alone anymore. Not if she didn't want to be.

"Thank you." The moment the words left her mouth, she knew they were not enough. There was so much she wanted to say, to admit. Her lips parted. "I—"

A whistle cut her off.

They pulled away from each other and looked up at Ellie.

"He's here," Ellie said, pointing her freshly sharpened blade at the forest across from them.

Kallie and Graeson both looked over. A flicker of light sparkled deep in the trees, as if the sun's rays had caught on metal.

Graeson, already on his feet, held out a hand. Without hesitation, Kallie grabbed it, letting him pull her up.

Once upright, her legs only trembled marginally. Loralaine's words swirled in the back of her mind.

Fear reminds us we are human.

Ellie's boots hit the ground with a loud thump as she jumped from the branch. "Army or no army, you've got this, Kals. Or else we all might be—"

"Euralys," Graeson hissed.

He was too late, though. Kallie already knew what Ellie was going to say: they would all be dead if Kallie failed.

I will not fail, she told herself, determination steadying her legs.

She took a step forward, but a calloused hand wrapped around her wrist, beckoning her to stop mid-stride. She turned and peered at Graeson.

"Together," he said.

Kallie nodded.

They would meet Domitius together, but the rest of this she would have to do on her own. She knew it, and he knew it.

With Graeson and Ellie on either side of her, Kallie began crossing the clearing. She focused on the silhouette clouded in shadows across the field. With each yard gained, more features came into the light. Domitius stood with his head tilted slightly up, hands clasped behind his back, shoulders relaxed yet rolled back. His feet were shoulder-width apart, planted and unwavering. Months might have separated them, but some things never changed. From this far away, Domitius was barely a blip compared to the forest behind him, yet he had the ability to tear the world apart. Today, that ended.

"Do you see her?" Ellie asked, scanning the trees.

"No," Graeson said, voice tight.

Other than Domitius, there were only two soldiers standing on the other side. They were several paces behind Domitius, their forms masked in darkness. Lysanthia, however, was nowhere to be seen.

"He's probably keeping her out of sight," Kallie said, pushing away the rising nausea. "We continue on as planned."

She could sense their hesitation, but Kallie ignored it. Rolling her shoulders back, she steeled her expression. Leaves crunched beneath their feet as they eliminated the space between them and Domitius, inch by painful inch.

Once they were halfway across the field, Domitius stepped out of the shadows at last. His white pants were impeccably clean for having traveled from Ardentol, and Kallie wondered when he had arrived. A day ago? Several? Had he simply been sitting in some posh inn, drinking whiskey while they waited?

At the thought, anger boiled inside her, and she tamped it down the best she could.

The two guards stepped out of the shadows, and a collective

gasp whipped through the air.

Large wings spanned out from behind the guards. One man bore a set of webbed wings as black as night, while the other had feathered wings that were made of molten ash, each feather a different shade of gray.

"Myra wasn't lying," Kallie whispered, voice haunted.

While she hadn't doubted Myra, seeing the winged men was entirely different from hearing about them. Suddenly, Kallie was regretting leaving Nyrri behind with the horses deep in the woods. Would the drakonis be able to hear them if they needed her? How long would it take Nyrri to get here?

"We agreed no armies, yet he brought two of his pets?" Graeson spat, a low rumble vibrating in his throat.

Kallie inhaled. "We knew he might try to pull something like this. The odds are still manageable." But she wasn't sure if she was trying to reassure the others or herself more.

Ellie tilted her head, her braid falling to her back. "How do you think they put on that armor?" she asked, eyeing the winged guards decked head-to-toe in armor.

"Now is not the time," Graeson retorted.

While Ellie observed the guards, Kallie's attention was fixed on Domitius. Unlike the guards, Domitius wore no armor. Kallie wondered what it felt like to be so sure of one's survival, to be so confident in one's ability to win, that one didn't even find it necessary to wear a chest plate.

A small smile graced Domitius' lips, but there was nothing gentle or warm about it. There never had been.

He had no power over her, not anymore, she reminded herself.

Her fingers twitched at the dagger strapped to her thigh. She hadn't bothered to hide the weapon. There was no point. He knew her well enough to know she would not come unarmed. He had trained her, after all.

"Where is she?" Kallie called out as both parties stopped fifty yards away from each other.

Domitius clicked his tongue against the roof of his mouth. "Have you fallen so far that you have forgotten how to greet those stationed above you, let alone your father?"

"You are *not* my father," she spat, hands curling into fists at her sides.

Domitius laughed, and the sound grated on her skin.

"I'd rather not waste time rehashing things we have already discussed. We have more important matters, do we not?" He looked past her, as if searching for something or someone behind her. "Is Myra not with you? I had assumed she would have wanted to be here for this."

"She is not part of this deal," Kallie said.

An amused smirk curled at the edge of Domitius' lip. "Ah, but is she not? We have her to thank, after all."

"Enough of this," Graeson said, stepping in line with Kallie. "Stop delaying. Where is my mother?"

Domitius' attention turned to Graeson, and he tilted his head, assessing. "I must say, I'm glad to see you didn't die when the tunnel collapsed. It would have been a pity to have lost someone so..." He paused, rubbing his jaw with his hand before smiling and saying, "*Special.*"

Kallie's brows twisted together, but before she could question it, Domitius waved his hand. Twigs snapped in the distance, forcing her attention away and toward the figure stumbling through the brush.

"Mother?" Graeson jerked forward, but Kallie quickly grabbed him by the wrist, yanking him back.

The woman lifted her hands to block out the sun. The chains on her wrists rattled.

"Ah, ah. Be a good little guard dog and stay put," Domitius

ordered as another winged guard led Lysanthia. "If you move before I say, she dies. Got it?"

As if to prove his point, the guard unsheathed his short sword, and the steel glinted in the sunlight. Without a sound, Lysanthia lifted her chin and kept marching forward.

Graeson went rigid beside Kallie, his chest rising and falling hard with every uneven breath. But he didn't move.

Domitius smiled at his obedience.

Lysanthia's ink-black hair hung down her face as if pulled by heavy weights. The guard pushed her to hurry her along. Graeson's mother stumbled but managed to steady her feet. She straightened, and her hair peeled back away from her hollow face. The seer's skin was pale, nearly translucent, as if she hadn't seen the sun in years.

"Now, Kalisandre," Domitius called, curling a finger inward, "be a good girl and come here."

Graeson's breathing hitched. But this was why they had come here. This was the plan: Kallie for his mother. That was the deal.

"Not until she is safe," Kallie said.

Domitius sighed as if annoyed. He beckoned the guard forward, and the man dragged Lysanthia by the chains. When he reached the halfway point, the guard shoved Lysanthia to the ground. Her knees buckled, collapsing beneath her.

"You bastard," Graeson hissed.

"I believe *you* are the bastard," Domitius countered.

Through gritted teeth and quietly enough Domitius couldn't hear, Graeson said, "I'm going to—"

"Nothing," Kallie interrupted, glaring at him as he shook with rage. "You are going to do *nothing*. He's doing this on purpose. Do not fall prey to his games, remember?"

The muscles in his jaw popped, but after a second, he nodded.

Kallie looked at Ellie and said, "No matter what happens, you protect her first."

Ellie nodded just as Graeson spat, "What? That wasn't the plan."

"I can handle myself, Gray. Trust me," Kallie urged. She needed him to believe in her. If they didn't save Lysanthia, she wouldn't be able to live with herself. Graeson wouldn't be able to live with himself.

Kallie faced the men on the opposite side. The third guard had already joined Domitius, his hands clasped in front of him. In the center of them, Lysanthia sat with her head down, her hair shielding her features. One foot after another, Kallie strolled forward. Each step she took became heavier than the last, but she kept going until she was beside Lysanthia.

When the seer dragged her gaze from the floor and looked at Kallie, her expression almost brought Kallie to tears. So much was visible within those gray eyes—Graeson's eyes—that Kallie had to blink away the water blurring her vision.

"You are even more beautiful than my visions led me to believe," Lysanthia said with a small smile. "And you have your mother's eyes."

"And Graeson, yours," Kallie said, the tears stinging.

"Do not cry, my dear," Lysanthia said. "I knew this was coming years ago, but some fates cannot be changed."

Kallie's brows pinched together. Lysanthia had seen this version of the future? The question was on the tip of Kallie's tongue, but before she could ask, the seer spoke.

"I am sorry for the pain that will come."

"The pain? What pain?" Kallie asked, her heartbeat thundering in her throat.

Instead of answering, Lysanthia only said, her voice a near echo, "Know that this was the only way."

The seer's words sank like a stone in a lake in Kallie's stomach. This was the end. Kallie could feel it in her gut, see it in the way Lysanthia looked at her.

"We do not have all day, Kalisandre," Domitius demanded.

Kallie peeled her gaze away from the seer. She had too many questions, but no time to ask. Swallowing them, Kallie moved.

But as she passed Lysanthia, the seer spoke once more. "A sacrifice was always needed."

Kallie stumbled, hearing the warning within the seer's voice.

Kallie's sacrifice would not be in vain. She would make sure of that. The others would live. Graeson deserved this. His mother deserved to be free, to have a life with the son she never got to see grow old.

"Bend the knee, Kalisandre," Domitius ordered when she reached him.

Kallie's head fell to the ground in submission. In her periphery, she saw Graeson run to his mother, pulling her up and tucking her into his arms as he squeezed her. She wanted to memorize the way Graeson's hair fell over his face, the width of his shoulders, the way his eyes peered into her very soul when he blinked them open to look at her over Lysanthia's shoulder.

Peering into those gray, tear-stained eyes, Kallie's heart cracked. She should have told him how much she cared about him, how much his encouragement and trust meant to her. That this sacrifice, while for the good of the seven kingdoms, was also for him. Mostly for him.

Because, bond or no bond, she would do anything for him.

For her entire life, Domitius had doubted her, believed she wasn't strong enough. But not anymore. Kallie called out to the swirl of power waiting eagerly within her. In an instant, it filled her veins, coating her tongue.

She lifted her head, a wicked smile peeking through the strands of hair that had fallen in her face. "I think it is about time you bent the knee to me, don't you, Kage?"

Wide-eyed, Domitius fell, his knees smacking the ground with an ungraceful thump.

One of the winged guards made to move forward, but a flash of silver sliced through the air, landing beside his toe.

"Next time, I won't miss," Ellie called out, twirling another jagged star around her finger.

The guard stepped backward, his fingers twitching at his side beside his sword.

Kallie's power hummed within her, a torrent of energy buzzing inside her. She was not afraid, not of herself and not of death.

"Actually, Ellie, I think I have a better idea," Kallie said as she observed the guards. "Join him."

One after the other, the guards' knees struck the ground, their wings flaring out in anger as they fell victim to her command.

"That's better, don't you think?" Kallie asked, looking down at the man whom she had looked up to her entire life.

She slipped the dagger from its strap and brushed the tip of her blade along the edge of Domitius' neck, enjoying the way his eyes widened in terror. She dragged the metal from his jugular to his jaw before tipping up Domitius' chin.

She had once admired him, respected him, wanted to *be* him. Now she only wished to drive a sword through his heart.

Although, a quick death would be a mercy for him. Domitius deserved to feel all the pain he had caused her, her family, and her friends.

"Tell me, *Father*," Kallie spat, the term that once held so much weight now leaden on her tongue. "How does it feel to be on your knees before me?"

"You think you're strong for holding steady? Is that it?" Domitius sneered, his nose still held high. "You do. It's laughable, really."

"I'm not laughing. Now am I?"

"Oh, Kalisandre, you still haven't learned, have you? What good does killing me do? You have *nothing*. Your so-called family, the ones who share your blood, they *despise* you. You're the very reason their beloved prince is dead. You have no friends, no home, no kingdom, no *crown*."

He was wrong, yet the blade shifted in her hand.

She couldn't have cared less about a title. It was the other claims that had her halting. Kallie wanted to believe she had earned a home with Graeson and Terin, but she had seen the way Dani looked at her. The stony stares and hushed whispers. They may have been on speaking terms now, but it didn't mean Dani had forgiven Kallie. Nor did Kallie want to be forgiven. There hadn't been a day that went by since Fynn's death when guilt didn't coat her tongue and taint her lungs. Every breath Kallie took was another reminder that Fynn no longer breathed, that his and Dani's child would grow up fatherless, just like he had.

As if knowing he had hit his target, Domitius drove the verbal knife in deeper. "Your brother—Fynneares, was it?—he's dead. But he has a twin, does he not? The crown has been passed to him. So where does that leave you, Kalisandre?"

"Kal," Graeson called out.

She shook her head. Graeson promised he would let her do this. She had to be the one to end it all.

For Fynn.

For her father.

For the innocents who had died because of Domitius' greed and her mistakes.

"I could have given you everything, Kalisandre," Domitius taunted.

"You used me!" she shouted, her anger snapping like a strike of lightning.

"Of course I used you! Do you think they won't?" he asked,

glancing at Graeson and Ellie. "You don't even realize the full extent of your ability!"

Kallie's blood buzzed, her power coursing through her.

"All you ever cared about was my ability, and you turned it against me. You manipulated my *mind*!" Kallie's voice shook, but she did not relent. "You're right about one thing, though: I no longer have a claim to a crown. For years, I have been chasing a hunk of metal. An accessory shaped and crafted, given some artificial authority because of the symbol it provided to the people. A crown means nothing when you have no one to share it with. When everyone around you either fears you or hates you.

"I may be without a crown, a kingdom, or even a penny to my name, but I at least can walk out of here with my mind intact. I can at least walk out of here knowing I didn't sacrifice my soul in order to achieve my goal."

She thought of Graeson and Ellie behind her.

She thought of Terin and Esmeray in Pontia.

She thought of Dani, her belly growing bigger and her and Fynn's child growing stronger every day.

The innocent lives across the seven kingdoms, who were suffering and would continue to suffer if the war went on.

Myra, who had lost her brother to madness.

The numerous guards Kallie had sacrificed in order to further Domitius' plans.

Graeson's mother, who had lived beneath the marble castle for almost two decades.

She thought of the father she never got to know.

She thought of Fynn in the Beneath and the promise she made to him.

Enough was *enough*.

Kallie knelt before Domitius, pressing the tip of her blade against his heart. "You have taught me many things. You taught me to fight, to wield my gift, to hold a sword. You turned me into a weapon. It is only fitting that the same weapon you forged years ago is the one that becomes your undoing."

But as Kallie went to drive her dagger through Domitius' cold, black heart, she hesitated as a coy smirk rose on his face.

And that hesitation cost her everything.

CHAPTER 32

KALLIE

"Drop the blade."

Kallie's grip unfurled around the hilt, and it slipped from her hand. The dagger bounced on the ground, then fell flat beside Domitius' knees. She tried to move, tried to snatch the dagger. But she couldn't. Her limbs were too heavy, as if dozens of weights were tied to the ends of them, cementing her in place.

Domitius smiled as he stood, the curve of his lips sinister and victorious.

"Kalisan—" Graeson started, but his shout was cut short, as if the words were shoved down his throat.

In the corner of her eye, Kallie saw the masked guard hold out his hands, his stance widening. Before she could see what the guard was doing, Domitius snatched her by the chin.

"We could have been spectacular together," Domitius said, his fingers digging into her cheeks as he forced her head up. His lip curled in disgust, and he shoved her face away. "Now, turn around. I want you to see what happens when you betray me."

As if her legs had a mind of their own, Kallie turned, obeying Domitius' command.

What was happening? Why was she listening to him? Why did she drop that godsforsaken dagger? This was not the plan. Domitius wasn't her. He couldn't—

Kallie choked on a gasp as she stared at Graeson, Ellie, and Lysanthia in horror. Her breathing became shallow; her heartbeat stuttered.

It wasn't possible.

She had to be wrong.

But before she could process the truth staring her in the face, Domitius spoke.

"Take off your helmet," he ordered.

With his right hand, the guard to her right reached for his helmet while keeping his other hand in front of him, as if he was shielding himself. He peeled his helmet off, and the metal clunked to the ground.

Kallie's brows twisted. She recognized that face. Those brown eyes, those short, tight curls. But where had she seen him?

"Moris?" Graeson choked out the guard's name as if it was a struggle.

Moris?

Another gasp filled her throat.

The Pontian who had accompanied them the first time to Ardentol, the one who had paralyzed her. He was *here*. He was one of *them*.

"Didn't anyone ever tell you never to leave a man behind?" Domitius questioned, looking at Graeson.

"Y-you were dead," Graeson said. The veins on his neck were prominent, as if he too was straining against the poison lacing the air that prevented them from moving.

"My men got to him just in time before he bled out on the floor in the temple on the day of the wedding," Domitius said. "I was minutes away from disposing of him, but then he showed me how useful he could be. I decided to give him another chance at life, a reward for being the first. Paralysis truly is a remarkable gift." Domitius looked down at Kallie and smiled. "I never got to thank the handmaiden before she ran out. A pity, really. She did a splendid job."

Kallie tried to speak, tried to scream, but her body was still frozen, rock solid, Moris' power drenching her.

"Chain her," Domitius commanded.

Moris yanked Kallie's hands behind her back. A cold, heavy weight was dropped onto her wrists, the sound of manacles clicking together, solidifying her fate.

Kallie could barely comprehend anything that was happening as she watched Domitius stroll toward Graeson, two of the guards trailing behind him, their wings fluttering in the wind.

Domitius glanced back at her, curiosity sparkling in his brown eyes. "Is it still true you cannot penetrate his mind, Kalisandre?"

Kallie growled, her voice stuck in her throat. Her bones vibrated with rage as she fought against Moris' power. But no matter how hard she tried, she failed.

Domitius rolled his eyes. "Speak," he commanded.

The words poured from her mouth in a rush. "Let him go!"

But she found that while she could speak, she was still paralyzed. Invisible shackles tethered her to the ground. Her gaze locked onto Graeson. Fear rippled between them as the two guards flanked him, Ellie, and his mother.

"Answer my question," Domitius demanded.

"I will not manipulate him!" she blurted.

"Will not or *cannot?*" Domitius asked. He was only a few yards away from Graeson and the others now. "The difference matters."

Kallie's gaze flicked to Ellie. Their gazes connected, a tense exchange passing between them in a matter of seconds. Kallie's ability stirred within her. The command hung on the tip of her tongue, but she didn't get a chance to release it.

"Silence, Kalisandre."

Her mouth snapped shut.

"Disappointing," Domitius said, shaking his head. Kallie could almost feel his sigh brush her cheek. He shrugged. "Then again, you've always been a disappointment."

He turned his attention to Graeson. "But with you, there is so much more potential, isn't there? A half-god, I've been told. And according to your mother, one that hasn't touched half of his power."

Kallie's gaze shot to Lysanthia, who stood beside Graeson. But Kallie couldn't make out the expression on the seer's face. Had they been wrong this entire time? Had Lysanthia betrayed them? Was this all some ploy?

"Tell me," Domitius asked, as the two guards unsheathed their swords, "is a god still a god if he bends the knee to a mortal king?"

Graeson's gaze flicked to Kallie briefly before returning to the king. Vitriol and hate spilled from every bone and muscle in his body. "I will never bow down to you."

"Never say never," Domitius warned, his voice sending a sickening chill skittering down Kallie's spine. He grabbed Graeson by the jaw, his fingers indenting Graeson's cheeks. "You *will* bend the knee."

Graeson's nose twitched.

Hope fluttered in Kallie's chest. Even if Domitius had stolen Kallie's power, Graeson was stronger than Domitius knew. Stronger than them all. He could fight this. His mind could not be—

No. No. No! Kallie screamed internally.

It wasn't possible, yet the bend in Graeson's knees was

indisputable. They hit the ground with a loud thump, the earth quaking as they did.

A gasp bubbled up in Kallie's throat as she watched Graeson's head fall down in penance. His jet-black hair fell in streaks across his face, casting his expression in deep shadows.

It shouldn't have been possible. Kallie had never been able to manipulate Graeson. His mind was impenetrable. Yet there Domitius stood, victorious.

"Chain him," Domitius called out.

When neither of the guards moved, confusion twisted Kallie's expression. Then horror consumed her as the last person she suspected shifted.

Lysanthia stepped forward, tears streaming down her sunken cheeks. She dug into her pocket and pulled out a key. With a twist, the chains around her wrists came undone. Graeson didn't move an inch as his mother approached.

Lysanthia reached out to her son, pulling his hands behind his back with long, nimble fingers. She placed the chains around his wrists, and the iron manacles snapped together with a finality that nearly shattered Kallie's heart.

Domitius snapped his fingers, and the other guard stepped closer to Ellie. He pressed the tip of his sword into her back, and Ellie blanched in horror.

"I gave you a chance, Kalisandre. Many chances, in fact," Domitius said. "Instead, you planned to best me. Did I not teach you anything when you were under my roof?"

Kallie's entire body trembled. She no longer knew if she was kneeling because of her own crumbling strength or because of Moris' power.

"Did you truly think I would not see through that flimsy little proposal? You should have known better. *I* taught you better.

Although you always were more arrogant than your ability and knowledge deserved. But you see, you have made a grave miscalculation. I no longer need you." Domitius bent down behind Graeson. Grabbing him by a chunk of hair, he wrenched Graeson's head back. "Now, let us see the true power of a god."

CHAPTER 33
GRAESON

THE GOD ROARED, HIS FURY SO BRIGHT IT SHOOK GRAESON TO HIS core as his knees buckled and hit the ground with a loud crack.

Graeson was powerless to stop Domitius' command from ripping through him and shredding his control. The moment the order left the bull king's lips, a numbness coated Graeson's limbs, as if he had been pushed into a half-frozen lake and his limbs had turned to ice on contact.

Not a single part of Graeson had wanted to obey the order, nor had he intended to bend the knee. Yet there he was, looking up at the man he loathed with every morsel in his body.

Graeson had been trapped inside his own mind plenty of times. He experienced it whenever the god took over. But this—whatever *this* was—was entirely different. Before, there was a sort of separation, a strange divide between what he could experience versus what was happening in front of him. When the god was in control, it was almost as if Graeson was looking through a fog-covered window. Some images were hard to decipher, some voices were difficult to parse, their words occasionally mumbled. This was not the god's doing, though.

Unlike when the god took control, Graeson could see and hear everything clearly, yet he had no control over his limbs.

He knew he should do something—move away, fight, *anything*—but he couldn't. It was as if a gate had been slammed shut, cutting off his connection to his muscles. He couldn't say anything. He couldn't stand. He was completely and totally under Domitius' control.

For the first time in his life, Graeson was powerless.

We are never *powerless,* the god hissed, seething from within. *Do you really wish to let this speck of a man overcome us?*

I have no control over my own limbs! What do you expect me to do? Graeson shot back.

"Chain him," Domitius demanded.

His mother's face appeared in front of him, and the betrayal fractured his heart as metal clanged. Yet, when his mother's eyes met his, sorrow flooded her expression. Graeson knew then that she too was under Domitius' influence. Cold metal touched his skin as his mother placed the manacles around his wrists. The heavy metal weight pulled his hands down.

Graeson's attention flicked to Kalisandre. Fear spilled from her wide-eyed expression. Her body was tense, nearly shaking with rage and frustration. And as he stared at her, realization struck him in the chest like a lightning bolt searing through the sky and striking a tree.

Graeson had never imagined—he had never dared to think—that Domitius could replicate Kalisandre's ability, but that was the only plausible explanation.

Anger vibrated throughout his entire body. Graeson saw Kalisandre's lips move, yet he couldn't process her words. They were too quiet compared to the roaring scream ripping through his mind.

With a slimy smirk, Domitius crouched behind Graeson. The

bull king hummed in satisfaction as Graeson knelt before him, unable to move. The king was barely even a yard away, yet Graeson could do nothing but stare back. Every nerve was on fire. His skin burned and thrummed. A red hue haloed his vision. His hold on the god was slipping.

If you wish us to get out of this, take control, Graeson demanded.

Do you still not understand what you are? the god asked, his tone taking on a sharp edge.

"I gave you a chance, Kalisandre. Many chances, in fact. Instead, you planned to best me. Did I not teach you anything when you were under my roof?" Domitius said, moving to stand behind him.

Rage and terror ripped through Graeson's body at Domitius' words.

It was a *fucking* trap, and they had all fallen for it so easily.

"Did you truly think I would not see through that flimsy little proposal? You should have known better. *I* taught you better. Although you always were more arrogant than your ability and knowledge deserved. But you see, you have made a grave miscalculation. I no longer need you."

A sharp pain laced Graeson's scalp as Domitius squatted behind him and tugged Graeson's head back. Domitius tilted his head so far back that Graeson's neck cracked, and a wave of pain spiraled down his spine.

In the corner of his eye, Graeson saw Ellie on her knees, the guard behind her pressing the tip of his blade to her back.

"Now, let us see the true power of a god."

The command that fell from Domitius' lips next sent an icy terror running through Graeson's body.

"Kill her."

Graeson wanted to scream as his limbs straightened. Unwillingly, he pushed himself off the floor, his legs and arms acting of their own accord as if they were not his to control. His fingers folded around the hilt of an outstretched dagger, and Domitius withdrew several steps. Fear ripped through him in an instant as he met Kalisandre's sea-blue eyes. His breath hitched, a panicked gasp catching in his throat. A cold sweat slicked his palms, yet his grip around the dagger remained firm. His heart threatened to shatter as the frantic drumbeat threatened to burst through his ribcage.

Kalisandre was his heart, his world, his every breath. He urged himself to turn the dagger, to press it against his own chest. He would rather rip out his own heart than take hers.

The taste of bile rose in his throat, a wave of nausea threatening to overwhelm him. But he couldn't shake the command that soaked his limbs.

The god screamed in protest, a violent roar that shook his bones. Still, Graeson's foot moved, his knee bending as he took a step forward.

Kalisandre deserved to live. She deserved to experience a family that loved her. She deserved the world. He couldn't take that from her. He *wouldn't*. There was no way—

His heartbeat faltered as his feet took a step in a different direction. But the relief was fleeting because gray eyes replaced blue.

His mother blinked at him, understanding flooding her countenance.

This wasn't…this wasn't what he wanted either. It was too soon. They hadn't had enough time.

Tears stung his eyes. One after another, droplets fell. The tears, cold on his skin as they rolled down his cheek and spilled onto the ground, were the only signal that some part of his mind was still connected to his body. A cruel reminder that it was truly Graeson holding the dagger. Yet, when he looked at his mother, not a single drop of fear shone in her eyes. He briefly wondered if she believed this to be a mercy after everything she had been through while in captivity.

Graeson wanted to tell her so much at that moment. He wished he could tell her that whatever she had done, however she had aided Domitius over the years, wasn't her fault. That he forgave her. That he wasn't mad at her for not being there, for not being able to see him grow up. He wished he could relay everything he had done in his life, how he had never stopped thinking about her, never stopped loving her.

But more than anything, Graeson wished he could drop the blade.

He attempted to loosen his grip; he tried to peel his fingers from the hilt. But no matter how much he strained or how much his blood vessels threatened to pop from the pressure, his fingers remained glued to the leather wrapping.

He didn't want to do this. He didn't want to be parted from his mother so quickly.

"Do not be afraid," Lysanthia whispered.

Afraid? He was absolutely fucking terrified.

Graeson had taken so many lives—too many to count at this point. It never got easier. Even when the god was in control, Graeson felt the weight of every soul pressing down on his shoulders, weighing him down with every step he took. He did not wish for her to be another name added to that long list.

This was not how it was supposed to be.

This was not how their plan was supposed to unfold.

Kalisandre was supposed to manipulate the king and his guards —and she had done so beautifully in the beginning. Yet Domitius had broken free of the command. And now she, too, would feel the weight of his mother's death.

"My son, I never stopped loving you," his mother said, voice still impossibly steady as Graeson lifted his head. "Know that there was nothing you could have done differently. I sealed my fate a long time ago. *This* was the only way."

Tears blurred his vision, and for a second, he thought he felt his hand tremble, yet it only rose higher and higher.

"Set yourself free," she whispered.

The dagger hovered over her chest, where he could faintly hear her heartbeat, its rhythm calm. Steady.

"Now!" Domitius commanded.

The blade jolted forward. Graeson's arm wrapped around his mother's back. He dug his fingers into her blouse and hugged her tightly to his chest. Her weight shifted, and the wet gurgle of blood filled her lungs as she took a quivering breath.

When the god of the Beneath came to fetch her soul, Lysanthia did not scream.

She did not cry.

She did not fight.

His mother died in silence, one hand wrapped around Graeson's and the other gripping his shoulder.

Somewhere a scream pierced the air, sending the birds in the field and in the trees scattering.

Graeson glanced at Kallie. Tears spilled down her face, but the scream had not come from her. No, the scream had come from *him*. It rushed from Graeson's throat like a roar. Rough, raw, and guttural.

Ice-hot fury poured through his veins as his mother's life bled into him. Every muscle, every nerve, every ounce of blood inside Graeson screamed out in pain and sorrow and frustration. His mother's lifeless body slipped through his hands, but he couldn't catch her as the rage overwhelmed him. His entire body burned as the grief and guilt and fury strangled him.

He fell, his knees and palms crashing against the ground. His bones twisted and contorted, cracking and breaking. Pain and panic surged through him. Dirt piled underneath his nails as he tore into the ground.

Every bone hurt.

Every muscle screamed.

His throat tore open as a feral scream left his lungs, an endless outpouring of rage.

The sky melted into a violent ruby hue, his vision bleeding red.

Finally, the god whispered.

Then Graeson came alive.

CHAPTER 34
KALLIE

THE ROAR THAT POURED FROM GRAESON'S MOUTH PIERCED KALLIE'S ears and shattered a piece of her heart. Even Domitius had retreated several steps at the sound.

As he screamed, Graeson collapsed to the ground, his back arching and limbs trembling. The fabric stretched across his arms, his sleeves tearing at the seams. His limbs jerked in unnatural ways, and Kallie could have sworn she heard several sharp cracks as bones snapped.

Panic seared through her, draining her complexion. What did Domitius do to him? Had he or Lysanthia stabbed Graeson with whatever poison they used to create the drakonises?

Kallie tried to yell out to him, but her scream caught in her throat and expanded as if she had swallowed a bone. Moris' spell was still wrapped around her limbs, keeping even her mouth sealed shut. All she could do was watch as Graeson transformed before her eyes.

Her heartbeat thundered, each thump crashing against her ribcage.

"What the fuck?" a guard sputtered.

Sharp spikes poked through the back of Graeson's shirt. His limbs grew, and sharp claws formed at the tips of his fingers. He tipped his head up, his neck stretching and revealing opalescent scales crawling across his skin. He screamed again, this time more violently. Kallie's heart stuttered as the sound smacked her in the gut. Something protruded from his shoulders, and his entire body began to take a new shape.

Kallie was wrong. This was *not* Domitius' doing. It couldn't have been. When she looked at the winged guards and recalled Nyrri's form, Sebastian and Domitius' creatures paled in comparison to the beast coming to life before them.

The creature Graeson was turning into was four times the size of Nyrri. But unlike Nyrri, Graeson had no fur. Instead, silver and black scales that shimmered like armor in the sun covered his entire body. He dug all four sets of claws into the ground, and the earth cracked. When he shivered, two terrifyingly beautiful, carbonate leather wings, which were darker than the shadows, flared out from his shoulder blades. He extended his long neck, the movement serpent-like, and released an inhuman screech.

Dragons were not myths, nor were they extinct. They were gods.

If Kallie hadn't seen him transform before her very eyes, she wouldn't have known the man she had grown to care for beyond measure stood in front of her. He was an entirely new being, a creature she barely recognized.

When he brought his head down, though, Kallie realized that wasn't true, not entirely. A pale scar ran from his brow past his cheekbone, nearly missing his eye. It was in the exact shape of the scar Graeson bore. Then, the dragon's eyelids peeled back. In an instant, they were on her, and Kallie couldn't look away. At first, black voids stared at her as if a bottle of ink had been spilled into his eyes. But as he adjusted to the light, the ink melted away, turning into mere slits and revealing the most stunning molten silver hue that glowed in the golden sunset.

This was who Graeson was. This was the monster living inside him.

And as impossible and as foolish as it was, Kallie was not afraid. Not in the slightest.

A menacing laugh filled the air, and Graeson ripped his focus from Kallie, his head snapping toward Domitius.

The king stood with a victorious grin. "Your mother was right. With you, I will be unstoppable." Domitius tipped his head back, joy spilling from his mouth.

Graeson, however, didn't seem to find anything amusing about the situation. His nostrils flared. When he exhaled, smoke poured from his nose. A tail nearly as long as his body swept out behind him, slicing the air and slamming against the ground. Those closest to him collapsed, the quake forcing them to the ground.

Domitius pushed himself onto his elbows. His brown eyes were wild, greed and hunger swirling within them. "Heel," he shouted.

A low growl rumbled deep in Graeson's throat as he lowered his head. But it wasn't in submission. Not at all. It was in preparation. A predator about to strike. His pupils darkened as he glared at the king. His top lip curled, revealing razor-sharp teeth.

Domitius cleared his throat. "I command you to—"

Graeson's front paw struck the earth, and Domitius' back hit the ground as the land trembled.

This time, Kallie fell with him. Her palms smacked into the dirt, and a spiral of pain soared through her wrists. Her fingers flexed on the grass.

She gasped, her breath hitching. It was as if a bucket of ice water had been poured over her, her limbs finally waking up. In the corner of her eye, she saw Moris pushing himself up.

Inches away, silver sparkled in the sunlight, and the ancient words stared back at her.

You are the holder of your fate.

Quickly, she peered at Domitius through her hair. He was shouting at Graeson, trying and failing to command the dragon. Kallie grinned and sprang for her dagger. She twisted around, striking Moris in the back of his head. His body slumped down, his leather wings sprawling across the ground.

With blood and rage pumping through her, she snapped her head up, readying to charge toward Domitius. But before she could, she was thrown back. Her back crashed against the ground, knocking the breath out of her. She blinked through the searing pain and the gusts of wind smacking her in the face. One of the other guards hovered over her. He dug his hands into her shoulders and forced her body into the ground, his wings beating rapidly behind him. In her periphery, she spotted Ellie struggling against the other guard.

Kallie snarled, her gift humming. "Let go of me."

The guard flew back in an instant.

"Ah, ah. Not so fast," Kallie hissed. None of them would leave this clearing alive. Not after everything they've been through. Snarling, she swung, her dagger lacerating his wings. Gray feathers fell.

With a screech, the guard collapsed, his tattered wing failing him. "You bitch," the man sputtered.

"Oh, so you do speak," Kallie mused, her fingers flexing over the hilt.

The guard charged, his wounded wing hanging low. Kallie dove beneath his legs. Swiftly rolling onto her back, she kicked as hard as she could, her boots slamming into him. The guard stumbled, barely catching himself before he landed face-first. Kallie didn't wait for him to steady himself. She jumped onto his back. She brought her elbow back and struck, her dagger digging into the spot where the wing sprouted. The guard arched back and howled in pain. Before he crushed her, Kallie jumped.

"Stay down," Kallie ordered.

The guard slumped on the ground instantly with a growl.

When she spun and sprinted toward the others, Graeson was no longer on the ground. In his place, shadows danced across the field. When Kallie looked up, there he was, his scales aflame in the golden light of the setting sun.

Domitius furiously barked orders, refusing to accept his failure to control the dragon, but Graeson continued to hover, as if waiting to strike. As if waiting for *her* to strike.

Kallie ran harder, her arms pumping at her sides.

"You've lost, Kage!"

At Kallie's voice, Domitius spun, a section of blond hair falling in front of his face. Yet a victorious sneer still sat on his lips. "The fun has only begun, Kalisandre." He threw up his arms.

All around the clearing, the leaves in the trees rustled, yet there was no breeze to blame. Not a second later, arrows shot across the sky, whizzing through the air. But not a single one was directed at her. They all soared into the sky.

Realizing their true target, Kallie screamed, waving her hands frantically.

Graeson's gaze snapped to her, his lip curling back further.

"Go!" she shouted.

But there was nowhere for him to go. The arrows came from every angle, at various heights, as if the archers were determined to strike the dragon down.

Graeson lurched back, his dragon-form arching, a high-pitched yelp filling the air.

"I never lose, Kalisandre," Domitius said. He brushed a hand through his hair, pushing the fallen strand back into place.

Kallie charged, teeth bared and dagger in hand.

Domitius spewed out a mangled laugh. Then when she was five feet away, he shouted, hand up, "Stop!"

Kallie's body jerked to a halt. She wobbled like a blade thrown into a tree trunk.

"Kill the girl already," he demanded, glancing at the last guard standing.

From the corner of Kallie's eyes, she saw the last guard flip Ellie over in one fell swoop. Her back hit the ground, forcing out a soft *humph* from her lips.

"No!" Kallie shouted in protest. "Re—"

"Silence!" Domitius shouted, his command slamming her mouth shut with a loud snap.

The guard's boot slammed down onto Ellie's chest. But the warrior wasn't giving up, not yet. With her weapons out of reach, Ellie clawed at the guard, using her nails to scratch at any uncovered skin. Red smeared across his flesh as she ripped into his leg without mercy or restraint.

Another heartbreaking screech poured over them, and Kallie's attention flicked to Graeson. He dove forward, a stream of fire spewing from his jaws as he roared. A tree went up in flames the moment Graeson's fire licked the decaying leaves. And one by one, the surrounding trees caught aflame.

Kallie gasped in horror as she watched, stunned.

Then another sparkle in the forest caught her eye. The setting sun caught on the metal tips of a dozen arrows from the waiting soldiers, like stars in the sky.

Domitius' laugh echoed in Kallie's ears.

Her gift stirred within her, but she couldn't speak. Domitius' stolen power clung to her skin like a layer of sweat. Still, the energy filled her.

Ellie's razor-sharp nails ripped through the fabric of the guard's trousers, and the guard laughed in amusement.

He had stolen so much from her already: her home, her family, her life, even her ability. But she would not let him steal her friends, too.

Move, she demanded. The invisible golden strands danced, rising higher as the guard lifted his sword, readying to strike. Sweat dripped down her face as the temperature of the fire rose.

Move!

Kallie stumbled forward just as a violent roar erupted, causing her to hesitate as the guard tumbled across the field with a shadowed form. Domitius shouted something, but Kallie didn't hear him. His protests were lost to the pounding in her ears as Nyrri rolled over and over, the guard struggling to push her off him.

Black webbed wings flared out. Blood spurted, spewing across the field. Nyrri shook and tossed the guard's head across the field as she discarded his limp form. The drakonis twisted around, ruby-red eyes aflame.

Kallie had never been so happy to see the drakonis.

She turned on her heel, ready to strike. But Domitius was no longer there. She spun around, searching, panicking. She jerked to a stop when she found the other guard missing. A shadow raced across the field, and her attention shot to the sky.

"No!" she yelled, spotting the guard flying away and Domitius' legs dangling over the guard's arms.

She started to run after them and shout a command, but the moment her lips parted, a flash of pain pierced her hamstring. Her command was replaced with a yelp. She dropped, her leg giving out.

Someone's hands were on her a second later, and she tried to bat them away.

"Stop moving! You're only making it worse."

"Ellie?" Kallie croaked, the pain blurring her vision.

"Who else, you idiot?" the warrior snapped. "I'm going to pull the arrow out, and it's going to fucking hurt. But don't move, got it?"

"Wait—"

Something was lodged into her mouth.

"Bite," Ellie demanded, giving Kallie only a second to do so before pulling out the arrow.

Kallie screamed around the makeshift gag, and hot tears rolled down her cheeks. Fabric ripped. As Ellie tied the fabric around her thigh, Kallie squeezed her eyes shut, the pain blinding.

"Come on," Ellie said, pulling the gag from Kallie's mouth with a disgusted grimace as a shadow fell over them. "We need to get out of here."

Ellie threw the wad of fabric away, and Kallie recognized it to be a part of the guard's trousers.

She wanted to throw up, but she shook her head, pushing through the pain. "We can't. W-we have to go after him."

"This entire area is going to be on fire in a matter of minutes. We don't have the time!"

Kallie trembled as she stared out at the destruction. The fire had spread further than Kallie had thought possible in the short time that had passed. Bare branches burned. Smoke and ash filled the sky, twirling in the wind. In the distance, Kallie could hear the shouts of the soldiers who had escaped the fire and the louder screams of those who weren't as lucky.

"But—" Her words were stolen from her as she and Ellie were swiped from the ground, Graeson's claws wrapping around her. A gust of wind swept through her hair as Graeson scaled the sky, his large wings thrashing in the air. To her right, Ellie dangled from his other paw. Her face was ghastly white as she screamed in terror. Kallie looked away just as Ellie's cheeks puffed up, her skin taking on a sickly hue.

A few seconds later, Graeson dove, heading toward the clearing. When Kallie thought they were going to hit the ground, he evened out, the force of his speed stirring up debris. Kallie sucked in a breath and coughed, inhaling dirt.

Graeson lowered his front legs. Kallie braced for a rough landing, but it never came. One after the other, he snatched up Moris and Lysanthia. Then he twisted around, flying toward the clouds once more.

Nyrri trailed behind them, her wings beating rapidly as she tried to keep up. Kallie's attention quickly slipped past the drakonis, fixing onto Domitius, who was now a mere speck, heading for the woods.

They couldn't let him escape. Frantically, Kallie slapped the nearest claw and shouted at Graeson to release her. She needed to put a stop to this. She had to before—

Graeson dove, his body zipping through the air as he tipped his head toward the ground.

A piercing scream tore at her lungs as she held onto him. Her thigh throbbed, but she ignored the pain and held on as tightly as she could. An intense heat smacked Kallie in the face, forcing her still. When she looked down, fire covered the terrain, sweeping across the grass and leaving a burnt trail in its wake.

Through the smoke and scorched earth, she searched and searched, looking for Domitius' remains.

Was he dead? Had Graeson killed him?

Graeson swept back up. As he flipped around, his tail lashing around angrily, Kallie saw the guard fleeing toward the forest.

Spotting them at the same time, Graeson turned. But before he could dive again, a screech poured from his mouth, then another. His body twisted as if he had been punched in the gut.

Quickly, Kallie scanned the parts of Graeson's body she could see. Black scales covered his form, intricately layered. Then she found them: a series of arrows sticking out from his sides, beneath his belly, across his tail. One had struck bare flesh. How many arrows had he taken? How many more *could* he take?

Arrow after arrow came flying at them. Kallie ducked, barely dodging an arrow that whizzed by her hair, slicing a piece near her ear in half. The next time, however, Kallie wasn't as lucky. An arrow drove into her arm, right below her shoulder, and she bellowed. Blood stained her blouse and dripped down her limb.

Graeson's gaze snapped to her. Anger burned in his glowing eyes.

She needed to get the arrow out, but she couldn't. Her other arm was locked against her, between her body and Graeson's paw.

She could see the hesitation in his eyes.

She shook her head, pleading.

With a huff, Graeson scanned the clearing, and Kallie followed his gaze, blinking past the tears springing to her eyes from the sharp pain of the arrow.

"There they are!" she shouted. "Do it!"

Graeson roared, and fire rained down upon the guard. His wings, doused in flames, blazed like an inferno as they beat once, twice, before failing entirely. The guard tumbled, his body aflame. He plummeted into the woods, like a shooting star darting across the sky.

Unable to turn away, Kallie's stomach dropped.

The burning forest swallowed the guard and Domitius.

Graeson hovered over the trees as the heat rose and drenched Kallie in sweat. The air became thick with smoke. The flames ate away at the trees. Graeson twisted around, flying away from the destruction.

There would be no survivors today. No one could survive the ferocity with which the inferno swept through the forest.

As the wind ripped at her hair, Kallie wept. She might have stopped a war, but at what cost?

PART TWO

BREAKING THE CHAINS

CHAPTER 35

MYRA

"THIS WAS NOT THE PLAN," SOMEONE NEARBY HISSED AS MYRA SLOWLY regained consciousness.

Her head spun as if someone had tossed her into a barrel and rolled it down a hill. She blinked, trying to rid her vision of the darkness that enveloped her, but it did her no good. When she opened her eyes again, shadows still consumed her vision. Her heart rate kicked up, her memory of leaving the inn returning. A large lump was forming on the back of her head where her attacker had hit her.

She attempted to steady her breathing, to overcome the rising panic.

Slow, quiet breath in.

She focused on her surroundings, the things she could feel.

Shadows did not blanket her; rather, someone had tied a soft cotton fabric around her head. As she exhaled, the heat of her breath came back into her mouth. Her tongue brushed against a rod.

She kept going, assessing the situation, taking in whatever details she could.

Her wrists burned, and something rough and itchy dug into her skin. She wiggled her fingers, and the pads scraped against a rough material she could only assume was the bark of a tree. Had they tied her to a *tree*?

She was blindfolded, gagged, and restrained.

Myra tried to recall what the man had said.

This was not the plan.

What wasn't? What *was* the plan if not to knock her out and tie her up? Who even were they? How *many* were there? Their voices were completely foreign to her, but so far, she had only identified two unique ones.

Why had they even taken her? Her mind reeled with the possibilities.

Tears pricked her eyes. Drool dripped from her mouth, dribbling around the gag and down her chin.

Through the darkness, vibrant red tendrils of anger swatted around her. But there was something else there, something beneath the violent slashes of hate. It coated her tongue and was as sour as an unripe lemon.

"Look," the second voice said, "she was the first one who came out and the easiest to grab. There was no time to question things. They'll come for her. I promise."

Beneath the blindfold, Myra's eyes widened. Fear wrapped around her neck, strangling her. Panic vibrated through her body, but she didn't dare move. Instead, she thought of Kallie. When the Pontians had ransacked their carriage on the way to Frenzia the first time, Kallie had not panicked. She had remained calm. She had discovered what their captors' intentions were before she had made her move.

Myra let the scent of late autumn calm her nerves—the warmth of the leaves, the notes of pine hanging in the air. She could do this. She could be like Kallie. She could—

"And if they don't?" the other demanded before Myra could finish building up her courage.

"They will," the first said. Although the man spoke with confidence, Myra caught a whiff of doubt, and her stomach twisted with nausea.

Perspiration coated her palms despite the cold air that brushed her skin.

Would Laurince and Rian come after her? While she considered them to be her friends, what if they believed she had abandoned them? What if they didn't know she had been taken until it was too late? How would they even know how to find her? Myra didn't know how long she had been knocked out or how far they had traveled. Once again, she was totally and completely useless.

"The woman promised they would," the man who had grabbed her added after a moment.

"Yeah, like you can trust a woman who sells drinks and beds for a living."

Myra went rigid. Did they mean the innkeeper? If so, why would she tell the men that Laurince and Rian would come find Myra if they took her? Why did they want—

They knew.

It was the only plausible answer. They knew Rian was the king. They were after *him*. And they were using her to get to him. She wanted to laugh, to cry. Her life was not worth the life of a king.

"If they don't, we'll just find out where they are going from her."

Even though she couldn't see the men, she could sense their eyes turning to her. Their attention was sticky and latched onto every pore.

"And if she doesn't tell us?"

"We'll get it out of her."

The man's promise sent a line of goosebumps crawling down Myra's spine.

Who was she kidding? She wasn't Kallie. She could barely even wield a sword despite Laurince's efforts.

"I don't hurt women," the other man whispered, vitriol staining his words.

"For this amount of money?" He huffed a laugh. "You'll do whatever needs to be done."

Leaves crunched. Footsteps approached. A boot lodged into her side, the man's toes smashing into her ribcage. Agony surged through her, and Myra released a sharp cry. One man grabbed her by the back of her tender head. White splotches filled her vision as she tried to hold back a sob as his palm pressed against the fresh wound.

"For your sake, girl," he hissed, his hot breath searing her skin, "you better hope your friends come."

The tears that had been gathering on her lash-line fell, soaking the blindfold. The damp fabric stuck to the tops of her pale cheeks.

Myra stayed silent, though, not daring to speak a word. She refused to betray Laurince and Rian. No matter what the men did to her, she would not break. Not this time. Not again.

Never again.

So as her ribcage throbbed and her wrists burned, Myra was stuck between hoping Laurince and Rian would save her and praying they wouldn't come at all.

She really regretted not taking that knife that morning.

CHAPTER 36

MYRA

FEAR OVERWHELMED MYRA'S TREMBLING FRAME. THE PAIN AT THE back of her head had only marginally subsided in the time that had passed. Her wrists burned from the rope digging into her flesh.

As the leaves crunched only a few paces away, the hairs on the back of her neck stood up. Panic surged through her as her captor's emotions wafted off him. Impatience, hunger, greed. But it was the feeling beneath those that scared her the most. Something more wicked and sinister.

She pressed her head back against the tree, trying to get as far away as she could. Still, the man came closer. His hot breath scorched her neck, sending a terrifying chill spiraling down her back.

"Hey," the second man called out, "what are you—"

"Hush," the man closest to her spat. "Perhaps our little friend here needs some convincing."

Myra heard something slide against leather. Then a sharp tip pressed against her knee, the pressure not strong enough to pierce but enough to be present.

"I wonder if we've made a mistake. Maybe you're not as precious to King Rian as we first thought," her captor whispered. His emotions whipped around her, red-hot and searing. A wickedness slithered beneath that turned her stomach.

"No response? Hmm. Perhaps you need some convincing." He dragged the blade higher up her thigh, increasing the pressure with each passing inch.

The blade ripped through her trousers, the fabric tearing, the sound like a crack of thunder. The tip broke skin, the pain bright. She choked back a sob. She would not cry. She would not—

Snap.

The man froze.

"What was that?" the other man asked with a slight tremble.

Myra stopped breathing.

She wanted to be wrong. Laurince and Rian weren't supposed to come. Not for her, never for her. She didn't want to endanger either of them, yet somehow, even before he revealed himself, she knew *he* was there. Every nerve-ending sparked, her heart thundered, and relief flooded her chest at the sound of his voice.

"Release her," Laurince demanded, his tone even sharper and deadlier than the blade that had just touched her skin.

The man jerked away. "Grab her," he demanded.

Myra was jostled as cold metal kissed her throat. A high-pitched, muffled yelp slipped from her lips as he held the blade steady. Tears stained the blindfold.

"Did you not hear me?" Laurince asked. "I said *release her.*"

"We'll gladly give her over if you give us King Rian," the man, who was now a few feet away, said.

Myra jerked in the other man's grasp, a muffled shout slipping around the gag as she tried to tell Laurince to turn around, that she wasn't worth it.

"Shut it," her captor hissed in her ear, the metal cold on her skin.

"Do you see a king with me?" Laurince asked.

Thank the gods, Myra thought.

But the relief was fleeting. Without Rian, Laurince was outnumbered. Even if Myra wasn't tied up, she would have been useless in a fight.

"Do not play dumb with us. We know you're traveling with him. That little innkeeper confirmed it." He clicked his tongue. "There's a pretty penny for that little red head of his—dead or alive. Although we'll get more if we bring him back alive."

"Just give me the girl," Laurince commanded, "and maybe I'll let you leave here alive."

"I don't think you're in a position to make threats," the man said, his tone sharpening. "Plus, I don't think I've had my fill of her yet. Not even a taste, really. We were just getting started, weren't we?"

The tip of the blade pierced Myra's skin, and Myra gasped, choking on the gag as tears fell.

"I said, *get your hands off her.*"

A whistle of air whipped past her ear. Myra froze as a wet scream sounded to her right, followed by a gurgle. Something splattered on her neck and face, and she squealed in horror as something dropped into her lap. The knife, she thought—she *hoped.* The tang of iron coated the air, and warm liquid soaked the sleeve of her shirt.

"Oh, you're going to regret that," the man spat.

Metal crashed against metal, each man grunting. Insults passed between Laurince and the assailant as they battled. But Myra was still blindfolded. She couldn't see anything. She couldn't tell who was winning or losing. Frantically, she scooted back, ignoring the weight pressing against her side. She shifted, sliding her head against the bark. The blindfold didn't budge. All her frazzled movements did was irritate the lump on her skull and snag her hair.

Someone hissed in pain. Her stomach lurched. She could have

sworn it was Laurince, the sound all too similar to when he fought Mynhos in Ardentol.

Her movements became more frantic.

Myra ignored the pain lacing the back of her head, the heat emanating from the rope, and the warmth seeping into her clothes. She tried to wiggle free of the restraints, twisting and yanking. She attempted to saw through the restraints using the bark of the tree. Every time she moved, though, her right shoulder screamed in protest. Still, she forced herself to push through.

Then she heard it: a gut-wrenching, wet sound of a sword sliding through someone's chest, the crack of ribs, and the squelch of blood spilling onto the ground.

Time stood still.

She didn't know if she was breathing or if she even could. She could have sworn her heart stopped as she thought of Laurince lying dead on the ground, of his sweet smile forever fading into the distance, never to be seen again.

She was going to be sick.

She was going to—

Her blindfold was yanked from her eyes, and the sun blinded her, blurring her vision. She peered through water-stained eyes. The figure before her was too foggy and bright to see clearly. Then he spoke.

"I got you, Haze."

The sob ripped through her.

Laurince wiped away a stream of tears with his thumbs, the pads rough yet gentle against her skin. The gesture was useless, though, as more tears came. Her anxiety and fear were an unstoppable flood.

Hushed words spilled from Laurince's mouth, but Myra barely heard them. She absentmindedly felt him reach around her. She faintly heard his blade slice through the rope, setting her free.

Unable to control her body, Myra crashed against his chest. She melted into a puddle against him, the pain of her shoulder, the wound on her inner thigh, and the burn around her wrists barely even a second thought. Tears rocked her entire form, but she didn't care how much of a mess she must have looked, not as Laurince wrapped his arms around her, pulling her closer to his chest.

"You're safe with me. I promise," he whispered. Weaving his fingers through her damp hair, he cradled her head in his palm.

Myra hissed on contact, the bump on her head still sore.

"Shit, Haze. I'm sorry," Laurince muttered, instantly removing his hand. "If they weren't dead already, I'd kill them again."

Myra pulled back slightly. At the bottom of her vision, the grass was stained red, her trousers splattered with blood.

"No, don't look over there." Laurince said, guiding her chin back toward him. "Look at me." His eyes danced across her features as he caressed the side of her face. His thumb slid across her cheek tenderly. A million unspoken words seemed to cross his face. His lips parted, but then snapped shut.

He had killed them.

He had ended their lives to save *hers.*

She didn't know how to feel about that. Her sense of morality, which, granted, was tainted, told her she shouldn't have been relieved. Yet when she considered the other outcome...

Shaking, Myra asked, voice hoarse, "Where's Rian?"

Laurince stiffened. His hold on her loosened, and his thumb halted its calming movement. "He's safe, too. Don't worry," he said, dropping his hand. The space where his hand had been instantly grew cold. He leaned back, putting distance between them.

Myra silently cursed, realizing her mistake. Still, she didn't have the energy to correct herself.

"He wanted to come, but I told him not to." Laurince stood, brushing the dirt from his knees.

As he did, Myra nodded but stopped when her vision blurred.

"Good," she said, chewing her bottom lip. "That's good. They..." Myra's gaze instinctively slid toward the man's body, but Laurince moved, shielding her from him. It was a small gesture, but one she was grateful for. She had seen death before, but it always shook her. "They were after him."

He held out a hand, and Myra took it without hesitation. Once upright, she wobbled on her feet.

Laurince caught her, his hands landing on her waist and steadying her. "Are you all right?" His gaze caught on her neck, where the man had nicked her with his weapon. His eyes trailed down her torso toward her thigh.

Myra slammed her legs together and swallowed the resulting curse. "I'm fine. I'm..." Her words trailed off.

She wasn't fine; she was terrified.

Wiping her hand across her neck, she scratched the droplet of dried blood. She looked back up at Laurince. She was alive. She was safe.

Because of him.

"Thank you for coming," she said quietly, dropping her gaze again.

He tipped her chin up with his thumb. "Did you think I wouldn't?"

"I—I didn't know. I wasn't sure," she admitted.

"Haze," he said, drawing out the name.

She stumbled, her knees buckling.

"Whoa," he said, catching her by the waist.

Her vision blurred, and her body grew suddenly cold, chills covering her flesh. "I think...I think I'm concussed..."

At least she assumed that was why her knees wobbled and why it was still hard for her to breathe. Although Laurince's presence, his closeness, and the protective shield he offered her without question, might have played a part, too.

Laurince wrapped his arm around her back, tucking her against him. "Lean on me then, yeah?"

CHAPTER 37
KALLIE

Kallie watched as the magnificent dragon flew over the trees, its tail the last part she saw before Graeson melted into the night sky.

Although they were upwind and the smoke wasn't as strong as it had been, it still soaked their clothes and their hair.

A wet snout nudged her hand. When Kallie went to pet Nyrri, she moved just right that the pain from the arrow returned, her adrenaline long-since drained.

"We need to get the arrow out and clean the wound before it's infected," Ellie said, grabbing Kallie's arm.

"We need to go after him," Kallie countered through clenched teeth. Her entire arm was throbbing now.

"Please tell me how you are going to chase after a fucking dragon with a wounded arm and leg?" Ellie demanded, hands on her hips.

"Nyrri can—" Kallie choked on her scream as Ellie ripped the arrow from her arm.

"Shit," Kallie spat, her nails biting into her palms. "A warning would have been nice."

"Next time, don't say stupid shit." Ellie splashed alcohol from a canteen onto Kallie's arm, and Kallie hissed. When she poured more on her hamstring, Kallie hobbled away.

"You're doing that on purpose," Kallie hissed.

Ellie glared. "I'm making sure your wounds don't get fucking infected. You can barely stand as it is." Ellie shoved Kallie's bad leg, and Kallie teetered without Nyrri's support.

Nyrri whined, and Kallie patted her side. "It's only a flesh wound. It'll heal."

Although when Kallie hiked up her bloody trousers, blood trailed down her leg.

"You'll be hobbling around for at least a few days. You're already a terrible rider. Sending you off searching for him will only put you in more danger. I enjoyed irritating Gray before, but now that he's a dragon?" Ellie swiped her hand across her forehead, smearing the ash with sweat. "We don't know how many men Domitius brought with him. He might be dead, but his men are not. At least not all of them. The best thing you can do right now is rest while you can. Gray will come back."

Kallie pursed her lips but nodded. It would be reckless to go after Graeson. While Nyrri had gotten better at flying, Kallie had yet to ride her. It would not be smart to do so now, especially in the sorry state she was in.

She hated when Ellie was right.

The warrior tightened the wrapping around Kallie's arm. Kallie bit back another groan.

"Thanks," she mumbled.

She looked at the sky once more. Graeson shouldn't be alone right now. He had been forced to kill his mother. He shouldn't have to bury her alone.

And what of the stolen guard—Moris? As far as Kallie knew, Moris was still alive. Was Graeson planning on killing him? What would happen when Graeson transformed back into his human form? *Would* he transform back?

"Did you know?" Ellie asked quietly as she finished wrapping the gauze around Kallie's thigh. She tied it in a tight knot.

"Know that Graeson was a dragon?"

Ellie nodded.

"No, I didn't," Kallie admitted. She still hadn't fully processed that Graeson was one.

She sat on the ground and rested her head against Nyrri's side. Kallie ran her finger over the frayed edges of the bandage on her thigh. "Did you?"

"No. The gods are...mysterious. The stories about them—the legends and myths that have been passed down from generation to generation—have shifted and changed with time. My people have spent centuries studying them, trying to decipher where the gods came from and when they left. Some gods have been known to walk on this plane, taking control of humans."

"Rian once mentioned that he believed the gods came by way of dragon," Kallie said, recalling the days spent with Rian in the Frenzian library. "That the dragons were the ones that burned the holes in the sky and made it possible for them to come to the mortal world."

Ellie nodded. "That is one of the stories, yes. There's even a children's story that claims the gods could shape-shift into different common animals."

A question sat on the tip of Kallie's tongue. It felt silly, stupid. She knew so little about the gods when she once thought she knew everything. But she needed to know if her guess was right. "Is it possible that the gods were, in fact, the dragons, then?"

"There have been stories of mystical beasts that appeared out of nowhere, such as dragons or the kraken. But the dragons have been missing for a long time. If the dragons are gods, perhaps that is why they disappeared?"

"Graeson's only part god, though. Lysanthia was mortal."

"Maybe the rage from his mother's death was the trigger?"

An ache pounded in Kallie's chest, a restlessness building within her bones. "Graeson always talked about a darkness lurking within him, but I don't think even he knew he could transform into a dragon. But to deal with that reality and his mother's death?" She shook her head, unable to comprehend what Graeson could be going through right now. "I wish—"

"Don't do that," Ellie said, immediately cutting Kallie off.

"Do what?"

"Do that thing you do," she said, flicking her hand in the air.

"What *thing*?"

"Take on the responsibility when it doesn't belong to you. You couldn't have done anything to save her, Kallie. Death happens. While we often wish to fight against it, we cannot stop it when the Fates come knocking."

Kallie's eyes widened at Ellie's words. They were similar to something Lysanthia had said before she had died.

Realization struck her in the chest, and Kallie gasped. "She *knew*."

"Who knew?" Ellie asked, confused.

"Lysanthia. Before she..." Kallie choked on her words and cleared her throat. "She said she knew this was coming years ago. I hadn't given it much thought since I assumed she was referring to the trade. But she knew her death was coming. That's why she didn't fight him. She knew." Kallie pressed her palms to her temples, ignoring the pain in her arm. "She said a sacrifice was needed. I thought she had meant me, that *I* would be the sacrifice. What if... what if *she* was the sacrifice? That her death was needed in order for Graeson to take on his true form?"

"It's…it's possible," Ellie said, more to herself than Kallie, her pitch-black gaze growing distant as she stared at the sky.

Kallie followed her gaze. They had heard no screams or roars. But somewhere, Graeson was flying through the smoke that blanketed Borgania. She wondered if he was all right. Was he safe? Was he hurt?

"Do you think…will he…" Kallie swallowed the question, unwilling to voice it.

"Will he return to normal?"

Kallie shook her head. She didn't care which form he took. To her, he was still Graeson. When he looked at her before he left, she could see it, see *him.* Graeson shifting back was not her concern. Not at that moment, at least.

"Will he come back?"

Ellie cocked a brow. "Do you even have to ask?"

While it might have seemed obvious to Ellie, Kallie wasn't so confident. Graeson had already viewed himself as a monster. What did he think now that he had taken the form of a dragon?

Ellie took off the thin armor and peeled up her shirt. Kallie grimaced at the sight of the dark bruises marking her skin. When Ellie poked one, her face twisted with agony. Tugging her shirt down, she lay on the ground, her movements stiff. "He was smart enough to take us far away from the fire and from possible threats. Although our horses are likely running back to Tetria as we speak, he'll come back. He traveled across Vaneria twice for you, remember? Gray doesn't give up that easily."

Behind Kallie, Nyrri released a soft exhale and shifted closer. Kallie smiled softly at the drakonis, but it didn't reach her eyes. She scooted further down, trying to get comfortable. Tilting her head up, she watched the sky, hoping to see Graeson's silhouette. Yet all that remained were twinkling stars, the smoke from the distant flames slipping slowly across them as it rose higher and higher.

He would come back, and if he didn't, she would just have to go after him instead.

CHAPTER 38
GRAESON

Graeson shivered as a breeze swept over him. He was cold. Freezing, actually. He attempted to move, to grab hold of a blanket or anything for some semblance of warmth, but every inch of his body cried out in protest. His bones hurt more than when Fynn had dared him to jump off a cliff into the Red Sea. Even the tips of fingers threatened to disintegrate the moment he dug his hands into the hard earth.

He took a deep breath, inhaling the frigid air and…smoke?

His eyes flung open. The early moments of dawn colored the tips of the trees. Or was the fire still hanging on?

His head spun. He wiggled his fingers, and blades of sharp grass poked his hand. When he lifted his hand, he didn't see a paw with sharp claws but *his* hand.

He was himself, in his own body. Not some monster.

Was it another nightmare, then?

Slowly and carefully, he pushed himself up, his body heavy and arms shaking from the pain. He looked down at his chest, his *bare* chest. Where the fuck were his clothes?

He barely had time to register his nakedness, though, when he noticed the ground around him. The surrounding field was either burned to ash or dried up. Had *he* done that?

Varying images crashed into him, one after another, wave after wave. It was like waking from a nightmare, but everything Graeson saw, everything he remembered, was real.

The flames spreading across the trees.

The wings tearing through the flesh between his shoulder blades.

The arrows flying at him—at Kalisandre and Ellie as he held them in his paws.

The thunderous roar that spilled from his mouth, and the blazing heat that followed.

The piercing, gut-wrenching screams of terror that sounded when Graeson had taken to the skies.

But most importantly, his mother's life blinking out in front of him, her very soul slipping between his hands.

Graeson spun, panic making his movements frantic as he searched the area. He had carried her here, hadn't he?

Graeson spotted Moris knocked out on the ground and his mother beside him. Anger spurred inside him at the sight of the traitor, but Graeson held it back. When he exhaled, he could have sworn he saw smoke rise from his mouth. His mother needed him. His mother—

Was dead.

He had killed her.

He knelt beside her and tried not to look at the stain covering her top. With a trembling hand, he swiped away the limp hair that had fallen in front of her face. Her wan skin was cold to the touch.

They were supposed to save her. They were supposed to free her.

Graeson pressed the heel of his palm against his eye and screamed. He let his anger, frustration, and grief pour out of him, unrelenting.

"You were a seer. You were supposed to know! You were supposed to—" Graeson choked on his words as his mother's final words came tumbling back to him.

"My son, I never stopped loving you. Know that there was nothing you could have done differently. I sealed my fate a long time ago. This was the only way."

She did know. She had known all along. *That* was why she didn't fight him or cry out. That is why she helped him push the blade when he struggled to fight off Domitius' commands. She had known she was going to die.

"And to think, all it took was a little push," Barinthian's voice slipped through the trees like a python and wrapped around Graeson's neck.

"Now is not the time," Graeson bit out. He swiped at the tears, but it was useless.

"Oh, but it is the perfect time," Barinthian said. "I told you this would happen."

"You did not tell me I would turn into some savage creature! You did not tell me I would kill her!" Heat rose in the back of Graeson's throat, the ice melting away.

A rumbling sounded in the back of Graeson's throat.

Graeson scanned the trees, searching for his cowardly father hidden among them.

Barinthian's voice washed over him. "You finally coming to terms with your true self is not the reason for her death."

Graeson scoffed. He had not come to terms with it by any means. He didn't even understand *how* he had shifted. One minute he was holding his mother's limp body, seeing her life slip from her eyes, and the next an icy-hot rage ripped through him, tearing at his muscles and breaking his bones.

He wasn't sure he knew how to do it again. Would someone he cared about have to die every time?

He reached for the god that lurked within. But when he reached the cage, he found it empty. The cell was blown apart. There was a weight that existed that hadn't been there before, a layer beneath his skin.

"Is this what you wanted, then?" Graeson asked. "For me to...to transform into a fucking dragon? And for what? What was the point?"

"The *point*, son, is that the humans have grown unruly. They believe they can take and give freely, that they can rise above their frivolous titles and become gods. But that is not how this world works. They have overstepped. They have created creatures that shouldn't exist. They have given abilities to those who are undeserving."

In Graeson's periphery, he spotted Moris still out cold, his wings spread out beneath him. How many more people like him were there? How many more Pontians had Domitius gotten his hands on before he died?

His hands curled into fists at his sides. "And my mother had to die because of that? Is this some sick fucking joke?"

"Am I laughing?" Barinthian asked.

For once, Graeson did not hear a single laugh slip from the god's mouth. The chilling sound had been absent during their entire conversation, a fact Graeson should have noticed immediately.

"Then why?" Graeson demanded. "You could have stopped this!"

"No, I could't have. The Fates made it so."

"The *Fates?*" Graeson was so fucking sick of hearing about the Fates. "You are a fucking god!"

"And even gods are bound by the tapestry woven by the Fates," Barinthian said, his voice hollow, almost pained. "Lysanthia—"

"Do not speak her name," Graeson said, cutting him off. Barinthian didn't deserve to. He was a coward and a fraud. He was a god, yet he did nothing to stop Graeson's mother from dying. There was no warning. No guidance. Even now, he remained hidden, not even giving Graeson the courtesy of showing himself.

"Your mother knew what the Fates had in store for her. She accepted it long ago. If you crumble now, if you refuse to accept the truth, her death will only be in vain. She never wanted you to fear yourself."

Graeson's knuckles turned white as he stared at his mother's lifeless body. "You do not know what she wanted."

"And you do not know everything," his father retorted.

A breeze swept through the woods and ruffled his clothes. Iron and smoke tinged the air. Fallen leaves skirted across the forest floor, rustling. When his mother's hair swept across her face, Graeson brushed it away.

"You are just like her," Barinthian said, his voice quieter than before. "Full of hope."

"Maybe before," Graeson said, struggling to hold on to the last dredge of hope that threatened to slip through his fingers.

"Before and now."

Graeson huffed. "What use is being a god, in being a dragon, if I can't even save those I care about?"

A small child's voice rang in his ears.

You won't save her.

The little girl had been right. Graeson had thought she was referring to Kalisandre, but it was his mother she was warning him about. If only he had known…

"This was how the tapestry was woven," Barinthian said, pity dripping from his tongue. "Once the stitches are made, there is no unraveling it. Now, you must do what needs to be done. You must become the reckoning the kingdoms need. You will remind the mortals who dare challenge the Fates, who fight against the natural order of the world."

"The war is over. Domitius is dead."

"No," Barinthian said. "The war has only begun. Kage has ignited the flame, and fire is spreading."

Graeson's nose twitched. He did not care about any of it. Why did any of it matter if their stories were already written? If there was no way to fight the inevitable?

"If the Fates have already dictated the outcome, what is the point?"

Barinthian sighed. "We do not have much time," he warned.

To Graeson's right, Moris stirred, his leg twitching.

"Your mother saw various versions of the future, and every time the outcome was different. The fate of the war remains to be seen."

"I need to bury her," Graeson said, grabbing her limp hand.

Leaves rustled.

"I will take her."

"You will not touch her! She deserves a proper send-off. She deserves—"

"I know what she deserves," Barinthian growled, his voice rattling the branches and sending the barely clinging leaves fluttering down.

"Did you love her?" Graeson asked, the question slipping free before he could pull it back.

He didn't know why he had asked. Of course, Barinthian didn't love Lysanthia. If he had, he wouldn't have abandoned them. He wouldn't have left Lysanthia at Domitius' mercy.

If he did, Barinthian would have said so, but he didn't. Instead, he whispered, "I will take her."

Graeson wanted to fight him. He wanted to refuse. But as bright silver eyes blinked between the trees and a large black wolf came forward, its fur melting into the shadows, Graeson was rendered speechless, his body immobile. The wolf was twice the size of a normal one, its paws nearly as large as Graeson's head and its body half the size of Nyrri. He should have been terrified, and he supposed a part of him was. But the wolf prowled closer, its movements slow and calculated.

"I-I don't understand," Graeson stammered.

The wolf arched a brow and huffed.

"Gods can take many forms. As the son of a god and a mortal, you can only take one," Barinthian said. But when he spoke, the wolf's mouth did not move, and Graeson realized he was simply hearing Barinthian's voice within his mind. Yet he knew without a doubt that the wolf before him was not an ordinary creature. This was his father. Or at least one of his forms.

The wolf nudged Lysanthia's body with his snout, shifting her.

"That doesn't...you can't..."

"I will not drop her," Barinthian said as he maneuvered Lysanthia's body onto his back. He looked at Graeson, his glowing eyes piercing into Graeson's soul. "You might not claim me as your father. But heed my words, son. Lean on the one you call yours. You may feel like a monster, but running from her will only make it worse. Let her be your humanity."

Graeson didn't respond. In silence, he watched the wolf disappear into the woods, his mother draped over its back, her long black hair blending into its fur. He stared at the spot the pair had disappeared for a while, his thoughts spinning too quickly for him to grab. But one thought was louder than the others: Lean on Kalisandre.

How could he do that?

He had seen the terror in her eyes. She hadn't accepted him

before, so why would she now after seeing him transform into a true monster?

His heart twisted as he thought of Kalisandre's screams of terror. They echoed in his mind, repeating in an endless loop.

A twig snapped behind him, and Graeson spun around just as Moris swung.

CHAPTER 39
GRAESON

GRAESON DUCKED AND ROLLED UNDER THE BROKEN BRANCH THAT WAS barreled toward him. His movements were slower than normal, his muscles still sore from the recent transformation and strain on his body.

Moris prepared another strike, his leather wings flaring behind him. But when his eyes locked onto Graeson's, Moris halted. "*Gray?*"

Heaving, Graeson narrowed his gaze. "Moris?" he said cautiously.

If this was a trick, Graeson was in trouble. His body needed time to recuperate, and he had no weapon. The last time he saw his scimitars, they were strapped to Ellie's back. He hadn't thought to take them when he had left the two women. He hadn't thought about a lot of things in those fleeting moments after the attack.

He rolled his hands into tight fists and shifted his stance, readying for the next attack.

But it didn't come. The branch fell to the ground, and Moris dropped to his knees, his wings tucking behind him.

"I-I'm so sorry," Moris sputtered, voice shaking. His head fell into his palms, and sobs rocked his body. "I had no choice. I—" Moris choked on his words, the tears overwhelming him.

Graeson stood and took a hesitant step forward, still unsure whether he could trust Moris. Once upon a time, Graeson had called Moris a friend—or at least an acquaintance. Now, he didn't know what to make of the man kneeling before him. "What do you mean you had no choice?"

"Domitius," Moris blurted in between sobs, "he made me. He—he can command people."

"Domitius is dead," Graeson bit out.

Moris snapped his head up. "What? You killed him?"

Graeson bit down on his tongue, but nodded. He remembered the bull king's body falling alongside the guard's, whose feathered wings erupting into flames.

"I thought I would never get out of there," Moris said, already on his feet and stumbling forward, his wings beating behind him and lifting him onto his toes. He grabbed Graeson by the shoulders and dug his fingers into the sore muscles. Graeson tried to shift away, but Moris only held on tighter, his strength surprising even Graeson.

"I should be dead," Moris said with a wild look in his eyes. "I was nearly dead, but then they did *this*. They made me into a monster. And when I saw you, I had no choice. When the order came…" He shook his head, anguish and disbelief coloring his brown cheeks. "I thought I was going to kill you, Gray."

Graeson pursed his lips. Part of him wanted to believe Moris, but another part of him distrusted him. Too much had happened within the past twenty-four hours that Graeson didn't know what to believe.

"Let go of me, Moris," he ordered, his words clipped.

Moris dropped his gaze to where his fingers were piercing Graeson's skin. He quickly snatched his hands back and flew back several yards, stumbling when he landed. He threw up his hands, and a few of his fingertips were red.

Graeson looked at his shoulder. Deep crescents marked his flesh. Some spots had been torn open.

"See? I can't control myself. I can't—" Moris' eyes went wide as he stared at the blood dripping down Graeson's chest. "Are you fucking *naked?*"

Graeson began to speak but halted, the back of his neck prickling. He held up a single finger to Moris, who froze, wings twitching. Before Graeson could search the woods for the source, though, Moris hissed and arched backward, his features twisting in agony.

"What the—" Moris gritted out through clenched teeth. He spun around, reaching toward his back.

At the sight of the bejeweled dagger, Graeson's lips twitched. He would recognize that dagger anywhere. He looked beyond Moris' flailing form and spotted the two silhouettes creeping toward them.

Kalisandre strolled forward, pulling out Graeson's scimitars from her back. Her brown hair whipped across her face as a gust of wind rolled in.

Gods, they look good on—

"Wait!" Graeson stepped in front of Moris, shielding him as he spotted Ellie rearing her hand back, her throwing knife at the ready. "He doesn't mean us any harm."

While Graeson might not have trusted Moris entirely yet, as far as he could tell, whatever command had poisoned Moris before had faded.

"He was working with Domitius!" Kallie said, her hands flexing over the twin hilts. Her gaze was a storm, the sea within a torrent.

"I-I don't want to hurt you." Moris made to step forward but halted when both women shifted their stances, readying to attack.

His wings folded back. "I *didn't* want to hurt you," he clarified. "That wasn't me."

"You just said you can't control yourself," Ellie retorted.

"I—" Moris looked around, frantic. He rubbed his hands across his head. "I can, but not when…when I'm triggered."

"Triggered?" Kallie asked, confused.

Moris nodded. "Yes. It's like some spark gets ignited within me. One moment I'm fine, but then the next…" He shook his head, terror burning in his eyes.

"That doesn't make me want to trust you. Quite the opposite, in fact," Ellie said. Her braid was nearly undone, and random pieces fell over her shoulder, giving her a wild look.

A low growl came from the opposite direction. When Graeson turned, he found two red eyes locked on Moris.

Moris stumbled and muttered a curse.

"Nyrri," Graeson warned. Dani would kill him if she found out Moris was alive and Graeson let him die. To all three of them, he said calmly, "If he wanted to kill me, he would have already."

And he probably could have easily. Graeson left that last part out, unwilling to admit to his weakened state.

"I'll tell you everything I know. I promise," Moris said, hands up. "You can even tie me up."

Ellie narrowed her gaze, but Graeson noticed how the muscles in her raised arm softened before she lowered her weapon.

"You trust him?" Kalisandre asked, weapons still raised.

Trust might have been too strong of a word, but then Graeson thought of Barinthian's warning about the war having only begun. If that was true, and if Moris knew something, they had to use him to their advantage.

"Dani would want him alive, and he might prove useful."

Kallie pursed her lips. Her gaze flicked across them, still hesitant. But as if deciding to trust Graeson, she called out, "Ellie?"

Ellie pointed her knife at Moris. "Come on, flyboy. Let's have a chat."

"With *you*? Alone?" Moris asked, glancing at Graeson, fear shining in his eyes.

An amused grin ticked at the corner of Graeson's mouth. He might have saved Moris from death, but he would not save him from Ellie's wrath. He was still pissed off at Moris for using his power on them.

As if sensing this, Moris let his head fall, defeat washing over him. He dragged his feet across the ground, his wings almost touching the dirt as he reluctantly followed Ellie.

"And you," Ellie called out before disappearing into the woods, pointing her knife over her shoulder at Graeson, "put some clothes on. You're burning my eyes."

Graeson rolled his eyes. He had nearly forgotten he was completely nude in the middle of the woods. "I would if I had some."

"Nyrri," Kalisandre called, and the drakonis came forward, his bag strapped to her saddle.

Graeson nodded in gratitude, grabbed a pair of trousers from the bag, and quickly pulled them on. As he did, a whistle sounded. Nyrri nudged him with her snout before heading after Ellie.

Alone with Kalisandre, his throat seized up. He could have sworn he saw a flicker of fear in those sea-blue eyes.

"Are you hurt?" she asked after a moment.

Graeson swallowed, unable to lie to her. Not only did his body hurt, the pain only marginally subsiding, his heart hurt, too. "I've been better. Are *you* all right?"

"I've been better," she said with a weak smile, never looking away from him.

Graeson looked her up and down, taking in her recent wounds. The bandage on her arm was already stained red, blood having seeped through the center. She stood with her hip cocked, carefully avoiding placing too much weight on her injured leg.

He tried not to let the guilt rise in his throat, but knew he had failed when his voice came out hoarse. "You should be resting."

"I will," she said with a shrug, making no motion to move.

He swallowed, realizing he couldn't avoid it any longer. Graeson didn't know where to begin, didn't know what to say. So much had happened in the brief span of twelve hours. "Kalisandre, I—"

His scimitars dropped to the ground with a clatter, cutting him off. In the blink of an eye, Kalisandre was hobbling over to him, tears rolling down her cheeks. Heart in his lungs, Graeson met her half-way. She barreled into his chest, her arms wrapping around his waist.

His eyes grew wide, but the shock was brief. He wrapped her in his arms, inhaling her. Graeson shoved his face into her thick, brunette hair, the smell of burnt lavender drenching him. He didn't know how she felt about him, but he needed his friend. He needed *her*.

"I'm so sorry, Graeson," Kalisandre whispered, nestling against him and tucking her chin in the crook of his neck.

And as she squeezed him tighter, Graeson finally broke. His tears soaked her beautiful, knotted locks. He didn't know how long they stood like that or how Kalisandre stayed standing with him leaning against her. He was just thankful she didn't let go.

His mother was dead. His mother, to whom he had said only a few words before she was taken from him again. Whose chest he had driven a blade through.

Graeson recalled the way Lysanthia had looked up at him. Not with anger or sorrow, but with acceptance.

His sobs rocked his body harder.

Kalisandre didn't speak. She didn't say it was going to be fine. She didn't say it wasn't his fault, nor did she try to take the blame like she was prone to doing. In silence, she embraced him, allowing him the space he needed to process his emotions and grief. Giving him as much time as he needed.

And while grief, Graeson knew, was not something one could get over in a matter of minutes or days or even months, he was thankful for the time she granted him. Because, if Barinthian was right, they would need to be on the move sooner rather than later.

When he finally loosened his grip some time later, he didn't let go of Kalisandre completely. He didn't think he could. If he did, he would probably collapse, his weight too much to bear on his own.

With the pad of his thumb, he wiped away the moisture from Kalisandre's cheeks. "How did you find me?" he asked, his voice hoarse and throat raw.

Her cheeks flushed. "I just...I had a feeling."

"A *feeling?*"

She nodded, chewing at the bottom of her lip. "I didn't understand it at first—I still don't, but it's like...like there's a thread connecting me to you. I think, no matter where you go or how far apart we are, I'd be able to find you."

A question sat in the center of her bunched brows. And for a moment, Graeson didn't think she would ask it, but she did. "It's the bond, isn't it?"

Graeson brushed a piece of hair behind her ear. "I've been told it's an even greater pull when a bond has been accepted."

Something flashed across her expression. Before he could identify it, she looked away. "Did you...did you bury her?"

Graeson shook his head.

"Do you need help?"

He closed his eyes, unsure how to explain that his father had visited him in wolf-form and had taken his mother. "It's... complicated."

"More complicated than being a dragon?" she quipped.

The corner of his mouth ticked up. "Surprisingly, yes."

She cocked her head to the side. "Did you know you could do that?" she asked, her face contorted as if she believed it was possible for him to keep such a secret from her.

"No. I had no idea. At times, I have felt odd in my own skin, but I never imagined…" Graeson shivered as he thought of the instances when he would be in cramped places and his panic would surge. Now though? Now, the voice inside his head was silent, as if his body was finally at peace with itself.

Kalisandre dragged her gaze across him as if she was searching for scales or talons, as if the dragon would appear at any moment. "Did it hurt?"

Graeson chuffed a laugh. "Like nothing else."

He hesitated to say more. He wasn't sure how to describe what the transformation felt like, nor did he believe it would help either of them. His silence gave him away, though.

"What is it?"

"It's—" He swallowed the rest of the sentence as Barinthian's words echoed in his mind.

Lean on the one you call yours. You may feel like a monster, but running from her will only make it worse. Let her be your humanity.

"I think we should sit down," he said.

When she nodded, Graeson wrapped an arm around her waist and guided her over to a fallen tree. He helped her sit down, careful of her injury. Then he sat beside her. A gentle breeze skated across them, though it did little to rid his skin of the beading sweat. He wiped his palm on his trousers, his leg bouncing beneath it.

Her hand fell on his, and she squeezed it. The light pressure momentarily calmed the rapid beating of his heart. The nervous tremor in his hands subsided slightly.

"Whatever it is, you can tell me, Graeson," she whispered. "I'm not going anywhere."

He pulled his gaze away from their hands to look up at her.

Maybe he was wrong before. Maybe she hadn't been afraid *of* him, but *for* him.

Exhaling a slow breath, Graeson let his shoulders drop, the tension within them easing just a fraction. Then he told her everything: what Myra had told him after the council meeting, what his mother had said about freeing himself, his father showing up and taking Lysanthia. He confessed it all, not bothering to hold back, not fearing that she would think differently of him. Because he finally understood that if he didn't lean on her, if he didn't tell her the truth, then it would only tear him apart.

CHAPTER 40

MYRA

"Maybe I should swear off women," Rian announced as he tossed the bread the innkeeper had given them away.

While Myra didn't believe the bread was poisonous, she did not voice her dissent.

Rian had gone on monotonously about how he was an excellent judge of character. Myra, however, quickly saw through his facade.

She had tried to convince him that he couldn't have known. Myra was honestly as shocked as he was that the innkeeper had betrayed them. The woman had most likely been forced to confess the truth to the assailants. When the trio had first arrived at the inn, Myra hadn't sensed any malicious intent, only curiosity and attraction from the woman. Although when they were leaving the inn, Myra recalled a strangeness coating the space. The woman had been more jittery, her aura coated with paranoia as she shifted on her feet behind the bar—something Laurince had realized only after Myra was gone.

"She told us eventually," Laurince said, looking over his shoulder as they rode. "We made it in time. That's what matters."

Rian glanced at Myra, remorse twisting his features. "I should have realized sooner. I shouldn't have been so careless."

"I was careless, too," Myra admitted, offering him a small smile. Maybe if she hadn't been distracted by the images of Laurince's legs entangled with hers, she would have noticed something was off with the woman sooner. "You cannot take all the blame."

"It comes with the title, does it not?"

Myra sighed. To some extent, if their arrangement had been different, Rian and Kallie would have gotten along well as a ruling couple. They both tried to take on too much.

As thoughts of Kallie came up, Myra looked away from Rian. Had she met with King Domitius yet? Was she safe? Was she—

"Mys?"

"Hmm?" Myra snapped her attention back to Rian and found him staring at her, concerned. Both he and Laurince kept glancing at her with that look. They were constantly checking in on her, afraid that something else had happened. That they hadn't gotten there in time.

But they had. Myra kept reminding herself that.

"Where'd you go?" Rian asked.

Ahead of them, Laurince shifted, side-eyeing them.

"Nowhere. I-I'm fine. I was just…thinking."

"About?" Rian prompted.

Myra pursed her lips, debating on telling him the truth. Although Rian hadn't brought up Kallie much during their time together, Myra didn't believe he cared for her. He had now been betrayed by not one woman, but two. And in both instances, either his life or someone else's had been in danger because of the woman's betrayal. That was something that only time would heal. Myra did not wish to impose her concerns about her former friend's well-being on him. Nor did she think it would do her any good to think of the what-ifs.

Her gaze locked onto the deep auburn hair peeking through the hood of Rian's cloak. A wicked smile crept across her face. Perhaps there was one good thing that came out of their stop at the inn.

"Why are you looking at me like that?" Rian asked, guiding his horse away from her. He glanced at the captain. "Laurince, she's being weird."

"Weird? What do you—" Laurince cut himself off when he looked back at Myra. "Haze? Why are you smiling like that?"

Her eyelashes fluttered across her cheeks. "Do we have time for a quick stop?"

"Do you really think that's a good idea? You were nearly killed," Rian sputtered. "*And* I have a bounty on my head, remember? It's probably not a good idea to go strolling through another town."

"I think that pretty little head of yours is the *exact* reason we should," Myra stated, looking from Rian's hair to Laurince.

"All right. Now you're *both* doing it, and it's creeping me the fuck out."

Myra and Laurince laughed, which only made Rian groan in frustration. Myra didn't care, though, because she had lied to herself before. Two good things had come out of stopping at the tavern.

MYRA SNICKERED as Rian scratched his head.

He dropped his hand from his hair and glared at her. "You said it didn't look bad," he whined from atop his horse.

Once a beautiful shade of copper, Rian's hair was now painted black, and Myra was still not used to it. When she had suggested the idea, Rian had refused. But after some coaxing and some choice words from Laurince in private, Rian relented.

Thankfully, they had found all the needed ingredients for the dye in a small village in Borgania the next morning. Laurince had accompanied Myra to the market while Rian reluctantly waited outside the village.

Growing up, Myra had watched her mother dye countless fabrics various shades in order to create her designs. The vibrant colors were one quality that made her mother's embroidery truly special. Her mother would use anything and everything—berries, walnuts, vegetables, bugs. Whatever she could find or afford. It was like magic, watching her work and seeing the beautiful colors she created.

"It doesn't look back," Myra promised, trying to hide the ghost of amusement on her lips. She didn't dare tell Rian that one ingredient in the black dye was crushed beetles.

Rian slowed his horse down to a trot in line with hers. "Are you sure?"

Laurince snorted ahead of them. "How many times does she need to boost your ego? It's not even permanent."

The dye would only last for a series of washes before needing to be reapplied—a fact they had to continue to remind Rian.

"Someone woke up on the wrong side of the ground this morning," Rian mumbled.

"For the tenth time, I'm *fine*."

"If you say so, Cap." Rian gave a two-finger salute at Laurince's back. Then he leaned closer to Myra and whispered quietly enough so Laurince couldn't hear, "You think he's cranky because he wasn't sleeping next to you last night?"

Myra kicked out her leg, narrowly missing Rian's foot. Her horse nickered in annoyance, and she yelped, gripping the pommel to steady herself before she fell over.

Laurince snapped his attention to her. "Are you—" He slammed his mouth shut as Rian laughed and winked at her. The captain quickly turned back around, his posture more rigid than before.

Myra silently cursed herself. She wasn't doing a great job of proving that she had no interest in the king.

Was this how it always was with them? The two men were around the same age and had grown up together. While Myra had a few more years on Kallie, she knew what it was like to be overlooked. As a handmaiden, her job was never to be seen or heard. She stood beside Kallie to ensure her corsets were tightened, her hair perfectly in place, and her tea served at the right temperature.

Was Rian's shadow just as large as Kallie's growing up?

Still, she couldn't imagine Laurince struggling to garner the attention of women. He was kind, strong, funny, charming. He could even sweep a woman across the dance floor if he so chose.

Her eyes dipped over his broad shoulders, down the length of his back. He was beyond attractive too. Likely the most attractive man Myra had ever laid eyes on.

"Perhaps you should tell him the truth," Rian said, leaning over again.

Myra straightened. "There's nothing to tell."

"Continue lying to yourself, Mys, if you must, but time is precious. Who knows how much of it we have?"

"Wow." Myra gasped dramatically and pressed one hand to her chest as she held the reins loosely in the other. "What an astute piece of wisdom."

"I'm not a king for nothing," he said with a smirk. The twitch of his lips was brief, his expression turning solemn. "Think about it, at least."

He didn't give Myra a chance to respond before he kicked his heels against his horse's sides. The horse trotted forward, joining Laurince. Rian asked the captain a question, but Myra didn't hear it or Laurince's response.

As she stared at the two men's backs as they rode through the woods, Rian's words settled in her stomach like a stone. Rian had a point. Domitius had declared war, and Sebastian was sitting on Rian's throne. It didn't matter how many men Laurince and Rian could gather from those they trusted. Blood would spill soon, and lives would be lost. Did Myra want to waste the time she had by hiding what she felt—as new as it might have been?

CHAPTER 41
MYRA

Myra knelt beside the river. She dipped her hands into the water, and the cold liquid nipped at her skin as she brushed it over her arms.

"Can I ask you something?"

Myra's hands stilled beneath the water at the sound of Laurince's voice. As he crouched beside her, Myra hoped he couldn't see her face flush red in the water's reflection.

"It's been bothering me for a while, but it's somewhat…personal," he said.

"What is it?" she asked cautiously, returning to washing her hands. Although she struggled to focus on the simple task as Laurince rolled up his sleeves.

He dipped them into the river and spread the water up his arms, scrubbing the grime from his skin. She tracked a droplet of water running down his arm, over the nook of his elbow, down his forearm. She licked her lips, suddenly feeling parched.

"Why didn't you use your ability?"

Myra nearly flinched at the question. "When?"

Laurince shook out his hands and sat back on his heels. He

draped his arms over his knees, and water dripped from his fingertips. "When you were captured. Why didn't you manipulate their emotions? Make them feel…sorry for you or remorseful? Or anything that would make them untie you?"

Myra blinked, speechless. Her tongue was like a stone in her mouth, a heavy weight that she couldn't move. After a moment, she whispered, "I—I didn't think to use it."

"Why not?"

Myra shrugged, and suddenly, her body grew cold. Her hands trembled, and she wiped them across her trousers, leaving a dark smear on the fabric. She curled her fingers inward. And although her palms stung as her nails etched half-moons into her skin, her hands at least stopped shaking.

"Myra." Her name was a whisper on his tongue, as if he feared she would run away and flee into the forest if he spoke any louder.

She took a deep breath. "I guess I didn't because…because I was afraid."

"Afraid of what?" Laurince asked, folding his legs beneath him as he sat flat on the ground. He placed a hand atop hers, and the sting of her nails lessened. "If you don't want to tell me, you don't have to."

"It's not…" She shook her head, struggling to find the words. "It's not that I don't want to…"

"But?"

"I don't know how, I guess?" Myra chanced a glance at him, and the look on his face nearly broke her, which was so incredibly silly. She shouldn't have been overcome by Laurince's sincerity, but no one had ever looked at her with such unmotivated interest. He did not view her as a tool or a specimen to be studied. He simply cared. And somehow, that made it less simple in Myra's mind.

"Can you try?" Laurince asked.

She wanted to try. She needed to.

She brushed her hair behind her ear and began, "When I was under Domitius' rule, I…I didn't have a say in what I did, where I went, who I spent my time with. Although I could walk the castle grounds and breathe fresh air, I was still a prisoner. I had tried, though…" Her voice became thick as thoughts of her past surfaced. "I had tried to alter the king's emotions on more than one occasion. Most of the time, especially when I was younger and didn't have full control over my ability, it was by accident. But he knew every time. When he realized what I was doing…" Myra rubbed a hand across her neck. Her throat seized, and breathing became harder. Her skin became clammy.

Laurince reached for her, but she leaned away. He immediately retreated and gripped his knees, as if to keep himself from reaching out again.

All Myra could feel was pain.

All she could smell was whiskey.

All she could hear were insults spewed from the king's mouth.

Arrogant, girl. You think you have power? I am *power.*

"It's all right, Myra." He placed his hand beside her, not quite touching her, but close enough to let her know he was there. "He can't touch you anymore."

Myra nodded, but it was unconvincing.

She wanted to believe Laurince, but it was as if his words danced around her, just out of her reach. She didn't know whether she would ever feel safe. Not until Domitius was dealt with. Not until Kalisandre won.

"I didn't manipulate their emotions because I was afraid of what would happen. Every time I used it to fight back, it only ever made things worse," she admitted quietly, tears springing to her eyes. As she thought of her parents, of her mother's sorrow-filled gaze when she looked at Myra before she was murdered, she could hear her parents' screams, Mynhos' cries.

Myra hadn't been strong enough when she was a child to save her family. Why would she be strong enough now? When the captors came, when the man pressed a blade to her throat, she had frozen. Nothing had changed. She was still the weak and powerless girl she had been when she was in the pantry beneath the floorboards.

"You're not weak."

Myra's gaze snapped up to meet his. She hadn't even realized she had said it aloud.

"I am," Myra argued. "Everyone knows it."

Laurince reached out again, his movements cautious and slow. When Myra didn't flinch away this time, he caressed her cheek. "You're not weak, Haze. You have spent most of your life as a prisoner, forced to make yourself small."

"I'm only a—"

"Don't," Laurince said, squeezing his eyes shut for a second. "Don't say it. You are not just a handmaiden, Myra."

"Then what am I?" It was a question she had been pondering since they had left Ardentol. A question that was more for her than Laurince, but a question she craved the answer to all the same. And to her surprise, Laurince gave her one.

"You are whatever you want to be, Haze. You're kind, caring, loyal, occasionally uptight but usually for good reasons."

A small smile poked at the corner of her lips. Laurince continued.

"You protect those you care about, even if it means risking your own life, your own happiness. You're stronger than you give yourself credit for."

"But when it mattered, I failed. When it mattered, I let fear get the best of me. My ability only hurts people," she said, voice shaking and her gaze falling to the river. The water rolled over the rocks, gliding across them as if they weren't even there.

Laurince shook his head. "Only if you let it."

There was some truth to his words, yet she struggled to believe them.

"Look at me." He tipped her chin up with his thumb, beckoning her. "The next time you are in danger, I want you to do whatever you can to save yourself. Promise me?" With his free hand, he reached behind his back and offered her the small knife he had given her before they left Tetria. "I gave this to you for a reason, but you didn't take it that morning."

"I'm not good at—"

When he shook his head, she snapped her mouth shut.

"While I promise to do whatever I can when it comes to protecting you, I need to know you have a way of defending yourself."

His thumb brushed across her cheek, and Myra wasn't sure if he even knew he was doing it. She didn't care, though, as long as he didn't stop.

"I c-can't kill someone. I'm not…"

"Like me?" he asked.

The rising guilt was sour on her tongue. "That's not what I meant."

"Even if it was, you wouldn't be hurting my feelings, Haze. I hope that you never have to use this. I hope that if the time ever arises when you need to, that you don't have to kill someone. Taking a life is not easy. It's not a weight I wish on anyone. But a war is upon us, and we are about to walk straight into the heart of it. I cannot…" Laurince's words became thick, and Myra didn't need to read his emotions to see the concern twisting at his heart.

His comrades, his friends, and his family lived in Frenzia. The three of them didn't know how bad things were inside of the capital, but they had seen the remains of the Tetrian village that was burned to the ground, they had seen the fear in the Borganian village that they had stopped at for supplies, the paranoid gazes, the closed doors.

"This time you were lucky, but who knows if you will be the next time? I need to know you will do whatever you can to survive." He stared at her, his gaze unwavering, as if he wished to sear his words into her soul. "Got it?"

Using her power should have been the first thing Myra did. Instead, she had hesitated. Instead, she had waited. She had tried to think of what Kallie would do. But Myra wasn't Kallie.

Maybe she didn't have to be.

"Yes," she said, opening her hand.

CHAPTER 42

KALLIE

"Let me get this straight," Ellie said, massaging her temples as she paced. "Your father shows up here as a fucking *wolf*, tells you that you're some reckoning, then carries your mother's dead body away? Anything I'm forgetting?"

Kallie squeezed Graeson's hand in reassurance. When he had first told her, she also had a hard time believing everything. But then she remembered it was only yesterday when she had witnessed Graeson morph into a dragon—something she had never deemed possible. It was time to stop questioning what was and wasn't possible.

Graeson scratched his head, the cotton fabric stretching over his arms. "That's kind of oversimplifying it, but…yes?"

"You forgot to add that he's a fucking dragon," Moris mumbled from the tree he was tied to. Because of his wings, he had to hug the tree. It would have been comical if Kallie had been in a better mood.

Ellie groaned. "No one asked you, traitor."

Moris' left cheek was red, a bruise the size of Ellie's fist marring his skin. When Graeson had asked Ellie about it, she simply shrugged, claiming Graeson was only upset that she did it first.

Kallie couldn't disagree with that. Whether or not Moris was one of their friends, the line between ally and enemy was currently blurry. Every time Kallie looked at Moris, she shivered, recalling the way her body refused to move under his spell.

"I already told you I didn't want to do any of that! Domitius had some hold over me. He brought me along with him only because of my power and because he thought seeing me would rattle you," Moris explained. "The serum they gave me—that turned me into this *monster*—didn't tie me to him. He *controlled* me, like she can."

Kallie sat up, discomfort soaking her bones.

Thankfully, neither Graeson nor Ellie looked at her for too long. They both knew how she felt about using her ability, especially when she was living with Domitius.

"And we're supposed to believe his control over you is suddenly gone?" Ellie snapped.

"You killed him, didn't you?" Moris asked, struggling to look at Graeson and Kallie from his position.

Graeson cracked his jaw, tension rippling through his body. "Yes."

"If you don't believe me, that should prove it to you, at least." He rolled his shoulders, and his back pressed against the binding that wrapped around him. "Plus, I could break free from this in a matter of seconds. Even if this rope was an iron chain instead, it would be no issue."

Kallie grimaced. "Well, that's comforting."

"But I'm not trying to! That's my point. I don't care if you tie me up. If you wanted to kill me, I would let you. I'm still me. I'm still—"

"We don't know that!" Ellie shouted. "You could betray us the moment we turn our backs on you."

"She's right, Moris," Graeson said, rubbing his palms over his knees. "We have to be cautious."

Moris groaned out of frustration. "Do you hear me arguing

with you about that? *Please* be cautious. Please *don't* trust me. I already told you. I can't control myself, but not because I wish to betray you or aid the other side. I am a danger to *anyone* around me."

"He hasn't tried to kill us yet," Kallie said, feeling bad for Moris. She understood what it felt like not to be trusted, and even more, she understood how painful it was not to trust one's own mind.

"Technically, he did attack Graeson," Ellie corrected.

"*Before* I realized it was him!" Moris exclaimed.

"We're straying from the point, are we not?" Graeson asked. He leaned his elbows on his knees and massaged his temples with his fingers.

Without thinking, Kallie reached out and set her hand on his thigh. He released a heavy exhale that ran through his entire body.

Ellie threw up her hands and faced them. "Why can't anything ever be simple when it comes to the two of you?"

Kallie and Graeson exchanged looks, but neither responded. They had no explanation or excuse to offer.

"It doesn't help that all this one could tell me was that Domitius had amassed an entire army of flyboys." Ellie shoved her thumb in Moris' direction.

"Stop calling us that," Moris groaned.

"I will when you give me something worthwhile to work with!"

Moris rested his forehead against the tree trunk and sighed, exhausted. "If I knew more, I would tell you. Just because Domitius turned me into one of his pets doesn't mean he trusted me with his plans or secrets. All I know is that he was in constant contact with the Frenzian king's brother."

"Sebastian?" Kallie asked.

"Yes."

Kallie's stomach twisted with nausea. Even now, she could feel the burn of Sebastian's hand around her throat. She could feel the hatred spewing from him. That night, there was so much fear running through her veins.

Now, there was only rage.

As if sensing her anger, Graeson squeezed her hand.

"Domitius was constantly visiting Frenzia," Moris said. "That's where the drakonises are being held. Something to do with cages for the dragons from way back when."

Graeson went rigid beside her, and Kallie swore she could see smoke billowing from his nose.

"That's not going to happen to you," Kallie promised.

Graeson nodded, but the tension remained.

Ellie plopped down on the stump they had brought over earlier. "How long do you think it will take until Sebastian knows about Domitius' fate?"

"Depends," Graeson said. "If there were survivors, who's to say where they went—back to Ardentol to put it all behind them or to Frenzia to alert Sebastian?"

"Domitius didn't trust many," Kallie said. "If he had trusted Sebastian to take care of the drakonises, he would be in close contact with him. Sebastian's arrogant, but he's not stupid. He will realize something is wrong when he doesn't receive a letter or a visit."

Graeson rubbed a hand over his face.

"We need to return to Pontia," Graeson said.

Kallie straightened, the blood draining from her face.

Return to Pontia? Ever since she left Tetria, she had put any thought of returning behind her. Once they killed Domitius, returning should have been the obvious next step, but everything else had distracted her.

With her mind elsewhere, Kallie barely heard the rest of the words spilling from Graeson's mouth.

Gather troops.

Army.

Plan.

End the war.

They were all passing thoughts, like a breeze sweeping by that barely rustled the fallen leaves. Kallie brushed her hand over the bandage on her upper arm. The wound was still sore.

"If Domitius is dead, is there a point? The war is over," Ellie said. "We did what we came to do."

Kallie forced her attention back to the present conversation.

"Did you not hear everything I told you?" Graeson asked, annoyed. "This is only the beginning. Sebastian was working with Domitius. While Domitius was not known for his caring personality or willingness to share, do you really think he was the only one who was given a new ability? Sebastian has an entire army of drakonises at his disposal. He might have been following Domitius originally, but do you really think he is going to stop now that Domitius is dead?"

"Fuck!" Ellie stood and started pacing again.

"Sebastian told me he wanted Rian's throne," Kallie said after a moment. "If Domitius' plans have given him a way to gain even more than just Frenzia, Sebastian will not shy away from the opportunity."

"Fine," Ellie bit out, tossing her hands in the air. "I'll return to Tetria then and make sure the Queen and my people know as well."

"No, we need to rest first," Graeson countered. "My body is still recovering from the transformation. And you and Kallie are both too injured to travel on foot for long."

Ellie folded her arms over chest. "I'm fine," she argued.

Graeson raised a brow. "Show me your ribs then."

Ellie stepped back, aghast. "I will *not* take my clothes off for you. Kallie, do you hear this?"

Kallie rolled her eyes. "That's not what he means, and you know it. Your ribs are broken, and if not broken, badly bruised."

"I'm fine. I can—"

"*No.* You need to rest. We all do." Graeson stood, and Kallie could see how tired he was, too. The bags under his eyes could have rivaled Terin's.

"Come on," he said, holding out his hand to Kallie.

"I thought you said we needed to rest?" Kallie asked.

"We do, and I know just the place to do that where we can also borrow some horses."

"Oh, are you friends with the local stableman?" Ellie prodded.

Graeson smiled down at Kallie as she took his hand. "Something like that."

CHAPTER 43
MYRA

THE EMBERS EMITTED A SOFT GLOW AS DUSK FELL OUTSIDE THE CAVE. The light from the fire bounced off the cave's walls, humming and pushing at the shadows that crept inside. The crackling wood and the soft rustling of leaves outside were the only sounds around the fire.

Myra wrapped her arms around her legs, squeezing them against her chest. It wasn't as cold as it had been on previous nights, but the light pressure was comforting and settled her nerves.

With a groan, Rian stood, stretching his arms to the sky. "I'm going to go take a lap."

Laurince swiftly shook his head. "I can go. You two should stay here."

"Unless you wish to help me take a leak, sit your ass back down, Lo," Rian said, waving him off.

Myra quirked her brows. "What about the bounty?"

Rian pointed to his head. "I'm unrecognizable, remember?"

"Not *entirely* unrecognizable," Laurince mumbled under his breath.

They would reach the capital tomorrow, which meant that

Rian's chances of being recognized had increased tenfold because of his proximity to the castle. They had done their best to avoid the villages where possible. When they were forced to pass through them, Rian kept his head down. But they could all sense the tension among the civilians. They had opted to avoid the inns at all costs, despite the knots in their backs and shoulders. But even in the deserted cave they had found, there was still a chance of hunters or soldiers searching the woods. They wouldn't be safe until the war was over and Rian was back on the throne.

Rian swiped his sword from the ground and twisted it in the air. "Happy?"

"Not even close," Laurince argued gruffly.

"Too bad. Maybe Mys can help you navigate your feelings, yeah?"

Myra's gaze snapped to Rian, who was backing away as Laurince poked the fire with a long stick, mumbling to himself. A rebuttal was on the tip of her tongue, but Rian was quicker.

He tipped his head in Laurince's direction and mouthed, "Do it."

She glared at Rian, realizing he was using this as an excuse to make her listen to his advice from the other day. But before she could argue, he left the cave, slipping into the woods with a mischievous grin on his face. Myra held her legs closer to her chest. Yet no matter how hard she squeezed them, her heart hammered against her ribcage. She kept her focus on the fire, praying that Laurince couldn't hear her rancorous heartbeat.

Minutes passed, and neither she nor Laurince broke the silence.

Restless, Myra shifted. She crossed her legs and slipped her hands beneath her thighs. Her knees bounced as she glanced between the fire and the entrance of the cave. Maybe Rian was right. Maybe she should tell Laurince.

Then again, what if she told him and Rian came back and overheard her silly proclamation? How embarrassing would that be?

"He'll be fine," Laurince said, poking a burning coal with a stick. The rock disintegrated upon contact.

"Hmm?" Myra hummed, dragging her attention from the fire to him.

He propped his leg up, throwing his arm over it. "I just mean that Rian knows how to use that sword of his."

Myra's brows scaled up her forehead. "Oh?"

"That's not—that wasn't—" Laurince rubbed his hand across his face in embarrassment.

Myra tilted her head, eyeing the captain. Was he *blushing?*

"What I meant was…" He cleared his throat and scratched the scar on his neck. "When I said I didn't want him to go before, it's not because I don't have faith in his ability to wield a sword. He's been thoroughly trained. I've trained with him many times. He can handle himself if he were to come across someone or something. Although I doubt he will. I just did a lap around the campsite not even half an hour ago. This area seems deserted."

"That's…that's good," Myra said, unsure why Laurince was babbling. He was sounding like her.

"So you don't have to worry."

"Do I look worried?"

"Well…" He gestured to her knee, which was still bouncing against the ground. "You haven't stopped fidgeting since he left."

"Oh." Myra froze. "*Oh.* You think I'm worried about his safety?"

"Of course."

If only it were that simple.

She hadn't realized Laurince paid that close attention to her. She sucked in her bottom lip and chewed on it nervously. When Laurince clocked the movement, her heart pounded. She released her lip immediately.

Dropping her gaze to the pebbles on the cave floor in front of her, she confessed, "I'm not worried about him."

"Then what's the matter? Are you cold? I can add more wood to the fire," Laurince offered, getting ready to stand.

"No, no," Myra said quickly. "You shouldn't."

"I can though. We can let it burn a little longer. I'm sure—"

"It's you," she blurted.

Laurince stilled, half-standing, half-sitting, frozen awkwardly in the middle.

She forced herself to look at him. The embers were like stars in his dark eyes as he gaped at her.

"*Me?*" he asked, pointing at himself as he slowly sat down.

Myra nodded, and the regret was instant.

Gods, she was so foolish. She shouldn't have said anything.

"Why me?"

"Because you…you…" Myra sighed, struggling to find the words. Why was this so hard? It shouldn't have been. Yet her palms were sweating, her tongue felt heavy, and despite the cold, her hair was sticking to the back of her neck.

"Wait, Haze," Laurince said, concern filling his voice. "Do *I* make you nervous?"

"No, of course not." She wiped her palms on her trousers. Then, she admitted quieter, "Maybe?"

Dejection, guilt, and regret twisted around him, and Myra didn't understand it. Had she said something wrong?

"Is it because of what happened back at the tavern?" he asked.

What happened at the tavern certainly didn't help. Myra was sure she had developed some kind of interest in the captain before then, but the tavern had caused something to change. It was there that she realized she couldn't deny she enjoyed his presence. She would have been lying if she said she hadn't thought about dancing with him, his hand on her waist, his—

She cleared her throat. "Maybe?"

Laurince nodded, but the movement was rigid. "I didn't mean—I'm sorry. Truly, I am."

"What for?" she asked, afraid of the answer. If she had been wrong—if she had misread his emotions—things were going to get awkward fast.

He pulled the cuff of his sleeve down, stretching the fabric over his hand. "For scaring you. I shouldn't have been so brutal, but it was as if something had overtaken me." He leaned his weight to one side, then the other. "When I saw you, I...I was so angry. More than I had ever been before."

"What could I have done to upset you?" she asked, suddenly regretting starting this conversation.

"*You?* You did nothing," Laurince said, aghast. "But I shouldn't have killed him. If I had missed him, I could have hurt you. It was reckless and stupid and—"

"By the gods, you are more foolish than I thought," Myra mumbled, shaking her head and standing.

Laurince tracked her movements, but Myra didn't think he was really seeing her. His brows were drawn tight, his brown eyes wide and full of sorrow.

"Yes, and foolish," he said as he nodded repeatedly. "I shouldn't have done it, but I had to do *something*. He had a blade pressed to your throat. If he had harmed you—"

Myra grabbed his head between her hands. The shock and panic puckered his lips and enlarged the whites of his eyes. In any other situation, his expression would have been comical.

"Laurince," she said, drawing out the syllables of his name.

"I know," he said, the words mumbled.

She loosened her hold, her touch melting into a caress.

He wrapped one hand around her wrist. His calloused fingers were a balm to her skin. "It was a foolish decision. It put you at risk, and now you're nervous to be around me because I scared you—"

The crease in the center of his forehead deepened as he looked at her quizzically. "Why are you laughing?"

"Because," Myra answered, chuckling, unable to contain her amusement, "you're not listening."

"Yes, I am." He pulled back as if offended, which only made Myra's smile widen even more.

"No, you're not. You're not a foolish man because you saved me. You're a foolish man because you believe I am scared of you for what you did when that couldn't be further from the truth."

"Then what...what is it?" His eyes flitted across her face, searching for the answer as if his life depended on it. "Why do I make you nervous?"

"Isn't it obvious?" Myra asked, her hands still resting on his sharp jawline.

"Apparently not," Laurince muttered.

Myra exhaled.

Are all men really this daft?

She had only been this close to him once when they were dancing, and even then, she didn't dare stare too long at his features out of fear of being found out. But what had she been afraid of? Why had she let herself go without seeing him this close up before? His jaw was sharp as a knife. The corners of his eyes were wrinkled from years of laughter, and softened the hard edges of his cheekbones. Her attention dipped to his mouth, where his lips were set in a flat line. She looked to the spot where she knew a small dimple hid. As she observed him, her breaths shortened, and the thump of her heart pounded harder.

"Haze?"

"Yes, Laurince?" His name was no more than a breath on her lips.

He swallowed, the bump in his throat rising and falling. "Why do I make you nervous?" he asked again, his voice low and his pupils dilating. He brushed her collarbone with a knuckle, sweeping a stray hair away. The touch sent a chill across her skin, and heat pooled low in her stomach.

The beat of her heart was an echo in her ears. It hummed, pounding, threatening to burst through her ribcage. Her eyes dipped to his lips again. He scraped his bottom lip with his teeth, and she wondered if he was even conscious of doing it.

"Myra," Laurince said, placing his hands on her waist, his fingers pressing against her. Layers of fabric separated his hand and her skin, yet goosebumps rose in the wake of his touch.

What had he asked her? She couldn't think straight.

She inhaled, hoping to steady her shaking hands. But it only made it worse because when she breathed, all she could smell was him: pine, crushed leaves, and smoke.

"Because," she said, her voice airy as Laurince's grip on her tightened ever-so-slightly, "when I'm with you, I can't help but think…"

"Think what?" he prompted.

Myra bit her lip, and Laurince's attention fell to it. When he dragged his gaze back to her eyes, none of the previous stars that twinkled from the embers pierced through the darkness. There were a million thoughts that passed through those all-consuming eyes. A silent permission.

"Use it, Myra."

Without any effort, Myra plucked the golden thread that whipped around them. Curiosity and tension danced across the thread in such a way that filled her entire being with a foreign, insatiable hunger. It was sweet yet sour. Warm like a hearth, yet it sent a scattering of toe-curling chills crawling down her spine.

She rose to her knees. Laurince snaked his hand further around her back, the warmth of his touch spreading across her skin and tickling her spine. He leaned forward, or she did. She didn't know, nor did she care, not when—

A crack of a twig and a quick hiss had both of them snapping their heads toward the cave's entrance.

Myra's nose crashed into Laurince's cheek as he smashed her against his body.

"Fuck," Laurince spat. A glimmer of steel sparkled in the corner of her eye, where he held his sword.

"Shit, sorry," Rian said, holding up his hands. "Am I...am I interrupting something?"

Myra jolted backward and out of Laurince's arms. She plopped on the ground beside him, unable to move any further, her limbs liquid.

Rian chuckled and rocked back on his heels. "I *hope* I'm interrupting something because if not, then I just walked around the woods for nothing."

Mortified, Myra dropped her face into her hands, mumbling a curse.

"Why don't you take another walk then, huh?" Laurince asked.

"Too late. I gave you plenty of time—more than I should have if I'm being honest." Rian strolled around the fire. He patted Laurince on the shoulder. "You've got to be quicker than that, Lo. If you need some pointers, let me know."

If Myra could scream without embarrassing herself more, she would have. Tomorrow, she would have some choice words with Rian—royalty or not.

Rian grabbed his bag and pulled out a blanket. He spread it across the ground. "But hey, don't mind me. You're more than welcome to carry on with...whatever that was."

Laurince looked at Myra, a brow cocked. She immediately shoved him.

"Ow," he said, rubbing his chest where she had struck.

She rolled her eyes, though a shy grin curled at her lips.

The moment was dead. She would not kiss Laurince with Rian

pretending to sleep right next to them—and doing a piss-poor job at that.

With his head propped up on his arm, Rian wiggled his brows at her.

Scoffing, Myra faced the dying fire. However, without Laurince's hands on her, she couldn't help but notice how cold it had gotten. Shivering, she leaned forward and held her hands closer to the embers.

Laurince scooted closer. His leg pressed against hers, his side against her side. He leaned into the crook of her neck, his breath warm against her throat. "You still haven't answered my question," he whispered.

She shivered even more. "What question?"

His lips grazed her neck. He didn't quite kiss her, but he was close enough for her to feel the smile that formed. He whispered his question against her neck, trailing it up to her ear. "What do you think about when you look at me?"

"If you two are going to flirt, can you at least be loud enough for me to hear so I can make fun of it later?" Rian called out. "I was left at the altar, you know. It's only fair."

Laurince released a laugh, his head dropping to her shoulder and shaking her. The sound was so pure that it sent an overwhelming wave of bliss over her, and she could do nothing but lean into it. Lean into *him*.

Laurince wrapped an arm around her and rested his chin on her head. "You should get some rest, too," he whispered.

Myra hummed in agreement, but she didn't move. She couldn't. Because if she moved, she was afraid that this moment would vanish forever. Tomorrow, they would reach the castle, and the true fight would start. She wasn't ready to face that.

Gathering her courage, she turned, her lips brushing his ear.

Then she finally answered him, her words barely a whisper. "I think about kissing you."

A wide smile stretched across Laurince's face, and he tucked her closer against him. "Maybe you should."

But she didn't. She wouldn't, not yet. Not while Rian was punching the air, at least.

Instead, she stayed next to Laurince for a little longer, soaking in his warmth and trying to delay the inevitable as much as she could. And perhaps hoping she would dream about what would have happened if Rian hadn't interrupted them. If she had actually kissed Laurince.

CHAPTER 44
KALLIE

Even miles away from the clearing, the air remained polluted, the smoke from the fire hanging over the area.

Kallie scanned the stretch of land. The crops across the field had long since turned into dry husks, as if the green hue had been stripped from the world. A single house sat on the property, a house where everything in Kallie's life had changed. This place was where she had found out Terin and Fynn were her brothers, that she was the daughter of the Queen of Pontia.

Reflecting on that night and the weeks that followed, there were so many things she wished she had done or said differently. She tried to squash the what-ifs and should-haves, but it was easier said than done.

As they approached, Kallie spotted the old farmer standing atop a ladder, a utility belt hanging low on his hip. Menz stretched up and slammed his hammer against a nail sticking out of a white shutter. The hammering must have masked their approach up the walkway because, when Graeson shouted out a greeting from below, Menz jolted. He spun around, about to fall as he grabbed onto the window ledge.

Graeson rushed over to steady the ladder. "Need some help, Menz?" he called up with an apprehensive smile.

Menz barely looked at Graeson, though, his attention immediately snagging on Nyrri and Moris. His foot slipped. "W-what are they doing here?"

Kallie grimaced as Moris straightened, his wings snapping back. Maybe they made a mistake bringing Moris and Nyrri with them. They had debated about having Ellie stay with them in the woods while they explained the situation to Menz, but Graeson had brushed off their concerns, claiming Menz was easy-going enough. Apparently, he was wrong.

Not that Kallie could really blame Menz' reaction. If she had seen a man and an enormous wolf with wings approach her unannounced, she would have had some choice words too.

"Neither of them will hurt you, I promise," Graeson said, his hands raised. "You know I would never bring anything or anyone here who would bring you harm."

Menz snorted. "Tell that to my flock of sheep that was stolen the other week."

"Wait, have you seen others like them?" Graeson dropped his hands as he peered back at their group.

Menz scanned the empty fields just beyond them, then slowly nodded. "A horde of them came through town almost two weeks ago."

"The village," Kallie whispered, her thoughts immediately turning to the homes that were attacked. "Have there been other attacks since then?"

"I've heard rumblings of attacks near the borders and have seen several hordes fly over," Menz said, his knuckles blanching around the side of the ladder.

Kallie looked at Graeson. His father was right; the war wasn't over.

Graeson scanned the sky, his hands flexing at his sides. "We should talk inside."

"What about them?" Menz asked as he descended the ladder.

"I can stay outside," Moris offered.

"No," Graeson said. "If a group flies over, we can't risk them spotting you."

Kallie stepped beside Graeson, her shoulder brushing his. Menz' gaze flicked to her.

"I know you're afraid and I know we're asking a lot," Kallie said gently when Menz reached the ground, "but he won't hurt you. On the off chance that he loses control, we can stop him."

The farmer had aided Graeson and the others when they had brought Kallie here, even knowing who she was and what she could do. He was a good man, one of the best.

Menz rubbed his jaw, hesitating. "Fine, but that one will not fit through my front door," he said, pointing at Nyrri.

The drakonis' ears went flat, and a small whine slipped out. Ellie scratched Nyrri beneath her chin, but it only placated Nyrri so much.

"She can hide out in the stable," Graeson suggested.

Menz flinched. "What about the horses!?"

"They might spook when they see her, but she won't harm the horses. She's used to being around them," Graeson explained. "If it makes you more comfortable, we can always leave her in the woods…"

Kallie held back a snort. She knew Nyrri would rather sleep atop the roof of the stable than be left alone in the forest again. It seemed she had developed some trust issues since the last time.

Menz looked between Nyrri and Graeson, still unsure. But after a second, he relented. "Fine. She can stay in the stable for the time being."

Graeson patted him on the shoulder. "Thank you, Menz. I owe you."

Menz huffed as Graeson turned and led Nyrri to the stables. The horses nickered as she entered, but Nyrri ignored them and plopped down on a pile of hay, knocking over various tools in the process.

Groaning, Menz shook his head as he opened the front door. "Come on then," he said, ushering them inside.

Kallie offered him a polite smile as she approached, and he rolled his eyes and pulled her into a tight hug.

"It's good to see you," he said, his voice as warm and comforting as a cup of tea.

When he pulled away, Kallie's smile was a little brighter.

She dipped inside, taking in the house and relishing its familiarity. Everything was the same as it had been the last time she was there, and the lack of change twisted in her gut. It was another reminder of how much had changed outside the house.

A small crash sounded behind her, and Kallie spun around.

"Shit," Moris cursed as he hurried to pick up a frame that he had accidentally pulled down from the wall. But as he moved, his wings smacked into a skinny table, knocking over another frame. "I—I'm sorry."

Menz groaned and shouted, "Please be careful where you're swinging those things, or you'll be in the stables, too."

"Sorry, sir. I'm so sorry." Moris fumbled to set the picture frame upright.

"I got it," Kallie said, taking the frame from Moris' trembling hands. She set it down on the table and brushed the dust from the frame. Beneath the glass sat a self-portrait of Menz' late wife, Lois. Her small signature was scrawled in the bottom corner.

"Come on," Kallie said, ushering Moris forward while keeping an eye on his wings.

As they headed deeper into the house, Kallie looked over her shoulder. Menz stopped beside the table, frame in hand. He swiped a finger across the painting. Longing spread across his countenance. When Graeson entered, he stopped beside the farmer.

Kallie turned around, giving them some privacy. Menz' wife had passed years ago, and this farm was all he had left of her. Perhaps they were asking too much of him.

"YOU'RE IN LUCK," Menz said, carrying a steaming pot into the dining room. "I already had a stew brewing because of the cold weather coming in. Go sit, and I'll bring everything out."

"That's really unnecessary, Menz. We do not want to intrude," Graeson said. "We only came to ask—"

"Food first. Then we can talk," Menz interrupted, setting the pot in the middle of the table.

Kallie's stomach rumbled loudly, and she pressed a hand against it. She hadn't realized how hungry she was until the aroma of garlic and broth hit her nose.

"Don't bother arguing with me about it, either. I would bet good money on the fact that you all haven't had a good meal in a while." Menz winked at Kallie, and she grinned.

"It smells delicious," she said. She sank into a seat, and her thighs all but thanked her for the relief. The journey to Menz' house, while short in the grand scheme of things, was longer than her body would have liked. Although she had ridden on Nyrri's back most of the way after protesting, her leg still ached. As much as Kallie wanted to get back out there and finally put an end to the budding war, they all needed the rest. She could almost hear the relief from Ellie sitting across from her, too. Even Graeson seemed to be relieved for the temporary haven.

Menz motioned for her bowl, and Kallie raised it as he dropped two generous scoops of steaming stew into it. "Eat as much as you'd like."

Kallie blew on the soup and took a bite. The flavors instantly transported her to the last time she was there with her brothers and Dani. But as she looked around the table and those sitting with her, a lump formed in her throat. She wondered how Terin and Dani were faring in Pontia and if they had made any headway in gathering troops for the war. She had yet to hear from Terin since he had first contacted her. If she didn't hear from him soon, they would need to get word to Pontia that while Kallie had been successful, she had failed at ending the war. They should have known that stopping a war would not have been as simple as cutting off the head of the snake.

As if reading her mind, Graeson asked, "Do you still have that messenger bird?"

Menz nodded as he sat.

Beneath the table, Graeson squeezed her thigh. "Do you mind if we send a letter to Pontia?"

"Of course not," Menz said, slurping down a spoonful of stew. "First, do you care to tell me what in the god's breath is going on and why you're hanging out with him?"

Moris glanced up from his bowl, his eyes wide and brown cheeks flushed pink. He sat at the head of the table with his chair spun around to make room for his wings.

Graeson took a deep breath. "It's a long story."

Menz arched a brow. "Good thing we have plenty of stew."

THE POT WAS bone-dry by the time they finished relaying the events of the last few weeks. It was hard to believe that not even a month

had passed since Domitius had declared war, yet it felt like a lifetime had gone by.

"I'll go grab those medical supplies and gather the bedding," Menz said, standing from the table.

"I'll help you," Graeson said.

Menz waved him off. "You're a guest."

"A guest who is likely asking far too much," Graeson countered.

A small grin appeared on Menz' face. "Come on then. I'm sure you're all tired."

The two men left the room, and inaudible whispers trailed them as they disappeared into the hallway.

Kallie spun her half-empty mug of tea between her hands. The drink was lukewarm now, but she couldn't stomach any more of it. Myra had always said tea was supposed to soothe her, but now it only made her anxious.

Moris rested his head in his left palm and tapped his fingers on the table with the other. "Well, he seems nice."

Kallie blinked. "He is…"

Moris looked at Ellie, a question on his face.

The warrior sighed and threw her hair over her shoulder before resting her head on her hand. "So, am I going to have to room with flyboy over here or not?"

"Huh?" Kallie asked, confused.

Ellie arched a brow. "Don't *huh* me. You and Gray have obviously made up."

Kallie's cheeks flamed red. "What's your point?"

"I would like to know if I need to sleep with a knife under my pillow or not," Ellie said, sending a lethal glare in Moris' direction.

Moris groaned, his wings ruffling behind him. "I already said—"

"No, no," Ellie interrupted, holding up a hand in protest. "You said you were a danger to those around you. If you snap or have some silly little nightmare and freak out, I will not hold your hand and rub your back."

"I wouldn't ask you to hold my hand," Moris said with a roll of his eyes.

Kallie rubbed her hands across her face. "He and Graeson will share a room, all right?"

"It's really no big deal," Ellie said. "I get it if you want some privacy with him."

"We're just…." Kallie swallowed, unsure what the end of that statement was.

"Ah," Ellie said with a nod. "You two still haven't talked about the soul bond thing, huh?"

"He finally told you?" Moris asked, eyes wide. "Thank the gods! That man has been moping around ever since I've known him. He was practically unbearable when we were traveling together. The little love sick—"

"Not helping," Kallie said, cutting him off. She leaned back in her chair and groaned. She massaged the growing headache, rubbing her fingers against her temples. "We haven't had the time to talk about it."

"It's because he can shift into a dragon, isn't it?" Moris asked, leaning his weight against his arms. "Kind of intimidating, no?"

"That's not—that doesn't matter."

Ellie scooted back in her chair. Standing, she pressed her palms onto the table. "Now might not seem like a good time either, but it might be your only chance. We're here for a few days, right?"

"Only chance for what?" Graeson asked from the door, a stack of medicine supplies resting in his arms.

Kallie glanced from him to the others. Moris and Ellie shared similar expressions: raised brows, pursed lips, amused glints in their eyes. But Kallie couldn't do it. Not in front of them. Not right now.

"For a decent bath," she blurted.
Ellie dropped her head and sighed.

CHAPTER 45
MYRA

A RIVER OF MUD FLOODED THE LOWER STREETS OF THE FRENZIAN capital as a storm rolled in. Myra tightened her cloak, pulling the hood down to shield her face from the pelting rain. The dirt pathway was slick, but they had no time to spare. They pressed on.

As they made their way closer to the castle, they spotted more guards patrolling the streets. And it seemed they were not the only ones who did not want to attract the guards' attention. Most of the pedestrians who were out also kept their heads down as they passed the guards.

Myra hurried after Laurince, determined to keep up with his quick pace. As the clopping of hooves sounded behind them, Laurince pressed her against the wall with his arm. She tried to shove him off, but he only tightened his hold.

"Don't move," he ordered.

Carefully, Myra peered around him and sucked in a sharp breath. She flattened herself against the wall as much as she could when a horse-drawn carriage came her way. The width of the wagon was just small enough to fit through the narrow street, but wide enough to leave little room for anything else. She swallowed as the carriage crept forward.

The driver snapped the whip beside one horse's ears. Instantly, the horses sped up, the carriage rattling over the stones behind them.

Myra squeezed her eyes shut as the horses darted past them. Hooves slapped against the puddles marring the streets, splashing water onto her cloak. Air whipped across face, and she made the wrong choice to open her eyes just as the carriage was less than a foot away from her face.

"Assholes," Laurince mumbled as the carriage passed. "They're not supposed to be down this road."

They peeled themselves away from the wall. Myra pressed a hand to her chest as she took in her first full breath.

Laurince grabbed her by the shoulders and knelt down to peek through the lip of her hood. "Are you hurt?"

Myra shook her head. Her hands trembled, and she shoved them deep into her pockets.

Laurince, of course, had already noticed them. He squeezed her shoulder. "We're almost there."

"This is ridiculous," Rian hissed, wiping the mud from his soaked cloak.

"A little mud won't hurt you," Laurince said, rolling his eyes.

"I'm not talking about the mud!" Rian spat. He waved his hand in the air. "I'm talking about this entire thing."

A few patrons walking on the opposite side of the street turned in their direction.

Laurince quickly stepped in between them and Rian, blocking their view of him. "I already told you," he whispered, leaning forward, "we can't go barging in. It's not smart."

"Smart? It's my—"

Laurince snatched Rian by the collar and dragged him down the street toward a nearby alley. As he was about to turn down the alley, he tore a poster from a shop window and glanced at Myra, brow raised in question.

Myra halted in her tracks and nodded, letting the two men slip into the alley as she waited at the corner. In her periphery, she saw Laurince shove Rian in the shoulder. A slew of hushed words spilled from the captain's mouth, the spoken words mere white noise under the cover of the rain. Taking a deep breath, she peered into the window of the nearest shop, but she barely paid any attention to the trinkets on display. Her attention was fixed on the posters plastered to the window. Someone had drawn a rough sketch of a man with a sharp chin and thick eyebrows. In another poster, a young woman with an oval face and high cheekbones stared back at her. Their likeness to Rian and Kallie was uncanny.

Heart pounding, she forced herself to refocus on the task at hand. She scanned the faces that walked by, their reflections faint in the mirror. Her gift hummed inside her, waiting.

She recalled what Laurince had said by the river. Her power was not evil, nor was it only a tool for her to use to betray her friends. It was *hers*, and no one else's.

As the occasional curious eye dipped toward the alley, she snatched the threads, feeding notes of indifference down them. One by one, the people walked away.

With each person she successfully turned away, the guilt lessened. It might have been a violation, but it would not harm them. If anything, using her gift would prevent a brawl from breaking out if a guard correctly identified Rian.

Nightfall was less than an hour away, and the overcast sky blanketed the capital in shadows. When a swift breeze blew in and nipped at her fingertips, Myra buried her hands deep into the pockets of her trousers beneath her cloak.

When Laurince returned with Rian on his heels, she asked cautiously, "Everything all right?"

Rian muttered something unintelligible, tugging the cloak further down his face. The heavy fabric spread shadows across his features. His hair might still have been black, but there were more people who would recognize him in the capital, especially with his face plastered on every corner.

"We're good. The place is just around the corner," Laurince said, sweeping past Myra. But before he passed her completely, he squeezed her hand. The touch wasn't long or drawn out. It was quick. A mere pulse. But it was his way of saying it was going to be fine. Laurince might not have been able to read emotions like she could, but he had learned to read her tells quickly.

Turning around the next corner, Laurince halted in front of a building. The sign hanging from the post above the door was worn from time. Squinting at the etched markings where the ink had long-since faded, Myra read the words scrawled across the wood: *The Drunken Dragon.*

Myra tugged on Laurince's arm, stopping him from reaching for the door handle. "I thought we were done with taverns?"

"Don't worry. We're not staying long. I know the owners. We'll be safe here."

She peered at the tavern's opaque windows that were crusted with dirt. She could barely see through them to make out the oil lamps hanging from the ceiling. The faces of the patrons inside were a blur, their silhouettes masked in heavy shadows. She looked over her shoulder at the guests walking down the other side of the street. Further away, a guard surveyed the area, his fingers tapping along the hilt of his longsword that sat at his hip.

"Do you trust me, Haze?" Laurince asked, holding out a hand.

Without hesitation, she grabbed it.

As the door clattered shut behind them, a strike of lightning burst across the sky. Thunder rumbled and sent Myra bumping into Laurince. Several patrons looked over at them, and Rian stared at the ground as he strolled inside behind them.

"Sorry," Myra mumbled to Laurince.

"I thought we were done apologizing for silly things?" Laurince quipped.

Myra's lips parted. But before she could respond, he snatched her hand in his.

"Come on. Let's grab a table. I told him to be on time in my letter, not a minute late." Laurince led them through the tavern.

Only a few oil lamps hanging from the ceilings lit the space, casting dark shadows across the patrons. There was no music or dancing in the half-occupied tavern. They easily snagged an empty table in the back. Laurince pulled out a seat for her, and Myra quickly took it. Laurince took the seat next to her.

Sitting across from them and away from the rest of the patrons, Rian folded his arms on the table and tapped his fingers along the surface.

At a nearby table, a server poured ale into a glass. Once he finished, he turned around to head toward them. When he took them in, he stumbled, ale sloshing over the rim of the pitcher. Laurince went rigid beside her as the server hurried over to them.

"You shouldn't be here," the stranger hissed, glaring at Laurince. The man glanced at Myra and then at Rian. He did a double-take at the king. Rian offered him a tight smile.

Laurince slapped the server on the arm as he went to bow. "Not now," he demanded.

"I told you not to do that anyway, Han," Rian added.

Myra's gaze bounced between the men, trying to figure out their relationship to one another. In the dim lighting, it was hard to get a good look at Han's features, but there was something familiar about him she couldn't quite put her finger on.

"We wouldn't have come if we had any other choice," Laurince said, calling Han's attention away from Rian.

"We've all been worried sick about you," Han said, setting the pitcher on the table.

"They can't know," Laurince urged. "Not yet."

"Not yet? What do you mean not—"

"Cousin, please."

"*Cousin?*" Myra sputtered. She surveyed the man again and nearly gasped. She should have realized it sooner. Laurince and Han shared many of the same features. Their jawlines and dark eyes were clearly a familial trait. Unlike Laurince, though, Han had a dark mustache and a small beard. He appeared to be around the same age as Laurince and Rian, maybe a little older.

Han held out a hand. "Name's Han, and you are…?"

"Myra," she answered, taking his hand.

He offered her a small smile.

"We won't be here long," Laurince explained. "We only needed a place to meet someone, and this was the safest place I could think of."

The muscles in Han's jaw ticked. "If your mother finds out you were here and no one told her, she'll be—"

"Pissed, I know."

"*Pissed?* She'll cut my fuckin' head off."

"She can't know, Han. Not yet. We have to…" Laurince swallowed and rubbed a hand across his face.

"I'm sure I can guess what it is," Han said, eyeing Rian. "Since you've left, things have been different around here."

An eerie prickle ran down the back of Myra's neck, and she straightened, looking around them. A few of the patrons were getting curious. Her gift stirred in the pit of her stomach, but before reaching for the threads, she nudged Laurince. "Order something."

"What?" he asked, blinking down at her, confused.

Rolling her eyes, she said to Han, "Three ales, please."

"But—" Han began before Laurince cut him off.

"You heard the lady. Three ales," he said, finally noticing the curious faces turning toward them. "Actually, make it four."

Han bit down. "Fine," he gritted out. "We're not done here, though." He turned around and walked away.

As Han weaved through the tables and stopped to refill a few empty glasses, Rian leaned forward. "How long are we going to wait?"

"Just a couple more—"

The bell above the door rang. All three of them turned toward it. Beneath the ringing bell walked a broad-chested man walking inside, his head swiveling over the crowd. His hair was cut short, nearly to the scalp. Myra's mouth grew dry as she instantly recognized the newcomer. He might not have been wearing armor, but she knew without a doubt that he was a guard. And he was bee-lining it toward them.

She gripped Laurince's arm, her fingers digging into the muscle as fear wrapped around her throat. "Laurince—"

"He's here."

CHAPTER 46
MYRA

"Am I glad to see you," the stranger said, shaking the rain from his hair.

"It's good to see you, too, Bax," Laurince said, standing to greet the newcomer. He pulled Bax into an embrace, both slapping each other on the back. Myra momentarily wondered if it was some competition to see who could slap the other harder, who could show the other they missed each other more.

When the two pulled apart, Bax looked at Rian. "Your—"

"Sit down, Bax," Laurince urged, holding his hand out to the empty chair beside Rian.

Bax nodded in the king's direction in place of a bow. Rian offered him a polite smile in return, but the stretch of his lips was strained. A river of guilt and remorse poured from Rian, washing over Myra's senses. Since they had arrived in the capital, Rian had grown more tense, his movements more rigid, and his patience thin. Myra could only imagine what it felt like to walk through one's kingdom as a mere ghost, hidden beneath a cloak.

As Bax sat, Laurince shifted, and his hand brushed the side of

Myra's thigh. Instinctively, she relaxed, her shoulders dropping as she let Rian's emotions slip through her fingers like sand.

"Bax, this is Myra; Myra, this is Bax," Laurince said.

"It's nice to meet you," she said.

Bax responded with a polite nod.

Laurince leaned closer to her. "He was one of the men under my command."

"Was?" Bax asked with an arched brow. "Found a replacement for me already?"

Laurince snorted, a half-smile pushing at the corner of his mouth. "I could never replace you, and you know it."

"Oh, do I. Who else would you get to do your grunt work?"

Laurince laughed. "Don't act like I didn't give you your money's worth for those jobs."

Before Bax responded, Han came around and dropped off four pints of ale and a basket of bread. "Anything else I can get you while you're here?"

"You've already done plenty," Laurince said with a sincere expression.

Han tucked the empty serving tray against his side and shifted his weight, as if wanting to say more. But as his gaze slid to the other patrons in the tavern, he simply nodded and returned to the bar.

Bax took a swig of ale. As he brought the cup down, his eyes widened as he looked at Myra again. He leaned forward, ale spilling over the rim of his mug as it smacked the table. "Wait, aren't you—?"

"Yes," Myra said, already knowing what he was going to ask. "Well, I *was* her handmaiden." She took a long sip of her drink.

"*Was?* Is she dead?"

Myra nearly choked on the ale.

"By the gods, Bax," Laurince mumbled, rubbing a hand across his face. He brushed his other hand against Myra's thigh, drawing small circles with his thumb. "She only meant that she isn't her handmaiden anymore."

Myra wiped her mouth. "As far as I know, she's still alive."

"Oh." Bax gave her an apologetic smile.

Laurince bumped her knee with his. "She's all right," he reassured quietly.

Myra nodded. She had to believe Kallie was safe. Right now, she couldn't afford to think otherwise.

"Can we get to the point of this little meeting?" Rian asked, tapping his fingers along the side of his untouched drink.

Laurince scooted toward the edge of his seat, the serious captain returning in an instant. "What's the status inside?"

Bax ran his fingers through his short, sandy brown hair and grimaced. "How much time do we have?"

"Not much, so make it quick," Laurince said.

Bax nodded and began. "Since you've left, groups of soldiers have been disappearing left and right. None of us knows where they've gone. Sebastian's been running a tight ship, and the men in his favor are keeping their lips sealed shut."

"Of course they are," Rian mumbled.

"Money and security is all it takes for some to switch their loyalties," Laurince mused.

Myra nodded in agreement. For her, security and safety were the main reasons she had stayed silent for all those years. She now understood the actual cost of her compliance.

"Some are probably getting some money, but I don't know. Sebastian's been strategic. He knows which soldiers he can lead astray and pull to his side. At first, many of us believed the lies he was spewing, the kidnapping and treachery. However, lately, he's become more vocal about his opinions on how to rule and the direction the kingdom will turn in the coming months. King Domitius has been around more frequently, and if he's not here, then Sebastian's visiting him. But something feels off. He's been sending troops to villages, raiding homes, and dragging civilians back to the castle for interrogation."

"Domitius and Sebastian have declared war," Laurince whispered. "Raids and interrogations are unsurprising, unfortunately."

"They've been bringing *children*, Laurince," Bax said, his knuckles turning white as he gripped the mug. "Sebastian claims a group of traitors who sought to hurt the Crown led the attack the day of the wedding. He says he has it on good authority that the people who had attacked were not working alone. He has ordered a kingdom-wide search of civilians' homes to snuff out anyone who holds any ill-will to the Crown. Men and women, old and young—it does not matter. Dozens upon dozens of people have been taken. Some have returned after having been deemed loyal, but others remain missing. Children have been ripped from their parents. Some children have been left abandoned and forced to live on the streets." Bax shook his head, and color flooded his cheeks in anger. "It's not right."

"You said soldiers were disappearing?" Myra asked, feeling sick.

Bax nodded.

She looked at Laurince and Rian. "Do you think…?"

"It's possible," Laurince said, rubbing his jaw.

"What's possible?" Bax asked.

Laurince glanced at Myra. She understood Laurince's hesitancy. Few would believe the truth about the experiments if they hadn't seen it themselves. But if they wanted to take back Rian's throne, they needed people on their side.

"Tell him," Rian ordered, spinning his mug between his hands. "The people deserve to know who they are following."

"YOU HAVEN'T SAID a single word, Bax. Spit it out already," Laurince said, leaning back in his chair.

They had finished telling Bax everything they knew. Or almost everything. Laurince primarily focused on the drakonis experiments, leaving out the fact that some people, like Myra, harbored unique abilities. She hadn't expected Laurince to sway away from that or hide it from Bax, but she appreciated him not relaying something as private as her gift to another without her consent. Even without the knowledge of the powers, the drakonises were already hard to wrap one's mind around.

Bax grabbed the pint and took a small sip. His throat dipped as he swallowed, and apprehension seeped from his pores. He scooted closer to the table and glanced at Rian. "You truly did not know about any of this before?"

Rian shifted in his seat uncomfortably, but didn't retreat. "I will not lie to you. A day or two before the wedding, Sebastian presented one of his experiments to me as an early wedding gift of sorts. I should have known then that his intentions were not pure. I should have asked more questions."

"Why didn't you?" Bax asked, his voice taking on a sharp edge.

With creased brows, Laurince moved to speak, but Rian held up his hand, halting the captain.

"I do not admit my failure lightly," Rian stated. "For a long time, I was sick with grief after my father's passing, but that is not an excuse. I had a duty to protect this kingdom, to protect you all, and I failed every single one of you. Because of my mistakes, many of those I care about have been injured or put under a needle against their will. *I* have been under that needle." Rian's throat dipped as he glanced at Laurince. The two exchanged a look before Rian continued. "I aim to make that right. Sebastian is no king, and he must be dealt with."

"That's going to be harder than you think. He has turned many of the guards to his side," Bax said, looking nervous.

"Which is surprising. No one even liked him before he was on the throne," Laurince mused.

Bax shrugged. "Money and power, Lo."

Laurince hummed in agreement.

"He's your brother, though. What if it comes to the worst?" Bax asked after a moment.

Rian cracked his knuckles. "After what he's done to our kingdom, after he attacked our brothers and sisters, our elders and children, he is no brother of mine."

Bax massaged his jaw, a tense expression passing across his features. But when his hand dropped from his face, he leaned forward, resolute. "What do you need me to do?"

Laurince gave him a wicked smile. "How do you feel about staging a coup?"

CHAPTER 47

GRAESON

As Graeson lay on the small bed, he heard the patter of light footsteps across the creaking floorboards outside. The hinges of an old door screeched open and clicked shut. He pressed the heels of his palms against his eyes, and white splotches filled his vision.

"Want to talk about it?" Moris asked from the second bed.

"Talk about what?" Graeson asked, digging his fingers into his hair.

"Her, you. Whatever," Moris said, casually flicking his hand in the air. As if any of those things were casual.

Graeson turned to his side. "No. Go to sleep."

"I was just offering."

"Well, don't."

"I didn't think it was possible for you to get even broodier. I would have thought after saving her, you would have been more tolerable. I guess I was wrong."

Graeson groaned. He had forgotten how nosy Moris was. "I just said I didn't want to talk about it."

"*And* you don't have to. I was just thinking out loud."

"Maybe don't," Graeson grumbled. He was rethinking these

sleeping arrangements. He would have preferred sleeping in the stables with the horses and Nyrri. At least they wouldn't pry into his business.

"Fine." Moris' bed creaked from his weight as he shifted. Releasing a heavy sigh, he broke the brief silence. "You're lucky your wings disappear."

"You're lucky your bones don't break every time you shift in order to gain them," Graeson retorted.

Moris snorted a laugh. "I suppose that's true."

The quiet returned, and Graeson sank into it. Before he could get comfortable, though, Moris spoke again.

"Have you tried transforming again?"

"It's none of your business." Graeson pressed the sides of his pillow against his ears, hoping to drown out the conversation.

It didn't work.

"So you haven't then."

"No," Graeson admitted, letting the pillow flatten. He peered into the darkness that spilled over the room. Graeson had cracked the window before getting into bed, and the slight breeze was a welcome reprieve. It brushed over his skin and cooled his rising temperature. Graeson had always run cold. But ever since he transformed, his skin was hotter than normal, and his temperature was harder to regulate.

"Will you?" Moris asked.

"Will I what?"

"Try to shift?"

Flashes of the fire raking through the forest sent a chill down Graeson's spine. He had always known he was dangerous. Many people in Pontia already feared him because of what he could do before. What would the people think of him when they learned he could become a dragon? If he transformed again, there would be no hiding it. Word would spread. But could he prevent the transformation?

Did he want to if it would help them defeat Sebastian and his army?

"I'm not sure I have a say in the matter. The first time was involuntary," he confessed after a moment. "I'm sure it's bound to happen again, whether or not I want it to."

"Dani is going to freak out when she finds out."

"She'll freak out when she discovers you're still alive," Graeson retorted. "Both she and Sylvia were a wreck after they found out you sacrificed yourself."

Moris sighed. "There was no other choice. You and Terin needed to go after Domitius and Dani. I did what had to be done."

"I would have done the same thing if it was me," Graeson admitted. "Still, I'm sorry it was you. And I'm even more sorry for everything you have been through since then."

"It's…"

"Not okay," Graeson said when Moris struggled to finish.

"It's not, but the blame doesn't rest on your shoulders, Gray."

"I was the one who brought you here."

"And I agreed to come. The blame is on Domitius and Sebastian. You've gotten rid of one. We just have to get rid of the other."

"You say that as if you are laying claim to Sebastian's head," Graeson mused.

"I suppose I am. It's the least I can do after what went down the other day," Moris said, his voice filled with guilt.

Graeson snorted. "Good luck with that. Even if Dani's pregnant, I would wager that she'll still find a way to cut off that bastard's head."

The other bed creaked. "Dani's pregnant?"

Graeson rolled over onto his back. "Yes."

"Fuck," Moris breathed out. "That's why she was sick, wasn't it?"

"Yes. She tried to hide it. She didn't want the rest of us to treat her differently or to count her out because of the pregnancy. Terin's been acting like a mother hen ever since, though."

"Oh, boy," Moris muttered. "It's got to be worse now that she's home. Her parents probably aren't letting her out of their sight."

Graeson chuckled. Dani's mother was probably over the moon that Dani was pregnant. Sorinia loved all her grandchildren. He could already imagine the fight that would break out between the pair when Terin and the others returned and Dani demanded to fight. The entire kingdom would fight for Dani to stay behind. She wasn't just carrying a child; she was carrying Fynn's child, the future of Pontia.

But if Graeson knew Dani, she would find a way to be on that battlefield.

THE NEXT MORNING, Graeson awoke before the others. He made his way down the creaking steps and wandered outside the farmhouse. The crisp morning air bit his fingertips, and he welcomed the cool air on his scorching skin. He headed toward the stable and found Nyrri sleeping on the ground, her body half outside the stall.

He leaned against the opening. As the wood groaned from his weight, Nyrri peered at him through heavy eyes. She huffed, and a puff of air billowed from her nose in the cold. She hated confined spaces as much as he did.

"Soon, girl," he promised.

Nyrri whined and plopped her head back down.

Graeson pushed off the post and made his way toward the fields, needing to stretch his legs. His body was less sore than the day before, and his muscles begged to be moved.

The cornfields were nothing but tall dried husks, and he

wandered through them. The dried vegetation rustled as the wind swept across the field, and leaves brushed against his cloak, catching on the wool fibers.

He walked for a while, his thoughts a dull buzz. When the house was no more than a blip behind him, he stopped and stared at the sky. The sun was rising, the night sky melting away and turning into a brilliant combination of purple and orange hues.

Closing his eyes, he inhaled, the cold air a relief in his lungs. When he exhaled, a puff of smoke slipped from his mouth. His fingers buzzed, and his back twitched. He rolled his shoulders, trying to shake the sensation spreading across his skin. He could almost feel where the wings would sprout, the exact places where the bones would break and his body would contort into a new shape.

You must become the reckoning the kingdoms need.

With a shudder, Graeson opened his eyes.

The sky was expansive and endless. A part of him yearned to see how far it would go. How long would it take him to reach the end? Until he reached the stars? Once he reached them, could his fire burn a pathway to the world of the gods?

He wondered if there were others like him. Although Barinthian hadn't mentioned others, Graeson was not so egotistical as to believe that he was unique enough to be the only demi-god alive. Were the others in hiding? Or was the beast that lived within them waiting for the moment to come out?

As Graeson stood there, thoughts of his mother came flooding in, and he finally released the emotions he had been harboring.

CHAPTER 48
MYRA

"Are you sure we're in the right spot?" Myra asked when they reached a dead end of a dark alley after having parted ways with Bax. The buildings were so close together on this side of the capital that the opposing brick walls were only a few yards apart.

"Yes," Laurince said as he began rifling through the trash and pushing various items to the side.

The plan was simple. Since several squadrons of soldiers were assisting with raids throughout the kingdom, castle security was lighter than usual. Bax mentioned that a guard had raised concerns about their thin numbers, but Sebastian had brushed it off. Apparently, the sitting ruler believed he was untouchable within the castle. Now was the best time to act. Bax went to the castle ahead of them to inform some trusted guards about their plan to reclaim the throne, while Myra, Laurince, and Rian came here.

Surveying the dim alley, Myra questioned their supposedly simple plan.

The storm had yet to let up. Their cloaks were soaked, Myra's shoes were drenched, and her socks were soon to follow.

"Can you at least tell us what we're looking for?" Rian asked, grimacing as he stepped in a massive puddle and soaked the toes of his boots.

"It's—" Laurince ran his palm along a brick wall. "It's here somewhere. Just—A-ha!" He sprinted to a bin and shoved it away. Bending down, he ran his fingers around the sewer drain, scraping at the edges to find purchase. The metal was slick from the storm, though, and he struggled to pull it up. "Give me a hand?"

With a groan, Rian hurried over, and the two lifted the grate up and heaved it aside.

"Please don't tell me we're going down into the sewer," Myra said, her voice raising an octave as she leaned forward. Inside the sewer, nothing but darkness greeted her. She sniffed, expecting a rancid smell, but the storm must have hidden the sewer's scent. How far was the drop? Would the current sweep them away?

Laurince gave her an apologetic smile. "That's the plan."

For whatever reason, Myra had not been privy to this part of the plan, though. She sent a quick prayer to the gods.

"Your Majesty, will you do us the honor?" Laurince asked, ushering Rian forward.

"Oh, so now I get to lead," Rian retorted, stepping forward. He sat down on the wet ground, and his feet dangled over the ledge.

"For a second at least," Laurince said.

"Bax better come through or else this will be for nothing," Rian grumbled.

"He will," Laurince said. "He should already be inside the castle and gathering the others."

Rian arched his brows, a hint of disbelief wafting off him. "See you both down there," he said before pushing off and jumping. A second later, there was a loud smack as Rian hit the ground.

"It's dark as shit down here," Rian called up, his voice echoing in the tunnel.

Myra's stomach turned as Laurince offered his hand. Taking it, Myra hesitantly stepped closer and peered into the sewer.

"Scared of the dark, Haze?"

It was meant to be a jest, but as Myra stared into the shadows filling the sewer, her body trembled. The darkness instantly transported her to the cell in Ardentol. Screams of prisoners and victims echoed in her ears, as though they had followed her all the way here. The grief, pain, and agony of the past mingled with that of the streets of Frenzia. The emotions overwhelmed her, flooding her senses.

Calloused hands cupped her cheeks. "Hey," Laurince beckoned, suddenly in front of her. "He holds no power over you, remember?"

Myra gulped. Her gaze bounced across Laurince's face, trying to ground herself in the present.

"You don't have to go. Staying back doesn't make you weak. It doesn't mean he won. You can—"

"No," Myra interrupted with a shake of her head. She wasn't in a cell. She wasn't trapped. She refused to let Domitius get to her. He wasn't here in Frenzia. If all had gone according to plan, Kallie had already dealt with him.

Her pinky brushed against the knife tucked in her pocket. She wasn't defenseless anymore. "I'm going."

Laurince swept his thumbs across the sides of her face. "That's my girl."

As his dark brown eyes danced across her face and a million concerns spun in her mind, Myra stopped thinking. She stopped waiting. She reached up, grabbed him by the shirt, stood on her toes, and kissed him.

For a moment, Laurince was frozen, his lips unmoving. But then, just as quickly, he leaned into her. His hand slipped to the back of her neck, and he deepened the kiss.

His lips were sweet and soft and so at odds with the chest muscles beneath her palms. She could taste the faint trace of ale on his lips mixed with the rain. And she cursed herself for waiting this long to taste them, to feel their heat against hers. As she melted against Laurince, everything else disappeared. All her worries and concerns. All the fears. But nothing this good could last forever.

A whistle sounded from the sewer, ending the moment.

With a small sigh against her mouth, Laurince pulled away. He rested his forehead against hers. His breathing was labored and matched her own, and she wondered how they could have been so out of breath from such a brief kiss. As short as it was, though, it rivaled all the other kisses she had experienced in her lifetime.

"We should probably get going," he whispered.

"You're probably right," Myra said, voice breathy. "Maybe not the best time to "

"There's never a bad time for that, Haze," Laurince said, interrupting her. His touch softened. "I'm just sorry for not having done it sooner."

Myra pursed her lips, but for once, she didn't care that her cheeks turned pink. She smirked as she looked at him, noting the raindrops running down his cheek. "Who's the one apologizing now?"

Laurince laughed and pressed a quick kiss to her forehead and stepped back, hand outstretched. "I'll be down right after you," he reassured her, squeezing her hand when she took it.

Myra sat on the cold ground and shimmied across the wet stone. With her feet dangling over the edge of the sewer, she released Laurince's hand, then rolled onto her stomach. The ledge dug into her ribcage as she took a deep breath.

Then she fell into the void.

MYRA EXPECTED to land in a pool of water. Instead, her feet hit a small puddle. The hard drop sent a vibration soaring through her limbs, and she stumbled backward, bumping into whom she could only hope was Rian.

"You all right?" Rian asked, steadying her.

Her ankle stung, but luckily she didn't think she had sprained it. "Yes, I think—"

Rian yanked her as a shadow fell over them. A *whoosh* of air whipped across her face, blowing her hair back.

"Everyone good?" Laurince asked once his feet hit the ground.

Myra nodded, but when she realized he couldn't see it in the darkness, she responded, "Yes."

Boots slapped against puddles, sending water kissing her ankles. She reached out, searching for a wall to guide her. She hit something solid. A hand grabbed hers.

"There you are," Laurince whispered, finding Myra even in the dark. He lifted her hand and pressed a soft kiss on the top of her knuckles.

Rian cleared his throat. "I might not *see* you, but I can hear you. You're panting more than a dog, Laurince."

"Oh, shut it," Laurince said, twisting them around toward Rian's voice. Then he said, "Wring out your cloaks as best you can."

Myra peeled off her cloak and twisted it, draining the water from the fabric. As she put it back on, shuffling sounded beside them.

"It's fucking dark down here," Rian said. "How are we going to—"

A spark burst to life as Laurince struck a match and pulled a small torch from inside his cloak. The glow of the fire cast an eerie light across Laurince's features, but Myra had never been more thankful for the flame.

"Well, that solves that," Rian said. "Now, which way are we—"

"This way," Laurince answered, weaving his fingers between Myra's and pulling her behind him.

"I guess I'll stop asking questions, then," Rian mumbled.

"Probably for the best," Laurince mused.

The flames bounced off the rounded walls of the sewer, and moisture glistened across the stone. But beyond a thin puddle that spread across the floor from the rain, there was no sign of water damage along the walls. Even the smell was better than she had imagined it would be.

"I thought this was a sewer," Myra said.

"It was supposed to be, but an engineer messed up the plans and didn't connect it to the main sewage line," Laurince explained with a shrug.

"How did I not know about a tunnel that runs directly to my castle? And why didn't you tell me?" Rian asked, glaring at Laurince.

"There are a lot of things you don't know about your own castle and kingdom, remember?" Laurince arched a brow at him. "After all, you didn't know about the experiments happening in the other tunnels."

"At least I knew those tunnels existed."

"But you never went to scope them out, did you?"

"Neither did you," Rian spat.

"Does anyone else know about these tunnels?" Myra asked, diverting the conversation as she nervously scanned the shadows ahead. Thick spiderwebs hung from the ceiling, and she did her best not to look at them too closely. She hated spiders.

Laurince shook his head. "Not that I'm aware. I accidentally discovered this tunnel when I was studying the layout of the castle. Some maps had slight differences around the location of the sewers, and I started digging into it. It took a long time to figure out."

"What's to say no one else knows, then?" Myra asked. "If you found out, then others most likely have, too."

"Are you questioning my ability to uncover something no one else has?" Laurince asked, looking over his shoulder and smirking at her.

"No, I just…I don't want to be caught surprised."

"Well, let us hope Laurince is as special as he thinks he is," Rian said behind her.

They made their way through the tunnels, the glowing light of the torch guiding them. Their soft breaths and footsteps on the concrete were the only sounds that broke up the silence. As they headed further into the tunnel, the air became tenser. Based on the eeriness seeping in through the ceilings and dripping onto the floors, Myra knew instinctively that they were nearing the castle. When she first visited Frenzia, she didn't know why paranoia and fear gripped her throat when she would wander the halls. Now she knew all too well what horrors were taking place underneath their feet. The atrocities and secrets that had been occurring without Rian's knowledge. She thought of the animals in the cages. Their thrashing and screeches were an incessant echo in the back of her mind as they continued.

She only hoped that Laurince was right and that this tunnel didn't connect to the others.

"We're getting closer, aren't we?" Rian asked.

"I think so," Laurince said. "Once we're inside, we stick to the plan. This should take us near the west wing. Bax will meet us in his room."

Soon, the light hit a wall.

"Great," Rian said with a disgruntled grunt. "It's a dead end."

"Haze, will you hold this for a second?" Laurince held out the torch.

Myra took it and held it up for Laurince as he swiped his hand across the wall. He pressed his palms against a brick. Then something clicked.

"Ready?" Laurince asked, glancing back at Rian and Myra.

They both nodded.

"Put the fire out," he instructed, and Myra only hesitated for a second before dousing them in darkness.

CHAPTER 49

GRAESON

By the time Graeson was making his way back to the farmhouse, voices floated through the air.

"Come on. Is that all you've got?" Ellie asked.

He didn't hear the response, but he could hear some grunting and gravel shifting. He started running.

Had the soldiers come after them? Had—

He skidded to a stop as he rounded the corner of the house. To his relief, there was no attack. Instead, Ellie and Kalisandre stood in the front yard of the farmhouse, both panting.

Graeson leaned against the side of the house, crossing his arms over his chest. His cloak hung over his arm. It was high-noon, and the day had quickly warmed up.

Kalisandre wiped the sweat from her forehead. Gritting her teeth, she charged at Ellie. Kalisandre swung, her fist slicing through the air. Ellie swatted it away as if it was no more than a fly buzzing around her face. Kalisandre groaned, but she didn't let up. She quickly adjusted her stance and swung again. Ellie, predictably, dodged it. But Kalisandre had learned from her mistakes and already had a secondary maneuver lined up. She dropped to the ground and swept her leg across the earth, sending dirt flying and Ellie crashing to the ground as she struck.

Graeson smirked as Ellie let out a curse.

"Nice one," Menz shouted from the gardening bed, pausing his work to watch the two women spar.

"Good job," Ellie grumbled, pushing herself onto her elbows.

Grinning with pride, Kalisandre stood. But her adrenaline was gone. She mistakenly leaned her weight on her wounded leg and hissed out, grabbing her hamstring.

Graeson was there before he had even realized he was moving. "Are you all right?" he asked, panicked.

"I—yes," she stammered, eyes wide. "I'm fine." But when she straightened, she grimaced again and nearly collapsed.

Graeson caught her by the waist. "Maybe we should check on that wound, yeah?"

Kalisandre waved him off, and Graeson frowned. If she wanted to fight in whatever battle came next, she needed to heal first.

"You should be resting," he said for what was likely the one-hundredth time.

"We rested yesterday."

Graeson arched a brow. "I would hardly call the journey here a day of rest."

"Sebastian's not resting."

Graeson ran a hand through his hair. "That doesn't mean you need to push yourself to the point where you can't even walk."

"I can walk just fine," she snapped, stepping away from him. Kalisandre took one, two, three steps before her knee gave out. She released a groan of frustration.

Graeson crossed his arms. "You were saying, little mouse?"

She shoved him in the chest. But a small smile pushed at the corner of her lips, one she tried and failed to hide. "Fine, maybe it still hurts."

"When was the last time you changed the wrapping?"

"Last night."

Graeson hummed. "You should probably check to see if the stitches opened."

Kalisandre straightened, favoring her good leg. She pushed her fingers through her hair and sighed. "Fine," she grumbled. "Ellie, do you mind?"

"Not at all. I'm kind of famished, anyway. A break sounds good to me."

Graeson looked between the women, aghast. "A *break*? I thought you were going to rest."

Both women shrugged, and Ellie said, "If her stitches are fine, I don't see why we can't continue."

A retort was on Graeson's tongue, but Kalisandre nudged him, calling his attention to her before he could voice it.

"Will you help me? It's a hard spot to see," she asked, almost bashfully.

Graeson blinked, and his lips parted. "Sure, of course."

Kalisandre nodded and hobbled toward the house. Graeson, still stunned, stared after her for a moment before he shook himself from his stupor and followed.

GRAESON, simple man that he was, was transfixed as Kalisandre peeled her loose trousers over her knee and tugged the pant leg past her thigh. With each inch of skin she revealed, his heart pounded harder and harder. It was only her leg, yet he stood there dumbfounded all the same.

The last time they were alone together was in the forest when he had told her about his father. Something had changed that day between them. Neither of them had spoken about it, and Graeson was afraid to bring it up. It was still too new.

There were so many things he wanted to say to her—there always were. But he struggled to speak, the words stuck in his throat. More than anything else, he was surprised she had asked him to help her. He was trying hard not to dwell on it or figure out what it meant, but it was harder than he cared to admit.

Kalisandre cleared her throat. "Can you—?"

"Oh, of course," Graeson mumbled, dropping to his knees behind her. He reached for the cotton wrapping and placed his other hand above her knee to hold her in place.

The moment his palm touched her skin, Kalisandre gasped. Graeson struggled to keep his attention focused on the task.

He swallowed hard.

Blinking away the haze that filled his vision and the emotions that stirred within him, Graeson unpeeled the bandage, being careful not to put too much pressure on the wound in case it was still sore. Once unraveled, he let the fabric fall to the ground.

"How does it look?" Kalisandre looked over her shoulder, struggling to see the wound.

Graeson brushed his thumb lightly across the bruised skin. The skin around the wound was a little red and a little warmer than the rest of her leg, but there didn't appear to be an infection. "It looks good," he said, his voice thick.

"What's wrong then?"

"Hmm?" he hummed, peeling his gaze away from the wound.

"You look upset. Did the stitches come undone? Ellie said she knew how to sew up a wound, but maybe she was lying."

"No, no," Graeson said, shaking his head. "The stitches look fine. None of them have ripped, either."

"Then what is it—*oh*." Kalisandre turned to face him, causing Graeson's hands to fall limp in his lap. She tipped his chin up with her hand, her thumb brushing against the faint scruff that colored his jawline. "It's only a small wound, Gray."

He stared up at her, speechless. How did she know where his thoughts had gone?

"It's *not* your fault."

"But—"

"No," she interrupted, shaking her head. "You do not get to take the blame for this."

"I could have lost you," he said, voice shaking.

"But you didn't." She pressed her other hand to his face, cocooning either side of him.

He squeezed his eyes shut as she dug her fingers through his hair. Her touch was a comfort he hadn't realized he had missed until that moment. His forehead kissed her bare thigh, and he took a shaky breath. He let the scent of lilac and sweat calm him.

"We both have a habit of taking on too much, of bearing the weight of too many," she said, her words gentle. "We need to stop. If we have any hope of facing Sebastian and his army, we need to keep our heads clear. Got it?"

"I'm not sure I know how to do that."

"Then we can learn together, yeah?" she said with a small smile.

His gaze bounced between her sea-blue eyes, their depth drawing him in. His breaths became shorter. He could see the quick rise and fall of her chest, the tension in the room tightening.

She tugged at the hair at the base of his head, tipping his head further back. "Graeson."

His name was a plea on her lips. Didn't she remember what that did to him? The effect she had on him when—

Fuck.

Graeson groaned and closed his eyes as she bit her bottom lip. This woman would be the end of him.

Then again, he wouldn't want it any other way.

When he opened his eyes and a slight gasp slipped from her lips, he knew she could see the beast within him, the dragon that lived inside him, begging to come out. He brushed his knuckles along the side of her calves as he made his way up her legs. Goosebumps peppered her skin in the wake of his touch.

"We shouldn't," he warned, pressing a light kiss to her thigh, his gaze never leaving hers.

Her lashes fluttered across the tops of her cheeks. "You're right, but…"

"But?" he prompted, his exploration stopping and his hands halting right above the backs of her knees.

She smirked down at him. "But I—"

A crash sounded from the door. They both jerked around and snatched their hands away from each other.

"Shit, I—I'm sorry," Moris blurted as he crouched and picked up the pieces of a shattered bowl. "I didn't know you two were…were doing whatever it is you were doing." His wings smacked into the wall as he reached for a ceramic shard.

"You're fine. We were just—" Kalisandre hesitated, a blush heating her cheeks in the most delectable way.

Graeson cleared his throat. "I was helping her with the wrapping."

"Of course, of course. That's exactly what it looked like, not something else," Moris said, gathering the remaining shards and standing. "Maybe you should just," he cleared his throat, "do that in a more private place than the living room? We wouldn't want the old man to see." Moris scurried out of the room. The sharp *tink* of shards bouncing on the ground echoed down the hall, followed by a whispered curse.

Graeson shook his head and leaned onto his heels. He returned his attention to Kalisandre.

She had buried her face in her hands, and through her fingers, she mumbled, "By the gods."

Graeson tried to hide his amusement. He was not easily embarrassed. He had thought Kalisandre wasn't either, but the current situation was proving otherwise.

"Want me to re-wrap this?"

"Please," she said with a nod. She peered through her fingers. "And quickly. Menz will kill us if more dishes break."

CHAPTER 50
MYRA

Myra had forgotten how dark and cold the Frenzian castle was because of the lack of windows. Scattered candles lit the quiet halls, casting an eerie glow across the floors. As her gaze swept over the stone walls, she missed the beautiful stained glass of Tetria. Silently, they crept down the hall.

When the heavy rhythm of footfalls sounded around the corner, Laurince pulled them into a nearby alcove. The tight fit was snug for the three of them, but they slipped inside it. Myra tried not to think about who she was touching—or possibly *what* she was touching. With no room to move, there was no point in worrying about it. Laurince's breath was warm on her neck, his exhales blowing gently across the tip of her head and sending stray strands of blonde hair flitting in the air. A piece stuck to her mouth. She tried to blow it away, but the sound felt like a thunderous crack in the silence as they waited for whoever it was to pass.

The footsteps paused, and Myra wasn't sure if any of them were breathing anymore.

Sweat dribbled down her back, soaking the top of her shirt. Steeling her nerves and forgetting the annoying strand of hair,

Myra reached out and grabbed the unfamiliar loose thread twisting in the air. Suspicion laced the string of emotions. With a deep breath, she squashed it as if it was a bug.

The steps continued down the hall, passing the hallway they were hiding in. When the steps faded in the distance, they all sagged in relief, exhaling simultaneously.

"Nice work, Haze," Laurince whispered in her ear as they filed out of the alcove.

With her power dancing at her fingertips, Myra beamed at the praise.

Laurince grabbed Myra's hand and pulled her forward, leading them in the opposite direction of the stranger.

As Myra followed him, the corners of her mouth turned down when a strange feeling washed over her. Laurince and Rian's emotions spun around her, and she tried to push past them. Goosebumps scaled her skin as she dug deeper. She choked on a gasp and reached out to warn the others, but she was a moment too late.

"Laurince?"

The captain skidded to a stop at the sound of the feminine voice, and Myra crashed into him. His hand slipped from hers as he turned and faced the woman who had snuck up behind them.

"Ferencia?" Laurince called out.

The woman lifted the candle she held, casting its flames toward them.

"It *is* you," she gasped, pressing her hand to her chest. "You disappeared, and I thought—" The woman swallowed, her eyes flicking to the spot where Laurince and Myra's hands were previously intertwined.

Myra reached for the woman's emotions, and waves crashed into her, one after another. The woman's emotions were so tangled,

Myra struggled to parse them. Notes of longing and sadness and fear dripped from the thread.

"We had some things to take care of," Laurince said, his voice strained with discomfort.

Myra could have sworn he shifted away from her. She was tempted to read his emotions, but stopped when Ferencia's attention turned to Rian.

Ferencia blinked several times before gasping and falling into a curtsy. "Your Majesty, y-you're back."

Laurince's eyes widened as he realized his mistake, but it was too late.

"Oh," Ferencia exclaimed, eyeing their appearances and the dark cloaks draped over their shoulders. She glanced down the hallway and at the trail of water left in their wake. "If the guards see you..." Her words trailed off. She nibbled her nails, anxiety pouring out of her. "We have to go," she demanded, spinning on her heels.

After a few steps, she must have noticed no one followed her because she looked back. "Well, come on. Are you simply going to stand there and let them catch you?"

"This is *my* castle," Rian argued.

"Not anymore."

Rian flinched as Ferencia's words struck him in the chest.

Myra glanced at Laurince, questioning what they should do. But it seemed their choice was being made for them as several pairs of steps sounded. A belly-deep laugh ricocheted off the walls and sent a chill down Myra's spine. The side of her hand brushed against the small blade pressed against her thigh. There was no time.

Myra turned to Laurince and spoke so only he could hear, "Do you trust her?"

"Uhm..." Laurince glanced at Ferencia, who stood wringing her hands together nervously. When he returned his attention to Myra and Rian, Laurince nodded. "Yes, I do."

"Then let's go," Myra said, ushering the captain forward.

"At least one of you is sensible," Ferencia said, peering past them and checking the hall. "This way."

One after another, they followed Ferencia through the halls. As Myra oriented herself in the castle, she soon realized the woman was taking them to the southwest corridor. Fear laced Myra's throat as she recalled several important figures staying on this side of the castle.

"Isn't this where—"

"Shhh," Ferencia hushed, immediately silencing Myra. She turned down another hall, then stopped at a door.

Myra's brows bunched together. But when she glanced at the two men, neither of them seemed as concerned as she about their location. If a lord or lady saw them, word would spread like wildfire, quickly falling to Sebastian's ears.

Myra leaned closer, popping her head between Ferencia and Laurince. "Whose room is this?" she whispered as Ferencia pushed the door open and ushered them inside.

"Mine," Ferencia said just as Laurince answered, "Hers."

Myra's heart stuttered as Laurince swiftly entered the room and tossed his wet cloak on the coat rack without a glance, as if it was his own room. He wiped the dirt off the soles of his boots on a quaint pink rug, and Ferencia smiled warmly at him.

Were they—had they—?

Myra jumped as the door locked shut behind her.

Laurince cast an inquisitive look in her direction. "Myra, is everything all right?"

"Mhm," she hummed, hurrying out of Rian's way as he tried to slip past her.

Myra. Not Haze or Mys. Laurince rarely called her by her actual name. She was probably only paranoid, yet she couldn't shake the jealousy and strangeness that covered her skin.

Laurince unbuckled his sword and sat it on the table. He pulled a wooden chair out and sat on it backwards, his arms resting over the back. He looked like he belonged there. It was almost as if Ferencia had chosen the purple curtains purposefully to accentuate the warmth in his deep brown eyes.

Rian whispered something in Laurince's ear.

"It's fine," Laurince responded, batting him away.

Rian groaned and yanked his cloak off. Tossing it over an empty chair, he rubbed a hand across his hair.

"The black hair suits you, Your Highness," Ferencia said as she rested her hip on an elegant vanity table that sat beneath a large silver mirror framed with rubies.

Myra quickly averted her gaze, not wanting to witness her frazzled state in the reflection. Especially not with Ferencia standing there, her hair falling in perfect ringlets, wearing a satin dress that miraculously bore no wrinkles.

"Thanks," Rian mumbled.

Myra fiddled with the buttons on the top of her cloak. She couldn't tell whether she was hot or cold. Either way, the wool was suddenly uncomfortable and irritated her skin. She began undoing the buttons. It should have been a simple task, something that was mindless, yet helped distract her from the awkwardness that hung in the air. However, it was taking her far too long to undo them. The others must have noticed, too, because she could feel their eyes on her. When she finally undid the last button, she hung it up beside Laurince's and turned, facing her next predicament. She wasn't sure if she should sit or stand. She felt out of place here, uncomfortable even among friends.

When Myra looked at Laurince, he tipped his head to the seat beside him, and Myra plopped down in the chair. As the others exchanged awkward pleasantries, Myra rubbed her hands across her arms, regretting having taken the cloak off. At least it had provided some layer of protection.

"Do you need something for that?"

Myra snapped her attention to Ferencia. "Pardon?"

Ferencia arched a brow and pointed. Following her gaze, Myra found her sleeves were up to her elbows, revealing patchy red skin. Her cheeks flamed in embarrassment and horror, which only made the redness on her arms worse.

"If it's infectious, you probably should not be so close to others, no?" Ferencia asked, glancing at Laurince sitting only a foot away from Myra.

"Oh, I—" Myra struggled to speak, her tongue suddenly feeling thick in her mouth.

Could one be allergic to embarrassment? If so, then she most definitely was.

She made to stand, but a large hand grabbed her thigh.

"Leave her alone, Ferencia," Laurince demanded, removing his hand from Myra's thigh only once she settled back into the seat.

"I'm only looking out for you, Lo." The bitter tang of annoyance and frustration slipped into the air as Ferencia narrowed her gaze at the captain. "But you never were good at listening to me, were you?"

"If this is going to be a problem, we can leave," Laurince said, his jaw popping. He began to stand. "On second thought, this was a bad idea. We should go."

Ferencia's shoulders dropped, her eyes widening. "Wait, no. I'm sorry," she sputtered as she ran her palm down the front of her dress, smoothing out the fabric. "It's been a little tense around here. I didn't mean—" She swallowed and looked at Myra. "I'm sorry if what I said was offensive."

A pang of jealousy hung in the space between the women.

"It's fine, really," Myra said, tugging the sleeves of her shirt down.

Her gaze swept across the room. A pile of pointe shoes sat in the corner. Then she noted the way Laurince sat comfortably in the chair, how he didn't look around the room to take it all in like he normally did when entering an unfamiliar place, his casual tone with Ferencia.

Myra's lips parted.

Ferencia had to be the dance instructor's daughter. The one Laurince had a crush on growing up. How long ago was that crush? Had he gotten over it?

"Your brother will not be happy to see you, Your Majesty," Ferencia said, changing the topic.

"Is that so?" Rian asked, his tone taking on a sharp edge.

"We all know Sebastian is not one to hide his feelings. He's grown quite comfortable on that throne," Ferencia explained.

"You mean *my* throne," Rian said through clenched teeth.

Ferencia nibbled on her thumbnail but quickly removed it when her eyes met Myra's. "This conversation would be much easier over some brandy, don't you think?" she asked, strolling toward a side table. "I believe I still have your favorite, Laurince."

"Fine," Laurince mumbled, raking a hand through his hair.

Myra tried—and failed—not to think about why Ferencia had Laurince's favorite brandy. Myra didn't even *know* his favorite brandy, let alone that he even liked the alcohol.

Ferencia grabbed the decanter and peered into it. "Hmm," she hummed, shaking the bottle. "We seem to be out. Let me run and grab some."

"That's really unnecessary," Laurince argued.

"Oh, nonsense. I'll just be a moment," she said, heading for the door.

"But—"

Ferencia was already gone, though, the door clicking shut behind her.

Laurince sank back into his chair. "Stubborn woman," he muttered.

"She always was," Rian said with a roll of his eyes.

"So...are you two...?" The question slipped from Myra's mouth before she could stop herself, the jealousy reaching a tipping point.

"We were," Laurince admitted, straightforward.

"Oh," Myra said, fiddling with her fingers.

Laurince paused his fidgeting and looked up at her. He arched a brow. "Are you...jealous?"

"What?" Myra blurted. "No, of course not. Why would I be?"

"She's definitely jealous," Rian agreed with a small smirk. "Did you see how her jaw ticked when Ferencia mentioned having your favorite brandy?"

"I am *not* jealous."

"If you say so, Haze," Laurince said with a wry grin.

She hated how her body reacted to the nickname.

Laurince leaned toward her. "If it's any consolation, I think Ferencia is more jealous than you are."

Rian snorted, claiming the seat next to Myra. "Without a doubt. I thought she was going to punch you the moment she saw you holding hands with Mys."

"She wouldn't," Myra said with a gasp.

"Oh, Ferencia has done far worse," Rian claimed.

Myra looked to Laurince for confirmation, and he shrugged.

"She nearly cut my head off when I ended things with her," Laurince said nonchalantly. "And that's not an exaggeration."

"When did you end things? It seems..." Myra hesitated.

"Recent?" Laurince supplied.

She nodded.

He scratched the back of his head. "I suppose it is, although it feels like years ago now. After the fire, I was focused on making sure Rian was all right. However, when no one would let me see him, I refused to listen. I searched for him everywhere. It took up most of my time and energy, and Ferencia grew annoyed since I was spending less time with her."

"Isn't that a little..." Myra bit her lip, not wanting to insult the woman whom she barely knew, especially one who had saved them from getting caught.

"Selfish? Callous? Rude?" Rian suggested with a shake of his head.

Laurince sighed in agreement. "I ended things after that."

"I would have loved to see how that went," Rian said, resting his chin atop his palm.

Laurince snorted. "I'm sure you would have gotten a kick out of it."

Rian shrugged, but didn't deny it.

"Anything else you want to know, Haze?" Laurince asked.

"Oh, no. I wasn't trying to pry. Your history is none of my business," Myra said, leaning back.

"I really don't mind. I'm sure if I met any of your partners, I would be five times as jealous as you are now."

"I already said—"

"You're not jealous," Laurince said in playful mockery, pulling a small smile from Myra that she tried to stifle.

"Well, you don't have to worry about meeting any of mine," she said.

"And why's that?"

"They were Ardentolian guards. Well, the last one was actually a Pontian spy pretending to be a guard."

"Oh, a Pontian, hmm? Did he also have one of your special abilities?"

Myra chuckled. "Yes, he did."

Laurince leaned closer, his knees knocking into hers. "So, tell me, Haze. What was so special about him?"

"His hearing."

"His *hearing?*" Laurince repeated.

"Yes, he could hear very well."

The door swung open then, and they all turned toward it. But it wasn't Ferencia who stood in the doorway. Myra's jaw hung open, her neck flushing red as fear skated up her skin.

"*Exceptionally* well, actually."

"Armen?" Myra stammered as she gaped at her former partner.

Armen sneered at her, flashing sharp, white teeth as he leaned an arm against the threshold. "Hello there, *Haze*. It's been a while."

CHAPTER 51

MYRA

MYRA JUMPED AS LAURINCE'S CHAIR CRASHED TO THE GROUND.

"Who the fuck are you?" Laurince demanded, standing.

"Oh, come now, Mys. Aren't you going to introduce me to your new friends?" Armen hissed, his head cocking to the side in an almost birdlike fashion.

Myra's former lover stood in the middle of the doorway, blocking their only exit. Shadows painted the hall behind him. His blond hair was cut short in its normal fashion. His shoes were impeccably polished, and the light in the room bounced off them perfectly. Yet there was something off about him, something that Myra couldn't quite pinpoint.

When she reached out for the invisible strand, it lashed out at her. Her gift recoiled, retreating inside her. She thought they had parted on good terms, but the way Armen surveyed her suggested otherwise.

"I'm Armen. Although, I'm sure you've heard of me," he said with a wink.

Laurince shrugged, though his fingers twitched at his sides. "Name doesn't ring a bell, actually."

Armen clicked his tongue in dismay and looked at Myra. He pressed a palm to his chest. "Ouch, Mys. That hurts."

Myra stood there dumbfounded.

"What? Are you not happy to see me?"

"W-why are you here? I thought you were in Pontia," Myra finally forced out. Her eyes dipped over the armor he wore. Not a single scratch marked the metal. Was it new? It looked different.

Armen smirked. "It's a long story. Perhaps we should sit and chat, no? I think we have some time."

As he stepped further into the light, the shadows followed him.

Myra stumbled backward. Her back hit the table as she gasped in horror.

She had been wrong. Those were not shadows at all. Instead, dark, webbed wings twitched behind him as Armen strolled forward. The corners of his new wings bent as he forced them to fit through the door.

"The staff really needs to work on widening these doors," Armen said, glancing around the pink and purple room.

"Why?" Myra squeaked, her attention fixed on the wings. How many victims had fallen prey to the serum? Armen and Myra might not have been a couple anymore, but she had cared about him once. "Why did you do it?"

Armen swiped a finger over his lips and revealing a smug look. "The king gave me an offer I couldn't refuse."

Myra's heart cracked, the consequences of her actions once again slapped her across the face.

Armen turned to Rian, who had been maneuvering toward the other side of the room. "Don't even get me started on what King Domitius will give me when I hand *you* over to him."

"That's if he's still alive," Rian spat.

Myra prayed Rian was right.

Armen's lips parted, a retort on the tip of his tongue, but before he could voice it, Laurince charged, sword in hand. Armen ripped his sword from its sheath and blocked Laurince's attack.

"Shit," Rian hissed, unsheathing his sword.

Laurince and Armen swung, their blades clashing with each strike, with each block. Rian bounced from one foot to the other, trying to find the best time to join the fight.

Laurince's sword crashed into Armen's, and his muscles strained against the fabric of his shirt as he braced himself. He spotted Myra out of the corner of his eye. "Get out of here!"

Myra hesitated, her heart racing and panic surging through her.

"Not without you!" Rian ran forward. But before he could reach Laurince, two more guards filtered into the room. One man bore charcoal-feathered wings, and the other had small brown ones.

"You should have left when you had the chance, Your Highness," the first guard hissed with a saccharine smile.

"Fucking traitors," Rian spat. He charged, his sword held high.

"Myra, go!" Laurince shouted in between attacks.

But Myra refused to abandon him. He hadn't left her behind, so she wouldn't either.

Myra palmed her small knife and stormed toward the other guard with the smaller set of wings. She repeated Laurince's training over and over in her mind.

Elbows up. Legs spread apart. Balance even.

When the guard saw her coming, he grinned, amused. "Stupid—"

The man yelped as Myra slid between his legs and sliced an ankle with her blade. Laurince had always said that her speed was her greatest asset.

In her periphery, she spotted Laurince swinging his sword. Armen quickly avoided his attack, spinning around and knocking Laurince's sword from his hand. The weapon slid across the floor, stopping a few feet from Myra.

On her hands and knees, Myra scurried forward, reaching for

the sword. But when it was only inches away, the ground moved. Pain spiked in her ankle as the guard grabbed and yanked her back. Her shirt rode up, and her skin burned as the guard dragged her across the carpet. Sweat coated her palms, and she tightened her grip on the hilt of her blade, determined not to drop it. She kicked out frantically, not caring what she hit as long as she hit something. Then she heard a loud *oof*, and her foot crashed to the floor.

Myra scrambled, rolling over and pushing herself up to her feet. She sprinted, raising her weapon. But as she made to strike the guard, she stumbled, her right foot sliding on the slick floor.

The man grabbed her arm and twisted her around. Her jaw slammed against the wall, and she yelped. The man smashed her wrist against the wall, and the dagger clattered to the ground.

Grunts and clangs of metal sounded behind her, but every sound was drowned out as the guard twisted her hands behind her back. Her shoulders made a popping noise. A bright white pain sliced through her arm, and she screamed.

She kicked and thrashed. She did whatever she could to escape the man's grasp. But the man was stronger than she was, more skilled. Tears slipped from her eyes as he grabbed her hands in one of his and yanked her back toward him. His scruff scratched the side of his cheek.

"Oh, am I going to have fun with you," he snarled.

She squirmed against him, but it didn't stop him from skating his hand up her neck. His fingers wrapped around her throat. He squeezed, cutting off her airway.

Someone shouted behind her. Laurince maybe. She couldn't tell. Her ears were ringing; her vision was blurring.

"Silly bitch. You thought you could beat me? You are powerless," the man hissed, and spit splashed onto her cheeks.

But Myra wasn't powerless. She didn't have to suffer and take the pain that was handed to her.

When she reached for her power, it sprang to greet her. Snatching the man's emotions, she tugged and poured everything she had into them. Anything and everything to get him to release her.

In an instant, Myra fell to her knees, gasping for air.

Through blurry vision, she spotted another set of knees hitting the ground a few feet away from her. A shriek ripped from her throat as Laurince fell forward and his head smacked against the ground. She cried out and scrambled to reach him just as Rian's limp body was thrown down beside him.

Sobs overtook her, and Myra struggled to breathe and regain control of her muscles. She grappled for her power, but it was sluggish. She was nearly drained after using it in the village.

She reached for Laurince, and a sharp heel slammed down onto her hand, nearly piercing it. Before Myra could look up to see who stood above her, a familiar voice sounded from the entrance.

"I must say, that wasn't very fun to watch. The Venerable King and his captain defeated in less than a matter of minutes. Despicable, really," Sebastian scoffed, and his voice caused a spout of nausea to rise in Myra's throat. "You did well, though, my love."

The heel lifted from Myra's hand, and her fingers screamed in agony. Myra looked up to find Ferencia sneering down at her.

"You bitch," Laurince spat, his voice heavy and eyes half closed.

Armen slapped him across the face, and Myra winced. Laurince spat blood onto the rose-colored rug, and it dribbled down his chin.

"That was imported!" Ferencia whined, stomping her foot.

"I've always"—Laurince spat again—"hated that rug." Blood stained his teeth. The scar he had earned from Mynhos had reopened, and blood dripped from it.

"Gag him already, will you?" Sebastian demanded.

With a slight roll of his eyes, Armen tied a gag around Laurince's mouth, earning a bite or two from the captain when he got sloppy.

Armen clocked Laurince in the back of the head, and the captain went limp. Myra screamed.

"Knock her out, too," Sebastian ordered with a dismissive flick.

"No!" Myra shouted, tears blurring her vision. Her panic and fear flooded her system so violently that she couldn't reach a single ounce of her power.

A guard tugged her up, and Myra screamed as loud as she could through the sobs that tore her throat. She heard the gust of wind as the guard reared his hand back. Right before he struck, Myra saw Sebastian's silhouette crouch beside Rian and yank his head up.

"You should have stayed away, brother. Maybe then you would have survived. But you never could let me have anything, could you?" He dropped Rian's head, letting his forehead smack against the floorboards. "Take them away. We'll deal with them later."

Then it all went dark.

Myra had thought she was done with dungeons, but when she awoke, she once again found herself locked in a cage.

Somewhere in the dimly lit cell, droplets of water plunked, hitting the cold stone ground. The air was thick with moisture and clung to her skin. The smell of mildew and decay made her nose itch, the scent turning her stomach.

She summoned her gift, needing to find the familiar threads of her friends. Her power was limp in her palm as if it too had been knocked out and was slow to wake. All she could sense was a deep hopelessness that soaked the walls.

With trembling arms, Myra pushed herself off the floor and crept toward the front of the small cell in search of Laurince and Rian. Her knees scraped against the rough pavement, the coarse stone tugging at her trousers. When she grabbed the bars to pull herself up, a rod hit her fingers, and she yanked her hand away with a yelp.

"It's always the pretty ones who seem to waste their lives, isn't it?" The guard tilted his head to the side, his gaze skimming down the length of her. His hand curled around the bars, and he eyed the metal, his fingers dancing across it. "All it would take is for me to snap these bars like a twig, and then you would—"

"Get away from her!"

Myra nearly collapsed at the sound of Laurince's voice.

The guard snickered as he turned to the cell next to Myra's. Myra eyed his brown wings. One was bent more than the other. A bit of pride blossomed in her chest for at least harming him. At least she wasn't completely useless.

"What will you do if I don't, *captain?*" he asked, spitting Laurince's title at him.

Before Laurince could respond, someone called the guard.

"Enough, Tomlin. The king wishes to see you."

A retort was on Tomlin's tongue, his gaze slipping back to Myra, but the other guard called out again. With a groan, Tomlin left.

Once his footsteps faded into the distance, Laurince whispered, "Haze, are you hurt?"

Myra's throat seized up. The back of her head throbbed, but she was alive and so was Laurince. And as images of Laurince's limp body surfaced, that was all she could hold on to.

"I'm fine. Are you?" she asked, moving closer to the wall they shared.

"I've been worse."

Instinctively, she sought the thread of his emotions, and her stomach churned upon contact. Agony rippled across the thread, coating it in a sickening red hue that twisted at her insides and made her keel over. Her power was still sluggish, but she tightened her hold and pushed away Laurince's agony.

Laurince exhaled a shaky breath, and she heard a faint *thump* as if he had rested his head against the wall that separated them.

"You didn't need to do that. You should save your strength."

"It's the least I can do." Myra leaned her head against the wall, wishing she could offer him more than a temporary bandage.

Movement flashed in the corner of her eye, and she nearly jumped in fright. But when she recognized Laurince's hand, she exhaled a breath in relief. She reached out, and the tips of their fingers brushed, the distance too great to weave them together.

"Where's Rian?" she asked.

"Still knocked out, I think."

Myra chewed on her lip and hoped he was all right.

"This is all my fault. I shouldn't have trusted Ferencia. I'm so sorry. I never wanted this."

"You couldn't have known she was helping Sebastian," Myra said.

"I should have, though. She's always strived for more. I often thought she was only with me because she couldn't be with Rian. I should have been more careful. And now..." His words drifted off, and she didn't feel the need to push him.

No matter what she said, Laurince would still blame himself for their fate.

CHAPTER 52
KALLIE

KALLIE ROLLED OVER ONTO HER SIDE. ON THE BED ACROSS FROM HER, Ellie lay fast asleep, snoring softly.

The pads of her bare feet touched the ground. Pushing off the bed, she tiptoed toward the door. As her hand gripped the doorknob, she recalled the last time she had been in this very room with Dani knocked out and a letter opener the only thing to defend herself. This time, she wasn't planning on escaping anything but her own nightmares.

She cracked open the door and peered into the hallway. No candlelight flickered beneath the door across the hall where Graeson and Moris slept.

Closing the door behind her, she made her way to the stairs and descended them on light feet, her palm sliding against the wall.

Once she was outside, she let the cool air filter into her lungs. Head down, she headed over to the stable. One stall was open, and a large black snout peeked past it. At the sound of Kallie's footsteps, Nyrri blinked an eye open and huffed.

"Are you really that predictable?"

Kallie halted, her gaze sweeping across the stable, searching for him. Movement atop a tall pile of hay caught her attention, and she looked up.

Graeson sat on the hay, one leg swinging in the air while the other was bent, his arm draped across it as he peered down at her with a curious brow.

"I—" She struggled for a response.

Graeson chuckled. "I'm only kidding, Kal." He cocked his head to the side, his gaze dipping down her frame and sending a flush of heat coursing through her. "Unless you really are escaping, then..."

Kallie smirked. "Not this time."

"Good. We both know how that ended last time."

Flashes of him atop her, his hands pinning hers to the ground, came to mind. Her gaze raked over him.

Not the time.

She cleared her throat and held up her hands. "Only wanting some fresh air."

"Can't sleep?"

Kallie shook her head.

"Come on up." He patted the spot beside him on the hay bale.

Shrugging, she reached up and dug her hands into the hay, trying to gain purchase. As she went to step up, she felt something pushing up her injured leg. When she looked down, she saw Nyrri lifting her foot with her nose.

"Thanks, girl," Kallie said. Using her good arm, she reached for the ledge as Graeson grabbed her forearm and hoisted her up. Once safely atop the hay, she offered him a small smile in gratitude and then adjusted her cloak before sitting down.

"Does it still hurt?" Graeson asked, glancing at her injured arm.

"Not as much," she admitted. Over the past few days, the pain had lessened to a dull ache. She still needed to rest it more before she could fully use it again without grimacing. But progress was progress. "The arrow didn't go deep enough to cause any serious harm."

He brushed his knuckles on the side of her arm, and the touch was warm and soothing. "I'm…I'm sorry. I should have been more careful. I shouldn't have—"

"Hey," she said, cutting him off. "We're alive, right?"

Graeson nodded, but she could still see the guilt in his gray eyes.

She turned toward him, her knee bumping into his thigh. She laid a hand on his cheek, the stubble beneath it scratching against her palm. "I'm okay. It's not your fault."

"Says the woman who is known for taking the blame for things," Graeson retorted with a small smile.

Kallie playfully shoved him in the shoulder, and he laughed, the previous tension and concern fading.

Kallie rubbed the hay from her trousers as she scanned the stable. Most of the horses were sleeping, and Nyrri had plopped beside the hay bale as if not wanting to be too far from them.

"Why are you hanging out up here, anyway?" Kallie asked, curious.

Graeson lay down, propping an arm behind his head. He arched an eyebrow at her. "Lie down and find out for yourself."

She followed his instructions, carefully maneuvering backward so that her legs were stretched in front of her. Once beside him, she looked at him expectantly. "Now what?"

"Look up."

Kallie turned her head toward the roof. Menz had added a new skylight where a leaky hole had been. Past the glass, a sea of stars covered the night sky.

"You came in here for this?" she asked, curious why he hadn't gone outside instead.

"No, not intentionally. After Moris fell asleep after his nightly ramble, I couldn't sleep. So, I came out here to check on Nyrri and the horses. I didn't really want to go back inside, so I sat up here for a moment. And, well, a moment turned into several."

She sensed his gaze turn to her, but she couldn't get herself to look at him, her eyes darting from star to star. "What's it like?" she asked.

"What's what like?"

"Flying."

Graeson hummed as he thought of his response. "When I flew on Nyrri for the first time, it was absolutely terrifying. She almost killed me multiple times."

Kallie smirked. "I guessed as much after finding you almost crushed by her weight."

"I think she was trying to push me off the first few times we flew together," he said, facing the roof again. "She wasn't too happy about the saddle."

Below them, Nyrri huffed in response, and Kallie chuckled.

"After a while, I got used to it, but it still felt…awkward."

"And now that you've flown on your own?"

He scratched his chest. "I've only done it once, so it's too early to tell, but…it felt different. When I woke up the morning after, I barely remembered that night. But the memories have slowly come back. I think I was too terrified to truly appreciate what was happening."

"Maybe next time will be different."

"Maybe," he said, though his voice was strained.

"Are you nervous about shifting again?"

He brushed his hair away from his face. "I don't know if 'nervous' is the right word. It was probably the most excruciating thing I've ever felt, but it also was the most freeing. Before, I always felt like something was wrong, like something was out of place. It used to be so loud inside my head, as if there were two sides of me fighting to grab control. Now, there's a sense of peace that I can't quite explain." Graeson released a nervous laugh. "It sounds silly now that I've said it aloud, but..." He shrugged.

"It doesn't sound silly," Kallie said quietly. "While I obviously don't know what it feels like to shift into a dragon, I understand the feeling that something isn't right, that you're not entirely you." She might not have known Myra had manipulated her emotions, but now that she was free of it, it seemed so obvious. "It's a relief once you get to be...you."

"Yeah," he said. He took a deep breath. As he exhaled, he sank into the hay. "When I left you and Ellie, it got lonely flying after a while. I never realized how big the sky truly is."

Kallie turned her head toward Graeson, observing him for a moment. His eyebrows were pinched, and he seemed to have retreated into himself. She could only imagine how big the world would feel from the clouds. But she also believed it could be freeing, too. To soar through the sky, unbound by roads or mountains or seas.

Her hand twitched at her side, and her pinky brushed against his. "Maybe next time..."

"Next time what?" Graeson prompted, facing her. His hand slid atop hers, his fingers entangling with hers.

His eyes dipped to her lips, his pupils dilating.

"Maybe next time I can join you," Kallie suggested, swallowing the nervousness.

He quirked a brow, a smirk tugging at the corner of his mouth. "You wish...to ride me?"

Kallie's eyes widened, and she jerked upright. "That's—that's not what I meant. What I meant to say was that I could take Nyrri, and *we* could join you."

"Ah," he said, nodding dramatically. "*That's* what you meant."

"Of course," she said, lying back down.

He hummed as if in thought. With a tilt of his head, he said,

"Probably for the best. Even if we commissioned a big enough saddle, I'm not sure if you could hold on tightly enough."

Kallie scoffed. "I'm sure I could handle you just fine. You're not *that* big."

"Oh? Is that so?" Graeson propped himself on his elbows, a brow arched in challenge.

Kallie's cheeks burned bright red, the cold stable suddenly becoming hot as Graeson looked at her, amused. But Kallie refused to let him win.

"You're actually quite small for a dragon," she quipped.

"And you're so familiar with my kind, are you?"

"Based on the books I've read, they're supposed to be six times the size of humans."

"Did you see my wingspan?"

She shrugged. "Uninspiring."

Graeson laughed, the sound deep and full. "You're a terrible liar, you know."

She shoved him, nearly knocking him onto his back. "I am not!"

"Then tell me what you really thought when you saw me."

"I thought..." Kallie fidgeted, and Graeson lifted his brow higher, patiently waiting. She dropped her gaze to his cloak. Pieces of straw clung to the wool. Without thinking, she brushed them off and mumbled a response.

He leaned forward, his breath tickling the tip of her nose. "I'm sorry. I didn't quite hear that. What did you say?"

Kallie closed her eyes, as if she could hide from the embarrassment, and repeated herself, "I thought you were the most beautiful thing I had ever seen."

When she looked at him, she found him smirking, pride gleaming in his eyes. She went to slap him on his chest, but before she could make contact, he swiftly snagged her hand and tugged her toward him.

"You think I'm beautiful?" he whispered, his words lightly tickling her.

Kallie rolled her eyes. "Oh, don't get a big ego now."

"Too late," he said, beaming.

"You are insufferable."

"As long as I'm still beautiful, I'm fine with that," he said with a wink.

Kallie laughed, and the sound bounced around the roof of the stable. Her arm gave out, and she collapsed on top of him. Her fingers curled into the fabric of his shirt beneath his cloak. A horse released a loud huff as if annoyed, which only made both of them laugh more.

As her laughter died down, Kallie pushed herself up, her hair cascading and falling onto his chest. Graeson slipped a piece of hair behind her ear, the tips of his fingers brushing gently across her face like a whisper. His expression turned serious, and Kallie stayed silent, waiting.

"I am yours, and I will always be yours. But..." A deep groove creased his forehead, and Kallie had the strange urge to wipe it away. "But it is killing me not knowing where your head is at. So please, I need you to tell me. What are we doing?"

Kallie's lips parted, but she struggled to answer him. What *were* they doing?

She stared down at him, and he watched her. In the silence, she could feel every spot where they touched: her palm on his chest, his hand on her waist, her leg brushing against his. Layers of fabric still existed between them, yet heat emanated in those very spots and blossomed deep in her core.

Graeson had become a safe place for her, and sometimes she believed it had happened too quickly. But in truth, it had happened a long time ago.

They had nearly lost each other, and she struggled to grapple not only with that fact but with what it meant as well.

There were a million things she could say, but none of them were enough. None of them would prove to Graeson how much she cared for him, how much she needed him in her life.

So instead of saying anything at all, she bent down. Slowly and carefully, she ran her hand up his chest and neck. Her fingers curled into the ink-black hair at the base of his head. Time seemed to stand still, as if the world was waiting to see what she would do next. If she would let herself fall.

"I have waited years to have you, Kalisandre. I could wait longer if I needed to."

"But?" she prodded.

His hands tightened on her thighs, his thumbs brushing up and down tenderly, setting her core aflame. "But nothing. Take whatever time you need, little mouse."

She felt his chest rise as he inhaled a deep breath. She waited for the exhale, but it didn't come, as if he was waiting for her, giving her the power and the choice. Giving her *time*.

But Kallie didn't need time. Not anymore.

"I think I'm tired of waiting," Kallie said. Then, without giving him a chance to respond, she eliminated the rest of the space between them and kissed him.

His lips were soft and molded to hers immediately. Chills spread down her neck and over her spine as he gripped her thighs more firmly. Yet his kiss remained tender, sweet, and full of unspoken words and promises. She dug her fingers further into his hair. She gently tugged him closer, deepening the kiss.

This, this was what she wanted. What she needed. Not simply because of the closeness or the physicality of it all, but the security. The understanding and trust Graeson offered her.

For years, Kallie had thought freedom meant independence. She hadn't wanted to tie her life to another. But because of her fear of being caged, she lost sight of the beauty of the fall, the weightlessness.

She was done fighting the fall. She was done fighting *him*.

A golden warmth ignited at every point of contact—where their lips brushed, where her hand gripped his neck, where his thumb grazed the patch of skin at her hip. It spread like an inferno, traveling through her veins, to her core. Every limb buzzed with an intoxicating energy that set her body aflame.

Kallie gasped and pulled back. She stared at Graeson, awestruck. His eyes were as bright as the full moon as he blinked up at her with a similar expression.

Her lips parted, but there were no words to describe the feeling that consumed her.

"You feel that too, right?" he asked, voice trembling as if he believed he was imagining it all.

Unable to speak, Kallie nodded. A honeyed-warmth ran through her bloodstream, and her limbs trembled. Every nerve was on fire, and she wanted to drown in the flames. She had never experienced anything similar, yet she knew immediately what it was. The soul bond was snapping into place, wrapping around them and weaving their souls together.

"Are you...are you sure?" Graeson asked, brows knitting together.

She laid her palm on the side of his face and swiped her finger across his cheek. "As far as I know, this isn't something you can take back once it's done."

"I mean no, but if it was by accident, if you're not ready, we'll find a way. We'll—"

"Graeson," Kallie said, her smile widening. "I'm yours. I'm done fighting."

"I do not wish to own you, Kalisandre," Graeson said.

"I know." And she did know that, but she also knew her soul was irrevocably entwined with his, soul bond or not.

Graeson smiled back at her, and the emotion in his gaze did something to her.

One of his hands skated up to her hips as his other palmed the back of her head. Before he could pull her closer, she pressed a hand against his chest. "Wait."

"What is it, little mouse?" His pupils dilated, and a muscle in his jaw ticked as if he was hanging by a thread.

His slipping control only made her smile even wider.

"Promise me one thing," she said, drawing circles across his chest with a finger.

"For you?" he breathed out. "Anything."

She could have sworn a stream of smoke escaped his mouth. His grip on her waist tightened, his muscles straining, as he waited for her. She had a passing thought that he would wait forever if she asked him.

The thread connecting their souls hummed.

"Do not be gentle."

A wicked smile spread across Graeson's face, and Kallie couldn't tell if she was looking into the eyes of the man or the dragon. When he tugged her toward him and their lips met, she decided she didn't care who it was. They were one and the same.

As Kallie slipped her tongue inside his mouth, she first thought she had made a mistake, for Graeson's muscles tensed. But the next moment, her back hit the hay. He hovered over her, their kiss never breaking, not even for a second.

Graeson slid his hand up her calf. He took his time with her as if he were exploring her body, wanting to memorize every inch.

Or to torture her. Kallie couldn't tell at that moment as every muscle, every nerve, craved his touch. Craved *more*.

"You promised you wouldn't be gentle," she said, arching a brow.

"Just trying to make this last, princess," he said with a smirk.

His hand skated up her thigh, over the base of her stomach, and her legs twitched beneath his teasing touch. She hadn't realized how much she had wanted this, *needed* this. And she vaguely wondered why she had fought the bond for so long. It wasn't like the last time when they were together. This wasn't happening because she needed a release or a distraction. Kallie needed *him*.

Graeson picked up her hips and slid a hand to her lower back. Her slip dress slipped down her thighs, pooling in her lap. Holding her up, he grabbed his cloak resting beside him and slipped it beneath her. Gently, he placed her back down before lowering himself.

With his gaze still locked on her, he placed kisses down the center of her stomach and made his way down her body. He bunched the fabric of her chemise higher. Goosebumps trailed across Kallie's flesh as Graeson's breath tickled her bare skin. His lips brushed the apex of her thighs, and she arched back. He chuckled against her and blew on the sensitive area, sending another scattering of chills running up her body.

As if of their own accord, her legs widened. "Please," she whispered.

Graeson didn't make her wait any longer. He moved the fabric, then his mouth was on her, lapping at the sensitive bud. Tension pooled in her core as he worked her. And perhaps it was the heat of the soul bond or something else, but every touch, every kiss, every lick wound her up that much more. Her legs trembled as Graeson pushed her higher and higher. But she didn't want this to be over so soon. She wanted more. She wanted—

"Stop fighting it," Graeson said lowly, his voice vibrating against her.

"But I don't—I don't want this to be over yet. I—" Kallie moaned as he nipped her inner thigh.

"We still have the entire night ahead of us, and I have yet to hear you scream my name."

"But the others," Kallie said, her breathing labored.

"Are in the house with the windows shut." He licked the place where his teeth had just been, then blew on the damp skin. "Would it be such a bad thing for the world to know that I am yours and you are mine? For the Fates to know that we have won? That their tricks were no match for the likes of us? Don't you want to scream out your pleasure?"

With each question, he peppered another kiss on her skin, inching his way closer to her clit. When the last question left his mouth, all Kallie could do was release a soft, "Yes."

"I'm sorry. I don't think I heard you. What was that, little mouse?"

Kallie groaned and dug her fingers into his hair, tugging on the ends, her need too bright, too primal. "Yes, Graeson."

Then he devoured her, worshiped her. And Kallie fell blissfully over the edge. The stars that spread across her vision rivaled those she saw through the skylight.

As she fell down, Graeson looked up at her and gave her a wicked smile as he swiped his bottom lip with his thumb.

"Can you take more?" he asked.

Unable to form the words, Kallie nodded. She was already spent, but she wanted to feel him. She wanted him to feel what she was experiencing at that moment.

He slipped his trousers off, and she looked down as he palmed his full length in his hand. He pressed the tip against her, and she shuddered, her body still sensitive. With his length pressing against her, he slipped a hand beneath her neck and kissed her as he drove inside.

CHAPTER 53
GRAESON

Graeson admired Kalisandre as she slept. Not a single ounce of tension wrinkled her forehead, and she looked absolutely divine as she dreamed.

My soul bond.

He still couldn't believe it. If his entire body wasn't buzzing with a foreign energy, he might have convinced himself that last night was only a dream. But there was no denying the truth in front of him. He could almost see the golden thread that connected them, the invisible string that others had spoken of.

Knowing that Kalisandre accepted him, dragon and all, brought an unshakable smile to his face.

His cloak lay on top of them, and Kalisandre was curled against him, her body molded around his. Her beautiful hair was sprawled across her cloak. Pieces of hay were woven within the locks, and he plucked a piece of straw from her hair.

Kalisandre stirred awake. Her hair was a mess, and she wore his shirt, which was wrinkled with mismatched buttons. Sleep crinkled the corners of her eyes. She was absolutely stunning, wearing what might have been the brightest smile he had ever seen.

Her eyes dipped to his lips. Without any hesitation she leaned forward and kissed him.

"Good morning," she said, resting her head back on his arm.

"Morning," he said, smiling back at her. He spun the piece of hay between two fingers. "You should wear hay more often."

"Yeah?" she hummed, nuzzling against his arm as if still half asleep.

Even though Graeson would have rather stayed there forever, he knew they needed to get up. When he looked at the skylight, the sea of color was already melting back into the sky.

He squeezed her side. "Come on. We should get up."

Kalisandre whined and wrapped her leg around his waist, scooting closer to him and locking him in place. His length pressed into her.

The others would look for them if they weren't at breakfast, though. And if the other day was any indication, Graeson didn't believe Kalisandre wanted to be found on a pile of hay with him, their bodies entwined.

Still, he didn't move.

"Kal," he warned. Although he wasn't sure who the warning was for.

Kalisandre groaned, but instead of getting up, she rolled on top of him. "Can't we stay here?"

As she peered down at him, her deep blue eyes round and wide, Kalisandre looked so much like the girl Graeson had first known. When she was bright-eyed and afraid only of the dark. He brushed her hair behind her ear.

Her teeth scraped her bottom lip as she trailed a finger down the buttons of his shirt. "Just a little longer?"

Everywhere she trailed her finger, an insatiable fire followed in its wake. Still, Graeson hesitated giving in, even though he wanted to.

"How's your leg?" he asked.

"Never been better," she said with a smirk.

"Are you lying to me?"

She shook her head, but he narrowed his gaze, unsure.

"Fine," she said with a sigh. "It's fine, but if you don't want—" She pulled away, but Graeson tugged her back, catching her by the neck.

"A few more minutes couldn't hurt," he said, unable to deny her.

"That's all I need," she said, a devious smirk rising. Then she was crawling down his body and tugging at the top of his pants.

"That is not what I meant," Graeson said, craving the taste of her.

She blinked up at him, her eyelashes fluttering across her sun-kissed cheeks, promising anything but innocence. "Please?"

Who was he to deny her when she looked at him with a hunger that matched his own?

He pressed his head against the hay and released a curse.

Kalisandre's power brushed the edges of his mind, not to command him, but to coax him. "Eyes on me, Gray."

THE SUN STREAMED down from the skylight.

More than a few minutes had passed, yet neither of them had moved, both utterly and completely spent. Kalisandre's head rested atop his chest, one of her legs sprawled over his thighs and her arm hugging his torso.

Graeson would have been perfectly content to stay there like that for the rest of the day—for eternity, if he could. He didn't even care that his arm was falling asleep. He refused to ruin their moment of peace.

But apparently, the Fates had other plans for them. As Kalisandre drew circles on his chest, a toe-curling scream tore through the walls of the farmhouse.

CHAPTER 54

MYRA

Myra pried her eyes open. Fatigue and anxiety coated her eyelashes.

A guard stood above her. A sneer curled on his lips, but when she found no wings protruding from his back, she almost sighed in relief.

But not all monsters bore wings.

"Now," the guard demanded, yanking her up by the crook of her elbow.

He snapped a set of cuffs onto her wrists and ankles. The metal was cold and pinched her skin. He quickly shoved a gag into her mouth before Myra could voice a protest. Still, she tried, and spit dribbled down her chin. The nameless guard only pushed her forward. Myra stumbled out of the cell as another guard led Rian out of his. The king wore the same manacles and gag as she did. Their gazes connected, and rage and fear blazed within his green eyes.

Rian tried to say something, a warning perhaps, but Myra couldn't understand the garble that slipped around the gag. As the guard pushed him, Rian tried one last time to relay his message. He looked over his shoulder and glanced at the cell beside hers with wide, fearful eyes.

When Myra followed his gaze, her heart dropped.

"Where's wo-wence?" The gag warped her words, yet the guard deciphered her question all the same.

He snickered behind her, shoving her forward. "The old captain is getting what he deserves."

Fear snaked its way up Myra's neck. A large lump formed in the middle of her throat, one she failed to swallow. Hot tears slipped down her cheeks.

Her steps echoed in the space that threatened to swallow her. If only it had.

CHAPTER 55

MYRA

Myra's breaths grew shorter with every step she took, with every clang of metal that followed. Over a thousand voices slipped beneath the cracks of the closed doors and pounded against her eardrums.

She had imagined this moment going differently when they had started on this path—all three of them had. Rian was supposed to push open the doors to the throne room and stroll inside with his head held high. His people were supposed to greet him with open arms. Instead, the man who was supposed to put an end to this frivolous war and remove his brother from the throne was covered in chains.

Rian spun, elbowing one guard and kicking at another.

Myra reached for her power. She had to do something. She had to help get them out of this. They had to find Laurince. Her power was a dull thrum in her core, yet she latched onto it, coaxing it.

She sought the threads of the guards. Finding them, she tightened her grip. Emotions welled up inside her like a balloon, but before she could release them, they popped. The threads broke in her hands.

This wasn't right. She wasn't powerless. She wasn't weak.

But there she was, unable to stop the guard from slamming his fist into Rian's jaw. Rian bit the rod, and blood spilled out of his mouth, dripping down his chin.

Why would Sebastian do this? Why would he drag his brother, the king, into a crowded room chained? Did Sebastian wish to make himself an enemy of the people? Did he wish to turn them against him? Rian was their king, their ruler.

Before Myra could piece the puzzle together, two guards stepped toward the closed doors and thrust them open. As the crowd turned toward the sound, Sebastian's voice broke over the murmurs.

"The people of Frenzia, our king—my brother—has returned."

Gasps echoed through the vast chamber as a guard pushed King Rian inside the room, restrained and gagged.

A guard shoved Rian in the back, and Rian stumbled. When he steadied himself, his gaze swept across the room, his eyes narrowed. Confusion streamed off him and soaked Myra's feet.

Myra squinted down the aisle toward the man pushing himself off the golden throne. Anger rippled around Myra, twisting around her ankles. But she could no longer decipher her rage from Rian's, the two intertwining.

Although Sebastian shook his head in disappointment, the stench of victory seeped from his pores. The gold crown encrusted with red rubies rested on a plush pillow atop a pedestal beside him. Myra was marginally surprised it wasn't already sitting on Sebastian's head. By the way Ferencia and the guards spoke, she would have assumed Sebastian had already claimed it. Crown or not, it seemed Sebastian was one step closer to garnering the title as whispered conversations brushed her ears as they descended the aisle.

A few wandering eyes turned to Myra, but none stayed too long, their attention fixed on their king. Myra recognized a few of the people standing around the perimeter of the room—staff members whom she had dined with only a few months ago, handmaidens she had chatted with daily. When they looked at her, they quickly averted their gazes, letting their attention fall to the floor. She found Bax standing among the guards. When their gazes connected, he pursed his lips, and Myra sensed a faint trace of apprehension and failure drifting off him.

But he wasn't the only one who had failed.

She tried to tamp down her rising anxiety, but the rattling of the chains accompanying her every step only enhanced it. As she scanned the room, two things became abundantly clear: none of the winged guards were present, and Laurince was nowhere to be seen.

Sweat dampened her neck, soaking her hair.

Once they reached the front of the room, the guard forced Myra into a seat. She fell into the chair with an *oomph*. Several guards inched closer, their hands resting on the hilts of their swords. But Myra barely noticed them as she spotted Ferencia standing in the front row among some of the council members.

Myra's brows drew together.

Sebastian and Rian's mother was absent from the audience.

When Ferencia's eyes met Myra's, a small smirk rose to the woman's lips. Ferencia swiped a finger across a sparkling necklace adorned with a dozen brilliant rubies.

Myra curled her hands into fists. Her nails bit into the flesh of her palms as she sneered at the traitor. Laurince had trusted her, yet Ferencia had betrayed them. And for what? A shining new necklace from Sebastian? Was that the price of her betrayal?

Sebastian stood and approached the edge of the dais. He signaled for those gathered to sit, and everyone in the room obeyed his command.

Myra tried to grab the threads and shift them, but they slipped through her grasp like water. Not before she sensed the amusement and triumph coming from Sebastian in waves as he observed his brother.

"Kneel," the guard beside Rian ordered.

"I yam yer eng," Rian spat around the restraint, his words mangled, but the meaning clear enough.

The guard only sneered, as if Rian's title was meaningless. He grabbed Rian by the shoulder and forced him to his knees. Rian tried to fight him off. He tossed his hands in the air, and his chains clanged violently.

Myra looked toward the staff members, the people—to anyone who might help. But instead of friendly faces, she saw only the horrified looks of the onlookers as they watched their king lash out. How had Sebastian turned Rian's own people against him so quickly and effortlessly?

Then Myra felt it.

Beneath the anger and terror, pools of betrayal, dissatisfaction, and hurt soaked the throne room. And their emotions were all directed at Rian.

The whispers brushed her ear, sinking into her skin.

"Where has he been?"

"Has he been hiding away this entire time? While we suffered and grieved? While we buried our dead?"

"Why did he let those traitors into our kingdom?"

"Why didn't he protect us?"

The people believed Rian had betrayed them. They believed *he* had abandoned them. When they were grieving, when their temple had burned to the ground, Rian was hidden from sight. It was Sebastian who was there to hear their laments.

And this display? Rian's anger and refusal to repent were only making it worse.

Sweat dripped down her neck as the emotions of the room whipped around her.

When Rian locked eyes with Myra, she shook her head, silently begging Rian to stop resisting. Didn't he see he was only making it worse?

"It breaks my heart to see you like this, brother. It truly does," Sebastian said.

Rian paused, glancing around him. It was as if someone had poured a bucket of ice-cold water over him. He collapsed onto his knees, defeated.

The guard bowed to Sebastian, and the tiniest hint of a smirk twitched at the corner of the prince's lips. It was barely deducible to those far away, and the moment it appeared, the next second it vanished.

Sebastian folded his hands behind his back and looked at the people. "The return of one's king after months of searching and terror should be a joyous occasion, so it is with great sadness that we must bring forth our king in chains. However, sometimes drastic measures must be taken," Sebastian said, his voice steady. He took a deep, exaggerated breath and pressed a hand to his heart as he glanced at his brother kneeling before him. "Recent discoveries have brought to light that we have been deceived. As you all are aware, we have been searching far and wide for my brother after his disappearance. We were all horrified to hear that the Pontians dared abduct our king. However, we have since discovered that it was all a ploy. Our once-beloved king and his fiancé, Kalisandre, were colluding with Pontia and Tetria."

Gasps of horror slithered through the audience.

Rian shouted around the restraint, "Yew eyer!"

Sebastian frowned. "I know that these are grand claims. No one wishes to discover that their king has betrayed them. Learning about my brother's deceit feels as if he has stabbed me in my heart. But I would not lie to you. After all that we have been through, after we have been forced to live in terror after the attack. After we were forced to question the loyalty of those around us. Many of us in this room lost loved ones. My own mother has been locked in her room, overcome with terror. It has been a hard few months, but we are finally one step closer to bringing justice to those who have harmed our kingdom.

"We have recently learned that when Kalisandre was taken by the Pontians the first time, she forged an alliance with the Nadareans. Good men died trying to save her, but their lives were lost in vain. Kalisandre came here with malicious intent to begin with, only seeking a marriage with King Rian to gain his power and throne. But it wasn't enough. She had to turn our king against us, too."

Rian shouted over the gag in his mouth, but none of his panicked words were audible. Dread shone in his eyes as he looked across the room, begging the people not to believe his brother's lies. But no one believed him. The people looked upon their king with confusion and hurt.

The guards tightened Rian's restraints, restricting his movements.

"But do not take only my word for it," Sebastian said, raising his voice to speak over the growing whispers and disgruntlements. "Hear it from someone who has witnessed these atrocities from the beginning."

A guard's hand tightened around Myra's elbow, and she staggered to her feet with a muffled scream. Her face paled as she took in the overwhelming sense of treachery that spilled from each person in the room. And though there were some that appeared to be leery of Sebastian's claims, the majority were easily falling for his lies. She could see it in every glance, every twitch, every narrowed gaze, and furrowed brow.

Where is Laurince?

But Laurince would not save her this time. Nor would anyone in this room.

Sebastian peered down at her, malice brewing in his green eyes. "For those of you who do not know, this is Myra, one of Kalisandre's handmaidens and an alleged close friend. When the princess was first taken, the handmaiden was too. We have brought her in front of you today because she holds vital information that would be unjust to keep from you all." Sebastian waved someone forward. "We have the honor of having the esteemed Judge Lockwood here today. He will proceed with the questioning."

Her gaze snapped to Rian, and he looked between her and the judge cautiously.

A man in a well-tailored suit stood and bowed before approaching the dais. As he walked by Myra, his hand brushed hers. The patch of skin he touched tingled and crept over her body.

"You will speak the truth and only the truth, answering yes or no to my questions, understood?" Judge Lockwood said, facing her.

A mumbled *yes* slipped over the gag.

Myra's eyes widened in horror. She hadn't meant to agree. She hadn't meant to speak at all.

What's happening?

The question, one she had meant to speak aloud, was stuck inside her head.

Judge Lockwood nodded to the guard, who then took off the gag. Myra sucked in a sharp breath, yet the unobstructed air did little to soothe her fear. Her hands trembled even more than before as the judge began his questioning, her focus glued to him as if cemented there.

"Were you Kalisandre's handmaiden?"

"Yes," Myra said. Her response was immediate despite the desire to hold her tongue, to give this man and Sebastian nothing.

"Were you close to Kalisandre?"

Myra's panic rose higher as another resounding "yes" slipped from her mouth.

The faintest grin rose to Judge Lockwood's lips. "Did Kalisandre come here intending to steal the Frenzian throne?"

"Yes."

Tears sprang to her eyes as gasps of outrage flooded the room.

She hadn't meant to say that. She did not wish to betray Kallie even more than she already had.

Myra needed to rectify this. She needed to fix this. *Now.*

She tried to force out an explanation—that Kallie wasn't the one at fault, that Domitius was. But she couldn't. The words wouldn't come.

Judge Lockwood's gaze dipped down her as if he could sense her internal panic. Amusement tickled her nose.

Who was this man, and how was he able to pull the answers from her?

There could be only one plausible explanation. Yet, as Myra stared at him with horror, there was nothing she could do about it. She was trapped, ensnared by his gift, and there was no breaking free from it.

"Is it true that she planned to manipulate the king?"

"Yes."

"Was she successful in manipulating him while she was here?"

Rian shouted over the gag.

The answer was stuck in her throat, and her eyes widened. She couldn't say yes or no. The answer was more complex than that. His power didn't work if the answer wasn't clear. There was still hope.

Sebastian shifted, and Judge Lockwood cleared his throat.

"Did Kalisandre manipulate the king while she was in the castle?" the judge asked again, rephrasing the question.

"Yes," she squeaked out, the thin string of hope vanishing as quickly as it came.

"Did you and King Rian sneak into the castle yesterday intending to reinstate Rian, even if it required force?"

"Yes."

Judge Lockwood glanced at Sebastian, who gave the judge a curt nod. The muscles in Lockwood's jaw popped when he looked back at Myra, his stare intensifying. "Is it true that the king was performing tests on animals and humans alike?"

"Yes." Terror flooded her countenance. It was a lie, though. She shouldn't have been able to—

Myra gasped. Lockwood had not specified *which* king.

A guard restored her gag. As the judge stepped back, bowing to Sebastian, whatever spell he had put on her drained from her body like a fresh puncture in a bucket of water.

Her gaze snapped to Rian, who looked at her with horror and betrayal. She screamed around the gag, trying to explain that the judge had tricked her. But it was no use. The rod was lodged so far back that she nearly choked when she spoke.

The guard dragged her back to her seat.

Sebastian stepped toward the edge of the platform. "As the witness stated, yesterday King Rian snuck into the castle with the handmaiden and the captain of the King's Guard. Someone who is innocent of these crimes would never feel the need to infiltrate his own castle, yet here he stands today."

Rian shook against the restraints, his anger overpowering him. But all it did was paint him as the man Sebastian wanted him to be: a power-hungry, vengeful king.

Myra had to do something. She had to help. If Rian carried on this way, he would only make matters worse.

So, even though she viewed it as a betrayal, Myra reached out. With the last dredge of power she had, she coaxed Rian's senses with a tender touch, sedating his anger and rage.

When Rian calmed down, Sebastian glanced at her, a ghost of a satisfied smirk on his face.

Guilt twisted in her stomach, but she didn't regret her choice, not this time. She only regretted not having realized Sebastian's game sooner.

Sebastian addressed the crowd. "This is only a portion of my brother's wrongdoings, though. Rian has misused his power and the sacred knowledge Frenzia holds in order to build an army that would thwart any who spoke out against him. He has mutilated their bodies and minds. He has transformed innocent animals and turned them into wild beasts. Some of you may have heard rumblings of the ongoing attacks in Vaneria. For the safety of the kingdom, we have restrained many of them. We have done our best to undo my brother's work, taming the men he has already stripped of their humanity." Sebastian shook his head as if overcome with remorse and sorrow. "But we are afraid some of it cannot be undone."

It was lies. All lies.

Myra reached out to the crowd to persuade them to change their minds. The moment she did, two guards threw open the doors in the back of the room. Warning sounds filled her ears. Bax and a few other guards stumbled backward an inch in shock, yet Myra couldn't get herself to look. Every muscle in her body refused to move.

"If you still do not believe us, we have brought you further proof," Sebastian said. "I must warn you, though, what you are about to see is not for the faint of heart."

A feral scream cascaded down the aisle, and Myra finally turned.

People closest to the aisle nearly fell on top of their neighbors as they tried to back away from the edge.

Myra's knees wobbled, verging on collapse. She was seeing things. She had to be. This wasn't their reality.

But as the guards wheeled the cart over and the man on top of it came into view, there was no mistaking the truth.

Laurince was strapped to the cart, the traces of the serum running through his veins and agony rippling through him.

CHAPTER 56
MYRA

Myra screamed. She raged. She tossed and kicked at the guards as they grabbed her.

She was wrong.

Wrong.

Wrong.

Wrong.

A web of blue veins ran across Laurince's arms and neck as he bellowed.

Agony flooded her senses and forced her to her knees. Myra dug her nails into a guard's limb, and the man hissed, snatching his arm away from her. Another immediately replaced him. There were too many, and she couldn't fight them off. She had no weapon, and her power was beyond her reach as she spiraled.

This wasn't happening.

This *couldn't* be happening.

Myra couldn't breathe. Her lungs felt like they had collapsed. The air felt too thick. She was hyperventilating.

Laurince fought against the restraints, his muscles straining against them. One strap ripped free. His arm swung out and struck the nearest guard in the jaw as the man tried to hold Laurince down.

People in the audience shrieked in terror. Sebastian spoke, but Myra didn't hear him.

It was the first time Myra had seen the serum in action. Whenever Dr. Thorne had given his victims the shot, Myra hadn't stayed around for it to sink in, for the throbbing veins to turn blue, for the whites of their eyes to turn red.

Through her panic and sobs, she tried to aid him, but Laurince's fury was unquenchable. It lashed out violently and with a ferocity she had only come across once. But this was entirely different from Graeson, though. Laurince's emotions were wild, feral, and lethal.

Guards came forward, and Laurince fought them off as he freed his other arm. With a primal roar, Laurince broke free from his bindings. He snatched the leather strap holding his legs down and snapped it in half. In seconds, Laurince was on his feet, chest heaving and sweat dripping from his forehead.

The guards hesitated, fear freezing them in place.

"Chain him!" Sebastian ordered.

The men snapped into action.

Myra shouted a warning through the gag, but it was too late. A guard kicked Laurince from behind, and Laurince's knees buckled. The guards pounced, forcing him to the ground. One guard grabbed Laurince's right arm while another grabbed his left. Together, they forced his hands behind his back.

"This is the work of your king! This is what he's been hiding from you!" Sebastian shouted.

Laurince bellowed. His back arched, and his arms sprang free from the guards' grasps. He convulsed, and his palms hit the floor with a thunderous crack as another violent scream poured from his mouth. As his skin took on a green hue, the veins became more prominent.

Sebastian shouted more commands at the guards, and a few approached Laurince with frightened steps.

Laurince was in too much pain to even notice the guards. With his eyes pinched shut, he collapsed, his jaw smacking the ground.

Laurince's pain and torment wrapped around Myra and forced her to the ground along with him. She peeled her head up off the floor and gasped.

Something akin to bone ripped through Laurince's shirt, tearing the fabric to shreds. Laurince thrashed on the ground as the bone grew. Pieces of his shirt fell to the floor, leaving the torn collar hanging around his neck.

Bile rose in Myra's stomach, and she squeezed her eyes closed, unable to witness the transformation. But even with her eyes shut, she couldn't erase the image.

Fabric ripped.

Screams of strangers echoed off the wall.

Still, Laurince's painful bellow was the loudest. It pressed down on Myra, and she trembled beneath its weight.

The ground shook. At first, Myra thought it was only her body reacting to the pain, but then she heard nearby glass shattering, followed by feral shrieks echoing outside the throne room.

"We're being attacked!" Sebastian yelled.

She snapped her eyes open. Sebastian wouldn't.

Desperate screams filled the hallway as winged beasts flew into the throne room.

Sebastian had orchestrated this entire thing. He had attacked his very own people, all because he wished to paint Rian as the villain.

Those in the audience who sat closest to the doors fell backward. Some hopped over the benches, sprinting for safety, as drakonises poured into the room.

Bax, who had been held back by a set of guards when Laurince came out, broke free. He grabbed his sword as he charged at the drakonis that flew over the crowd. Several men followed him. Others ran toward Sebastian, surrounding him, their weapons drawn as they sought to protect him.

Even after meeting Nyrri, Myra was unprepared for the sight of the beasts. These creatures were rabid, not docile like the familiar drakonis who chased butterflies. These were the drakonises that Sebastian and Domitius had been creating together, the ones Sebastian was now claiming were Rian's doing. Each drakonis differed from the next. Some wings were nearly translucent, the glow of the torches peeking through the thin membranes. Others were covered in feathers. And if Myra's stomach wasn't in her throat from fear already, she would have admired the beauty in their varying shades of gray.

Their black and gray wings sent gusts of wind toward the crowd, pushing anyone close backward. Myra fell.

One after another, the drakonises swarmed inside the throne room. The beasts' feet smacked the ground with a crash that vibrated through the floors and rocked every nerve in Myra's body.

In the fray, the guard behind her had abandoned her. She frantically searched for Laurince, Rian, and Bax—for any friendly face—but chaos reigned around her. She looked toward the dais, but she could not find Sebastian. Had he sent the drakonises on them and then abandoned his people?

The people, once seated, were now running, tripping over one another and screaming in terror as chaos erupted. Some escaped the drakonises' claws as the beasts flew inside, but others weren't as lucky.

Myra turned as a beast opened its jaw and snatched a stranger near the back of the room. The man's scream pierced the air before a teeth-chattering crunch cut it off.

Somewhere, Rian yelled over his gag, and Myra spun around.

She made to move toward Rian, but movement to her right caught her eye.

Red eyes bore into hers. The drakonis kicked at the ground, lowering its head and curling its lip as its wings flared out behind it. Drool dripped from its razor-sharp teeth. Then, the beast charged.

With her hands still bound, Myra scrambled to her feet. One, two, three steps in and something twisted around her ankle. Her bottom hit the floor, sending a shock wave of pain spiking up her spine and knocking her breath from her lungs. She looked down at her feet and cursed.

The chain had twisted around her right foot, causing her to slip. She yanked at the manacles, trying to free her ankle from their grip. She didn't dare look up, afraid of what she would find barreling toward her.

Myra pulled and pulled, but the manacle wouldn't budge.

Then, with nothing left to do, she flung herself on the ground uselessly, slamming her eyes shut as she braced for impact.

And in that moment, as the beast sprang toward her, she nearly laughed. It was only fitting that she would die by the creatures Domitius had forced her to help create.

In the seconds before the God of Death greeted her, Myra did not beg for forgiveness. She could not be forgiven for the atrocities she had committed, for all the lives she had destroyed—Kallie and Mynhos and Laurince—and the lives her mistakes would surely destroy now. Myra was past the point of forgiveness.

So, as her death came for her, Myra did not cry.

She did not scream.

Death, she knew, was a mercy—something she did not deserve but welcomed either way.

She took one final breath, allowing the air to fill her lungs.

She thought of Laurince, Rian, Kallie, and the others—the people who did not deserve this fate. The people who deserved to live and to live freely. She prayed to any of the gods who were listening to protect the ones she loved. To let this war end before they suffered the same fate as she did.

This was how it ended for her—death by cowardice and weakness.

A heavy weight knocked into her side, and she slammed her eyes shut.

She waited for the pain, for the torment, for the drakonis' teeth to tear apart her skin. But it never came. All she felt was a slight pang in her spine where her back had smacked into something hard.

Someone said something unintelligible, and her brows bunched together.

Was the God of Death here?

She tried to peel her eyes open, but she was afraid to look the god in the eye.

Her body shook as someone grabbed her by the shoulders and pulled the gag from her mouth. "Gods, what were you going to do? Just sit there and let it trample you, Haze?"

Myra's eyes sprang open.

Concern and anger swirled within Laurince's dilated, red-streaked eyes. Sweat soaked his thick black hair, and pain still twisted his features. Yet he was here, with her.

"Laurince, you're—" She struggled to speak, and her heart hammered in her chest. "I'm not dead?"

Laurince scoffed, then grimaced as a spout of pain warped his features. He shivered and said through gritted teeth, "Not yet, but you might be soon if you don't snap out of it."

Laurince sat up and rolled his shoulders back, and Myra gasped.

With a shaking hand, she reached out. Her fingertips hovered over the violent red skin around his shoulder blades. His skin was twisted and so red that it appeared as if he had been burned.

"Laurince," Myra whispered.

"Not the"—he shuddered, and the muscles around his shoulders rippled—"*time.*"

He snatched the flimsy collar and ripped it from his neck. Then he grabbed her by the wrist and pulled her up to her feet, the chains rattling on the floor. "This might hurt."

Before she could question him, Laurince bent down and tugged on the chains, snapping them as if they were made of twine.

Myra's jaw dropped in shock. "How did you do that?"

"No time to explain." Laurince snatched her hand and dragged her behind a pew, the broken chains trailing behind her and scraping against the floorboards. He forced her down behind the seats and grabbed her shoulders, his grip almost bruising as he stared at her, his eyes bouncing across her face. "We're getting out of here."

"But—" Myra looked around them.

Havoc reigned in the throne room. The screams hadn't stopped and had only become more violent, more strained as the drakonises attacked.

"Stay down, got it?" Laurince pulled away, but Myra panicked. She grabbed his wrists, halting him.

"Where are you going?"

"I'm getting Rian. Then we're getting out of here."

Before she could respond, Laurince stood, the long chain in hand. "Keep your head down, Haze," he directed before he took off.

Despite his instructions, she peeked her head over the top of the bench and found him running toward the dais. Blood stained his back, dripping from the protruding bones. Myra had no idea how he was even moving.

A shadow fell overhead, and her hair was swept across her face as a snarling drakonis swooped in. The beast screeched, its teeth dripping with saliva as it rushed toward Laurince. The captain slid beneath the animal's head as it snapped its jaws, narrowly missing him. And though Laurince moved with speed, his movements were jerky, the pain of the serum still affecting him. Yet he pushed through it, his determination and adrenaline overcoming it.

How long could he last before he inevitably crashed? Before the adrenaline wore off?

Rolling over, Laurince grappled for something silver on the floor near a body. He stood and spun, facing the beast. He shifted into a fighting position, a small throwing knife in one hand and the broken chain in the other.

Myra's stomach lurched. Even she, barely trained, knew that a small blade would be akin to a needle prick to a creature that was as large as four men.

Myra felt a sudden weight release from her hands, and she turned to see the manacle clattering to the floor.

"Phaia?" Myra croaked, blinking at the woman, who now crouched beside her. Myra hadn't seen the Frenzian handmaiden in the crowd, but she must have been there.

"Hi," Phaia said, holding up a hand, where a set of iron keys dangled. Blood stained her blouse. Briefly, Myra wondered what Phaia had done to gain those keys, but now was not the time to ask.

"Can I unlock those?" Phaia gestured to the shackles around Myra's ankles. "Unless you prefer to wear them out of here."

A flash of hesitation and suspicion rose, but Myra quickly batted it away. She didn't have time to hesitate. Not as screams, grunts, and screeches continued to flood the room.

"Why are you helping me?" Myra asked carefully as Phaia unlocked the metal cuffs.

Phaia peeked up at Myra through her pin-straight black hair. "Because some of us would rather die than believe a single word Sebastian says."

The last cuff fell to the ground with a *thunk*.

A drakonis flew over them. Gasping, Phaia quickly pulled Myra beneath the bench with her.

"Thank you," Myra mumbled.

"Don't thank me yet," she said, looking over her shoulder. "We still need to get out of here."

"Laurince is getting the king now," Myra said.

Phaia moved from beneath the bench and peeked over it. "Shit," she hissed, falling back down and shoving her hair out of her face.

"What is it?" But Myra didn't wait for a response. She looked over the bench and swallowed her scream.

Laurince struggled against the drakonis, his forehead pinched in concentration and agony. He jumped onto the animal's back and threw the chain around its neck, catching it with his other hand. Choking the drakonis with the chain, Laurince held on tight, pressing his chest against the back of the beast's neck. With a deafening roar, the beast jerked, trying to throw Laurince off. But the captain pressed his thighs harder against it and tightened his grip on the ends of the chain.

The drakonis let out a guttural cry. It shook its head from side to side, its body twisting. Laurince miraculously held on. He couldn't hold on forever, though.

"We need to help him," Myra said. "We need to find His Majesty." The faster she found Rian, the faster she could help Laurince.

Frantically, her gaze bounced across the sea of chaos. In the fray, she struggled to spot Rian. Women and men ran around the room, trying to find an exit that wasn't blocked by a drakonis. Guards and those with weapons fought the beasts off as best as they could, but the drakonises were quickly overpowering them. Death spread across the floor as its victims clung to the last threads of their lives. A flash of auburn hair popped up in the crowd further ahead. Had Sebastian actually stayed to fight?

Then, further away, between the rows of benches, there was a flicker of movement.

"Come on." Myra pulled Phaia with her, hoping she wasn't misplacing her trust once again. Together, they ran toward Rian, jumping over the bodies that littered the throne room

Rian popped his head out, and his green eyes grew wide when he spotted them. Myra picked up her pace and crashed beside him.

Rian mumbled something, but the gag was still in place.

Myra pulled the gag out as Phaia said, out of breath, "You're smart to hide."

"I'm not hiding," Rian spat once he was free to speak.

Myra's brows bunched together. "Then what are you doing over here?"

He held up a short sword. "I was grabbing this."

"Where did you find—" Myra shook her head, cutting herself off, realizing she didn't want the answer based on the blood on the hilt and blade. Myra ushered Phaia forward. "Give her your hands."

"Where's Laurince?" Rian asked, his breath haggard.

"Fighting," she answered, as Phaia made quick work of unlocking the chains around Rian's wrists. Once done, she instantly moved to the ones on his ankles. "Weaponless, mind you."

"He's not weaponless," Rian said, a darkness swirling in his gaze. "He has become a weapon."

"Laurince isn't like the others," Myra snapped.

"Not yet. The transition is still happening. Who's to say—"

"Stop!" Myra pressed her palms against her head. She couldn't hear him say what she feared most.

"Now is not the time," Phaia said gently.

"Fine," Rian gritted out. He looked at Myra, his expression solemn. "But you are only delaying the inevitable."

"Maybe we should focus on getting out of here alive first, yeah?" Phaia suggested, dropping the last manacle.

Rian rubbed his wrists and thanked the handmaiden. Then all three of them peered over the bench. Quickly finding Laurince as if drawn to him, Myra watched in horror as the drakonis fell on top of Laurince.

Myra didn't hesitate. She didn't think. She didn't look at Rian for permission or guidance. She ran.

Feet pounded behind her, but she barely registered them. Myra didn't check to see if it was another drakonis or Rian and Phaia. She couldn't afford to waste any time. She stamped down her panic and sprinted harder.

Only seconds had passed, but Laurince had yet to emerge from beneath the beast's body. Was he hurt? Was he dead? She shoved the thoughts away.

In her peripheral vision, she saw Rian catching up, his arms and legs pumping faster than hers and quickly passing her. He skidded to a stop beside the fallen creature. His fingers dug into his dyed hair as he searched for Laurince. Then he sprang into action. He sprinted around the body and dropped to the ground, shoving at the beast's deadweight.

Myra hurried over and jerked back in fright. The creature had fallen on Laurince's lower half. The captain wasn't moving.

"No, no, no—"

"Help me!" Rian yelled, putting his hands on the beast's side and lifting.

Quickly, Myra slipped her hands beneath Laurince's shoulders and pulled.

And pulled.

And *pulled*.

"I can't," she wept, sweat dripping from her forehead. "He's stuck."

Phaia reached and quickly put her hands under the drakonis' belly. She nodded at Rian. "Come on."

Rian didn't hesitate. Together, they lifted the drakonis a couple of inches. Frantically, Myra tugged, finally freeing Laurince from the beast's weight. Rian and Phaia immediately dropped the drakonis' body once the captain's feet were free.

"Laurince?" Myra called out, brushing his hair back.

There was no answer.

Tears streamed down her face and splashed onto his cheeks.

"Is he all right?" Phaia asked.

Rian pressed his ear against Laurince's chest.

Myra's tears were an endless river as she waited with bated breath. She peppered Laurince's forehead with soft kisses, begging the gods to show him mercy.

"He's alive," Rian called out just as another voice spoke.

"You truly do have a death wish, don't you?"

At Laurince's voice, Myra nearly collapsed on top of him. Instead, she forced herself up and peered down at him.

Rian moved, and Myra quickly took his place at Laurince's side. "Are you…are you all right?"

"Are *you*?" he asked, swiping away her tears with a shaking hand.

"I'm not the one who got crushed by a drakonis," Myra argued.

Laurince shrugged. "Maybe not, but you kind of look like you did."

She scoffed, aghast.

"Care to let me up?" he asked, raising a brow.

Myra looked down. Her palms were pressed against his chest and stomach. She removed her hands instantly, cheeks flaming.

"Sorry," she mumbled, standing and holding out a hand. He grabbed it. His hand was large in hers, and she could feel the calluses covering his palm from years of wielding a sword.

Once on his feet, Laurince stared at her, his gaze dipping down to her lips. He caressed her cheek.

He was alive.

He was *alive.*

Myra didn't know who leaned in first, but before their lips met, a trickle of pain wrapped around her. Myra leaned away. Pain pinched his brow, and sweat dripped down the sides of his face.

"Laur—"

The captain keeled over, his back contorting.

"By the gods," Rian hissed, his gaze falling on Laurince's back.

Then, Myra finally saw it. The burn had spread down Laurince's flesh, and his tormented skin was smeared red.

"The tunnels," Laurince croaked, pointing to a wall.

Rian slipped one of Laurince's arms over his shoulder, and Myra immediately did the same. As she held onto him, she sought the source of the pain and sedated it as much as she could, as much as her draining power would let her. Phaia hurried after them as they bee-lined it to the hidden tunnel within the wall.

Behind them, the drakonises continued to wreak havoc, their hunger insatiable and unrelenting.

CHAPTER 57
KALLIE

KALLIE AND GRAESON BURST THROUGH THE DOORS OF THE farmhouse. The front door slammed against the wall, and the pictures hanging on the wall rattled.

"Watch the damn door!" Menz shouted.

"Menz?" Graeson shouted. "What is going on? Why did we hear someone—"

A loud *thump* came from upstairs, followed by a crash.

When Kallie and Graeson reached the living room, they came to an abrupt halt. Menz was sitting, chipping away at a piece of wood with a small blade. He lifted the small wooden object up to the window and squinted as he inspected it. He pointed his blade toward the ceiling. "They're upstairs."

"What's happening?" Kallie asked, wanting to know what they were running into first.

Menz shrugged. "I'm staying out of it. But if they damage any of Lois' paintings, I'll kill both of them. I don't care who's to blame."

Graeson looked at Kallie, and she already knew she would not like what he said next.

"Stay here."

Kallie snorted and pushed past him. These were their friends. If something was happening, she was better suited to take care of it than he was. The last thing they needed was Graeson to transform and destroy Menz' house entirely.

She ran up the steps, taking them two at a time. Graeson was right on her heels, matching her pace. When they reached Graeson and Moris' room, they stopped and gaped at the sight inside.

One mattress was skewed on the iron frame with half of it lying on the floor. Blankets were thrown across the room, and feathers were scattered across the floor. A pillow ripped in half lay on the ground, discarded. Moris' body was curled into a little "C", his limbs tied together like a pig. With his wings flattened beneath him, he strained against the bonds. When his eyes locked onto the pair at the door, Moris spoke around a belt that had been wrapped around his head, muzzling him.

"Nice of you two to show up," Ellie said, sitting cross-legged on the other bed, checking her cuticles. She blew a piece of white hair from her face as her attention flicked to them.

"What the fuck happened?" Graeson asked. "Why is he hog-tied?"

"Why were *you* not watching him?" Ellie countered. Her gaze slipped to Kallie, and she narrowed her black eyes.

Kallie straightened, her cheeks burning. Graeson's shirt was half unbuttoned, and the remaining buttons were mismatched after he hastily did them as they ran inside.

Moris mumbled something unintelligible around the gag. Drool trickled from his mouth and dripped onto his chest.

"Will you just tell us what the fuck happened already?" Graeson demanded.

Ellie waved at Moris. "Flyboy over here had a nightmare or some shit. He started mumbling. I tried to ignore him and fall back asleep. But then he started screaming, so I, being the nice and kind-hearted person I am, came over here to yell at the two of you," she said, pointing at Moris and Graeson. "Him for the screaming and you for—"

"Me?" Graeson interrupted, wide-eyed. "Why me?"

"For not shutting him up and for allowing him to interrupt my beauty sleep!"

Kallie snickered in amusement.

Ellie glared at her with a knowing look.

"So…" Kallie said, shifting the heat away from her, "You hog-tied him because he woke you up?"

Ellie scoffed. "Of course not. Although I wouldn't put it past me. Flyboy is tied up because he *punched* me when I checked on him."

Moris muttered what sounded like a disagreement.

"And he punched you because…?" Graeson prompted, skeptical.

Ellie rolled her eyes. "*I* didn't start it, if that's what you're suggesting. He woke up all wild-eyed, like a god was possessing him, and punched me. Then he tried to tackle me to the ground, and well…you can see how that ended."

Moris grumbled again. He stopped fighting the restraints, though, and his breathing was calmer than when they had arrived.

Graeson folded his arms. "Why is he gagged?"

Ellie shrugged. "He was annoying me."

Graeson groaned and approached Moris. Crouching down beside him, Graeson took the belt off, allowing him to speak.

"I'm sorry. I—I didn't know it was her," Moris sputtered. He looked at Graeson. "I swear I didn't. I thought—"

Graeson grabbed Moris by the shoulders. "Breathe, Moris. Calm down. It's fine."

"Tell that to my new bruise," Ellie muttered, poking her swollen cheek and wincing.

Kallie shook her head and joined Graeson. Her power stirred within her, a pool of humming energy standing by. She pressed a hand on his arm. "Ignore her. We just want to understand what happened," she said calmly.

Moris took a deep breath. "I—" He swallowed, choking on the words. He squeezed his eyes shut, deep grooves marking his forehead.

Kallie frowned. They wouldn't be able to help him if Moris didn't tell them what happened. Kallie took a deep breath. When she exhaled, her power buzzed, and Moris started talking.

"In my nightmare, I was undergoing the transformation. It was as if it was happening for real. Every inch of my body burned. It felt as if my blood was on fire. Then, the wings started growing. Bone snapped, skin ripped. And once the transformation was complete, all I could feel was rage. All I could *see* was rage. One minute, I was fighting Domitius, then when I blinked, she was above me."

"Is this normal?" Kallie asked.

Moris grimaced. "The nightmares happen every now and then."

"What about the blinding rage? Is *that* normal?" Graeson asked.

"When my emotions become heightened, they can be all-consuming, yes," Moris admitted, ashamed.

"Any emotion?" Graeson asked carefully.

Moris nodded. "Yes, but anger is the most potent."

"He's lucky I didn't kill him," Ellie said from the bed. "He almost gave me no choice."

Graeson glanced at Kallie, and something flashed across his features. Worry or fear, she couldn't tell.

"Whatever they did to us," Moris said, his voice haunted, "it changes something within us. One second I feel fine. But then, like the strike of a match, it all changes in an instant."

CHAPTER 58
MYRA

CRACKING OPEN THE EXIT, RIAN PEERED OUT. THE BRISK AUTUMN AIR seeped into the tunnel and sent a chill down Myra's back. Laurince's hand tightened around her shoulder.

Myra had calmed the pain just enough for Laurince to walk and not hiss with every step. But based on the sweat dripping from his forehead, the pain was swiftly returning, her gift's hold on him draining.

"Oh!" Phaia bounced on her toes as she slipped outside the tunnel. "I know exactly where we are! Come on." She hurried forward, beckoning them to follow.

As they headed down the alley, faint screams sounded from those escaping the castle behind them. Myra glanced at the sky. She could have sworn she saw drakonises flying above the castle, but she couldn't be sure. The shadows melted into the dark sky as night fell over the capital.

"My house is down here," Phaia said after a while.

"You don't live in the castle?" Myra asked.

Phaia held up a hand, and the four of them halted. She peered around the corner and whispered, "I did. But when Sebastian acted in His Majesty's place, I no longer enjoyed being in the castle. I needed an escape. I wasn't the only one either. We can stay at my house."

"We can't," Rian rushed out. "If there are others...I can't...we can't trust anyone right now. We shouldn't even be trusting you."

"That is probably true. I head what Ferencia did, but I'm not her."

Myra glanced at Phaia. Although her gift was weak, she could still feel Phaia's emotions. There was no malicious intent. No pangs of jealousy. Phaia wasn't Ferencia.

At least Myra hoped she wasn't.

"If you don't want to stay with me, you don't have to."

Laurince's weight collapsed on top of Myra as he keeled over in pain. Rian slapped a hand over the captain's mouth, muffling his groans.

"Rian, I don't think...I don't think we have a choice," Myra whispered, looking between him and Laurince. The captain was barely hanging on. He needed to rest.

"Your Highness, I have never betrayed you, but it is your choice," Phaia said.

Rian bit down, his jaw popping. But Myra could see the moment he relented.

"Go," he said, tipping his head forward.

Phaia nodded and dipped around the corner. She ran up the steps of a small bungalow and dug into her pocket, pulling out a key. After unlocking and opening the door, she waved them inside.

"Here, I got him," Rian said, wrapping his arm around Laurince's waist.

Myra reluctantly let go and followed them inside, her gaze trained on Laurince the entire time.

Phaia scanned the empty street and slipped inside before locking the door. "It's not much, but please make yourselves at home."

"It's perfect," Myra said, offering her a tired smile. All the adrenaline drained from her body, and the exhaustion smacked into her.

"Is there a place we can..." Rian tipped his head in Laurince's direction.

"Oh, yes!" Phaia scrambled past him. "This way. I have a small spare room. We can set him up in there."

"There's really no—" Laurince bent over, his words cut short.

"Laurince!" Myra cried out and ran toward him. She threw one of his arms over her shoulder.

"Fuck," he bit out, his jaw popping.

"Come on," Rian said, throwing Laurince's arm back over his shoulder and taking most of the captain's weight from Myra.

They followed Phaia into a room with a small bed and a single nightstand. Carefully, they lifted Laurince onto the bed with Phaia's help and Laurince's protests. The captain tried to shake them off, but another spike of pain halted his complaints.

Once on the bed, Laurince arched back, baring his teeth.

"Here," Rian said, unbuckling his belt. "Bite down on this."

Laurince shoved the leather belt away.

"Do you want to lose your fucking tongue?" Rian shouted.

Myra stepped forward. "Let me," she said, hand open.

Rian rolled his eyes but gave her the belt.

She moved to the head of the bed. "Laurince."

He blinked, struggling to focus on her. She brushed her hand across his sweat-slicked forehead.

"Please," she begged, raising the belt.

Grimacing, Laurince nodded and pried his mouth open half an inch. She slipped the belt between his teeth. She held the side of his face as he bit down, his body convulsing as another spike of pain overtook him.

"Is there anything I can get him? Maybe some tea?" Phaia suggested, shifting on her feet.

"That would be great, Phaia," Rian said, his attention focused on his friend.

Phaia nodded and hurried out of the room, her footsteps a soft clatter against the wooden floors.

Rian sat on the edge of the bed and gently placed a hand on Laurince's shoulder. He glanced up at Myra. "Can you—is there anything you can do?"

Myra scraped her teeth against her bottom lip. "I'm weak, but it would be easier if…" She glanced at the spot Rian was currently occupying. "Contact helps."

Rian immediately stood and offered her his seat. "Please, anything. Just help him."

Myra took his seat. She wiped her hand gently across Laurince's forehead, and he moaned, squeezing his eyes shut tighter.

"He's burning up," she whispered. "We should get a wet rag, something to help cool him down." She made to stand, but Laurince's hand immediately wrapped around her wrist. The leather fell from his mouth.

"Don't leave," Laurince croaked, chest heaving. The whites of his eyes were streaked with red as he looked up at her.

"I'll go," Rian offered, pressing a gentle hand on her shoulder before leaving.

Myra settled on the bed. "I'm so sorry, Laurince," she said, voice trembling as tears bit the backs of her eyes.

"It's not your"—he hissed out in pain—"fault."

Frowning, Myra dug deeper into her core. She found every droplet of power she could and poured it into Laurince. She would give him every drop if she could. Anything that would help him. Anything that would save him.

Laurince's eyes snapped shut once more as agony rippled across his face, his muscles contorting. Silently, she slipped the belt back into his mouth. She brushed his hair back, wishing she could do more for him, wishing she could make it all go away. But pain, she had found, was the hardest feeling to extinguish.

Footsteps sounded, but Myra didn't look to see who it was, as if afraid to take her eyes off Laurince.

"Here's the tea," Phaia said, placing it on the nightstand.

Myra nodded. Then a rag appeared in front of her, and she grabbed it, mumbling a quiet thank you. She dabbed the damp fabric on Laurince's forehead. Sweat soaked his entire body.

"We should turn him over so we can clean his back," Rian suggested.

Myra nodded and got up. Laurince groaned as they moved him. The moment they did, Phaia gasped and ran out of the room. Myra faintly heard the handmaiden retching somewhere in the house.

Laurince's back was even worse than it had been when they had left the castle. Right between his shoulder blades and around the protruding bone, his skin was torn open, a strange liquid oozing from the wound.

Laurince instantly screamed out the moment the wet cloth touched the wound. Myra ripped her hand away, muttering an apology.

"It's—it's fine," he said over the belt in between heavy, labored breaths. "Just—be careful."

Nodding, Myra gulped. She lifted the cloth, but she struggled to touch the wounds again. Her hand trembled as it hovered over the raw skin.

Rian placed a hand on her back and reached for the rag. "I can do it," he offered quietly.

"No, I got it," Myra said, swallowing the hard lump in her throat. She returned to her spot on the bed and bit down on her cheek. Gingerly, she dabbed at Laurince's back. She wiped the blood and liquid from his skin as carefully and as softly as she could while soothing the pain.

Rian brought over a pail of water, and she wrung out the rag. The water turned dark immediately. Rian hurried out of the room and returned moments later with a fresh pail and a new rag. She took it, soaked it with the fresh water, and gently laid both rags across Laurince's back on the two wounds, letting the fabric cool his burning skin.

"I think we're going to be here for a while," Myra said.

Rian ran a hand over his head and nodded. He glanced at the door, hesitant. "I'll make sure she's all right and that any guards outside didn't hear anything," he said after a second. "Do you…?"

"I got him," Myra reassured. Although Laurince's breathing was still ragged, his muscles had finally relaxed—at least marginally, allowing him to settle against the bed.

Rian gently squeezed Laurince's ankle, then left, shutting the door behind him.

Myra looked down at Laurince. His head was turned to the side toward her, his eyes were shut, and deep wrinkles marked his forehead. Without questioning it, she laid beside him. The bed was small for the two of them, but she fit when she turned on her side. She rested her hand beside his, brushing her pinky across his. His eyelashes fluttered at the touch, but he didn't open his eyes.

Myra took a shuttering breath and grabbed his hand, entwining their fingers. She squeezed his hand gently, letting him know she was there and wasn't leaving.

CHAPTER 59
GRAESON

Standing in the center of the cornfield, Graeson took a deep breath. He relaxed his body and dug deep within himself, coaxing the beast within. The dragon writhed beneath his skin. He rolled his shoulders back as a shudder rippled over his back.

Graeson was going to have to shift eventually. If it meant winning this war, what other option was there?

Moris' outbreak the day before had proven that they needed to get going sooner rather than later. If there was an army of winged soldiers, how long could Sebastian contain them until they grew antsy? If they were unleashed on the people of Vaneria in their rage-filled states, the likelihood of them being able to discern their enemies from the innocent was small.

Graeson, though, could even the odds.

Still, when he thought of transforming, a nervous spout of energy and terror rippled through him.

He had seen the damage he had caused to the forest. The smoke had just cleared from the skies. Did he really want to risk burning down the world?

"Maybe it's too soon. If you can't do it, you can always try again another day," Kal said.

"I can do it. I just..." Struggling to explain his anxiety, Graeson closed his eyes and shook his hands out at his sides.

What was he doing? This was idiotic.

Leaves crunched, and he spun. He held up his hands and blurted, "Wait, you shouldn't get close."

Kal entwined her fingers with his and lowered their joined hands. She gave him a gentle squeeze. "It's okay to be afraid."

"I'm not afraid." Graeson sighed when Kalisandre arched a single brow at him. "Fine, I'm *somewhat* afraid of having my bones break again."

"Maybe it will be easier this time?"

"Maybe."

Truthfully, he wasn't so sure.

Kalisandre made to say something, but before she could, something caught his attention in the sky. He grabbed her and dragged her to the ground, shielding her with his body.

"Wh-what's going on?" she said from beneath him.

He put his hand over her mouth. "Shh."

Graeson didn't move as the dried cornstalks shifted in the wind. Four drakonises flew over them, heading south, led by a smaller winged figure that looked to be a guard. Kallie froze beneath him, spotting them, too.

After a few minutes passed and Graeson could no longer hear the beating of their wings, he stood. He held out a hand to help Kalisandre to her feet.

"Where do you think they're going?" she asked, concern flooding her voice.

He wrapped an arm around her waist, tucking her against him. "I don't know. But wherever they are going, they seem to be in a hurry."

CHAPTER 60
MYRA

Myra didn't know when she had fallen asleep or what time it was based on the soft shadows in the room. All she knew was that there was a heavy weight pressing on her chest. She peered down and found Laurince's arm resting on her. Looking back at his face, she noted his pinched brows and the flat line of his mouth.

With the fog of sleep still blurring her vision, she slipped her arm from underneath the blanket and went to grab his arm to adjust their position—

Laurince's eyes sprang open.

Myra barely had time to inhale before she was flipped over. In one fluid movement, Laurince was on top of her, holding her arms above her head. His eyes were wide, gaze frantic and unfocused. His chest rose and fell as fast as Myra's heart rate.

"L-Laurince?" Myra breathed out, shock making her voice tight.

Gasping in horror, Laurince released her wrists instantly and sat back. "I—I'm sorry. I didn't mean—" He choked on his words. His hands trembled as he held them up.

Yet, for some reason unbeknownst to her, heat rose low in

Myra's core as she felt Laurince's thighs barricading hers and heard his heavy breaths. She forced her gaze back to his face.

Her jaw dropped, and she was struck utterly speechless.

Myra knew without a doubt that it was Laurince who sat atop her, yet he was not the same man whom she had fallen asleep next to.

"What? What is it?" Laurince asked, twisting around to see what had caught Myra's attention.

A painting hanging on the wall fell, and Myra ducked.

"What the fuck—" Laurince jumped off the bed, but it only made things worse.

"Laurince," Myra called out, maneuvering to her knees. "Calm down. It's going to be—"

"No, no, no," Laurince repeated over and over.

His panic only made him spin faster as he tried to get a full glimpse of the new wings that had grown overnight. Various items fell as the wings knocked over everything in their path. A small vase shattered as it hit the ground, and dozens of ceramic pieces littered the ground.

With each frantic movement, the surrounding air crackled with trepidation and horror. It wrapped around Myra's throat. Her fingers curled into the blankets as she tried to ground herself and not let Laurince's emotions consume her.

When Laurince finally caught sight of the wings that had sprouted from his back, disbelief washed over him. Myra stared at them in awe.

Where Armen and Mynhos' wings were all webbed shadows, Laurince's wings were nearly incandescent when the slivers of light from outside hit them. The feathers were as white as pearls. Some feathers even had a sheen to them that in the light made them shift colors, as if tiny opals or diamonds had been woven throughout them. They were, simply put, breathtaking. And as much as Myra wanted to tell Laurince that, she knew now was not the time.

She erased any drop of terror from her expression and crawled to the end of the bed. She held up her hands, trying to calm him down. "Laurince, it's all right. It's going to be—"

"Nothing about this is all right!" he shouted. "There are fucking—"

"Wings," Rian gasped, having burst through the doors. "You—you have wings."

"Get rid of them! Cut them off!" Laurince demanded, spinning around.

Myra dodged a wing that came straight toward her.

Laurince shoved Rian out of the way, and Rian flattened himself against the wall as he tried to evade the wings. But when Laurince tried to leave, his wings blocked his exit. He yelled out in frustration and shoved them through the door. A white feather ripped free and fell to the ground.

On the other side of the wall, Phaia squealed as the captain stormed past her. The sound of shattering glass followed in Laurince's wake, and Myra ran after him, Rian on her heels.

In the small kitchen, drawers opened and slammed shut as Laurince rifled through them. He dug through the contents, tossing them onto the floor carelessly as he searched and searched. "Where are the knives? Where are—"

Myra and Laurince saw the knives at the same time. She charged, knocking him back and grabbing him by the shoulders. Rian ran behind her and snatched the block of knives before Laurince could grab one.

"Give those to me!" Laurince breached for the knives.

Myra dug her nails into his shoulders. "Laurince," she shouted. "Laurince, *stop!*"

"Cut them off! I want them off! *Now!*"

"Look at me, Laurince," Myra demanded. She would not let him harm himself. She refused.

Laurince struggled to meet her gaze, as if by doing so, he would only see what he feared to be true. But Laurince was not a monster, no matter what he believed or what the wings suggested. No matter how Rian and Phaia were looking at him as he screamed and fought them in the quaint kitchen.

When Laurince finally looked at her, the whites of his eyes were red, and water collected on his lash-line. "*Please.*"

His plea broke her. Because no matter how much she tried to calm him, no matter what she said, she could not change this. Cutting his wings off would only hurt him more. And who knew whether they would grow back? Myra had witnessed how much pain he was in yesterday; she would not let him suffer even more.

"We can't cut them off, Laurince."

A teardrop slipped free at Myra's words. "I don't want to be one of them."

Myra slipped her hand to the back of his head and wove her fingers into his hair. "You're *not* one of them."

"But—"

"No, you're still you, no matter what. Got it?"

Tears slipped down his cheek, and he squeezed his eyes shut, sobs shaking his body.

"We *will* get through this." Myra wrapped her arms around him, careful not to touch his wings. Not because she was afraid of them or what they meant. In fact, they were perhaps the most beautiful wings she had ever seen. She avoided them only to prevent more unnecessary pain.

Laurince collapsed against her. He wrapped her in his arms, squeezing her waist. His shoulders shook as he cried, his sobs dampening her blouse.

Myra only held him tighter.

IT TOOK Laurince a while to calm down, to release all his anger and grief.

No one said anything.

No one rushed him or complained.

At some point, Phaia and Rian had retreated to somewhere else in the small house. Occasionally, she heard the *ting* of glass being swept up.

Myra remained with Laurince. She would stay there for as long as he needed.

Eventually, Laurince peeled their bodies apart. "Is there..." He cleared his throat, his voice raw. "Is there a mirror?"

"Come on," she said, sliding her hand down his arm and interlocking their fingers.

She led him through the house, down the hallway, and toward the bathing chambers. Faint whispers came from the other bedroom, but she ignored them.

At the bathroom, she faced Laurince and blocked his entry, her arms spread out. "Are you sure you're ready?"

Laurince glanced behind her and nodded. "There's no point in delaying the inevitable," he said, rolling his shoulders back. She didn't comment on the sparkle of fear in his brown eyes.

She moved to the side and let him pass.

Wanting to give him some privacy, she went to close the door as he shuffled past, but then Laurince froze just beyond the threshold. His hands were trembling. She had the urge to reach out and grab hold of them, but she wasn't sure if he wanted that. Some people preferred to grieve alone. Kallie was like that. Myra had also dealt with her own struggles and grief in solitude, unable to seek support. Sometimes, it seemed like Laurince was the opposite, but she wasn't sure if he wanted company in a situation like this. This was personal, transformative, life-altering. Something many would want to face alone first.

"Will you stay with me?" he asked quietly.

Myra blinked. "Of course."

He offered her a small smile in gratitude and moved further into the room. Myra shut the door behind them, offering him as much privacy as she could. Pressing her back against the door, she rested her hand on the doorknob, ready to pry it open at a moment's notice in case he needed to escape.

Laurince's footsteps were slow, as if it took every ounce of strength he had to walk toward the sink where the mirror hung on the wall. When he reached it, his head hung low, his gaze fixed on the floor. His wings were folded back behind him. The room was just large enough for them not to touch the walls. He grabbed onto the sink, his fingers curling around the basin. The veins in his arms were prominent, but they had lost some of their eerie blue hue they had the day before.

Myra laid her hand on his, and the trembling lessened marginally.

Laurince took a deep breath. When he exhaled, he finally lifted his head. The color drained from his face as he took in the wings behind him. His lips parted, an intake of breath, but no words followed. Not right away, at least.

Myra didn't dare move, giving him the time to process everything. Although, she wasn't sure if there would ever be enough time.

"They're—" He swallowed hard.

"Beautiful," Myra answered, the word slipping free before she could stop it.

His gaze snapped to hers in the reflection. A rebuttal was on the tip of his tongue, yet it never came.

The wings twitched, and he looked back at them. The lit sconce made the wings appear warm, its light catching on the tiny iridescent notes in the feathers.

"I...I suppose they could be worse," he said, a small flicker of a smile forming. But it was there and gone before it truly took shape. He reached up and gingerly touched the sides of his wings. At the contact, the feathers ruffled and his body shuddered. His eyes widened in shock.

"You'll get used to them," she promised.

"Will I?" He stared at his reflection, doubt marking his features.

Myra didn't know whether it was rhetorical. Still, she answered, knowing he needed to hear the words either way. "In time."

He took a deep breath. "I never wanted...I didn't want to become one of them."

She slipped her hand over his shoulder. "You're *not* one of them, Laurince."

"But..." His throat dipped, his brows furrowing. "Look at me. Look at what I've become."

"I am looking, and all I see is a kind, courageous man who would do whatever it took to protect those he cares for and those who cannot protect themselves. The wings do not change that." She slid her hand up to the back of his neck and gently squeezed, beckoning him to face her.

Laurince stared back at her as if searching for the lie hidden within her words. But he wouldn't find any lies. Myra meant what she said. Now, he only needed to believe it, too.

"They do not change *you*," she said.

He nodded, but it would take him time to believe it.

"Do you feel different?" she asked.

He looked down at his hands. "I...I don't know. Everything feels *more* now."

"More?"

He nodded. "Yes, like the light is brighter than normal. Sounds are louder, like a thunderstorm in my ears. Everything is too much. It's as if my senses are overloaded, going insane at every sound, every sight."

He grew silent, and Myra drew circles on the back of his head with her thumb, unsure how to support him but wanting him to know he could talk to her.

He squeezed his eyes shut at the movement and breathed out, "Every touch is—" He swallowed hard.

Myra immediately stilled her hand. "I-I'm sorry. I didn't mean to hurt you." She quickly dropped her hand, but Laurince caught it before it could fall to her side.

He shook his head. "No, you misunderstand me." When he looked at her, there were so many emotions flitting about his irises that she struggled to comprehend them all. "Your touch…it's the one thing that doesn't hurt."

A blush rose to her cheeks. "*Oh*."

Smiling softly, he brought her hand up to his cheek and leaned his head into her palm. "Thank you."

"For what?"

"For being here, for being you. I remember only bits and pieces of yesterday. I think the pain was too great, but…" He brushed the tips of his knuckles across her cheek. "I remember you, being there. Staying."

Myra looked up at him. He spoke with such earnestness that the cracks within her heart, the emptiness that she had felt for so long, felt a little less.

"I'll always stay if you ask me to."

CHAPTER 61
KALLIE

KALLIE YAWNED AND SHIFTED ON THE BED. SHE PRESSED HER HANDS into the sheets—

Her eyes flew open as her fingers dug into the sand. Above, a cloudless blue sky greeted her. She pressed her palms against the soft ground, the grains of sand shifting from her weight. With her head spinning, she sat up. This time, she ignored the pile of rocks and turned toward the trees lining the springs, already knowing who waited for her.

Terin strolled toward her, his jaw set and steps heavy. The bags under his eyes were impossibly heavier than the last time she saw him, and his tanned skin was slightly green.

Something was wrong.

"Is Da—"

"We're on our way," Terin interrupted, words clipped.

"What?" Kallie sputtered as she stood. "On your way where? What happened?"

"The Royal Seer had a vision."

"A vision? About what?" Kallie pressed, meeting him.

Terin clenched and unclenched his fists at his sides. "We know very little. All we know is that a battle is going to break out in Frenzia's capital."

"Are you sure?" Kallie asked, her knees growing weak. Immediately, she thought about the hoard of drakonises she and Graeson had seen when he was trying to shift. The group had been heading south. Were they heading to Frenzia? Was it possible that Sebastian was already calling for his troops' return?

Graeson's father was right. The war was not over, not even close.

"Yelsania's visions haven't always been the clearest or most reliable in the past, but this one was different. This one she was adamant about what she saw. She showed Mother it, and…" Terin swallowed, his eyes wet. "It's not good, Kals."

"Does…do…" Kallie struggled to string her words together. There were too many questions to ask, too many people she needed to stay alive. She dug her hands into her hair. Her nails scraped her skull as she tried to keep the worries and fears from taking over.

This couldn't be happening. They had won. She had ended the war.

"We don't know who, but many people will die. Domitius and Sebastian will unleash their army, and death will reign."

Kallie snapped her gaze up. "Domitius is dead." The words felt sticky in her throat, but she pushed past the feeling. She would not grieve the man who ruined not only her life, but so many others.

Terin blinked at her as if she had slapped him. "Are you positive?"

"Yes, he—" She swallowed, recalling the fire that consumed the Borganian forest, the guard's wings bursting into flames, his body tumbling into the trees, Domitius along with him. She cleared her throat. "Graeson burned him."

"What do you mean he *burned* him?" Terin asked, narrowing his eyes. "Graeson doesn't set people on fire. That's not—that's not who he is, what he does."

Kallie pinched the bridge of her nose. She shouldn't have said anything. This was not her secret to tell. Graeson was terrified that the others would not accept him for who he was. He deserved to be the one to tell them.

"Kallie, if Graeson has lost control, if you all are in danger—"

"Graeson is not dangerous!" she blurted.

Terin jerked back. His lips parted and closed as his eyebrows drew together. "What happened, Kalisandre?"

Kallie chewed on her nails and began pacing. "A lot has happened since we parted ways in Tetria. Graeson…he's different. He's a demi-god."

"That is not news, sister."

"It's more complicated than you thought—than anyone thought. He's…" Kallie took a deep breath.

"We do not have the time for this. Tell me," Terin demanded.

"Domitius was getting away. As we were flying, Graeson—"

"What do you mean you were *flying*? You're not making any sense."

"Graeson's a dragon!" The words tumbled from her mouth.

Terin's jaw grew slack, his entire posture curling inward. "A *dragon?*"

"Yes," Kallie said, rubbing her hand over her chest where her heart thumped loudly.

Terin squinted at her in disbelief. "Like a fire-breathing dragon with wings and scales?"

"Yes!" she repeated. "I would not lie about this. As you said, we don't really have the time, now do we?"

"Shit," Terin hissed, spinning around as he pressed his hands against his temples. "That's insane. That's—" He shook his head, struggling to comprehend it. But Kallie knew he would not truly understand it until he witnessed it himself. "Is he all right?"

Kallie wrapped her arms around her torso and hugged herself tightly. "He's dealing with it."

He nodded, his head shaking on a constant loop.

Kallie glanced around her. The sky was still bright, the shade of blue vibrant and bordering on unnatural. The space between worlds was still intact. But how long would Terin be able to keep them here? She needed to know more about the vision.

"When is it happening, Terin?" she pressed.

Terin blinked as if he had just recalled the reason for infiltrating her dreams. "W-we don't know. It could be in a couple days, right now, or in a week. We've sent word to Tetria, and we should be in Frenzia soon. I tried to reach you sooner but couldn't. Even now, the connection is shaky. It's as if—" Terin paused and gaped at her. "Where's Graeson?"

Kallie's cheeks flamed red. "He's sleeping, like the rest of us."

"*Where?*"

Kallie rolled her eyes. She didn't see why it mattered, but she relented, mumbling, "Beside me."

"His proximity to you must be shielding you from me. I could never infiltrate his mind unless he granted me access. But that would mean..." Terin trailed off, and a knowing smile graced his lips. "You did it, didn't you?"

Crossing her arms, Kallie lifted her chin. "I don't know what you're talking about."

He raised a brow.

Kallie expelled an annoyed breath. "Fine. Not that it's any of your business, but yes, I accepted the bond."

A wide smile spread across her brother's face. "I'm happy for you, sister."

Kallie offered him a small smile in return, but it quickly faded. "I'll tell Graeson and the others. We're at Menz' house now, so Frenzia isn't terribly far. We can assess the situation."

"What about Lysanthia? How is she doing?" Terin asked, frowning.

Kallie's heartbeat stuttered. How much more information could Terin handle? It already seemed like he was fraying at the edges, ready to combust at any moment. Rubbing the discomfort from her chest, she forced the truth out. "She didn't make it."

"Did Domitius…?"

Kallie's vision blurred, but she blinked the tears away. "He made Graeson do it."

Terin's mouth fell open, at a loss for words. He stammered, struggling to process what she said. "But Graeson would never do that."

"He didn't have a choice. Domitius found a way to replicate my ability and commanded him. He *made* Graeson do it," Kallie said quietly.

Graeson had barely talked about his mother's death since she had found him after the attack. It had been one event after another, with very little time to process any of it. But when he thought no one was looking, Kallie could see the grief in his distant gaze. The underlying pain he tried to squash.

"I—I don't even know what to say," Terin mumbled. "If Domitius wasn't dead already, I would kill him myself."

Kallie held herself tighter.

Then, with his brows bunched together, Terin said, "You said the others. If not Lysanthia, then who is with you other than Ellie?"

"Moris," Kallie said immediately. Then she scrunched her nose, forgetting one small thing.

"Moris is *alive?*"

Apparently, she was revealing everyone's truths tonight.

"Alive but different. Domitius forced him to take the serum. He's…"

"One of them?" Terin breathed out. "A drakonis?"

"He's still *him*," Kallie reassured. "But his emotions are out of whack. He's quick to anger, he's stronger, and…"

"And what?"

"He has wings now," she confessed.

"By the gods. This is…"

"A lot?"

Terin huffed. "And then some."

Fear rose in Kallie's throat by the hesitant expression coloring her brother's face. "How is Dani doing?"

"She and the baby are both fine. Despite our best efforts, Dani demanded she come with us, even if only to oversee things from afar. But she's healthy."

"Good, that's…good," Kallie murmured. It, of course, wasn't good that Dani was going to be returning to the mainland when a bloodbath was about to wash through the streets of Frenzia, but at least she was healthy.

Suddenly, Terin straightened as if remembering something else. "There's one other thing," he said, voice grave. "We received word from Tetria that Rian, Myra, and the captain ran off. They believe they went to Frenzia to take back Rian's throne."

Kallie groaned and flung out her hands. "Are they daft? Do they truly think they can take back the throne with only the three of them?" Kallie gasped, connecting the dots. "Do you think…do you think they're the reason for the battle?"

Terin shrugged. "I don't know, but we can only assume that they play a part in it. It only makes sense."

The surrounding scenery wobbled, the colors dulling as if Terin's grasp on the dream was fading.

Terin looked around them, tracking the distortion. "I know things between you two are still tense, to say the least, but…"

Kallie nodded, remorse filling her stomach. While they hadn't resolved things yet, Kallie still cared about Myra. She had been her best friend at one point, and those feelings, despite the betrayal, had not gone away overnight.

"I'll tell the others," Kallie confirmed.

The world around them shattered. The ground shook, and the waterfall crumbled as the dream ripped apart.

Terin reached out, and Kallie grabbed his hand before he was pulled away. He squeezed her hand tightly. "We're coming, Kals. We'll be there as soon as we can."

KALLIE JERKED AWAKE, tossing the sheet from her hot skin.

"Another nightmare?" Graeson asked, already reaching out, concern dripping from his gaze.

Her hands tightened around the blankets. It was moments like these that she was thankful they had changed their sleeping arrangements. "Not a nightmare. Although it might as well have been. Terin made a visit."

Graeson sat up. "Did something happen? Is Dani all right? Is there something wrong with the baby?"

"Dani and the baby are both healthy," she said. She inhaled and expelled a shaky breath. "Your father was right. This war isn't over. The Royal Seer had a vision."

Graeson scoffed and glared at the ceiling. "Yelsania's visions are mediocre at best. They rarely amount to anything."

Kallie grabbed Graeson's hand, forcing his attention back to her. "This time is different, Gray."

CHAPTER 62

MYRA

THE DOOR CLICKED SOFTLY BEHIND MYRA, AND SHE PADDED down the hall to the small bathing chambers to relieve herself. After she washed her hands, she opened the door of the chambers and nearly yelped in fright.

A flickering candlelight in the living room painted grotesque shadows across Rian's ominous form. He leaned on the opposite wall with his arms crossed over his chest.

Myra pressed a hand to her heart to calm her breathing. "C-can I help you?"

"We need to talk." Rian pushed off the wall and headed toward the living room.

Myra glanced at the bedroom door where Laurince was asleep. The transformation had taken a huge toll on his body, and he hadn't even stirred when she left the bed. She yearned to return to him, but she supposed he would have to wait. While she considered Rian to be a friend, he was still a king first.

She wiped her slick palms on the long slip Phaia had let her borrow, then pulled her sweater tighter around her torso before following Rian.

When Myra entered, he barely glanced at her. Instead, he held out a hand toward the couch. "Sit."

With a curt nod, Myra scurried over to the couch and sat. She folded her hands in her lap, twisting her fingers.

Instinctively, she reached out. Apprehension, fear, and anger dripped from Rian's pores.

Rian ran a hand over his hair. The dye had faded marginally, turning his hair into a dark burgundy shade. "You risk your safety staying in that room with him."

A knuckle cracked, and she shook the sting from her hand. "He's not a danger. He's still him," she argued.

Rian halted his pacing, and his hands fell to his sides in tight fists. "We do not know that."

"He hasn't hurt any of us since he woke up." If Laurince couldn't stand up for himself, she would do it for him.

"Yet," Rian bit out.

The word twisted in her gut uncomfortably.

"See!" he spat, waving his hand at her. "Even you and your hopeful optimism cannot deny that. There is too much we do not know about the effects of the serum. It would be unwise of us not to consider the potential side effects. You were there when he woke up the first time. He moved through the room like a tornado. We're lucky he didn't find those knives first and stab one of us."

"He wouldn't have done that!"

"He *could* have," Rian countered. "And that is precisely my point. He is stronger than all of us combined."

Myra bit the inside of her cheek.

Was this why Rian wished to talk to her? To berate her and her choices? It wasn't Laurince's fault that he had been subjected to the poison.

Myra lifted her chin. Rian might have been a king, but she was done cowering at the feet of royals. "He needs support. He needs to know we are here for him."

Rian sneered. "And what do you know of his needs, hmm? It was only a week or so ago when you denied your feelings for him."

Myra's lips parted, her voice catching in her throat. Where was this anger coming from? This was not the Rian she had come to know.

"Our relationship, as new as it may be, is none of your business, Your Highness," she hissed. "He is my friend, too. Have you seen how scared he is? Have you *felt* his fear? His anxiety? His rage?"

Rian's lips formed a flat line.

"No?" Myra asked, struggling to keep her voice quiet lest she wake Phaia and Laurince. "Well, I have. He is scared and frightened —more than you can even imagine. And right now, what he needs the most is not to feel alone. If that puts my life at risk, then so be it! But it is my risk to take, not yours to deny."

Rian curled his hands tighter, and his body seemed to tremble.

"If the roles were reversed," Myra pressed, "Laurince would be right by your side, doing the same thing I am."

Rian groaned and collapsed into the chair behind him. Myra froze as his head fell into his hands. His shoulders shook as regret and remorse weighed heavily on him.

After a moment, he cleared his throat and swatted at the fresh tears. "Laurince has always been a better man than I. He would jump in front of an arrow for me. It's what makes him such an excellent captain. But…" He ran a hand across his head. "He's so much more to me than that. He's been more of a brother to me than my own flesh and blood. I'm scared and I…I don't know how to help him."

Myra leaned forward, her hands resting on her knees. "We're all scared, Rian."

"After the way things went at the trial, I don't even know if I have a title anymore. If I did…If had access to the castle, I could have the best healers observing him, searching for a way to reverse the serum."

"Perhaps instead of thinking about how to reverse the serum, we should put our energy into being there for him? We don't know if there is a cure, and right now, that doubt only makes it worse. Laurince needs to know that no matter what happens, we will be there for him."

Rian pressed the heels of his hands against his eye sockets and nodded. He exhaled a shaky breath.

"Was this…was this what you wished to talk to me about?"

He shook his head.

"I didn't think so," Myra whispered.

Rian peeled his hands away from his face. His sad, green eyes bore into her, and when she looked into them, feelings of hurt and betrayal seeped from them.

"Why did you do it?" he asked, the question barely above a whisper.

"I'm sorry?" Myra's brows twisted together.

"Telling my people that Kalisandre manipulated me is one thing. It's not something I would have said so easily, but to tell the judge that *I* was the one performing tests on animals and humans? To give my people the impression that I am to blame for the drakonises? For Laurince? Why did you do it? Why did you lie?"

Myra's mouth went dry. With everything else that had happened, she had nearly forgotten about the judge's questioning. She wiped her hands on her knees. "The judge…I-I think he had some ability. I could only say yes or no to his questions and only the truth."

"But it's not true! I had no part in it. Sebastian may have shown me Nyrri, but I didn't condone it. I didn't—" Rian shook his head, stumbling over his words. "I thought you knew me better than that. I thought…"

Myra gasped, panicking. "No, listen to me. The judge found a loophole in his questioning. He asked me if the *king* was performing tests on animals and humans. He didn't specify *which* king. You might not have, but Domitius did. I was forced to tell the truth. I tried to say no, but it was as if the intention of his question was sewn into his words."

"Are you…are you sure?" Rian asked, the mistrust written clearly across his countenance.

"Yes," Myra promised. "I would never betray you."

She knew how those words sounded. By now, she knew her word held little weight. While Myra believed, deep down, that she was a loyal person, her actions for the past century suggested and proved otherwise. But when she spoke those words aloud now, she meant them with every fiber of her being. She was done aiding the other side.

"Whatever you need me to do to prove to you I meant it, tell me. I'll do anything," Myra said, standing.

Rian held up a hand. "I want to believe you," he whispered. "My own insecurities are making it hard to do that, though."

"Rian—" Myra began, but stopped when he shook his head.

"What's done is done. Now I have to figure out how to undo the damage."

He rubbed his hands over his knees, his brows scrunched, creasing the center of his forehead. "Phaia believes there are still some people who remain suspicious of Sebastian's claims, despite everything that happened during the trial. Whether it is because they believe in me or they just hate my brother remains to be known. Although I'm not sure if it matters at this point. Maybe… maybe if we gain enough allies, we will still have a chance to save them from Sebastian. I refuse to abandon my people. I refuse…" Rian choked on his words, a wave of emotion consuming him.

"Rian," Myra breathed. An apology was on the tip of her tongue, but she knew an apology would do little to nothing to help him.

He peered up at her, and the bags beneath his eyes were a dark purple shade, weighing heavily on his face. "There is one thing you can do."

Myra stood and took a step forward. "Whatever you need."

"Go be with Lo. *Help* him," he said, tipping his head toward the hallway.

Myra chewed on her lip, but nodded and forced her feet to move. When she reached the entrance to the hallway, she glanced back at Rian. His head was once again in his palms. And though his shoulders didn't tremble, there was still too much weight bearing down on them.

CHAPTER 63

KALLIE

"Did you really expect Rian to stand by while you went off to save Vaneria?" Ellie asked, her tone sharp.

After Kallie had told Graeson what Terin had said, they had woken the others and informed them of the news as well. While most weren't surprised about the prophesied battle because of Barinthian's warning, most were surprised that Rian and the others ran off. When they were in Tetria, everyone had advised Rian and the captain not to return to Frenzia until things were settled and it was safe to return.

Ellie, however, was not surprised in the slightest.

"He has a kingdom to look after," she said, continuing, "and he has been away for months now. It was only a matter of time before he tried to take action, too."

Kalisandre massaged her temples.

"Maybe they're not there yet," Moris suggested, hopeful.

Ellie snorted. "We all know that's wishful thinking. They're a smaller party than we were when we made the trip for the wedding. They probably left Tetria shortly after we did."

Kallie wanted to believe Moris was right, but Ellie had a good point. And the Fates had never been kind. If there was a battle in Frenzia, Rian would be in the middle of it.

Ellie stood and stretched her limbs. "So, when are we leaving?"

"Hold on," Moris said from a dining chair he had brought into the living room. "You can't go barging into Frenzia. Did you not hear what they said? If troops are gathering, that means we will be outnumbered."

"Did you forget that he's a fucking dragon?" Ellie shouted, slamming her fist against the coffee table and pointing at Graeson. "He can just burn the entire fucking place down."

"And kill hundreds, possibly *thousands*, of civilians and innocents?" Graeson retorted. "I don't think so."

Menz' face paled, Ellie's words finally sinking in. "Wait—did she just say you're a *dragon*?"

Graeson groaned, rubbing his hand over his face as he muttered something unintelligible.

When Kallie peered at Menz, she couldn't tell if the farmer was on the verge of collapsing or falling over in laughter. They had all conveniently left Graeson's latest development out of the conversation. Moris and Nyrri's presence were already plenty for Menz to deal with. There had been no point in mentioning that Graeson was even less human than they all had thought before. When Graeson had tried to shift, Menz was in town, none the wiser.

"It's a long story," Graeson said, scratching his head, cheeks flushed.

Ellie ignored the interruption entirely. "What good is it then, huh? They need our help. If *she* was the one in danger, you would run back with no question."

Kallie straightened as Ellie pointed a finger in her direction. Kallie wanted to deny the claim but couldn't. When she looked at

Graeson, she knew Ellie was right. He would burn down the entire world if it was Kallie instead.

By the gods, he would likely do it if she simply asked him to.

However, neither Kallie nor Graeson wanted more innocent lives to be lost if they could help it.

"Rian needs our help," Ellie said. "If your refusal is because he almost married your soul bond, then you need to get over it, and quickly."

"I did not say I refused to help them. I am simply hesitating to burn an entire capital to ash. An irreversible action any normal person would heavily consider before doing."

"Well, you're not normal, are you?" Ellie retorted. "You're a god. Gods don't have feelings or morals."

"I am only *part* god," Graeson corrected, teeth clenched.

Kallie shifted closer to Graeson. "We don't even know where in the capital Myra and the others are. We need to think this through first," she said.

Ellie exhaled a loud groan. "Fine. Then what's the plan?"

Graeson massaged his jaw, some of the tension releasing from his stiff posture. "I'll go to Frenzia and—"

"No," Kallie interjected, already knowing what he planned to say next. He would not leave them behind.

Graeson looked at her, confused.

"You will not leave us here and go to Frenzia alone." Folding her arms, Kallie arched a brow. "Don't even bother telling me that wasn't your plan."

"It'll be safer if—"

"I do not care! We are going with you."

Graeson turned toward her and grabbed her hand. "We don't know what we're up against, Kal. I don't want anything to happen to you," he whispered.

So many months had passed where Kallie's fire had dwindled to smoking embers, but over the past few days, she had felt them slowly return. She refused to let them blow out now.

"I might have only spent two months in Frenzia, but I wish to fight for them. You will not have me carted back to Tetria just to lock me up again. I thought we were past this?"

"It's not that I do not trust you. I—" Graeson pinched the bridge of his nose. Dropping his hand, he released a heavy exhale and looked at Kallie, pleading.

Within his fear-filled gray eyes, Kallie could see everything he didn't say aloud. He thought they had defeated the Fates. He believed they had chosen the path that would allow them to stay together, one that would keep them both protected, that would keep *her* protected. But it seemed the Fates were still playing with them, determined to keep them apart. If Kallie came with him and a battle started without the support from Pontia or Tetria, Graeson feared what would happen.

But Kallie had made a vow to herself that she would never allow anyone to control her. *She* was the holder of her fate. No one else.

She grabbed Graeson's hands, gripping them tightly, and whispered so only he could hear, "Fuck the Fates."

He tilted his head to the ceiling and took a deep breath. When he exhaled, a wisp of smoke circled them. "All right, but I wasn't planning on riding horseback," he said, with a hint of challenge in his eyes.

The flames within Kallie only grew brighter.

CHAPTER 64
MYRA

A FLURRY OF WHITE, OPULENT FEATHERS BLURRED PAST MYRA AND sent a gust of wind pushing back her blonde hair. Myra bit the inside of her cheek, unsure whether to follow or stay put.

"Is he…is he going to be all right?"

Myra's attention flicked to Bax. The guard sat on the edge of the chair across from her. He leaned forward, his palms digging into his thighs, as he peered down the hallway where Laurince had disappeared.

Myra ran a hand across her throat. "He will be."

That morning, Phaia had slipped into the castle through the tunnels to gather intel. There, she had learned that the hospital ward was overflowing with victims of the attack. Civilians, guards, and staff members alike were fighting for their lives. Many had died during the attack. Those who survived were riddled with fear.

The news of the trial had spread across the capital, and the people of Frenzia no longer knew who to trust. Many had yet to leave their houses, afraid of encountering the beasts that had wreaked havoc in the throne room.

Although Phaia said some people were hesitant to believe that

King Rian was behind the attack, others took to Sebastian's lies easily. Even Bax had admitted that many of the guards who previously mistrusted Sebastian were now hesitant to act against him. Myra refused to give up, though. For her entire life, greed and cruelty ran free and unchallenged. It had to be stopped.

They had spent the past three hours discussing how they could put an end to Sebastian's reign of terror. And while their options were limited, there were options.

Even though many of the guards were turning a blind eye, Bax believed they had allies in Freniza. Myra had also suggested reaching out to Tetria. Rian had initially opposed the idea, not wanting to drag other kingdoms into internal affairs. However, this was not only a civil matter. Sebastian had already attacked several Tetrian villages. The people of Frenzia might have been told that these attacks resulted from Rian's actions, but they knew the truth. Sebastian wanted not only Frenzia but the seven kingdoms.

"You should go, Bax," Rian said, his attention fixed on the floor, "before anyone gets suspicious."

Bax frowned. Sighing, he pushed himself to his feet. "Don't lose hope, Your Majesty. There are guards who saw how you fought against the drakonises."

"Yet they believe I created them," Rian mumbled, his hands clasped together in his lap.

Bax's lips parted, but he swallowed his response when Phaia placed a gentle hand on his arm. She shook her head.

They had spent the entire day cooped up in the house, trying to plan their next move. Rian was clear about his desires. He still wanted to take back his throne, but without a proper army, there was no easy way to do it.

"I will see what I can do," Bax offered.

Rian remained hunched over, his head in his hands.

"I'll walk you out," Phaia said to Bax, leading him toward the back door.

"Thanks," Bax mumbled.

As they walked away, Myra held back a sigh. Their hope was dwindling faster than she wanted.

"Do you have everything you need?" Myra asked, hugging the satin chemise Phaia had let her borrow. She stood with one foot inside Laurince's room and the other outside.

Laurince nodded, riffling through the clothes Bax had delivered.

Bax had left nearly two hours ago. When Phaia had returned, Rian had followed her into her room, where hushed conversations slithered beneath the door. For a while, Myra had kept to herself, not wanting to disturb the others. But then she heard a commotion coming from the guest room. When she had knocked, a low grunt answered. She pushed open the door and found Laurince tossing clothes all around the room. She debated leaving him alone since he was clearly upset and working through everything, but she couldn't bear to leave him alone.

"I could get you some tea?" Myra offered.

"No tea," he mumbled, tossing another shirt to the side.

Myra shifted on her feet. "Do you want to talk about it?"

He grabbed another shirt and held it up. He turned it around and around. Then he chucked it across the room. "Talk about what?"

"For starters, maybe why you keep tossing perfectly good clothes on the ground?"

Laurince shoved the clothes away and plopped down on the wooden chair. He sat on it backwards, the only comfortable position for his wings. He rested his arms on the back of the chair and set his chin atop them. With a wave of his hand, he said, "None of them fit."

"You and Bax are similar sizes, aren't you?"

"The size is not the problem."

"Then what—" Myra's mouth fell open as her attention flicked to the large wings. "Oh."

Laurince hummed.

She pushed off the wall and set her chemise on the bed. Snatching a shirt from the ground, she inspected it. "Well, that's an easy enough fix. We can cut the fabric here and here." She drew invisible lines with her finger across the back. "Then we can add some buttons, and you can slip it on like the shirt you're wearing now, but this won't be backwards. It'll look...normal."

"*Normal,*" Laurince said with a snort. "As if any of this is normal."

Myra frowned. Folding the shirt over her arm, she tipped up his chin, forcing him to look at her. "This is your new normal. Things change. Sometimes in ways we least expected them to, but that doesn't mean it has to be a bad thing."

Laurince sighed, and his lashes brushed the tips of his cheeks as he closed his eyes. "I know. It's just..." He ran a hand through his hair, pushing the thick strands off his forehead. "It's going to take some time."

She squeezed his arm. "Of course it is. You need time to adjust. But you know what we can do in the meantime?"

His eyes fluttered open, and gold flecks swam in his dark brown irises from the warm glow of the candles. "What?" he asked, his pupils dilating.

Myra held up the shirt between them. "We can cut all these shirts and adjust them so you're comfortable."

Laurince moved the shirt aside. His eyes locked onto hers before dipping to her lips. "Or I could go shirtless."

Myra's brows shot up. Goosebumps skated across her skin. A

small smirk rose on Laurince's face, and Myra suddenly had the strange desire to kiss it.

He's hurting, she thought. *This is not the time.*

She cleared her throat. "Laurince," she warned.

Amusement crinkled the corners of his eyes. Grinning, he stretched his arm, then scratched the back of his neck. The backwards button-up bunched up at his chest, and the collar poked his chin. "Sewing really isn't my forte."

Her mouth suddenly felt dry. "I-I can sew. You can cut."

"Hmm. I suppose we could do that."

Her heartbeat was in her ears. "Should I go get a sewing kit?"

"Or..." He grabbed the shirt from her hand, their fingers brushing.

"Or?"

He trailed his fingers over her arm, across the scattering of goosebumps. A sinful glint sparkled in his heavy, brown eyes. "I could show you other things I'm good at."

"I—" Flustered, Myra choked on her words.

Then, before she knew it, she was rushing out of the room, chemise in hand.

CHAPTER 65
MYRA

MYRA PRESSED HER BACK AGAINST THE DOOR OF THE BATHING chambers. The satin fabric crumbled in her fists as she held it against her stomach. She rushed over to the mirror and gripped the porcelain sink. Her chest rose and fell rapidly, her breathing labored.

What were they doing? Laurince was recovering. He was avoiding his feelings.

Myra blinked at her reflection. *She* was avoiding them too, wasn't she? After all, she had just run from Laurince, a man she was interested in. Beyond interested, really.

She was infatuated, consumed, and overwhelmed by him.

Was that all this was, though? Was Myra simply physically attracted to him?

Her fingers loosened around the sink, and the nightdress slipped from her grasp, landing at her feet.

Myra knew it was a lie the moment she questioned it. Her interest in Laurince went beyond physical attraction. The captain was funny and kind. He was protective, but not aggressively so, like some of her past suitors had been. He didn't want to shrink her down. Instead, he sought to arm her, prepare her, and push her. He even trained her—something no other man had ever taken the time to do. Armen had even joked about how ridiculous it would have been for her to wield a weapon. Laurince's instructions were always respectful but never lenient. And while Myra was terrible at wielding a sword, Laurince never gave up on her.

Even over the course of the past two days, he had frequently asked if she was keeping up with her exercises. When she had lied the first time, he had gently chastised her and encouraged her to keep practicing. She hadn't lied since.

That was the type of man Laurince was. Rather than focusing on his own problems, Laurince always checked on her. He checked on everyone.

Laurince was more than an excellent captain; he was a good man.

Yet Myra had run from him.

She tipped her head back and groaned. She was such a foolish woman.

Her gaze fell on the satin green fabric pooled at her feet. She could still rectify this.

Myra snatched the flimsy fabric and threw it on. Once changed, she stared at her reflection and frowned. She should have inspected the garment more closely when Phaia had given it to her. The green fabric melted over her curves, and the neckline framed her breasts almost obscenely. She tugged on the flimsy straps that were barely the width of her pinky.

Sighing, Myra pushed her hair over her shoulders, letting it fall over her collarbone. Her blonde hair wasn't as thick as Kallie's and barely covered her bare skin. If she walked out of this room, there would be no hiding.

She eyed her discarded clothes. She could change back. She could go ask Phaia for a sweater. Or maybe a burlap sack.

Turning away from the mirror, Myra leaned her hips against the sink and rubbed a hand across her face. She didn't know why she was suddenly feeling shy. The men she had been with before had seen plenty more of her, yet this felt different. *Everything* felt different with Laurince.

Maybe Laurince would already be lying down by the time she returned. If she blew the candle out right away, he wouldn't have the chance to notice what she was wearing.

By the gods, she was being ridiculous.

She didn't think she was misreading the signs, but he could have changed his mind since she left.

Would he still want her to sleep in the same room as him, though? She practically ran away screaming.

Myra winced. He probably thought *he* was the problem. She had to at least apologize to him. Since the attack, she had made it a point to ensure they all treated him the same. Had she just ruined all of that work?

She pushed open the door and poked her head into the hall. Phaia's door was still closed, and there were no flickering lights coming from the living room. She scurried across the hall. When she raised her hand to knock, she heard grumbling on the other side. Cracking open the door, she started to call out Laurince's name but stopped short. Laurince struggled to undo the middle buttons on the back of his shirt. He reached for them, but his wings kept getting in the way.

Slipping inside, Myra shut the door and hurried over. She dropped her clothes on the trunk that sat at the foot of the bed. "Here. Let me."

"No, I can—" Laurince started but stopped when her hand touched his back. His entire body went rigid, the fidgeting coming to an abrupt halt.

"I got it." She swiftly undid the rest of the buttons.

Laurince stood immobile for a second, then another. Ever-so-slowly, he slipped his arms out of the fabric and gripped the shirt in his hands. "Thanks," he mumbled, the syllable tight.

"You're welcome." Frowning, she took a step backward, giving him some space. "Laurince, I wanted to—"

"Don't," he gritted out.

Myra flinched at the interruption. But before she could say anything else, a faint crackling noise sounded. Her gaze dropped to the chair where Laurince's hand curled around the wood. The tips of his knuckles were stark white, the blood drained. Then, the wood snapped in half.

"Laurince!" she gasped. "Are you all right? Let me help."

"Stop!" he blurted, jerking away from her.

Myra's eyes glossed over. "Laurince, I-I'm sorry."

Laurince didn't respond, though. He stood, unmoving, unspeaking.

Was this because she had run out of the room before? How could she prove he wasn't the problem? That *she* was the one who needed a moment?

"Please," he said, his words tight, "remove your hand."

Myra blinked. "What?"

"Remove. Your. Hand. *Please.*"

Myra looked at her hand. Her palm lay on his back with her fingers woven into the white feathers. With a gasp, she snatched it away.

Laurince nearly collapsed against the wall, his hand flying out just in time to catch himself. He slumped his head forward and took several sharp breaths.

She hadn't even realized she had touched his wing. Were they still causing him pain? The surrounding skin was less red than it had been yesterday. Its normal warm shade had almost returned completely.

Myra stepped forward.

Snap.

Lifting her foot, she spotted the splintered wood on the ground. She crouched down and started cleaning up the pieces. The last thing they needed was someone to get a piece of wood stuck in their foot. She was lucky she had been wearing a pair of Phaia's slippers.

"Don't," Laurince nearly growled.

Myra rolled her eyes and reached for the wood. "I will not leave pieces of wood around for one of us to—"

"Please, Haze. I need…I need you to stop moving."

Myra halted at his strained, yet soft, voice. She took a moment to really *look* at him. Laurince stood with his head hanging, his right hand curled against the wall in a tight grip. His shoulders were hunched toward the wall, and his wings were flared out behind him. His entire body was trembling. She had never seen him so shaken before. Not even when he had found her after the two men had abducted her.

Fear rose in her throat, but not fear for herself, fear for *him*.

"What's going on, Laurince?"

He clenched and unclenched his fist. "I'm having some…trouble maintaining control."

"Control?"

"Mhm."

"Is there anything I can do to help?"

"Just…" He cleared his throat. "Don't move. When you move, I—" He swallowed, and his hand twitched.

Silence filled the space between them. With each passing breath, the space grew larger and larger until Myra couldn't take it anymore.

"You what?" she asked. She didn't understand what was happening. Was he this mad at her?

The veins in Laurince's arms became more prominent, and the muscles in his back rippled as a shudder tore through him.

"Fuck," he groaned and tipped his head back. "Haze, I—I think you should go. Get Rian."

"But you said not to move," she said, confused.

"I know what I said," he said through clenched teeth. "But if you don't go, I might do something I regret."

Whatever was going on, Laurince didn't trust himself. But Myra didn't believe running was the answer.

In the light, silver flashed on the table, and her gaze darted to the blade he had given her. The logical side of her told her to grab it, just in case. But she couldn't move, her entire body telling her not to reach for it. If it came down to it, Myra knew she wouldn't be able to use the weapon against Laurince. But more than that, she didn't believe Laurince would hurt her—as ignorant as that might have made her.

"I'm going to stand up," she warned, moving slowly. As she got to her feet, the muscles in Laurince's back rippled. Her gaze slid over to his wings. In the torchlight, the pearlescent feathers were like tiny flames. They were mesmerizing. As if entranced, she found herself inching toward them, reaching for them.

Before she could feel the soft feathers brush her fingertips, the room spun around her in a flurry. Her back hit the wall, and she released a soft *oomph* as her hair whipped across her face.

Laurince pinned her hand to the wall. His breath was hot on her flushed cheeks.

"Haze, you didn't listen," he said, voice low.

Unable to refute his claim, Myra gawked at him, her eyes darting between his. They were wild and consumed by darkness, yet she felt no anger dripping from him. Not a single ounce, despite his words. Instead, something else saturated the thread of emotions, something just as red and bright and…alluring.

Myra's breathing quickened as heat gathered low in her stomach. A scattering of chills ran up her neck and over her arms. Chest rising, she swiped her tongue across her lips.

Laurince's gaze dipped down. But just as quickly, he snapped his eyes shut. His grip on her waist tightened. "Don't look at me like that."

"Like what?"

"Like…like…" A low rumble sounded in his throat.

Then she realized the feeling she was sensing. The warmth between her legs made her fidget, her need growing. His hand flexed around hers.

This is not the time, she reminded herself. Yet Myra couldn't deny what she was feeling, and she suspected Laurince didn't want to deny it either.

"Laurince," she whispered lowly. "Tell me what you need."

"No, I can't. I—" He shook his head, eyes still shut. A deep wrinkle creased his forehead. "I can't." His jaw popped.

How long would he be able to deny his needs? Did Myra want him to? No, that much was clear. She wanted anything but for Laurince to deny what was between them.

It had been too long since the last time she had been with a man. And while she didn't want to rush things with Laurince, she also knew she was lucky to be standing there in front of him. He had almost died. They all could have.

Myra often ignored her own needs, but she wanted this. She wanted *him.*

And more than anything, she trusted Laurince.

Maybe it was time that both of them stopped sacrificing their needs and succumbed to them for once—while they still could.

Carefully, Myra placed her hand on his chest. The moment she did, Laurince's eyes snapped open. The brown hue was nearly nonexistent, wiped out by a sea of black that melted over his irises.

"What are you—"

She kissed him. It was clumsy and rough. Her teeth smacked into his, but Laurince didn't retreat. He moaned and pressed his body against hers. His erection pressed against her sternum.

She was right. This wasn't rage at all. This was a feral, ravenous *need*, and Myra had just opened the floodgates.

He released her pinned hand and palmed the back of her head, his fingers curling into her hair. Everywhere their bodies touched, an intense wave of desire poured into her. It was pure and real in every sense of the word.

Suddenly, though, he jerked back.

"Tell me to stop," he demanded, his entire body trembling beneath her hands. "Tell me no."

She sucked in her bottom lip, and she could taste him on her. And it wasn't enough. For either of them.

"*No,*" she said. Laurince closed his eyes and dropped his head onto her neck in relief and disappointment. He exhaled a shuddering breath that sent a shiver down her spine. But she wasn't done. "Don't stop, Laurince."

"Fuck, Haze."

Laurince grabbed her by the thighs and lifted her up, pressing her back against the wall and raising her. She wrapped her legs around his waist. His need poured into her as he tugged at her bottom lip with his teeth. He ground into her, and his length pressed against the thin fabric of her chemise. With each kiss, each touch, the heat deep within her core intensified. She was an inferno on the verge of exploding.

With a moan, Myra tipped her head back. "Laurince," she breathed out.

He ran his hand over her curves. His thumb skated close to the apex of her thigh, and she could feel the dampness build.

Her eyes fluttered shut, and her breathing quickened.

"Can—can I—" He struggled over the words, whether afraid to ask or unable to.

"Yes, please." She grabbed his hand and pushed it down, the need for his touch overwhelming her. She helped him shift the fabric. When he brushed a finger over her mound, she nearly cried out. He was barely touching her, yet she was already melting against the wall.

Then he worked her, his hand circling the sensitive bud. He slipped a finger inside her. When he pulled it out, he spread the slickness around. She squirmed against the wall as Laurince easily found the rhythm that made her heartbeat stutter.

Myra dragged her hands up to his neck, pulling him closer. Desire quickly rising, she ground awkwardly against him, needing more, craving more.

"I'm feeling a little ravenous," he hissed against her lips.

Confused, Myra pulled away. But her confusion only grew when he pressed a kiss down the column of her neck. "D-do you need something to…eat?"

"Mhm," he mumbled, the vibration tickling her. He slipped his finger inside her, curling it.

She swallowed another moan. "I-I could—"

"Lean back and hold on to my head," he instructed, cutting her off.

"What?" Myra questioned. Her entire body was trembling.

He pulled his finger out, and she whined. The sound should have mortified her, but it didn't. Not even as Laurince chuckled.

"Just lean back and hold on to me, got it?"

Although she was still confused, Myra nodded, trusting him. She pressed her back flat against the wall as she curled her fingers into his hair.

Satisfied, Laurince hoisted her up. She gasped as he swiftly flung her legs over his shoulders one at a time, careful to avoid his wings.

"Comfortable?" he asked, staring up at her from between her legs.

"Wh-what are you doing?"

Laurince gave her a devious smile. "Feasting," he said before devouring her.

Laurince feasted on her as if he was truly starving, as if he hadn't eaten in days, weeks. She slapped her other hand over her mouth to cover her shriek as he swiped his tongue across her sensitive skin. Her head tipped back, slumping against the wall. She bit the flesh of her palm, muffling her moans as he lapped at the sensitive bud.

Her legs trembled, and her core ached. She was right on the edge, her entire body shaking, sweating. As her orgasm swelled within her, Laurince pressed a hand against her stomach, steadying her against the wall. He murmured her name against her clit, sending a shockwave of pleasure soaring through her.

Her vision wavered. Her head spun. The world flipped upside down.

Myra squirmed against him, the fall after the climax disorienting. She uncurled her hand from his hair and reached up. Her fingers brushed something soft. Blinking away the fog, she found her fingers touching the glimmering white feathers. Lightly, she ran the tips of her knuckles down the silky material.

Laurince growled, the sound vibrating against sensitive, bare skin. He shifted his hold on her and slid her down the wall, one hand on her back for support. He dropped her onto his lap. "You will be the death of me, Haze."

She blinked at him, wide-eyed and still foggy. "W-what did I do?"

"The wings, Haze."

"What about them?"

He wrapped her legs around him, and she felt him beneath her swollen clit.

"Oh," she mumbled, cheeks flushed.

He pulled her against his chest and wrapped his arms around her. His lips brushed the side of her neck as he leaned into her. "Mhm."

Her eyes widened, finally realizing what had triggered him before.

Myra had touched his wings when she was unbuttoning his shirt. "Is that why…?"

"Yes," Laurince grumbled against her neck. "Apparently they are rather sens—" He gasped and snatched her hand away from his wing.

She snickered, unable to help it. "Sensitive?"

"Yes," he hissed out.

"I don't really see the problem."

"The *problem* is that I am"—he sighed, a shudder raking through him—"still getting used to this new normal. And while I want to take you on that bed right now, I'm afraid I would either break the bed or…"

Myra leaned away, already suspecting what he was going to say next. "I trust you, Laurince."

He gave her a half-smile and brushed her sweat-soaked hair from her face, his touch gentle. "I know. But right now, I don't trust myself. And when I take you to bed, I want to be fully in control."

CHAPTER 66
KALLIE

"THIS IS A BAD IDEA," ELLIE GRUMBLED, SHIFTING NERVOUSLY ON HER feet in front of the stable.

Kallie held back a snort as Nyrri gave Ellie a side-eyed glance, as if the situation equally displeased the drakonis.

After Graeson and Kallie agreed they would go to Frenzia together, Ellie decided she would meet the Tetrian forces on the road. Should Graeson transform again, the others needed to know he was not a threat.

Now, however, it seemed Ellie was regretting the choice. The last time Ellie had flown—granted, involuntarily so—the warrior had gotten sick all over Graeson's paw multiple times.

"The saddle has a buckle," Kallie pointed out. But based on the glare Ellie sent her way, the reminder wasn't as helpful as Kallie thought.

"Do you remember what happened when she crashed with Graeson on her back? He nearly had a stick go through his back. The saddle will not protect me."

Nyrri released a disgruntled snort, sending a plume of debris flying into the air.

"It was barely even a scratch," Graeson said, waving the hay from his face. He pulled on the strap, tightening the saddle. He had borrowed thread from Menz to repair the ripped strap. While his stitching was a little rough around the edges, it would suffice. At least Kallie hoped.

Ellie lifted her chin. "Well, it would be my luck that if it were to happen to me, it would go all the way through."

"It'll be quicker this way," Graeson reminded her. He scratched Nyrri behind her ears, earning a low purr. "Now that Nyrri is comfortable with a rider, she'll be able to cut the distance in half. You can meet up with the troops and then meet us in Frenzia."

"That seems like a wasted trip, does it not?" Moris asked, standing beside a stall. When he had first entered and leaned against the door, the horse inside the stall had tried to nibble at his wings. Now, he leaned against a post with his wings tucked away from the curious horses.

Ellie shook her head. "My place is by Medenia. She will likely be leading the charge. My oath is to her. There is no other option."

"So mount up, Euralys."

Ellie groaned.

Kallie cocked her head to the side, observing the warrior whose pale face had grown a pinch green. "Are you afraid of heights, Ellie?"

"What?" Ellie snapped. Scoffing, she folded her arms over her chest. "No, of course not."

Kallie arched a brow.

Ellie looked around the room—everywhere but at Nyrri. "Maybe. I don't know." She pointed a finger at Graeson as she narrowed her dark eyes. "Nyrri nearly killed you several times."

Graeson rolled his eyes. "And like I said, Nyrri is better trained now."

Kallie scratched Nyrri's head. The drakonis peered up at her with a bored and annoyed gaze. "You won't kill Ellie, now will you?"

Nyrri considered the warrior as if debating. Her nostrils flared, and she flexed her wings at her sides as she tilted her head. Then the drakonis released an exasperated huff.

"Why does she sound upset?" Ellie asked, glancing at the four of them. "She sounds upset, doesn't she?"

Menz shrugged, unfamiliar with the drakonis' habits.

"Kind of," Moris admitted with a shrug.

Ellie glared at Moris.

"What? You asked!"

"You're lucky you're going with them, flyboy," Ellie said, sneering. "Or else I'm not sure Dani and Sylvia would ever get the chance to see you."

A retort was on Moris' tongue, but a groan from Graeson cut him off.

Graeson shoved his hands into his pockets. "We're wasting time as it is, Ellie. Make up your mind. You can either take a horse or let Nyrri take you. It's your choice, but make it quickly."

Ellie glared at Nyrri.

Unfazed, Nyrri simply licked her paw, cleaning the debris that had gathered between her claws.

"Fine," Ellie said, stomping her foot. "Let's get this over with."

Kallie grabbed her hands. "It's going to be fine."

Ellie snorted. But Kallie didn't miss the small, thankful smile that momentarily twitched at the corner of the warrior's mouth.

Ellie took a deep breath and approached Nyrri. When she grabbed the pommel, Nyrri looked back at her and snarled, sharp canines gleaming.

"Oh, stop that," Kallie scolded, booping Nyrri in the snout.

Ellie tilted her head to the sky. "Nerva, help me," she implored, praying to the goddess of strength. Then she hoisted herself onto the saddle, using the new stirrups to help propel her.

Stepping back, Kallie gave the pair two thumbs up. "Go easy on her."

Ellie scoffed. "I'll try."

Kallie's smile wavered. "I was talking to Nyrri."

Ellie rolled her eyes and fixed her attention on Graeson. "Leave some of the fight for me, yeah?"

"No promises," he said, giving Ellie a rueful grin that sent a chill down Kallie's spine as the dragon surfaced.

Nyrri nudged Graeson's hip. He scratched behind her ear and planted a gentle peck on her forehead. "I'll see you soon," he whispered.

Nyrri licked his face, leaving a trail of saliva on his cheek.

With a shudder, Graeson bunched his nose in disgust and patted Nyrri on the side.

The drakonis sprang into action, her paws smacking the ground as she sprinted. Dirt spiraled into the air, filling Kallie's nose with the scent of freshly turned soil. Ellie squealed and promptly choked on dirt, coughing.

"Keep your mouth closed!" Graeson hollered. "It helps keep the bugs out."

Ellie tossed Graeson a vulgar gesture over her shoulder.

Nyrri jumped, her leg muscles rippling with power. With a scream, Ellie lurched forward, grabbing the pommel with both hands and pressing her stomach against Nyrri's back.

In a matter of seconds, they were off, soaring into the sky. Ellie's scream faded the further they climbed. Her white hair was like a beacon of light against Nyrri's black scales and wings.

"Not the most subtle, is she?" Kallie crossed her arms, her elbow bumping into Graeson.

"Nothing Ellie ever does is subtle," Graeson answered.

When his smile faded, Kallie reached for his hand, entwining her fingers with his. He squeezed it in gratitude. The four of them watched Ellie and Nyrri fly over the trees.

"She probably should have taken the beast on a test run first, no?" Moris mused, approaching the edge of the stable. He had rarely been outside since they had arrived, the fear of someone seeing him keeping him cooped up. However, now that they were all leaving soon, there was no point in hiding.

Graeson shrugged. "Ellie's more the type to dive head-first than to ask questions."

"Not sure if that was the smartest move here," Menz said, watching the pair.

Graeson snorted. "Perhaps not, but if she had any more time to consider her options, she wouldn't have taken off on Nyrri."

Kallie nodded in agreement. She knew Ellie didn't want to waste any more time than they already had.

A cool breeze swept through the stable, and goosebumps skated down her neck. Swallowing the lump in her throat, Kallie hugged herself tighter. Graeson's arm brushed hers, and she inhaled a slow breath.

When the pair was only a speck in the sky, too far to even distinguish from the birds, Graeson at last turned to Kallie.

"Ready, little mouse?"

"Are *you*?" Kallie asked, failing to hide her concern.

"I'm ready if either of you care," Moris interjected, leaning forward and waving a hand between them.

Kallie laughed. Although the joviality was short-lived before the nerves returned. She wasn't sure what she was more nervous about: riding a dragon or seeing Graeson transform again. She had witnessed how gruesome the transition was when he had shifted the first time, and she didn't care to see Graeson go through that sort of pain again.

However, he didn't really have a choice. This was who he was, who he had always been. Was it not worse if he denied this part of himself?

Kallie recalled how it had felt not to use her gift the past few months. It had been a painful itch that wouldn't stop.

Maybe this time it would be easier for him. At least, she hoped.

CHAPTER 67
MYRA

THE FRONT DOOR SWUNG OPEN, AND PHAIA AND BAX STORMED inside, slamming the door shut behind them. Their fear instantly wrapped around Myra, tying her to the chair.

Bax pressed his back against the wall, his breathing labored. "You need to get out of here."

"Why? What's happening?" Laurince asked, rushing over.

Rian swatted at the captain's wings when Laurince barreled past him toward the window. Even after several days, Laurince was still getting used to the new appendages. When Laurince tried to peek through the curtain, Bax slapped his hand away.

"Don't," he ordered.

"Then tell us what's going on," Laurince demanded, his wings going rigid at his back.

Myra was at Laurince's side in an instant. She intertwined their hands, calling his attention to her. His eyes were wild, his frustration rising at a dangerous pace. She squeezed his hand, and he took a deep breath.

Ever since the other night, Myra had been paying more attention to Laurine's emotions. The serum's effects extended beyond the new wings. His emotions were often all over the place. At his request, Myra did her best to sedate them when necessary, but it was proving to be more challenging than she thought. It was like they were running for miles on end. Every time she caught up with them, the emotions sprinted further ahead.

"They're coming," Phaia said. "You need to get out of the city. *Now.*"

"What? Who's coming?" Rian asked, joining them near the window.

"The guards," Bax breathed out.

"Are they coming *here*?" Laurince asked. "Do they know we're here?"

Before Phaia or Bax could answer, Laurince was throwing more questions at her. "Did someone betray us? Does Sebastian know we're trying to gather forces?"

"I-I don't know." Phaia dug her hands into her hair. "I—"

"Are the winged guards among them?" With each question, Laurince stepped closer, as if his proximity would force the answers out.

"I don't know!" Phaia repeated.

"What the fuck do you know then!"

"Laurince!" Myra chided, stepping in between him and Phaia. She pressed a hand to his chest and pushed him back. Laurince's body was rock solid, his muscles taut beneath her palm. She glared at him and Rian. "Maybe if both of you gave them some space to breathe, they could tell us what they *do* know."

Laurince's lip curled.

"Laurince," Myra called out, beckoning him to listen.

Slowly, he looked down at her, his mouth drawn in a flat line. His emotions whipped through the air, wild and erratic. She slipped her hand up to his face, caressing his jaw. He released a shaky breath and relented, retreating a step and mumbling an apology under his breath.

Once she trusted Laurince not to charge at them, Myra encouraged Phaia and Bax to proceed.

Bax placed a hand on Phaia's shoulder. "This morning, they stormed through the guards' chambers and were gathering soldiers to be questioned. I barely had time to slip through the tunnels before they got to my room. They know we've been trying to gather allies. They're looking for anyone who they suspect has allegiances to either of you," he said, looking at Rian and Laurince.

Anger and frustration soaked the floorboards as Bax's information settled across the room.

"How do they know we've been gathering forces?" Rian asked.

"I don't know," Bax said. "Someone must have let it slip by accident. Thank the gods we hadn't told anyone the plan yet."

"That's because we never had a fucking plan!" Laurince shouted, his control slipping. He dug his hands into his hair, and the veins on his neck became more prominent, straining. "We've been flying by the seat of our pants this entire time."

"No pun intended, right?" Bax said, chuckling nervously.

Groaning, Myra tilted her head back. *Wrong move,* she thought as a low growl vibrated in Laurince's throat.

She quickly tightened her hold on Laurince's emotions, doing her best to sedate them. "Now is not the time," she said, her words clipped.

"If their focus is on the guards in the castle, why do we need to leave?" Rian asked, putting the conversation back on track.

"Because they're gathering most of the troops and sending them out, fully armed," Bax explained.

"Then shouldn't we stay here?" Myra asked, trying to force her voice to remain calm despite her rising panic. "If they're leaving the city, then it's best to stay put, no?"

"I don't think they're leaving the city," Phaia said.

"They're checking the houses, aren't they?" Laurince asked, his voice turning cold.

Bax nodded. "I overheard some guards saying they believed His Majesty was still in the capital."

Laurince ran his fingers through his hair and tugged on the ends, threatening to rip chunks out. "It's because of me. Sebastian knows we wouldn't have gone far because of the transformation, that we would have needed to lie low until it was done."

Bax pursed his lips, his silence confirmation enough.

Heart pounding, Myra asked, "If we were to see soldiers marching down the streets, wouldn't they anticipate us running?"

"Most likely," Laurince said, rubbing his jaw.

Rian nodded in agreement. "Sebastian would probably rather risk that chance to get us to come out. We would be easy to spot in a crowd. It's not like we can hide a man with wings."

"Rian," Myra chastised.

"What? It's true. Do you know how many times those things have hit me?" Rian asked, pointing to Laurince. "His wings are massive."

"Rian's right," Laurince said.

"Shit, shit, shit!" Rian stomped and spun around, his hands flying to either side of his head. He froze when he faced them again. "How the fuck are we going to get you out of here without being spotted?"

Silence fell across the room as they all stared at Laurince's wings. They were too large to hide behind a cloak.

"There's no use," Laurince said. "If we stay here, they'll find us unless there's some hiding spot in the house we don't know about."

They all turned to Phaia, a seed of hope hanging between them. But a single shake of her head obliterated that hope in an instant.

Laurince took a deep breath. "If we leave, they'll see me. There's only one option."

"Which is?" Myra asked.

A sick feeling twisted in her gut when Laurince didn't look at her.

"No," she said, backing away and shaking her head. "No. There has to be another way."

Laurince frowned. Defeat curled his shoulders inward. He caressed her cheek and gave her a sad smile. "I wish there was, Haze."

Myra grabbed him by the shirt, wrinkling the fabric. "We're *not* leaving you. You have already sacrificed enough."

"Leaving you?" Rian spat. "That's your grand plan? Over my dead body, Laurince. You came and saved me! I'm not letting you get caught."

"It's better than all of us getting caught! At least if I provided a distraction, you two would have a chance to flee." Laurince's gaze flicked between them, pleading. Begging them to let him do this.

Rian snatched the captain by the shirt, his fingers curling into the fabric. "Listen here. We will *not* abandon you."

"What other choice do we have?" Laurince asked. The pain and sorrow glossing over his brown eyes nearly shattered Myra's heart.

Rian's lips parted, but no words came out.

Myra chewed on her nails. Was there another option? One that would end with all of them getting out of here alive?

"Oh, I have an idea!" Phaia said. She looked at Laurince, assessing him. "How do you feel about small spaces?"

CHAPTER 68
GRAESON

Graeson shook out his hands, then his legs, expelling the nervousness from his limbs.

Peering at Graeson wearily, Moris leaned over to Kallie. "Maybe we should back up? Give him some room?"

"Wouldn't be a bad idea," Graeson said, stretching his arms above his head. He didn't know if stretching would help the transformation, but he could at least hope. Dusk had come and gone in the blink of an eye. He hoped the darkness would help shield his form. He didn't want the entire world to know dragons were back. Not yet anyway.

"Oh, wait!" Kal jogged over to him. With a big grin, she grabbed him by the collar and tugged on the fabric.

Graeson cocked a brow, his hand slipping to her waist. "What is it?"

She arched an eyebrow. "Unless you wish to have no clothes when we arrive, take this off. Last time, you destroyed the clothes you were wearing."

Graeson chuckled and leaned closer. His lips brushed her ear, causing a shiver to ripple through her body. "If you wish to get me out of my clothes, all you have to do is ask."

She shoved him playfully and leaned away from him. "I'm trying to do you a favor," she said, trying to sound serious, but it was hard not to hear the amusement in her voice.

"Mhm, I'm sure," he said with a cocky grin. He reached for the back of his shirt and pulled it over his head.

"Woah, woah!" Moris slapped his hands over his eyes and spun around. "Why do I keep getting myself into these situations with you two?"

Laughing, Kal held out her hand. She let her attention dip over his chest, not bothering to hide the way her heated gaze seared into him.

"Kal," he warned, his control hanging on a thread.

She smirked and grabbed his shirt, stuffing it into a bag. When she straightened, she adjusted the scimitars strapped to her back.

He took in the sight of his scimitars on her back. "My blades look good on you," he whispered. The other day, Graeson had noticed her eyeing them. He had offered them to her, intending to show her how to use them. Little did he know, she had already been trained with the blades.

"Yeah?"

"Mhm." He motioned for her to spin. When she turned, Graeson tightened the straps. "Better?"

"Yes, thank you," she said, facing him again. She tipped up her chin, a devious glint in her eyes. "I'm thinking of keeping them. About time I stole something of yours, don't you think?"

Graeson brushed his knuckles across the bottom of her jaw. "You already have."

"By the gods," Moris groaned, still turned around. "I'm going to throw up."

Kal chuckled, and any trace of apprehension buzzing at Graeson's fingertips vanished.

"We should go," she whispered.

"Wait, one more thing," Graeson said, pulling her back when she retreated a step.

"What is it?"

Graeson dug into his pocket. "You should have this." He held out his hand, palm open.

Kal's gaze dropped to the dainty ring sitting in the middle of his hand. "You still have it?"

"Of course," he said. "It's yours—it's always been yours. Your parents helped create it."

"But don't we need to have a ceremony or something?"

Graeson shrugged. "We're soul bonds, Kal. That's all that matters to me."

Biting her bottom lip, she nodded and took the ring, slipping it back on to her hand.

"When you're ready—when this war is over—we'll celebrate with everyone."

"Everyone?" she asked.

Graeson chuckled, recalling how big her last wedding had been. "Maybe not *all* of Vaneria, but those who matter to us."

A small, shaky smile curved at the corner of her mouth.

Graeson grabbed her waist and pulled her closer to him. Her hands landed on his chest, her eyes widening slightly. Then he kissed her. It was shorter than he would have liked, but she was right. They needed to get going. But he would be damned if he didn't feel her lips on his one more time.

When he pulled away, he swept his thumb across her cheek. "Stand back, all right?"

She nodded and walked away. But before she made it back to Moris' side, she spun around and called out, "Wait, your—"

Graeson threw his trousers to her, and she caught them in her hands with a gasp. He winked and turned. He didn't need any other distractions, or they would never make it out of here. Then Moris would really have something to complain about.

Graeson tilted his head back and stared at the sky. Heat filled his core and spread throughout his chest and limbs. His body vibrated with a volcanic energy. His bones shifted, snapping and cracking. But this time, Graeson was ready. This time he was expecting the tearing of his muscles, the burning of his flesh as silver and black scales emerged across his flesh. A shudder ran through his entire body, and he trembled. Smoke billowed from his nose, and the monster within breathed to life.

Time seemed to warp as his limbs grew and his body contorted into his new form. In the blink of an eye, his hand turned into a massive paw. He lifted it, inspecting the sharp, deadly claws. A deep growl ripped through his throat and morphed into a screech.

Graeson swung his head around, the movement awkward as he adjusted to his new skin. When he spotted Moris, fear shone in the man's eyes. Even though Moris had seen Graeson change before, it was still terrifying to experience.

Yet a few yards away from him, Kalisandre stood tall. Not a single drop of panic shone on her countenance. Instead, something akin to admiration and pride sparkled in her blue eyes.

Carefully, Graeson lowered his head, approaching Kalisandre with caution.

She smiled, wide and bright. She lifted her hand but paused, halting it in midair. "Can I?"

Graeson gave her a small nod.

With his permission, she stepped forward and ran her palm over the scales that ran across his cheek. His eyes shuttered shut at the contact. When her hand fell from his face, he looked at her, curious.

"Ready?" she asked.

Instead of nodding, he turned around, careful not to step on either of them. Then he laid his tail out beside Kal and looked back at her, waiting.

Her eyes widened. "You want me to fly up *there*?" she asked, pointing to his back.

Graeson chortled, the sound strange on his tongue. He shrugged haphazardly.

Kal had said she was up for the challenge. He wasn't sure if she would prefer riding astride rather than inside his hand, but he was curious to see if she would take the offer. He started to turn, but she called out to him.

"Fine," she said. "But if I fall, you better catch me."

As if Graeson would let her fall.

Kal crawled up his tail, the climb slow and laborious. When she was more than half-way up, Graeson sighed and flicked his tail. Kalisandre released a high-pitched yelp, but a second later, he felt her land near the base of his neck. Then he felt her strike him—or at least he assumed that was what the light jab was.

He glanced back, his neck long enough for him to spot Kalisandre seated between two spikes as if the spot had been created just for her.

She closed her eyes for a moment as she took a deep, shuddering breath. When she exhaled, she said, "I'm trusting you here."

He huffed again and looked away.

"Are you…*smiling*?" Moris asked him, scratching his head.

Graeson glared at him.

"Ha! You were!" Moris shivered. "Gods, that's terrifying."

He began walking towards Graeson's tail, but before he reached it, Graeson launched into the air.

Moris shouted after him, but Graeson ignored him. He peered at Kalisandre as they rose above the farmhouse. She held onto the spike in front of her with a white-knuckle grip. As if sensing his attention on her, Kal peeled her eyes open. When her gaze locked onto his, a huge smile spread across her face. Graeson bristled at the overwhelming joy spilling from her.

"That's fine!" Moris yelled. "I have wings, too, you know."

Graeson snorted as Moris flew toward them, his wings beating rapidly to catch up. Meanwhile, Graeson glided through the air, his wings flapping at a fifth of the speed.

Graeson looked back at Kalisandre, a silent question sparkling in his eyes.

She nodded and shouted over the wind, "Do it!"

With a wicked smile that probably made him appear crazed, he swung back around, dipping over the clearing.

The wind muffled Moris' shouts.

With one quick swipe, Graeson snatched their bags with his rear claws. Then he charged forward, his gaze set on Moris.

Moris twisted in the air to look back at Graeson. His eyes widened when he realized Graeson was heading straight for him. He tried to dive, but he was too slow. Graeson reared. With his other back paw, he snatched Moris from the sky.

Shouting, Moris smacked one of Graeson's claws, the jab barely more than a prickle.

Graeson barely heard Moris' disgruntlements as Kalisandre's laughter filled his ears. The sound was pure and full, untainted by the weight of the world and what was to come.

His lips curved into a makeshift smile. Because he didn't know when, or even if, he'd hear it again, Graeson savored the moment.

CHAPTER 69
MYRA

THE WAGON CREAKED NOISILY OVER THE COBBLESTONE PATH. THE wheels scraped against the stones, the sound echoing down the narrow street. Piles of vegetables were strewn on top of a faded black tarp. As Bax forced the wagon over a lip in the path, a small onion jumped out and rolled onto the ground. A muffled "Ow" escaped from the vegetables.

Myra's brows shot up, but she flattened her expression as a stranger passed by the trio. Rian quickly rubbed his arm and twisted his shadowed features into a pained expression. The woman raised her brows at Myra but carried on down the street, not giving them a second glance.

"Really?" Myra mouthed at Rian, horrified that the woman thought she had smacked him.

Rian shrugged as Bax jostled the wagon.

"Shut it," Bax hissed at the vegetables as a potato rolled down the pile, revealing a soft, white feather.

Myra swiftly rearranged the produce as they hurried through the crowded streets of the lower district.

Laurince had been appalled when Phaia had suggested that he

hide in the wagon. But without an alternative solution, he begrudgingly crawled inside it. The wagon was barely wide enough for the tall captain. He had to fold his wings around himself and curl into a ball just to fit.

All around them, pedestrians walked with brisk paces, their heads on a constant swivel as they glanced over their shoulders. Across the street, a man hurried over to a woman and a child who were peering into the window of a bakery. Slipping a hand around the woman's waist, the man whispered into her ear. The woman's eyes widened, and she tucked her child closer to her side as they rushed down the street.

Word of the incoming soldiers was spreading fast across the capital. Apprehension and panic drenched the streets, pouring down them like a heavy stream during a storm. All around them, doors slammed shut, shutters banged closed. Those who hadn't heard about the rumors yet were quickly noticing the uneasiness of the others, their steps quickening.

"We need to hurry," Rian whispered, head low.

The soldiers hadn't made it to this part of the capital, but they would be here soon. It was only a matter of—

A high-pitched scream sounded behind them.

The pile of vegetables shook, and a few rolled to the side.

"Don't look," Bax ordered, his shoulders raising to his neck. But even he had a hard time not looking when a woman screamed in terror.

Despite knowing they shouldn't, all three glanced over their shoulders, and the wheels of the wagon halted. Up the street, a guard shoved a woman against the window of a store. Her head hit the glass so hard that a crack spider-webbed across it. Those nearby stumbled in their tracks, their faces paling in horror. Many quickened their paces as a result.

The guard shouted at the woman, spit flying into her face with each syllable. "Where is he?"

"I-I don't know," the woman stammered, her brown skin taking on a sickly hue.

"You do not know where your husband is?" the guard demanded.

"No, I—he ran to the market."

"Yet he is not there. So again, tell me, where is Han Morecaster?"

Myra sucked in a sharp breath at the mention of Laurince's cousin. Another potato rolled to the side as the pile vibrated more violently. Returning the vegetables to their places, Myra reached for the thread of emotion beneath them. The temperature was rising, and quickly at that. She poured calming thoughts down the line, and the produce stopped moving.

It would sedate Laurince for now, but not for long. It was a bandage and nothing more.

The guard yanked the woman by the elbow.

Fury rose within Myra, and even though she needed to preserve her strength, she would not let the guard harm Han's wife. She gripped the guard's emotions. Frustration, anger, and greed soaked the thread so violently she nearly released it in horror. But she held onto it, digging deep within herself, finding any emotion, any memory she could use to her advantage. She poured it down the thread of emotions.

The guard's hand uncurled around the woman's arm. He fell to his knees and sobbed as the new emotions of embarrassment, shame, and horror overtook him.

"What the—"

"We need to go," Myra interrupted Bax, charging forward. She didn't have time to explain. The woman was already running away from the guard, no questions asked. That was what mattered.

But when Myra didn't hear the creaking of the wagon's wheels, she spun around and glared at Bax, who stood still, dumbfounded.

"*Now*," she demanded.

Bax finally looked away from the guard crumpled on the ground.

"Nice work," Rian whispered in her ear as he hurried down the street beside her.

Despite the praise, guilt sat heavily in her stomach. Myra refused to think about it too long, though, lest she wished for it to pull her down. She had to get Rian and Laurince out of there. They were outnumbered. If the guards found them again, she didn't think Sebastian would let them escape a second time.

They made their way down the streets, passing more guards who were too busy breaking into shops and houses. They ignored closed signs and locked doors, kicking them down instead of waiting for someone to unlock them.

Myra did her best to keep her gaze forward. More than once she caught Rian glancing back, hesitating. While most of his features were cast in shadows from his low hood, his mouth was set in a grim line.

"Keep moving," Bax commanded, his voice tight.

Rian reluctantly put one foot in front of the other. He couldn't help his people if he were dead.

At every slam of a door, Myra jumped. At every cry, she grimaced. She helped as many people as she could, turning guards away from their victims, immobilizing them with an overabundance of emotion. Myra's well of power was deep, but she feared what would happen when she inevitably reached the bottom, when she could no longer help those escape the onslaught of the guards.

Some of the nearby pedestrians began jogging instead, dipping down the nearest street to get away from the guards. But their trio was slower, the wagon preventing them from running. Myra spotted someone eyeing them and whispering to their friend about abandoning the wagon if they were them. But Myra would not let that happen. They were all going to get out of there alive.

Glass shattered as a person flew through a nearby window.

A guard jumped through the broken window, his boots crunching the glass. Slipping two fingers in his mouth, he whistled, and a squadron of guards came sprinting through the streets. The guard shoved his thumb toward the building he had exited. With his other hand, he snatched the man who was trying to crawl away by the collar.

"Han," Myra gasped, recognizing Laurince's cousin. She tried to reach out, to grab the guard's emotions, but they slipped through her hands. The emotions were too bright, too violent.

"No, no, no," Myra mumbled as she scrambled to find more of her power. She was reaching the bottom of her well, and she was too far from the guard to get a strong enough hold.

Banging sounded from inside the building the guards had entered. A group of men came storming out, swords swinging.

Bax cursed, and the wagon stopped moving.

"Take it and go. I'll catch up," he instructed, ducking beneath the bar and racing to the side of the wagon. He pulled out a short sword and brandished it as he sprinted toward Han.

Rian glanced between the wagon and the fight, hesitating.

Myra tugged on Rian's arm. "No, you can't. You heard Bax. We need to go. *Now.*"

"I can't leave them!" Rian tugged his arm free. "I can't abandon my people."

The guards outnumbered them two-to-one. Han's right eye was swollen, and another man was limping, blood trailing down his leg.

"If they see you, you're dead. How are you going to help your people, then?"

Rian looked at Myra, and she already knew he had made up his mind.

"I'm sorry, Mys."

"You'll die!" she said, her vision already blurring.

Rian pulled out the sword Bax had swiped for them from beneath his cloak. "I'd rather be dead than be known as a king who ran from his kingdom. Take him and get out of here."

Then he was off before she could even respond.

"Shit," Myra hissed, pressing her hands against her head. Her heart was pounding in her chest. She looked at the bar of the wagon.

Strangers ran past her, the desire to be inconspicuous long since abandoned as a brawl broke out in the middle of the street. Bax was already at the center of the fight. He ripped a guard off one man who was struggling to stand his ground. As Rian sprinted toward them, a guard turned around. His eyes widened momentarily before raising his weapon. Rian attacked, but the guard blocked the strike. Metal clashed against metal as the two men struck again and again.

As Bax fought his opponent, he spotted Rian in the corner of his eye. But he couldn't voice an objection as the guard swung at his head. Bax rolled, narrowly missing the blade.

A few feet from them, Han was on the ground, fighting off another guard.

A hand popped out of the wagon, and Myra raced over, trying to shove it back. "No, you can't. If the people see you—" Myra choked on her words as Laurince ignored her pleas and burst through the pile of vegetables. His eyes bled black, his rage pouring from him.

She reached for him, but his wrath slipped through her fingers, the anger and rage too bright to diminish.

"Get out of here!" Laurince shouted.

Myra lurched forward, but Laurince was quicker. He shot through the air, sword in hand.

When he met his first opponent, Laurince was merciless. His

blade sliced through the air like water. Upon seeing the man with wings, the remaining gawking civilians ran in terror, screaming.

Myra felt for the small knife he had given her inside her pocket. She palmed the hilt, shifting from one foot to the other. But who was she kidding? If she joined, she would only get in the way. Her few training sessions with Laurince did not make her a fighter. Yet she needed to do something.

An explosion shook the ground, and a plume of dark smoke billowed into the air. Screams filled the streets. Feet pounded on the ground. A flurry of guards and civilians ran toward them. Fights broke out on every corner.

Another explosive went off, and she reached for the wagon to steady herself.

Explosive after explosive sounded. Her ears rang. Her legs trembled.

She spun around, searching for a safe path out. But there were no tunnels. There was no escape. All around her, guards and civilians fought. Glass shards and blood quickly covered the pavement.

Her attention flicked back to the brawl where her friends fought. Brilliant wings sparkled in the sunlight.

Myra tightened her grip around the hilt.

She was not weak.

She was not a burden.

She was not afraid of death.

With a war cry spilling from her mouth, Myra charged.

CHAPTER 70
KALLIE

THE WIND WHIPPED THROUGH KALLIE'S HAIR AS THEY NEARED THE capital. Her thighs and hips ached from riding astride, but she didn't dare complain. All she had to do was hold on; Graeson was doing most of the work as they soared through the sky at a grueling pace.

They traveled under the cloak of night, Graeson's onyx scales blending into the sky. During the day, they rested wherever they could. Graeson's speed was unmatched, and he reduced the time to get to the Frenzian capital by half. Before Kallie knew it, a forest of massive trees was ahead of them. Although the Frenzian forest looked different from above, Kallie recognized the sequoia trees instantly.

Graeson slowed his pace, his wings straightening as he glided through the ominous clouds. He peered back at her, his gaze narrowed and nostrils flared.

They were close.

Kallie inhaled a slow breath to clear her raging thoughts. But when the air hit the back of her throat, she coughed, inhaling smoke. She squinted and peered through the thick smog.

Kallie gasped.

Flames covered the capital.

She flattened herself against Graeson's back, tightening her grip just before he dove.

CHAPTER 71

MYRA

Myra swallowed her scream as agony flooded the streets.

It had happened so fast. Once the guards marched down the streets and the explosives went off, chaos ran rampant.

As the screams of terror rang in her ears, Myra didn't think it could get worse. Then, the drakonises came. Their claws ripped through anything the beasts encountered: stone, brick, flesh.

In the havoc, those fighting didn't have time to wonder who released the beasts—Rian, Sebastian, or someone else entirely. They had no time to place the blame on anyone. Not as they fought for their lives, as they struggled to survive.

All at once, Myra was back in Pontia when the Frenzians had stormed the castle and burned the coastal village to the ground.

Explosions erupted in every direction.

Windows shattered, and the broken glass mixed with the gravel.

Iron tinged the air.

Blood splattered across the walls, and ripped-off limbs lay forgotten in the streets.

Panic and fear rose higher and higher. It wrapped its fiery

tendrils around Myra's throat as the emotions of the ravaged city fell upon her shoulders, forcing her to her knees.

She struggled to breathe. Struggled to move, to fight, to run.

She couldn't see beyond the blood on her hands. She couldn't even recall if it was hers or someone else's. If she had caused the pain or if she had tried to stop it.

A shadow fell across her, and she was swept from the ground. As the frigid wind nipped at her cheeks, Myra had no fight left in her. She didn't scream. She didn't call out. She stared at the ground below her as horror flooded the street.

The beast carrying her headed toward an alley. When her feet landed on the ground softer than she had expected, Myra blinked.

Inhaling, she choked on smoke and coughed. Swatting at the debris wafting around her, she spotted white wings stained red and black.

"Laurince?" she croaked, her throat dry.

Laurince's arms wrapped around her before he pulled back and gripped her shoulders. He bent down to her height and peered at her. She struggled to maintain his eye contact. Although his broad frame and wings blocked the scene behind him, she could still hear the screams, the cries, the snapping of bones.

"Look at me, Haze," he said, squeezing her shoulders gently.

Myra peeled her gaze away from the smoke filling the night sky.

"You need to get out of here."

Myra shook her head and took a step back. She wouldn't abandon him. She *promised*.

Tears hung on her lash-line, her vision blurring and distorting Laurince's features.

"Myra, *listen* to me." His fingers dug into her sore shoulders. "I will be right behind you."

"No, you won't," she said through clenched teeth as she held back the tears.

"The others need you—the wounded and the dying. They need you to help them," Laurince pleaded.

"*You* need me," she whispered, the tears escaping.

"*I* need you to be safe."

She chewed on her bottom lip, hesitating. "I can't help them," she said at last. "I'm not a healer."

It was something she recalled saying to Domitius before when he had asked her to assist with the experiments. She had no choice but to listen then, and look where that had gotten them.

Laurince tipped up her chin, beckoning her to meet his eyes. "You helped *me*, Haze."

Another explosion erupted, this one even closer than the last. The earth beneath their feet quaked. Laurince held her tighter.

"You can do this, Myra. Your gift is a blessing, and those who are in pain will be grateful for a single ounce of it. Phaia will go with you."

"Phaia? But she's—" Myra choked on her words as the woman appeared beside Laurince.

Phaia's blouse was disheveled, a sleeve torn as if someone had snatched it. A smear of soot was spread across her forehead as if she had wiped the back of her hand on it. She carried a small blade. As if tracking Myra's gaze, she slipped the stained weapon behind her back.

"We'll go together, yeah?" Phaia held out her other hand with a trembling smile. She was afraid, too. But she wasn't giving up. That much was clear.

Myra glanced at Laurince. She saw the plea in his eyes, and although she hated to part from him, she knew she would only be a distraction.

She nodded.

"I—" Laurince cut himself off though and wrapped her in his

arms, squeezing her tightly. "I'll find you afterwards, all right?" he whispered into her ear.

Tears soaked Myra's cheek and fell onto his shoulder. Her throat swelled up, stealing her voice. Squeezing her eyes shut, she nodded, holding him tighter. He kissed her cheek.

Without another word, Phaia snatched Myra's hand and peeled her off Laurince. Phaia ran in the opposite direction of the castle, pulling Myra behind her.

Myra looked back, but Laurince was already returning to the fight. And as she stared at his disappearing figure, she couldn't help but wonder if that was truly what he had wanted to say or if he had been going to say something else before he had stopped himself. She wondered if she would ever get the chance to know.

CHAPTER 72

GRAESON

GRAESON JUMPED INTO HIS TROUSERS, SWIFTLY BUTTONING THEM despite his trembling fingers.

The transformation still hurt like nothing else he had ever experienced, but the breaking of his bones was marginally easier this time. Unlike last time, he was only knocked out for a few minutes before Kallie was shaking him awake.

He had landed in a clearing just before the forest outside the capital's perimeter. It was as close as he was willing to get without knowing the full scope of what was happening.

As Graeson tossed on his shirt, Kallie held out his scimitars.

"Thanks," he said, grabbing one and placing it in its sheath. He reached for the other, but she held it out of reach.

"Are you sure you don't need to rest?" she asked, hesitant.

Graeson swept his hand through his hair, shoving the thick locks away from his face. They hadn't flown as far as the night before, but Graeson had flown harder today. Still, he wasn't tired. Quite the opposite, in fact. Since he was no longer fighting half of himself, his energy wasn't spent on caging the beast within. Now it was as if he was overflowing with energy. The tips of his fingers buzzed at his sides.

"I'm good," he said, holding out his hand for the weapon.

Kallie eyed him warily. "Would you tell me if you weren't?"

Graeson smirked and wiggled his fingers. "Depends."

Her groan only made him smile wider.

She handed him the second scimitar, and he slid it into its sheath. "I am fine, though. Honestly. Flyboy over there, on the other hand…"

Moris grumbled, clutching his stomach as he bent over a shrub. "Flying myself is one thing; being carried through the air is another entirely. I—" He pressed a fist to his mouth. "I don't like it."

"I told you he should have ridden on your back with me," Kallie mumbled, elbowing Graeson in the side.

Graeson snorted. "I am not a pack mule."

Kallie rolled her eyes and hiked the bag onto her shoulders.

"All right," Moris breathed out, straightening. "I-I think I'm good."

Kallie pursed her lips and observed him. "Are you sure?"

Graeson didn't wait for Moris to respond, though. Instead, he headed toward the forest. They didn't have time to cater to Moris' needs.

"Hey!" Moris called out. "Not so fast."

"If you can't keep up, then that's your problem," Graeson said over his shoulder.

"By the gods, nothing ever changes with you, does it?"

Graeson rolled his eyes. When Kallie caught up with him, she nudged him in the side, and he chuckled.

THEY HURRIED through the forest as fast as they dared. The smoke from the distant fire crept over the ground, and the smog obscured the glow of the moon.

Moris hissed out as a branch caught his wing, and he swatted it away with a sneer. Graeson shot a glare over his shoulder when the thin branch snapped in half and fell atop the fallen leaves.

Moris raised his hands as if to suggest the tree was to blame.

Shaking his head, Graeson made to move forward when the crack of a branch sounded up ahead. He snatched Kallie by the waist and pulled her against him as he slid behind a tree. Hearing it too, Moris dove behind the tree next to them.

Graeson held up a finger.

Keeping Kallie tucked against his chest, Graeson shifted and peered around the tree. Several yards away, he saw a flicker of movement. Then he heard them.

The sobs and hisses of pain.

He pressed his mouth against Kallie's ear. "Stay here."

Slipping out from behind the tree, he crouched and weaved his way toward the voices with careful, silent footsteps.

Looking around a tree, Graeson could make out a figure as the voices intensified. Scattered across the forest was a large group of people. Cries of pain, sorrow, and grief filled the air.

Beyond the trees, he spotted the watchtowers on the capital's walls, but the distance made it impossible to tell if they were manned. In the far distance, screams echoed, and a rumble shook the earth. Graeson's attention snapped back to the people huddled before him. As he scanned the area, he realized there wasn't just one group but dozens scattered throughout the forest outside the city.

Nearby, a man cradled a woman's leg in his lap as she leaned against a tree. Even in the dim light, Graeson could see the gruesome wound. Her calf was nearly torn apart, the skin appearing to sizzle as if burned. He couldn't tell if it was from the fire engulfing the capital or the explosives that had rocked the earth. But one thing was abundantly clear.

"They're civilians," Kallie breathed out.

Graeson snapped his head in her direction. He hadn't even heard her approach, too focused on the atrocities in front of him. "You were supposed to stay," he hissed.

She scoffed. "I am not a dog." She shooed him away.

"Neither am I for the record," Moris said on Graeson's other side.

Graeson cursed.

Couldn't at least one of them listen to his instructions? Or did they both wish to give away their positions?

Kallie stood, and he grabbed her wrist, tugging her back down. "What are you doing?" he asked. They might have been civilians, but he had seen several weapons lying around.

"Look at them, Graeson. Most of them are wounded or dying."

"That does not mean they're our friends."

She snatched her hand away. "No, but—" She gasped, swallowing the rest of her argument.

Then she was running.

"Fuck," he spat and took off after her.

CHAPTER 73
KALLIE

Kallie was seeing things. She was having another nightmare, and any second, she would wake up. There was no other explanation for the sight before her.

A cold sweat slicked Kallie's palms as she ran, struggling to breathe. Each inhale was a desperate plea for air as she gaped at the pale body on the ground. Myra lay face-up, her blonde hair draped over a woman's lap and the moon's glow kissing her freckled cheeks. Blood dripped from her nose, and the woman cradling Myra's head dabbed her face with a stained cloth.

"No, no, *no*," Kallie repeated as she ran.

Myra was not dead. She couldn't be. They hadn't resolved things yet. They hadn't had time to discuss everything they had gone through, everything they had put each other through. Even though Kallie was still angry at Myra, she had never wished for this.

Kallie pressed her hand to her chest as the years of manipulation, lies, and hidden abilities squeezed her heart. They were both victims. Two children taken by a heartless man.

Her nails dug into her chest, nearly tearing her blouse.

She could hear Graeson on her heels and the gasps of horror

coming from the strangers they passed, but she didn't stop. She had to know the truth.

She crashed on the ground beside Myra's body. Questions tumbled from Kallie's mouth in a flurry, so fast the woman struggled to answer a single one. Kallie's hand hovered above Myra's face. Her cheeks were smeared with soot, and her normally bright blonde hair was dull from the ash.

An arm wrapped around her waist. Graeson tried to pull her away, saying something about giving Myra space. Kallie shoved him away. Teardrops lined Kallie's bottom lash-line, their weight tugging on her lashes and blurring her vision.

They were too late. They were—

Kallie's breath hitched. She choked back her tears as she tore her gaze from Myra and looked at the woman. She had to have misheard her.

"Phaia?" Kallie croaked, finally recognizing the woman.

The handmaiden gave her a weak smile.

Kallie shook her head, struggling to understand. "W-what did you say?"

Phaia exhaled, exhaustion tinting the warm beige skin beneath her eyes. "She's not dead."

"Sh-she's not?" Kallie's arms buckled beneath her, but Graeson was there to catch her before she collapsed.

There was still time. She could still fix this. *They* could fix it.

Phaia wiped away the blood from Myra's nose, and Kallie finally noticed Myra's chest rising slowly, as if she was in a deep slumber.

"No, she's not. I think she pushed herself too far. She was running around, helping as many of the wounded as she could. Then she passed out. I think that's why she's bleeding—" Phaia paused. A line formed between her brows. "Why are you here?"

Kallie looked at Graeson, her words jumbling in her mouth.

"We were in the area. When we saw the smoke, we came as fast as we could," Graeson explained, leaving out the fact that they had flown here after hearing about the Royal Seer's vision.

Kallie nodded absentmindedly as Graeson helped her to her feet.

"Why were you in the area?" Phaia asked, skeptical.

Kallie didn't hear Graeson's response as she inhaled a shuddering breath. The coppery tang of blood and smoke overwhelmed her. Around them, hundreds of people rested, an orchestra of moans filling the forest. The gentle pressure of Graeson's hand was a comforting contrast to the icy chill that clung to her skin as she took in the injuries of the wounded. Nearby, a man slept on the ground, his pant leg ripped off, revealing a ghastly burn. He should have been screaming, yet he slept, his features only marginally twisted. Several others had similar injuries, yet none screamed. It was as if their pain had been sedated.

"Kals?" a quiet voice croaked.

Kallie fell to her knees.

"Mys?" she called out, grabbing Myra's limp hand. Had Myra used her gift to lessen the pain of the wounded? How many had she helped soothe to sleep? Was her state the result of burning out?

Myra blinked, her hazel eyes unsteady. For right now, they would put the past behind them. When the war was over, they would have that talk.

"Are you—are you all right?"

Wrinkles creased Myra's forehead as she looked around. "Laurince? Wh-where is Laurince?"

Kallie's lips parted, but she quickly shut them, peering up at Phaia for an answer.

"He and King Rian are still in the capital fighting," Phaia said, gently brushing a strand of hair away from Myra's face.

"I—I have to help—" Myra tried to get up, but her limbs were too weak. They wobbled beneath her, and she fell back onto Phaia's lap.

Kallie placed her hand atop Myra's. "We're here, Mys. We'll help him," she whispered.

Myra nodded haphazardly before exhaustion pulled her back under, her hand once again going limp.

Kallie looked toward the capital, where smoke filled the sky. The tips of the flames peeked over the walls, their torrent unending.

"What happened?" Kallie asked Phaia.

Hesitation shone brightly in the handmaiden's eyes, her fear of trusting them and telling them the wrong thing evident.

"We're on their side, Phaia," Kallie urged, gesturing to Myra. "We came to help. But we can only do that if we know what happened."

Phaia took a deep breath and nodded. "After the trial, we—"

"What trial?"

Phaia blinked. "You don't know?"

Kalie and Graeson shook their heads.

"Sebastian captured King Rian, Laurince, and Myra when they snuck into the castle. Someone betrayed them. Sebastian made the king stand before everyone and blamed him for the creation of the drakonises."

Kallie gaped. "That's absurd! He had nothing to do with them."

Phaia frowned. "Not everyone believes Sebastian's claims, but he was able to turn many against the king by calling Myra up as a witness."

"Myra betrayed Rian?" Kallie asked, apprehensive. Was Myra still working for Domitius? Had she tricked them again? Kallie's suspicion was hard to swallow, yet somehow she knew she was wrong even before Phaia shook her head.

"She hadn't meant to. Sebastian and the judge twisted her words somehow and tricked her into speaking lies."

The ground shook, and Graeson's grip on her tightened.

Phaia barely flinched from the quake and continued, forcing Kallie to tuck away her questions. "I think even more distrust

Sebastian now after the drakonises escaped from confinement during the trial and then again today. Some even believe Sebastian released the drakonises intentionally."

Phaia then told them how the fight broke out after the soldiers began raiding the capital in search of Rian. The capital was quick to fall into mayhem. Brawls broke out, the Frenzian grenades tore through the city, and then the drakonises were let loose.

When she finished, Kallie and Graeson struggled to formulate a response. As Graeson's lips parted, a scream ripped through the forest, pulling their attention away.

"Traitor!" a man shouted. "We have a traitor in our midst!"

CHAPTER 74
KALLIE

Shouts erupted from the wounded. One man stood, clutching his side with a hand as he dragged his sword through the dirt with the other. Kallie squinted, looking beyond the stranger as two others dragged a body toward the crowd.

"Shit," Graeson hissed as the moon's glow spilled onto a pair of wings being dragged through the dirt.

"Oh no," Kallie mumbled.

"Is he…is he with you?" Phaia asked, peering at Kallie and Graeson.

"Unfortunately," Graeson mumbled.

Kallie slapped him on the side. "He's *your* friend."

"Dani's actually," Graeson corrected, rather unhelpfully.

Kallie glared at him. She had seen how worried Graeson was when he first saw Moris in the clearing. She had also witnessed the playful banter between the two, the faint smile that would appear on Graeson's face whenever Moris teased him. Although Graeson believed he was alone in this world, he was surrounded by people who cared about him.

"What? He's more of a companion of mine," Graeson said. "Really an acquaintance."

Kallie groaned.

"Whoever he is to you, if you care about him, you better do something and fast," Phaia urged, as an angry horde gathered around Moris. "He won't stand a chance against a mob, even an injured one."

Kallie didn't bother to say that Moris would have no problem handling an angry mob. Instead, she hurried over, vaguely hearing Graeson groan before following her.

When they reached the crowd, Moris was trying to talk sense into the buzzing mob. His control was slipping, though, as more shouts sounded. Kallie could see Moris' eyes darkening, his veins straining along the trunk of his neck as he became more frustrated. They needed to control the situation before Moris' emotions got the best of him.

Shoving her way through the bodies, Kallie jumped in front of Moris and tossed out her arms. "He won't hurt you!"

Piercing shouts bombarded her ears instantly.

"He's one of them!"

"Did you see what one of those beasts did to my wife?"

"Who are *you* to make demands?"

"You would rather defend him than put an end to this fight?"

Kallie tossed her hood back. "Many of you may not know me, but—"

A gasp rippled through the crowd.

"That's her! The princess who betrayed us!"

"*She's* to blame!"

Kallie retreated a step on instinct as the mob grew angrier. At the cacophony of snarls, her skin prickled. Her power stirred inside her, her core buzzing with untapped energy. Each insult shot at her only pushed her power up higher and higher. Beyond the chaotic fray, a distant rumble shook the leaves of the sequoias, a stark reminder of the battle waging on within the capital.

They were wasting time. She had to do something, and she had to do it *now*.

She threw her hands up. "Stop!" she demanded, her voice soaring over the crowd.

The shouts were swallowed in an instant, an eerie silence befalling the forest. Not only had the people gone silent, but they had stopped altogether, as if frozen in time.

She glanced at Moris, who knelt on the ground behind her with his jaw hanging open. The men who had dragged him over had since released him. Kallie frowned, her power sinking back down. Was the people's silence the result of his power?

Putting the question aside, Kallie stepped forward cautiously. "*We* are not the enemy. Sebastian is. The Prince has been leading your kingdom under the false pretense that the true king of Frenzia was sick and then abducted." Kallie looked at the weary crowd, hoping they could still hear her in their frozen state.

She swallowed and continued, "Hear me when I say that is a lie. With the king of Ardentol's help, Sebastian has been working to overtake Vaneria and put it under one rule. To further their own agenda, they falsely accused Rian and me of being unjustly taken in order to start a war. The truth is more complicated than that.

"Sebastian is to blame for the drakonises. *He* has taken your loved ones—your friends and family, your neighbors—and has turned them into weapons. He has brought civil unrest into your kingdom. At this very moment, your king is out there fighting. He is putting his life on the line for *you*, his people. Meanwhile, where is Sebastian? Did anyone see him fighting in the streets?"

At her question, the people stared at her, and she struggled to read their expressions. Were they even listening? Did they believe a single thing she had said?

To her relief, Phaia shouted a resounding *no*. When their gazes met, Phaia gave her an encouraging nod.

Kallie pressed on. "I have not known His Majesty for long, but one thing is certain: Rian cares for the people in this kingdom and their well-being more than anything else. He would rather risk his life than let the crown fall to his brother, someone who seeks to destroy the peace the seven kingdoms fought for one hundred years ago."

Kallie took a deep breath, hoping and praying some of her words reached open ears. But as the crowd shifted on their feet, their paralysis wearing off, her hope lessened.

Someone in the middle of the crowd was the first to speak out. "Even if what you say is true, we're outnumbered. How do you expect us to fight wild beasts and an entire army?"

Others murmured their agreement.

Her nails bit into the flesh of her palms. "Reinforcements are coming," she said, holding onto her fleeting hope as tightly as she could.

"When?" someone else demanded.

Kallie swallowed hard. The answer was stuck in her throat.

She didn't know when the Tetrian or the Pontian troops would arrive. Terin had told her they were coming, but how long would it take them? What if they didn't bring enough troops? What if they were too late? He said he sent word to Tetria, but what if the letter never arrived? What if Ellie was on a fool's errand? What if the troops from Tetria never came?

Her stomach churned, a nauseous knot coiling tighter with every unanswered question.

As if sensing her inner turmoil, Graeson shifted, causing her attention to snap to him.

Despite everything they had been through and everything the Fates had thrown at them, Graeson had never lost hope. He kept fighting for them. Even as he stood there amidst a fear-filled throng of injured and tired strangers, he still had hope for a brighter tomorrow, a brighter future.

She had to hold on to the hope that they would make it out of this.

She dug her heels into the ground. "They're coming. But we need to hold on until they arrive unless we wish Sebastian to win. We—"

Kallie stopped mid-sentence, startled by a snapping twig and a hushed voice coming from the north, closer to the walls of the capital. Those standing around her straightened, their eyes widening as fear gripped them.

Kallie reached for the weapon tucked in the holster strapped to her thigh.

As the shadows shifted in the forest, Kallie looked over her shoulder. Graeson was already in front of Kallie, scimitars in hand. A puff of smoke plumed from his lips, curling in the moonlight.

"Protect them," he said, tipping his chin toward Myra and Phaia.

Kallie wanted to argue. But when she saw Phaia gripping Myra's limp body to her chest, trembling, Kallie relented. She sprinted toward them just as the first soldiers burst through the trees, blood-soaked swords hanging at their hips.

Baring his teeth, Moris dug his fingers into the ground, scraping the top layer of soil. The muscles in his legs strained against his trousers, and his wings stretched out behind him as he prepared to take flight.

With whatever miscellaneous weapons they found, the civilians ran toward the soldiers.

"Stay back!" a man said, raising his weapon as the first line of soldiers appeared.

Heart pounding, Kallie strained to see the enemy cloaked in the shadows.

A gasp sounded behind her. Shuffling sounded, but Kallie didn't dare take her eyes off the enemy.

"Stay behind me," Kallie ordered.

"But—" Myra was cut off when a woman shouted at the soldiers, demanding they leave.

One soldier made to speak, but another civilian threw something at him before he could. The object bounced off the soldier's cheek.

"Was that a fucking *rock*?"

Kallie froze, her brows knitting together. The voice was familiar. But before she could place it, the civilians charged, swinging branches and swords wildly. Someone threw dirt at the soldiers. Others quickly picked up the tactic, grabbing handfuls and tossing dirt at the soldiers. Between the debris and the shadows, the fight became a hazy blur in front of Kallie.

Kallie squinted. Was the darkness playing tricks on her? She could have sworn Moris' wings were webbed.

"Laurince?" Myra croaked.

Kallie was jostled as Myra swayed, suddenly standing beside her. Kallie quickly grabbed hold of Myra, steadying her. But Myra pushed against Kallie, trying to break free. She stumbled, and Kallie reached out.

"It's Laurince!" Myra said, pushing against Kallie.

"Laurince? Where?" Kallie asked, tightening her hold around Myra's waist.

Myra pointed, her hand trembling as it hung in the air. "There."

Kallie squinted, searching for the familiar face. Had Sebastian's men brought hostages to toy with them? To threaten those who were injured?

As her heartbeat thundered in her ear, she nearly missed the captain, her gaze fixed on the feathered wings that sparkled like opals in the moonlight. Kallie's mouth fell open. Laurince was one of them. He was—

"It is him! He's alive!" Myra cried out as she tugged on Kallie's shirt. "They're both alive!"

"Both?" Kallie asked, panicking.

"Laurince and Rian."

Kallie frantically searched the faces of the soldiers. More civilians had joined the attack, and Kallie struggled to identify friend from foe. She looked for Graeson, their connection tugging at her. She did a double take, blinking at a man struggling a few feet from Graeson. She could have sworn she knew that face, yet the man's hair was different. This man's hair was as dark as night. His arm was wrapped around another person's back. He struggled under the man's weight but refused to release him. As he shifted his weight, he lifted his face, and familiar green eyes connected with Kallie's.

Rian's lips parted, as did Kallie's.

This wasn't Sebastian's army. This was *theirs*.

But those who were attacking hadn't realized it yet.

"Take her," Kallie commanded, passing Myra to Phaia.

She rushed forward, shouting. The cries and grunts of those fighting were too loud and masked her voice. A sword clashed against another. Others charged with their sticks, their teeth bared. A rock pelted Rian in the side, and he grimaced. Then a man with a longsword came charging forward, a war cry pouring from his mouth.

Kallie's head pounded. She spun, her hands digging into her hair. Where was Moris? He could stop the attack.

Her power twisted in her stomach, but there were too many.

There.

Kallie called out to Moris as he raised his weapon and pulled his elbow back, preparing to strike. But he didn't hear her. Moris' blade hit the man's armored brace and clanged against the metal.

Kallie skidded to a halt. Sweat soaked her neck as she took in all the people. She had to try. If she didn't, who knew how many would suffer?

She took in a deep breath, her power rising through her stomach and up her throat. When it reached the tip of her tongue, she unleashed the command. "Stop!"

Her voice reverberated against the trees, causing the leaves to shake. In an instant, those at the front of the charge halted, their heels sinking into the dirt.

Her chest rose rapidly as her gift hummed beneath her skin. Kallie flexed her hands at her sides.

She did it. She had commanded them.

Graeson looked back at her, panic shining in his eyes and a question on his lips. She pointed at the soldiers. As Graeson followed her finger, someone else shouted, "It's the king!"

Branches and rocks dropped to the ground as the people fell to their knees. Rian grimaced, his face twisting with agony, exhaustion, and something else Kallie couldn't quite pinpoint.

She turned her attention to those who surrounded him. Not all the soldiers wore armor. Some wore simple leathers; others wore casual tops and trousers. All were battered and bruised. Ash coated their hair. Soot, dirt, and blood stained their faces. The marks of battle were etched into every wrinkle, every cut, every stain. Some could barely stand, their arms wrapped around the shoulders of another. And as Kallie took in the faces of the Frenzians who stood with King Rian, she realized what she had seen in his expression.

Defeat.

CHAPTER 75
MYRA

MYRA WINCED AS SHE PLUCKED A STAINED FEATHER FROM THE tattered wing. Laurince's muscles grew tenser with every one she removed. Feathers were missing in various spots, and others were stained black and red, the evidence of the brutal battle soaking them. Even in the fire's radiance, the wings' usual pearlescent sheen was nonexistent.

A sparkle glimmered in the fire, catching Myra's eye. She separated a clump of matted feathers, revealing a glass shard piercing the skin. She nimbly grabbed the shard. With a shaky breath, she pulled it from the tough muscle.

Laurince hissed, his fingers digging into the dirt.

"I'm sorry," she whispered, dropping the glass on top of the pile beside her. The shard clattered as it hit the rest of the broken pieces. It tumbled down the side of the small mound and landed on the ground.

Blinking away her tears, Myra turned to continue her search, but Laurince reached back, grabbing her wrist. "Sit with me?"

Her gaze fell to the ground where loose feathers circled her. "But the glass—"

"Is gone," Laurince said. He rolled his shoulders back, the muscles along his back rippling from the movement. His wings twitched, the movement awkward. "I don't feel any others."

Myra gave him a dubious look.

He pointed at the pile. "You got them all, Haze. And if not, they will be there for you later to pluck out when you can't sleep tonight. For now, can you please…" He sighed and ran a hand across his face. They were a few yards away from the fire, but even in the shadows, Myra could see the heavy purple bags beneath his eyes. "Sit with me?"

Her shoulders sagged. Too exhausted to argue with him, she wiped her hands on the sides of her trousers to brush off the debris from her fingertips. "Fine," she said, taking a seat beside him.

Laurince wrapped an arm around her waist and pulled her closer. Their thighs pressed against each other, and his warmth spilled into her. Myra sank against him, her side nestling perfectly against his. She exhaled, and her breath twirled in front of her mouth.

"Are you cold?" Laurince asked, shifting. "Do you want to go sit by the fire?"

Myra grabbed his thigh, halting him. "I'm fine over here."

While she had been cold before she sat, she was quickly warming back up. His wing at her back shielded her from the icy breeze.

"Very well." He rested his chin on her head. "How are you holding up?"

"I should be asking you that," she said against his chest.

"And you have—a dozen times." Laurince rubbed his hand against her side, coaxing the heat back into her body. "It's my turn to fret over you, I think."

Her lips parted, a dismissal on the tip of her tongue.

Laurince poked her side before she could say anything. "Don't even try to lie to me. Your exhaustion is plain across your face. You're not as good at hiding your emotions as you think."

"At least not from you," she mumbled.

He squeezed her gently. "That's because I'm more observant than the others, *especially* when it comes to you, Haze."

A blush tinted Myra's cheeks at the comment. Her rising smile was quick to turn down when Rian's voice brushed her ears.

Since the skirmish ended, Rian, Kallie, Graeson, and a few others had been arguing back and forth about the best course of action. With no knowledge of war strategy, Myra had sat away from the fire, not wanting to get in the way. She had expected Laurince to stay with the others and offer his own input, but found him taking a seat in front of her instead. As she plucked the glass from his wings, she couldn't help but listen to the conversation transpiring.

When Kallie had revealed that she and Graeson had killed Domitius, Myra froze in utter shock. Laurince had peered back at her, a question in his gaze. But Myra ignored it, choosing to focus on the glass instead. For her entire life, Domitius seemed untouchable, always three steps ahead. It was hard to imagine him meeting his end. She struggled to believe it. Myra wanted to press Kallie for more details, just to be certain, but she couldn't. Especially not when she took in Kallie's somber expression. Domitius might not have been her blood, but he had raised Kallie. Her feelings were bound to be complicated.

The topic quickly changed, and the discussion of plans took over. Even though Domitius was dead, Sebastian seemed to be set on moving forward with their plans to take over the seven kingdoms. He had already pushed Rian out of the capital.

As the conversation progressed, Myra had never seen Rian act so stubborn. Anything Graeson or Kallie proposed, Rian dismissed immediately, his resentment toward them apparent. The exchange was borderline hostile, the personalities and histories clashing.

Myra shifted away from Laurince. When they were traveling, Laurince had always been a source of reasoning. He balanced Rian.

Laurince bunched his brows. "What?" he asked, as if sensing her confusion.

"As captain of Rian's guard, shouldn't you be with them?"

Laurince scoffed. "There are too many co—I mean heads in that conversation already. Rian can come find me if and when he needs me."

"But they've only been arguing. Shouldn't you—"

He tipped her chin up with his knuckles. "I'm right where I want to be. My input is not needed right now. Trust me."

Her eyes flitted over his face. "Are you certain?"

Laurince nodded, tucking her against him once more. "Anyway," he said, his breath kissing the top of her head, "I'm not Rian's favorite person right now. Not after I practically dragged him away from the fight."

Myra drew aimless shapes on Laurince's thigh. "Deep down, I'm sure he's glad you did. If you hadn't, who knows what would have happened?"

"His Majesty does not see it that way, at least not right now," Laurince said, failing to hide his frustration. Myra could practically hear his eye-roll. He shrugged. "But that is neither here nor there. What's done is done. He is alive. Bax and my cousin Han are alive. I cannot say the same for many of my brothers who fought with us."

The group that had returned with Laurince and Rian was smaller than any would have liked. While they didn't know how many had died, the number of those who survived, escaped, and were on their side of the civil dispute was fewer than desired.

"Do you think the reinforcements will come in time?" Myra whispered.

Laurince's lack of response was answer enough. His hope, like so many others, was fading rapidly, like the embers of a fire that had long since been extinguished. They all wanted to believe the aid from Pontia and Tetria would make it in time, but most weren't foolish enough to put their faith in the slim chance.

"We're at least safe for the night," he said, holding her tighter.

"You don't think they'll attack?"

Laurince shook his head. "While there is always a chance, they're as tired as we are. The drakonises were called back before we retreated. They've closed the city gates. I think we can take that as a small sign of relief."

Myra nodded and peered at the treetops. Because of the smoke, she couldn't make out a single star.

Laurince brushed the tip of his knuckles across her jawline, and Myra closed her eyes. "Let's save the worries. For now, we are together. We should take that as a blessing."

She knew he was right. When she had left Laurince, she hadn't known if she would see him again. Now, sitting beside him, seeing the trace of the battle marking his body and clothes, a flurry of emotions rose within her.

Laurince's arm fell from her side. He leaned away from her. Before she could voice a complaint, he brought his hand to her cheek. His thumb skated across her skin, the touch soothing. He stared at her, his deep brown eyes soaking her in as if he was memorizing every detail.

He offered her a small smile. "Thank you," he whispered.

"For what?"

"For leaving when I asked." He swallowed, the bump in his throat dipping. "Knowing you were safe made a difference."

As Myra took him in, she realized just how much he meant to her. She had never meant to catch feelings for the captain. Although she wasn't surprised. She always did fall easily and quickly. It was something Kallie had frequently teased her about.

But with Laurince, it was different. It felt bigger. More.

And it scared her to her very bones. Come morning, the battle would begin again, and Myra knew that when the others raised their swords, Laurince would too.

She feared for his safety, but she also couldn't ask him to stay. She couldn't ask him *not* to fight. That would have been like asking him not to breathe. He was a soldier, a fighter. It was in his blood. Myra refused to ask him to change that. His loyalty to Rian, his willingness to sacrifice his own life for his kingdom, was something she admired most about him.

So, she would take this blip of time they had together and hold it close to her chest for as long as she could.

She stood, and Laurince reached for her, his lips parting and brows curling in question.

"Walk with me?" Myra asked with a shy, shaky smile.

Laurince blinked, momentarily confused, as if something he had said had upset her. Then he narrowed his gaze as she motioned toward the woods. "Haze, what are you up to?"

Myra's smile turned into one of amusement. For a man apt in military strategy, he could be quite dense at times.

"Is that a no, then?" she asked patiently.

He grabbed her hands. "Lead the way."

CHAPTER 76
KALLIE

RIAN PLOPPED DOWN IN FRONT OF THE FIRE, HIS HEAD FALLING INTO his hands. "We lost so many—*too* many."

"Which is why we need to wait," Kallie said, sitting across from him. Graeson shifted beside her, his leg pressing against hers. "Reinforcements are coming."

Rian lifted his face from his palms, and a forest on fire blazed within his green eyes. "So you keep saying, but my people are dying as we speak," he said, vitriol spilling into each word. "Do you know how many we had to abandon? How many we could not carry back with us because we had no more open arms? How many we had to leave because it was already too late for them? Not just soldiers, Kalisandre, but women and children and elderly who were too close to the brink of death. Those who you see in this forest? They're the lucky ones. They got out."

"You cannot save them all, Rian," Kallie said, her hands falling limp at her sides.

Graeson placed his palm on her lower back for support, as if he could see the weight of Rian's words pressing down on her.

When Kallie, Graeson, and Moris had arrived, they had been too late to provide support during the battle. If they had left sooner, if they hadn't waited until nightfall to hide Graeson's form, would they have been able to make a difference? Would they have been able to save those who died tonight? Maybe some, but not all.

Still, the questions haunted her.

Once Rian had ensured the injured were seen by the healers, he had immediately wanted to return to the fight, despite everyone's protests.

Kallie understood his desire to go back. But she, like the rest of them, knew returning would only be a fool's errand. Rian was exhausted—they all were. If he went back now, he would be sealing his fate away, letting Death claim him, letting Sebastian win.

They had to wait for reinforcements. There was no other choice if they wanted to win.

Kallie rolled her hands into fists to keep them from trembling. "Terin and Ellie will arrive with the troops. And when they do, we will take back the capital. We'll take back *your* kingdom. But until then, you need to rest."

Rian scoffed in disbelief. "You mean sit here and listen to the cries of the dying? Sit here and watch my kingdom, my *home*, burn to ash?"

"Like ours?" Graeson retorted under his breath.

Luckily, Rian didn't hear him, his attention and anger fixed on Kallie.

"If that is what it takes to see tomorrow," she said, "to survive until we have the numbers, yes. That is precisely what you must do. You cannot rule a kingdom from the grave, Rian."

Rian stood, the movement sluggish as if it took all his energy to get up. He gave his back to them and looked at the fire, the flames casting eerie shadows across his features. "You say that as if there will be a kingdom to rule after tonight."

Rian turned on his heel and headed toward the provisional

infirmary on the other side of the camp. Kallie leaned forward, about to go after him to talk some sense into him, but Graeson tugged on her hand.

"Let him go," he said.

"But—"

He shook his head. "You will not get through to him." He arched a brow. "Unless you wish to persuade him through other means. Is that your intention?"

Kallie gaped. "No, of course not!"

She would not use her power on her friends and allies—unless it meant saving their lives. Although Rian was clearly heated, she did not believe he would sneak into the city tonight. He could barely make it to where his friend Bax lay on the ground, nursing his wound.

"Then let him grieve," Graeson said.

Kallie hesitated. She had witnessed the cold interactions between Graeson and Rian. During the entire conversation, Graeson was no more than a foot away from her. At first, she had thought nothing of it since they had been fairly inseparable since the bond snapped into place. But then she had heard him practically snarl when Rian had dismissed her suggestions.

Graeson's protective nature aside, this was the first considerate statement he had made about Rian.

Kallie sank back to the ground with a sigh.

As the fire crackled, she rubbed a knot from her neck. Her entire body was sore from the ride. As she observed the figures sleeping in the shadows of the woods, she realized just how tired she was. Moris was already raked out beside one of the two tents they had borrowed from Menz. He had volunteered to sleep outside to let a couple of the healers use it.

"Must you always be the voice of reason?" Kallie asked, nudging him in the side.

Graeson chuckled slightly, the sound a strange contrast against the soft groans of the wounded. "I told you I'm right quite often."

She folded her arms across her chest. "So tell me, Mr. Always-Right, where do you think they're going?"

Graeson turned, spotting Myra and Laurince dipping into the woods, hand-in-hand. When he faced her, a sinful smile graced his lips. "It's obvious, is it not?"

Kallie hummed in agreement. "I wonder when that happened."

Graeson shrugged. "I think with what they've been through the past few months together, getting close is nearly inevitable."

Although it was hard not to consider the impact of the bond, the past few months strengthened her relationship with Graeson in ways she hadn't thought possible. When she thought her fire was gone, Graeson had reignited it. He had given her the time she needed to process her grief and had helped drag her out of it. Even when she had pushed him away.

Kallie was glad Myra found someone who seemed to do the same for her. She didn't know the details about Myra and Laurince's relationship, but she saw the way Myra looked at him, and he, at her. The two had been inseparable since Laurince had returned. Myra fell easily for people, but this time seemed different.

"Would you have preferred if it was your former fiancé?" Graeson meant it as a joke, but there was still some bite in the last word.

Kallie rolled her eyes. "She can have them both. It is of no concern of mine who it is. All that matters is that she is safe and happy."

Graeson stood and held out a hand. "We should get some rest while we can."

Nodding, Kallie let him help her up. Then Graeson kicked dirt over the fire, extinguishing the flames. She wove her fingers between his and followed him to their tent.

As Graeson lifted the flap, Kallie paused. She tilted her toward the stars. She wasn't sure if the gods were listening or if they were even on their side, but she sent a prayer to them either way.

CHAPTER 77
KALLIE

WHEN KALLIE STEPPED OUTSIDE THE TENT, SHE KNEW HER PRAYERS had gone unanswered. She found no new arrivals, heard no cheers of relief.

The sun had barely risen, and the leaves above blocked most of the creeping light from seeping into the forest. Across the ground, most people still lay asleep. Some were already up. A few men strolled into the camp, a couple of rabbits thrown over their shoulder. Another was gathering supplies for a fire.

With a yawn, Graeson stretched his arms high, then dug his hands through his thick, black hair. The gold rings adorning his fingers sparkled in the morning light as he tousled his hair. His cheek was red from sleeping on his arm. When his gaze met hers, he frowned. "What's wrong?"

"They're not here," she said, scanning the field as if she had somehow missed an entire army.

Kallie wondered if the gods were even listening or if the skies were so flooded with prayers that they were incapable of answering them. Or maybe this was part of the gods' plans all along.

Hadn't Barinthian told Graeson that the mortals needed to be reminded of the natural order off the world? That humans had started a dangerous game by creating creatures that shouldn't have existed and by granting powers to those who did not bear the blood of the gods?

"No word from Terin either?" Graeson asked.

Kallie shook her head and wrapped her arms around her torso tightly. Terin hadn't visited her in her dreams since he had informed them of the battle. She told herself it was because he needed to preserve his energy, but she also knew how tumultuous the Red Sea was to cross.

"They'll come," Graeson said, but he failed to hide his creeping doubt.

"And if they don't?" she asked, already knowing the answer.

"We press on with those who are willing and able. By fire or blade, Sebastian dies today," he said, his gaze locking with hers. "I can promise you that."

Kallie closed her eyes, tipping her head to the treetops.

Where are you?

She knew Terin could not hear her, but she couldn't help but try.

"Come on," Graeson said, wrapping his hand around hers. "Let's see if we can help with prepping breakfast."

Kallie sighed but followed. They wove through the sleeping bodies spread across the camp toward the small group preparing breakfast. When they offered their assistance, though, an elderly woman swatted them away.

"There are already enough cooks in my kitchen," the woman said.

Kallie didn't bother saying there was no kitchen, only a few rocks and a stump signaling the area. Instead, the two of them took a seat against a nearby tree on the outskirts of the small fire.

Kallie's leg bounced as she watched the flames burn to coals.

"Here," Graeson said, nudging her.

Kallie stared at the scimitar in his hands. "I don't think we're going to get attacked right now. If we do, I have my dagger."

"Sharpen it," he said.

At her confused expression, he placed a hand on her thigh. "You've been fidgeting since we sat down. It'll keep your hands busy."

Kallie took the scimitar from him and cocked a brow. "And this is your best idea to get my mind of things?"

Smirking, Graeson leaned closer, the tip of his nose brushing her ear. "Noreen might smack me if she heard my other ideas."

Kallie pulled away. "Noreen?"

Graeson tipped his chin toward the woman cooking. Noreen ripped a knife from the hand of a young man, who was skinning a rabbit, and shoved him with her hip.

"Smack you? She would probably slice you with that knife."

Graeson snorted and handed her a whetstone. With a shaking hand, Kallie took it and began sharpening the blade. After a few swipes, she paused. "Shouldn't you be staying busy too?"

His gaze dipped over, his eyes burning silver as he took her in. "I enjoy watching you handle my blades."

Kallie laughed. "Don't let Noreen hear you say that."

When she finished sharpening the first scimitar, Graeson inspected her work, angling it this way and that. With an approving nod, he handed her the other. Kallie beamed at the silent praise.

As more people woke up, the camp slowly stirred to life. Despite the somber atmosphere and the ash raining down on them, the people threw themselves into various tasks after breakfast. In the civilians' haste to flee the capital, a good handful had the forethought to bring weapons with them. The majority had not, though. When a group suggested scavenging for weapons, Graeson and Moris offered their assistance. Although most wandered in a different direction than Moris, no one denied his help.

Progress was progress, Kallie supposed.

Once they left, Kallie found herself strolling toward the wounded, providing a helping hand wherever she could. While she had little knowledge about medicinal practices, she could run for supplies or hold down an arm as a healer stitched it up.

As Kallie pressed her weight down onto a soldier's leg to keep it straight while the healer dug out an arrow, someone gagged behind her. Looking over her shoulders, Kallie found Phaia scurrying the other way.

"Do you need anything else here?" Kallie asked once the healer started wrapping the arrow-free wound.

"No," Gerald, the healer, said. "I'm all set here. Thank you."

Kallie nodded. She got up and washed her hands in a bucket of fresh water a teenager had fetched earlier. As she dried off her hands, she searched for anyone else who needed help. But the healers had taken care of most of the injured.

With nothing else to do, she aimlessly walked through the camp, stopping at some groups to chat. Since she had arrived, she had talked to many of the people in the camp. But her attention kept going to the children. There were so many of them, some with families, others without. A few of the younger children were playing in the woods, wielding branches as makeshift weapons. They jabbed at each other with wide grins, laughter spilling from their mouths when they tagged their friends. Some of the older girls were braiding the younger girls' hair. An older couple was telling a tale to a small group, the man putting his heart into his performance. It was only after the man started running around the circle roaring that Kallie realized the story was about a dragon.

These were the people they were fighting for today.

"I told you to stay busy, didn't I, little mouse?"

Kallie ripped her gaze from the performance and found Graeson leaning against a sequoia tree.

"I was, but then…" She shrugged.

There was only so much any of them could do while they waited for the orders to return to the battle. Wanting to get as much rest as they could to prepare for the coming battle, many had opted to sleep. Kallie had debated doing the same, but she knew it would be a lost cause. She had slept only as well as she did last night because Graeson was with her.

She leaned her back against the tree, and her shoulder brushed Graeson's arm.

"It puts things into perspective, doesn't it?" he asked, tipping his head toward the children.

A sad smile ticked at the corner of her mouth. "Back in Ardentol, I would often sneak away and wander into the village. It was one of my favorite pastimes. I would go into random stores and taverns just to experience the world through the eyes of the people. There was one house in particular that had five children who would constantly play outside until nightfall. It makes me wonder what they are doing now."

"The council should be stepping up in Domitius' absence," Graeson said.

"The council is full of a bunch of power-hungry lords who can barely see past their own noses. They're probably champing at the bit to gain his seat."

"Domitius never named you heir?"

Kallie shook her head. "His plan was always for me to marry another king," she said, spotting the very man who she was supposed to marry several yards away talking to Laurince and Myra. "I suppose it makes sense that he didn't, since I wasn't actually his blood."

Graeson snorted. "Did he expect to live forever?"

"Knowing him? Probably. Perhaps that was why he had been searching for a way to recreate our powers. Maybe he was looking for a way to become immortal."

"Wouldn't be surprised if that was the case," Graeson mused, folding his arms over his chest. His elbow brushed her shoulder. "Would you go back if you had the chance?"

She peeked up at him, trying to see if there was a particular answer he was looking for. But when she found only curiosity staring back at her, she shrugged. "I don't know. I guess I haven't given it that much thought. I care for the people, but I have no claim to the throne."

"Does anyone?"

"One of the lords will surely try."

"THIS IS INSANE, ISN'T IT?"

At Kallie's question, Graeson observed the people anxiously awaiting their orders. A look of scrutiny passed across his countenance.

Once they had realized that reinforcements would not arrive in time, preparations for the battle began.

Phaia had explained earlier that when the previous fight had started, many civilians had fled in terror. Some had helped guide the young and the elderly to safety before the city was ravaged. Others had carried the wounded out, refusing to abandon them. Now, the same people formed a makeshift army. People who had fled in fear now stood with courage. Retired soldiers, despite their families' protests, volunteered to dust off their swords. Women, who had been barred from the Frenzian military yet fought for their loved ones' escape, held their chins high.

Some of the more traditional Frenzians grumbled about the women joining, but a single glance from Rian silenced them. Kallie was surprised Rian didn't listen to their complaints. Months ago, he had claimed that while he wished for change, the kingdom held onto its traditions with a white-knuckled grip. Perhaps the past few months made him realize that change was unstoppable.

Either way, Kallie was glad to see Rian supporting the women's decisions to join the cause. Not only because they needed the people, but because they too deserved a chance to defend their homes if they wished.

After scavenging for supplies, everyone who had volunteered to fight was armed with something. Strangers handed weapons to those who were weaponless, and when there were still people without, they found whatever they could. People stuffed their pockets with rocks; others created makeshift javelins from broken branches, sharpened to a deadly point.

After inspecting the crowd, Graeson asked, "Do you want my honest opinion?"

"Always," Kallie said.

"If Dani were here, she would call us foolish for leading a troop of untrained people into battle. Menides, her father and the commander, would advise us against it."

"Real comforting," Moris mumbled, coming up from behind them.

"I wasn't done," Graeson said, rolling his eyes at the interruption. "They may be untrained, but even a trained soldier has no hope of winning a battle if they have no reason to fight. But these people? They're not fighting because we are paying them. They're not fighting because we have threatened them. They're putting their lives on the line because this is their home. Some of them could likely not care less about which Dronias brother rules as long as they have a home to return to. We are not forcing any of them to fight. They have chosen to, and it would be foolish of us to ignore their desire to fight. Their loyalty is to their family and their home, and that above everything else will be the sole reason that we stand a fighting chance against whatever waits for us in the capital."

Kallie nodded in agreement. Those gathered weren't soldiers, but they were fighters. She could see that in their narrowed gazes, in the curling fists, in the anger that oozed off them.

She wiped the sweat from her hands on the back of her Tetrian leather trousers.

"Are you ready?" Graeson asked, turning to Kallie.

She gathered her hair in her hand and tied a red ribbon Phaia had given her around it. She wore the armored corset that Medenia had gifted her before parting Tetria, the same one she wore when she faced Domitius. Although this time there was no hesitancy in her stance, no questioning whether she was ready for the fight.

"Ready," she said, her voice unwavering.

The three of them joined the small army standing in front of Rian. As Kallie observed the king, she wondered if he had slept at all. The bags under his eyes were heavy, and she could see the apprehension pouring from him as he scanned the crowd.

After a moment, he cleared his throat and addressed the crowd. "I know that I have failed you as a king."

Kallie and Graeson winced at Rian's start. Admitting his mistakes was admirable, but did he not see what the people needed? Kallie had attended court enough to read a crowd. Right now, the people needed to be encouraged, not reminded of past failures.

Rian licked his lips. "I know that some of you do not trust me and that your reasoning for joining the fight is purely to protect your home. No matter your reasoning, though, I want you to know that your aid will not be in vain. The lives we have lost will not have been in vain. Today, Sebastian's reign will end. Today, we will take back our city!"

Scattered claps sounded across the crowd, but as Kallie locked eyes with Myra, she could see it in her frown and the curve of her brows that the people were still afraid.

Rian's proclamation wasn't enough.

Before Kallie knew what she was doing, she was stepping beside Rian. He looked at her with a questioning gaze. But to her surprise, he did not stop her when she addressed the army.

"Today, we are not only fighting for Frenzia, we are fighting for peace. We are fighting for the future. Most of you were not trained to be soldiers." She looked at every person gathered, giving each of them the same attention as if she knew them, as if she had dined with them and met their children. As if they were friends and not merely strangers.

She was all too familiar with what it felt like to lose power, to lose one's home. She refused to let that persist today. And for a split second, she thought her mind was playing tricks on her because she could have sworn they immediately straightened when her attention fell on them. Shoulders rolled back, chins lifted, jaws flexed.

Kallie might have believed she no longer had power because of her lack of a crown, but the sight before her suggested otherwise. The surge she felt wasn't from her gift or lineage but because of who she was at her core. "You are bakers, carpenters, blacksmiths, merchants, dancers, mothers, fathers, sisters, and brothers. *You* are the foundation of this kingdom.

"Many of you are probably scared right now. Some of you, like myself, might have even been told that your emotions are a weakness, that to succeed you must squash your fear and anxiety." Kallie's fingers flexed over the hilt of her dagger, the words ingrained into it bolstering her courage. "But a wise person once told me that our fear reminds us we are human. Use your fear. Use your anger and rage and sadness. Use *everything* at your disposal when you enter the city. Whether you are entering the city to fight or to retrieve the wounded, keep going, keep running, keep fighting."

She scanned the crowd, seeing the strength surge within the people. Her gaze fell upon Graeson, and a proud smile flickered at the corner of his lips.

For her entire life, she had been fighting for a crown because she thought it would give her power. In reality, she only needed to use the power she already had.

She looked beside her, and Rian shook the surprise from his face. Their engagement might have been a ruse and a failure, but that did not mean Kallie could not support him, that a friendship could not one day bloom between them.

As though sharing the same thought, Rian put his hand on his sword and nodded at her in encouragement.

With as much vigor as Kallie could muster, she lifted her dagger, pointing it at the sky. "Today, we fight for our tomorrow! We fight for Frenzia!"

"For Frenzia!" the crowd shouted back, and Rian's voice was among the loudest, his sword joining the throng of fists, branches, and weapons.

Together. They would do this together.

Rian leaned over and whispered, "I had it covered, you know."

Kallie's smile widened at his light tone. "That's a funny way of saying thank you."

Rian snorted and wove through the army. People patted him on the shoulder, shaking him gently. The energy in the camp was rising. There was hope yet.

Kallie hung back as the people followed him.

Nearby, Laurince pulled Myra into an embrace. Over his shoulder, Myra's eyes locked onto Kallie's. Myra offered Kallie a sad smile.

They had both been made into weapons wielded by a king who misused them for his selfish ambitions. It was time they reclaimed their power.

Today, they fought for their freedom and the freedom of others who were just like them.

CHAPTER 78
MYRA

As Laurince squeezed her hands, Myra wanted so badly to tell him to him stay. But she didn't.

"I'll come back to you," he said, his voice hoarse.

She smiled softly at him, unable to speak for fear of tears.

Then he let go of her hand and followed Rian toward the capital.

It took all of Myra's energy not to crash to the floor as she watched him walk away.

CHAPTER 79
KALLIE

Four arrows shot through the sky, all hitting their marks. One watchguard fell over the edge of the stone tower and smacked the ground. Kallie flinched, and several people behind her gagged.

The air hung heavy with the coopery tang of blood and the acrid scent of smoke. Although the city was no longer on fire, ash covered the ground like a thin layer of snow. As they crept toward the massive iron gates of the capital, silence befell the small army. They stared at the grand gate blocking their path. Cutting down the archers in the towers was one issue. The gates were another.

"Is there another way inside?" Kallie asked, turning to Rian and Laurince.

Rian shook his head. "If this gate is locked, the others will be too." He scanned the towering walls, but there was no way to climb them.

"We'll take care of it," Graeson said, his eyes glowing as if he was pulling from the dragon.

"Ready?" he asked, looking over his shoulder.

Laurince and Moris nodded.

"What are you doing?" Rian asked, hurrying after them.

As Graeson wrapped his hand around the iron bars, Kallie thought of the cell door that had been torn apart in Tetria. She grabbed Rian's arm, pulling him back. "Just watch."

The three men wrapped their hands around the metal bars. Rian's jaw dropped. The metal creaked and groaned as the men bent the bars back, their muscles straining even with their inhuman strength. A collective gasp rippled through the army as they witnessed a hole form in the middle of the gate.

Rian rubbed his face and mumbled, "Now I'm going to need someone to fix that once this is over."

"That's not the only thing that will need fixing," Kallie said, peering through the hole in the gate. Beyond it, the city was in ruins. Rubble covered the streets. The wind whistled through the shattered windows of collapsed buildings.

"Fuck," Rian breathed out.

Laurince slipped through the new hole, maneuvering carefully to avoid snagging his wings on the metal spires. He waved the rest of them forward.

"Come on," Kallie said, beckoning Rian toward the gate. There was no time to waste.

Once beyond the wall, Rian tilted his head one way, then gestured for Kallie and Graeson to go the other. The army split off, one half going with the king, and the rest following Kallie.

The deeper they embarked, the thicker the scent of the smoke became. Throughout the city, piles of embers still burned. Entire houses had collapsed, the explosives destroying them. Inside one building, a faint cry sounded, and a few of the soldiers entered the building to inspect it. When Kallie looked over her shoulder a minute later, she saw them carrying out two children. The sight of the children covered in ash and soot squeezed her heart. Kallie struggled to wrap her mind around the catastrophe. Did Sebastian not care if he burned the entire capital down? Was that part of his plan? To start anew?

As they crept through the destruction, those tasked with helping the injured moved as quickly as possible, carrying those who could be moved back the way they came. Kallie hoped the healers and Myra had rested.

A rumble rippled through the streets. They halted, searching for the source. Graeson crouched down, feeling the ground as he stared at the sky, his nostrils flaring.

"This way," he said gruffly.

Their small squad headed deeper into the capital, inching their way toward the castle. The destruction grew worse with every block. Somewhere, a loud screech pierced the air, and Kallie gripped her dagger tighter.

Up ahead, she spotted a child who was no more than eight years old tugging on his mother's arm, pleading for her to get up. Large flakes of ash coated the child's dark brown hair. The woman sat on the ground with her head leaning against the wall. She must have stopped to catch her breath as they were running out of the capital, believing she and her son were safe enough. Her eyelids were closed, and blood pooled around her. Still, the child knelt beside her, his tears rolling down his round, brown cheeks. Even yards away, Kallie could hear the boy's sobs and futile attempts to wake his mother.

Another high-pitched, ear-shattering screech sounded from above, closer this time. Kallie tore her gaze away from the pair as a drakonis dug its talons into the brick siding, crushing the material and crumbling it into mere pebbles and dust.

In an instant, Kallie was sprinting, shouting at the child to move, but she knew he wouldn't abandon his mother and she wouldn't be able to get there in time.

The wind whipped through her hair, and a shadow rushed past

her as Moris flew. He scooped up the child in his arms as the corner of the building came tumbling down. Chunks of bricks smashed onto the ground where the child had just knelt. If they had arrived one minute later, the child would have been crushed.

Moris swung back around.

Graeson signaled for him to fly away. "Get him out of here!"

Moris nodded, held the child tighter to his chest, and flew past them.

Kallie's hands flew to her ears when the drakonis roared in anger, the sound pounding against her eardrums at an ear-shattering degree. As the sound reverberated off the surrounding buildings, the ground shook again.

Then she saw it.

A hoard of drakonises barreled toward them. She peeled her hands away from her ears as Graeson ripped his blades from their sheaths.

A dangerous glint glimmered in his moon-bright eyes as if the dragon within was nipping at the edges of its confinement, hungering for blood.

Kallie chanced one glance back, spotting Moris' silhouette disappearing down the street. She took in a deep breath and twisted the dagger in her hand. For the first time in a long time, she was thankful for the training Domitius had put her through. Although he had taken plenty from her, he had at least given her the skills to shout with enough confidence, "For Frenzia!"

CHAPTER 80

MYRA

As the battle began, the camp quickly fell into disarray. More wounded soldiers arrived, their comrades carrying them back to the camp. Everywhere Myra looked, pain soaked the earth. It drenched her feet and soaked the soles of her shoes. It was like walking through quicksand, but Myra refused to let the stream of emotions drag her down.

She took a deep breath, steadying her racing heart, and kept her back to the capital, where smoke once again filled the skies.

I'll come back to you.

Laurince's last words wrapped around her, and she held onto them as tightly as she could. She tried not to think about whether those would be the last words he ever spoke to her, and instead let those words bolster her courage. Hoping and praying he would not be the next body that lay in front of her in anguish as the God of Death dug his claws into his next victim.

She lifted her hand from the soldier's chest, his brow finally unfurling as she soothed his qualms. A familiar set of wings entered her peripheral, and she looked up.

"Anything?" Myra called out, both craving and fearing an update.

Moris shook his head. He already held the record for the number of return trips. Each time, he came back with no news of Laurince. Myra wasn't sure if that was a blessing or a curse.

"No news is often the best news," he reminded her.

Myra pursed her lips and swallowed the rising fear. No news also could mean that Laurince was already gone.

She tried not to think about that too much, though.

"Are Sebastian's troops letting up at least?" she asked, begging for something that would give her hope. The battle had already been going on for a few hours. How many lives would they have to lose before someone ended it?

When Moris' mouth fell into a flat line, she immediately regretted the question.

"Sometimes, it's best not to ask," Gerald, the healer, said quietly, peering up at Myra through his thin-rimmed glasses.

"I—I'm sorry," she whispered. "I'm not used to this."

"Most of us are not," the healer said as he tightened the tourniquet around his patient's thigh. "There hasn't been this bloody of a battle since the Great War. Even the skirmishes that have happened on the borders and the small rebellions here-and-there could not have prepared us for this."

"How do you keep going?" Myra asked.

"You stay busy," Gerald said, handing her a bucket and tipping his head toward the man Moris placed on the ground.

Myra took the bucket and began cleaning the stranger's wounds. Across from her, Phaia did the same. While she hadn't gotten over her distaste for the sight of blood, she no longer gagged every time she saw a wound.

A light hand fell onto Myra's shoulder. "I'll try to see if I can find something out."

Myra looked at Moris with more gratitude than she could have ever expressed. Thank you was on the tip of her tongue, but before she could speak, a scream ripped through the camp.

CHAPTER 81

GRAESON

THE FERAL DRAKONISES HAD OVERRUN FRENZIA'S CAPITAL, POURING from the castle in torrents with curled sneers and deadly talons. Rancid drool dripped from their tongues. Graeson's entire body reeked of it. His clothes were drenched and stuck to his skin. Every time he got a whiff, he recoiled in disgust.

As iron tainted the air, the dragon within roared as Graeson swung his scimitar. With every strike, the desire to shift intensified. His skin itched as the beast begged to break free. But with one quick scan, Graeson knew there were too many people who would get injured if he did. The streets were too narrow. If he transformed, it would only result in more chaos, destruction, and death. Instead, he kept his attention on the battle.

These drakonises were even more aggressive than Nyrri had been when Graeson first encountered her in that crate months ago. It was as if Sebastian had kept the beasts locked inside the cells beneath the castle without food for days, perhaps even weeks, to increase their hunger and anger. But Graeson would not be deterred.

He fought alongside Kalisandre, their movements in perfect

harmony. They had fought against each other on several occasions and trained together throughout the past few weeks. He knew when she would strike by the shift in her stance, when she would dip by the sharp inhale she would take. With the bond flowing freely between them, their movements were fluid, a ballad twisting around their enemies.

When he looked at her next, he did a double take that nearly cost him his ear.

Kal struggled against a drakonis. The beast chomped at her ankles, forcing her to tumble across the ground, beneath the drakonis' belly. On one knee, she twisted the dagger in her hand. While she was skilled with the blade, it required her to get much closer to the creatures than Graeson would have liked.

He yanked his scimitar from his most recent kill and swiped the blade across his trousers. As she somersaulted away from another attack, he slid across the ground, meeting her.

"Take it," he urged, holding out the clean scimitar.

"I'm fine," she argued.

He pressed the hilt into her hand, anyway. "Use it, Kalisandre."

Her hand wrapped around the hilt, and they reentered the fight, charging in opposite directions.

When the hoard had appeared, Graeson had debated telling Kalisandre to turn back. He didn't want her to get hurt. He wouldn't be able to handle it if she did. Their bond was still new, but he knew without a doubt that it would destroy him if it was severed.

He couldn't lose her. Not now, not ever.

But when he had looked at Kal and seen her readying for battle, her stance strong, unmoving, and unshakable, he knew his plea would be a waste of breath. Kalisandre's mind was set. There would be no changing it. Graeson knew that better than most.

Still, he would have been lying if he said his heart didn't quake every time a drakonis targeted her.

All around him, the motley crew of soldiers, both trained and untrained, fought valiantly. Blades sliced through the tough skin of the drakonises. Arrows drove into their chests, backs, and wings—anywhere that would slow them down.

Sweat dripped down Graeson's back, dampening his shirt and causing it to stick to his skin. He didn't let up, though. He kept fighting, as did everyone. He slashed his blade across fur and scales, spun away from webbed wings that threatened to knock him down, dodged the sharp canines of another. But at some point, between blows and grunts and despite his best efforts, Kalisandre vanished from his view.

Frantic, he searched for her. As he spun on his feet, a drakonis knocked him flat on the ground, stealing his breath away.

The need to find Kal, to ensure she was safe, surged through his veins. With the adrenaline pumping through him, Graeson sliced his scimitar across the beast's neck and rolled, narrowly missing the outpouring of guts and blood.

He leaped to his feet and scanned the street. The clash of steel rang in his ears. His muscles strained as he grabbed onto the jaws of his next opponent. Then he finally spotted her in the thick of the fray, shielding one of their soldiers.

Kal swung the scimitar with deadly precision, as if it had been made for her. But she was losing the battle, and the other soldiers were scattered across the area, too far to help.

The beast's jaw snapped in Graeson's hands. A mangled screech spilled from its mouth, and Graeson drove his blade through its heart before abandoning it.

Graeson ran harder as the drakonis towered over Kal. He whistled, and the creature snapped its head in Graeson's direction. Snarling, it turned, its tail swinging around and its previous victims forgotten.

As Graeson taunted the creature, Kallie slid beneath the creature's belly as the man she was protecting cowered in a crouch.

The drakonis bore its razor-sharp teeth, and saliva hung from its canines. An odious stench dripped from its mouth. As it inhaled, a small light ignited within the back of the creature's throat. The moment the creature was about to exhale a river of fire at Graeson, it choked on its scream as Kallie shoved her blade through its stomach. A cry poured from its mouth, the sound shattering a glass window into thousands of pieces.

As the drakonis collapsed, Graeson jerked forward, his lungs dropping into his stomach.

"Kal!"

What had he done? He grabbed his chest, his fingers curling into the fabric, threatening to rip it to shreds as he looked on with horror.

Silence blanketed the space as the soldiers turned toward them. The rest of the drakonises in the vicinity either had been slain or had flown off, escaping death. Most of their group had survived this first attack, but he had never thought Kallie wouldn't. He reached for the bond. It was still there, but he couldn't tell if his mind was playing tricks on him.

"That was close."

Graeson snapped his head up. His heart stammered as Kalisandre stood on the other side of the drakonis' limp form.

She tossed her hair back, shoving it away from her face. "Thanks for the assist, Gray," she said with a wink. She swiped her hand across her forehead, smearing dark blood across her skin. As if feeling the foreign liquid, she looked down at her hand and shivered in disgust.

"Thanks for the assist? You nearly died!" he shouted, running to her and grabbing her waist.

She placed her hands on his chest and smirked. Beads of sweat rolled down her forehead. "I had it covered."

He scoffed, shaking his head. "By the gods, woman. What am I going to do with you?"

"You've been chasing after me this entire time, and you're just now asking that?" She clicked her tongue. "I thought gods were smarter than that."

"*Half* god," Graeson corrected. He wiped the blood from her forehead, then brushed a stray strand of hair behind her ear. His eyes bounced across her face.

Kallie took a step closer, their breaths mingling in the space between them. He didn't know who leaned first, but he supposed it didn't matter. Especially not as a man stumbled over, interrupting.

"Thank you," the soldier Kallie had shielded said, panting.

Taking a step back from Graeson, Kallie nodded at the man and turned her attention to the soldiers. They both knew they wouldn't be able to sustain this pace for much longer. Throughout the capital, the fires had started up again after an onslaught of explosives early in the fight. Whether luckily or unluckily, Kallie and his party only encountered drakonises. The soldiers had to be somewhere, though.

"We need to find Rian and the others," he said.

"Which way?" Kallie asked.

Graeson closed his eyes and took a deep breath, calming his senses. He could hear Kallie's breathing slowly evening out. Behind them, he heard the scraping of a sword on the ground as a soldier stood on shaky legs. Groans and hisses escaped the lips of those wounded in the battle. Further away, though, there was the clash of metal, followed by the now too familiar screech of the beasts.

"That way," Graeson said, pointing.

Kallie's knuckles blanched around the hilt of her stained dagger. "We finish this. *Today.*"

Then they were off, sprinting down the street toward the cries of the dying. But as they ran, all Graeson could think about was that he hoped the day would not finish them first.

They rounded a corner, then another. The familiar pound of wings beating against the wind sounded behind them. Graeson spun as a soldier nocked back an arrow. Before Graeson could move, Kallie sprinted past him, shouting.

The soldier didn't hear her, though. The bowstring became taut as he inhaled. Then, Graeson's heart leaped into his lungs as the man took aim and Kallie ran in its path.

CHAPTER 82
KALLIE

THE SHARP CRACK OF GLASS SHATTERING, LIKE A THOUSAND NEEDLES clattering on the stone, pried Kallie's eyes open. She should have been dead or at least severely injured. Instead, she stood in one piece, unscathed.

"What the fuck were you thinking?" Graeson roared, eyes blazing like melted iron.

The soldier with the bow lay sprawled on the ground. Lips quivering, he pointed at the sky, his hand trembling as a dark shadow fell over them. "It's a drakonis. It's—"

Graeson cut him off with a snarl before turning his gaze on Kallie. Swirls of smoke came from his nose with every exhale. "Well?"

Kallie didn't balk at his icy glare and rolled her eyes at him, paying him no heed. Soul bond or not, she did not need to explain herself to him, especially when the answer was obvious.

Turning to the soldiers, who were shifting into fighting stances, she gestured toward the drakonis. "This one is friendly. If you kill her, you answer to me. Got it?"

"What? How do you—"

The soldier's retort was cut off as Nyrri landed hard. Her talons dug into the dirt to help stop her momentum, sending up a plume of debris. The drakonis flared her nostrils, inhaling the scent of the blood and saliva soaking the street. Her lip curled in disgust, and a low rumble slipped from her mouth. Kallie couldn't tell if Nyrri snarled at the sight of the dead drakonises all around them or the apprehension radiating from the unfamiliar faces.

Kallie glared at every soldier as she strolled over to Nyrri. Thankfully, none tested her threat.

Several soldiers nodded, fear widening their eyes as Kallie went to pet the beast.

Kallie smiled at Nyrri. It had only been a few days, but she had missed the ferocious beast. As she scratched Nyrri beneath her chin, Kallie said over her shoulders, "She will not harm you."

"But I might."

Kallie jumped at the voice.

Paper-white hair flew in the wind as Ellie leaned over to peer around Nyrri's head. She gave Kallie a coy smirk. "I didn't realize you would take an arrow for me, Kals. I'm touched."

"Don't be too touched. I didn't even see you, which is shocking because of your big head," Kallie jested. She would have been lying, though, if she said she wasn't happy to see Ellie.

Ellie gasped and pressed a hand to her chest. "Come on! My head is not nearly as big as Gray's. And to think I came all this way to save your asses." She clicked her tongue in dismay, feigning offense. "By the looks of things, we came just in time, too."

"*We?*" Graeson asked, looking between Ellie and Nyrri with raised brows.

Kallie looked down the street where the pair had come from.

There was no army to be found. Ellie was alone.

Yet Ellie smiled. "We're all here."

"All?" Kallie asked.

The Tetrian warrior nodded. "The Pontians too. Impeccable timing, to be honest. We ran into Terin and Dani as we reached the city's gates."

Graeson grimaced, throwing his head back. "Please don't tell me Dani is joining the fight," he said, pinching the bridge of his nose.

Ellie shook her head. "Last I heard, they were taking her to that camp of yours."

Graeson sighed in relief.

"But knowing Dani, who knows if she'll stay behind, even if it's in her best interest to do so."

Graeson cursed.

"She'll be all right," Kallie whispered, giving his hand a squeeze in reassurance. Dani was stubborn, but not foolish. She would not put her child at risk.

Ellie crossed her arms and leaned her hip against Nyrri's side. "So," she said with a click of her tongue. "Were ya'll just going for a stroll, or shall we get back to it?"

CHAPTER 83
MYRA

Myra felt a surge of fear rise among those remaining in the camp the moment the soldiers appeared. Warriors clad in black leather and armor moved through the trees, the dripping sunlight reflecting off the metal. Those closest to the intruders scurried back. Children ran behind parents, grabbing their legs.

Myra squinted at the intruders. In front of the group, a woman stumbled, her features cast in shadows. Several people jumped to her aid, their arms wrapping around her.

Myra gasped. Smiling, she gripped Moris' arm. "Moris, I think that's—"

A muffled scream cut her off, and a fierce gust of wind slapped Myra's face, whipping her hair around. When she opened her eyes, Moris was no longer beside her.

"Dani!" Moris shouted over the noise.

Dani leaned forward, clutching her stomach. Her long brown braids hid her face in shadow as she released another groan.

Myra spun around and called for the healer. "Gerald!"

"Yes?" the healer answered, pushing his way through the crowd that had gathered at the troops' arrival.

Myra pointed to Dani. "The woman—she's pregnant."

Gerald immediately dropped the soiled towel. "How far along?"

Myra hurried beside him as they rushed toward Dani. "I—I don't know," she stammered, unable to remember.

They quickened their pace. When they reached the crowd, Gerald shouted, "Move! I'm a healer."

The crowd split, and Moris stumbled to the ground, his wings spanning out behind him.

"Dani? What's wrong?" Moris asked, his hand shaking as he reached for her.

Dani shrieked when her gaze fell on the man who should have been dead. She tried to scurry backward, but the person behind her prevented her from moving.

"Mo-Moris?" the person behind Dani called out, tears glossing their amber eyes. Myra recognized Sylvia instantly. "You're really alive?"

"How?" Dani asked, her hand trembling as she touched Moris' cheek.

Moris gave his friends a nervous smile. "It's a long story."

"One we do not have time for," an unfamiliar voice bit out, her tone in direct contrast with how she gently stroked Dani's back.

But it was as if the woman had never spoken. Dani snatched Moris by the collar and yanked him forward, her fingers digging into his shirt. "If you ever pull that sh—" Dani's threat was cut short as she choked on another scream.

"Everyone needs to get out of the way," the woman beside Dani demanded.

A few of the soldiers started shoving people back. When one prevented Gerald from coming forward, the healer shoved the man's arm away. "Did you not hear me? I'm a healer."

"Let him through," the woman said. "He can assist me."

Myra shuffled backward, giving them space.

"Assist you?" Gerald said, as if offended. "Have you had twenty years of training?"

"Thirty, actually," the woman quipped with an arched brow, silencing Gerald. "Theenah, Pontia's Head of Medicine."

Gerald's mouth fell open, eyes wide in shock. "Y-you're Theenah? You're legendary."

Myra stifled her chuckle as she watched the encounter.

"The one and only. Now, are you going to gawk or help me get her somewhere more comfortable?"

"Take one of our tents," Moris suggested, refusing to leave Dani's side. He swatted Sylvia's hand away when they reached for his wing.

Sylvia frowned. They quickly ripped their attention away from the wings when Dani keeled over and bellowed.

Through clenched teeth, Dani gritted out, "If someone doesn't *move—*"

"Show us the way," Theenah ordered.

With a quick nod, Moris lifted Dani from the ground.

"Careful!" Theenah and Gerald shouted.

Moris grimaced as nervous sweat dripped from his face. He mumbled an apology and strolled down the middle of the crowd, heading toward the tents with Dani draped over his arms. Dani's head lolled to the side as she groaned. Moris wrapped his arms tighter around her.

As they passed Myra, Gerald gave her a tight smile. Myra's gaze followed them as they made their way toward the tent. Only when they disappeared inside did Myra notice the soldiers filing into the camp. She recognized the Tetrian leather immediately.

"They've come," Phaia said, stepping beside Myra and squeezing her hand.

Even though the reinforcements had arrived, Myra struggled to hold on to the flickering relief. It slipped through her hand like water falling between her fingers.

She only hoped that the troops had arrived in time.

CHAPTER 84
KALLIE

THE PORTION OF THE ARMY THAT KALLIE AND THE OTHERS HAD previously encountered was nothing compared to what awaited them as they rounded the corner.

Sebastian's army flooded the streets. Hundreds of drakonises and winged guards flew above the marching soldiers.

This was the famed Frenzian army—the one Domitius had offered Kallie's hand in marriage to secure. The one he had planned to use to conquer the seven kingdoms. And it was headed straight for them.

Behind Kallie, the clang of metal and rising shouts sent her whirling. Her pulse quickened as Terin emerged. Beside him, a tall figure strode forward. Based on his helmet, Kallie could only surmise he was Dani's father, Commander Ferrios. Medenia and Ophelia marched together, and Kallie's heart nearly shattered at the sight behind them. The Tetrian warriors, clad in black leather, were interspersed with the Pontian army, their dark armor absorbing the light and in stark contrast to the gleaming steel of the Pontains.

Kallie's chest fluttered. They had come.

But as she assessed the size of the battalions, her relief was short-lived.

"We're still outnumbered," she breathed out.

"It wouldn't be the first time," Ellie said, squeezing Kallie's arm. "Tetria faced worse odds during the Great War. Do not lose hope."

As if determined to prove Ellie's point, Medenia raised her weapon and released a war-cry. At her signal, Terin and Menides pumped their swords high as did their troops.

Fingers flexing over her two weapons, Kallie glanced at the motley crew behind her.

Graeson leaned toward her. "What are your orders, Nadarean?"

"*My* orders?" Kallie asked.

"We are yours to command. You've gotten us this far. Carry us to the end."

Kallie's gaze bounced across her face, unsure if she could do this.

Graeson gave her a curt nod in encouragement.

She rolled her shoulders back. "Let's end this."

Then, they were charging toward the enemy.

Steel crashed against steel as the opposing forces collided in the capital's streets. Every foe they met crumpled to the ground. Yet no matter how many enemies they slew, more stepped forth, taking their place.

Death and destruction quickly plagued the streets. Explosions rocked the capital. Claws tore through flesh. Soldiers swiped at the limbs that came from above.

They were quickly surrounded.

Soon, a shadow fell over Kallie, but there was nowhere for her to go. She ducked as the drakonis dove for her and braced for the inevitable impact. But it never came.

Before the beast had the chance to grab Kallie, it tumbled through the air, another form rolling on top of it. An angry roar filled Kallie's ears.

Nyrri's form was a blur as she struck the creature. Her talons ripped through the beast's neck. The moment the drakonis fell, four winged soldiers spiraled toward Nyrri.

Kallie screamed out in horror.

A flash of metal whizzed through the air.

"Not my drakonis, you ass!" Ellie shouted, grabbing another throwing knife from her holster and taking aim.

The next blade drove into the soldier's chest just as a flurry of stained ivory feathers whirled by, chasing after the third enemy. Laurince swung his sword with an inhuman ferocity. When his blade met its target, the Frenzian soldier bellowed. The two soldiers fell from the sky, crushing a pair of unsuspecting enemies.

"Kallie!" Terin called out.

She spun and gasped as a soldier rushed toward her, his sword raised, teeth bared, and eyes crazes.

Kallie braced against the attack, but her opponent broke free. As the soldier swung, Kallie spun to the right, dodging his sword.

Kallie drove her blade through his side.

Heart pounding, she scanned the rising chaos as destruction reigned, searching for Graeson.

To her right, Terin drove his short sword through an opening in a man's armor. As the body dropped, he parried a blow from another soldier.

On the other side, Medenia and Ophelia fought back-to-back, their swords swinging in tandem as they fought off their opponents. Their movements were fluid like water and as smooth as the breeze.

But where was Graeson? Where—

The bond hummed.

Kallie spun and found Graeson several yards ahead, clearing a path toward the castle, one winged guard at a time. Although his strength had yet to falter, even he was slowing down. Kallie could see it in the slight drag of his foot, the roll of his shoulder when he lifted his scimitar, the crack of his neck.

He was still alive. The Fates hadn't won.

Yet, she reminded herself. The single word the only encouragement she needed to keep going.

Pushing past the growing ache in her bones, Kallie lifted the scimitar to block her opponent's attack, again and again.

As SWEAT DRIPPED down Kallie's back, Rian ran past her, weaving through the masses.

"Sebastian!" he bellowed.

Kallie glanced at him, her heart thundering.

"Go, Kals!" Terin shouted over the noise. "I got him!"

Kallie turned to her brother, who had made his way toward her. "But—"

"Help Rian!"

Kallie nodded and ran. She slipped through the maze of bodies as she followed Rian. She was only a few yards away from him when her attention snapped to Sebastian. He drove his sword through an unarmored soldier's back. Blood was smeared across Sebastian's dragon-shaped helmet.

Kallie's lip curled in disgust.

Sebastian was no dragon.

"You traitor!" Rian yelled, shoving past a soldier.

Sebastian turned toward his brother, and a rueful grin split across his blood-splattered face. He shoved the lifeless body aside. "I was wondering if I would get to meet you on the streets or if you'd get yourself killed before I got the chance."

"How could you do this?" Rian demanded. "How could you destroy our home?"

"Sometimes one must destroy to rebuild." Sebastian twisted his sword in his hand and leaned to the side as Kallie stepped beside Rian. "I see you brought your wife. Or wait—ex-wife, is it? I'm still a little unclear as to your relationship."

"You're a disgrace," Kallie spat, tightening her hold on her weapons.

"I must say it's rather poetic," Sebastian said, ignoring her insult. "Your relationship started this war, and now your deaths will end it."

Kallie and Rian charged. But Kallie made it only a few steps before someone snatched her wrist and yanked her back.

A blade pressed against her spine.

"Kallie!" Rian shouted, looking back at her.

"Don't let—" Kallie was cut off as the person swiftly wrapped his arm around her and lifted his sword to her neck.

"I was hoping I'd see you again."

Kallie's body went rigid.

She would never forget that voice.

Myra had told her Armen had betrayed Pontia again. Kallie just didn't think she would be lucky enough to face him on the battlefield.

Rian called out to her again, panicked and hesitant to abandon her.

"Get Sebastian!" Kallie shouted. "I got this one."

A laugh brushed her cheek. "Do you now? The way I see it—"

Kallie shoved Armen's arm away and ducked beneath it. Spinning around, she glowered at the Ardentolian crest stamped on his new Frenzian armor. For a moment, her attention was so fixed on the crest that she barely noticed the wings sprouting from his back.

"Does loyalty mean *nothing* to you?" she spat.

"I am loyal, darling," Armen said, his wings flaring out behind him. "I'm loyal to myself. And I gotta say, I'm going to enjoy finally putting my blade through that cold heart of yours."

He swung, and Kallie dodged it. In the corner of her eye, she saw Rian's and Sebastian's swords colliding.

"You'll have to actually hit me to do that," Kallie said as she blocked his next attack.

The serum might have increased Armen's strength, but his moves were still predictable. Armen had always used too much momentum, too much force. Whenever she found him training in Ardentol, she always predicted his moves with ease. Some things even a serum couldn't change.

They parried, their blades crashing against one another. In her peripheral, Rian narrowly dodge Sebastian's attack.

Kallie fought harder.

When Armen's sword swiped through the air, Kallie blocked it with the scimitar.

Nearby, Rian slid across the ground and jabbed, his blade slipping into the bare joint behind Sebastian's knee brace. The prince hissed out, and Rian pushed forward.

Refocusing on Armen, Kallie fought with just as much ferocity. She could taste the end of this battle, and she would not stop until she finished it. Until they both did.

Armen braced against her attack. Spit foamed on his lip. His eyes were bloodshot and crazed. He dug his heel into the ground and leaned more of his weight against her.

His strength nearly overwhelmed her, and Kallie's arm shook as she braced herself. The recent arrow wounds in her thigh and arm throbbed. Sweat dripped down her forehead. But Kallie had fought powerful men before, and one thing always remained true: they never knew when to give up.

She slid her weapon down and spun around him, dodging his wings as he twirled toward her. Kallie raised her dagger, and Armen blocked her attack. In his haste, he had ignored her other weapon. The curved blade slid across his thighs, and Armen collapsed, his knees striking the ground.

"You always did have a hard time kneeling," Kallie retorted. "Or at least, that's what Myra told me."

Snarling, Armen tried to stand, but his legs folded beneath him. "That bi—"

Kallie tugged Armen's head back, cutting him off. "Bite your tongue, or I will cut it out for you."

Armen laughed, the delirium sparkling in his eyes and twisting his mouth into a smirk. "You think you've won, don't you?" he asked as Kallie pressed the point of her dagger against his chest.

"Look around you, Armen." Kallie tipped her chin toward Rian, who now held the upper hand in his battle against his brother. "Sebastian will be dead soon. You've lost."

Armen chuckled. "Oh, but he is just a pawn. We all are. Can't you see that?"

Kallie scoffed. "You are more delirious than I thought."

His smirk curled into a smug smile. "You don't know. Do you?"

"Know what?" Kallie asked.

He threw his head back and fell into a fit of laughter. Mangled words slipped out. His veins became more prominent and turned a vibrant blue. Spit dribbled down his chin.

Kallie shouted at him, but no answer came.

His laughter overtook his body, and he convulsed, slicing his throat on Kallie's blade.

Kallie gaped as collapsed at her feet.

Her stomach churned, and she quickly looked away, only to find Sebastian swinging for Rian's neck.

Kallie screamed out a warning as she sprinted.

Rian ducked, then swung out his leg, tripping Sebastian.

"I trusted you," Rian said, hovering over Sebastian, "yet you betrayed me. You stole my throne, my kingdom. You turned my people into test subjects!"

Sebastian pushed himself up and glared at his brother. "They should have never been yours to begin with! I should have been king. I should have been the one to rule. You were always the weak one!"

"It didn't have to come to this," Rian countered, his sword lowering an inch. "It still doesn't. Yield, Sebastian."

The prince huffed. "It was always going to come to this."

A flash of silver caught Kallie's eye, and she lunged.

She wrenched Sebastian's hand back moments before he drove a broken blade into Rian's thigh. Kallie ripped the blade from his hand and pressed it against the prince's back.

Sebastian tugged, but Kallie's grip didn't budge.

He tipped up his chin. "I will never yield to you, so do it. Kill me."

"I don't want to do this. You're my *brother*," Rian said, his hand trembling.

Sebastian scoffed. "Even now, you're weak. You are not fit to be a king. You never have—"

Kallie slapped her hand over her mouth as Rian drove his sword through Sebastian's side.

Rian dropped to his knees. He grabbed Sebastian and held him against his chest. A streak of tears ran down Rian's cheek.

On shaking legs, Kallie stood and looked out. All around them, the sounds of war continued to ring.

Hesitating for a second, she reached out and rested her hand on Rian's shoulder. "Rian—"

"It didn't have to be like this," he whispered, trembling.

"It's over, Rian," Kallie said gently. "Give the order."

He peered up at her, his eyes stained red. His lips parted, but before he could say anything, the world turned sideways as Kallie was thrown to the ground.

When she opened her eyes, she found two silver ones boring into her.

"*Graeson?*" Kallie sputtered. "What are you doing? Sebastian is dead. The battle is—"

"You nearly got yourself killed!" Graeson shouted, chest heaving. Sweat ran down his forehead and over his scar. His black hair stuck to his face, like ink staining parchment.

She grabbed his face and forced him to look at her. "Did you not hear me? The battle is over."

He shook his head. "The battle is not over. Not even close."

"What? What do you mean?"

He moved and helped her to her feet.

As Kallie stood, she looked around. Drakonises still zipped across the sky as soldiers fought on the ground. Explosives still shook the capital. Screams still pierced the air. All around her, the battle continued.

Kallie took a jilted step backward.

The fighting hadn't stopped.

She didn't understand. Those nearby should have stopped. They should have put their swords down and fallen to their knees. Did they not realize Sebastian was dead?

"Rian—" Kallie began but cut herself off when she found Laurince kneeling beside Rian, a Frenzian soldier dead beside him.

As Laurince told him something she couldn't hear, Rian snapped his attention to Kallie. His grip on Sebastian slipped, and horror flooded his features.

Graeson grabbed her wrists and bundled them between his hands. "The war is not over, Kal. Not yet."

Kallie looked from Rian to Graeson. The same fear and shock shone in Graeson's usually calm demeanor.

"How? We won—We—"

Graeson's grip on her hands tightened. "Kal, he's alive."

"Sebastian? No, Rian killed him. He's right there—"

Graeson shook his head. "Not Sebastian, Domitius—he's still alive."

"No." Kallie tried to take a step back, to put space between them, to breathe, but there was nowhere to go. "You're wrong. You're—"

"Look, Kalisandre," Graeson demanded, pointing toward the castle.

Kallie shook her head. Her entire body trembled. "No, you're wrong. You killed him! He can't be—"

"Kalisandre!" Graeson grabbed her shoulders and shook her gently.

Kallie blinked.

"*Look*," he demanded.

Kallie swallowed and looked toward the castle sitting on the hill.

There, beyond the battle raging in the streets, stood a figure astride a black stallion, towering over the winged soldiers who surrounded him. Although Kallie could not make out the man's features, she recognized the curl of the iron horns that adorned the metal helmet. Only one person owned a helmet in the shape of a bull.

"It's not possible," she breathed out. "It has to be someone else. It has to be—"

"It's him, Kals. Domitius lives. I failed."

CHAPTER 85
GRAESON

Time stood still as Graeson watched Kalisandre look out toward the hill. The truth was no longer deniable as she witnessed the man sitting atop a black stallion, the horns of his helmet gleaming in the sunset.

This army wasn't Sebastian's. It never had been. Sebastian might have been their commander, but their true ruler—the one orchestrating this entire battle—stood before the castle's gates.

As if sensing their attention on him, Domitius snapped his reins, spurring his horse into action. The heavy iron gate slammed shut as he disappeared beyond the hill, swallowed by the shadows.

A tumultuous storm came to life in Kallie's eyes. She made to move, but Graeson grabbed her hand before she could head after Domitius.

"Kal, wait."

"Let me go!" she urged.

"So you can do what?" Graeson demanded, his heart thundering. "Charge through his army of soldiers, who are clearly under his command?"

Kalisandre had to have noticed it too—the way the enemy

soldiers fought with an inhuman focus. None of Graeson's victims flinched or begged for mercy when his blades were at their necks. They simply gave their lives to the cause, allowing the soldiers behind them to take their place.

At first, Graeson hadn't given their behavior much thought. But as the fighting wore on, it gnawed at him. Most men fought to survive, but these soldiers—both the winged ones and the wingless—were practically sacrificing themselves, as if their lives were nothing more than offerings for someone else's victory.

When he had seen Armen grab Kallie, Graeson charged. He cut down one enemy after another.

As he drove his sword through a soldier's stomach, the man's gaze locked onto Graeson. Before the light within them went out, a familiar milky haze coated the soldier's brown eyes. It had made no sense. Kalisandre was on their side, yet there was no mistaking what he had seen. It was the mark of being manipulated. He had seen it in Kallie's past victims. But Kallie was not the one controlling them.

Then Graeson heard Armen say that Sebastian was just a pawn, that they all were. And between the fits of laughter, Armen sputtered, so softly that Kalisandre's mortal ears could not hear, "He lives."

Armen's words were sticky and incomprehensible at first. But then Graeson looked up. And there was the bull king, sitting astride his horse, wearing that accursed helmet.

Kallie tugged, trying to free her hand from Graeson's tight grip. "I have to do something!"

Thousands of men stood between them and Domitius. By the time they fought their way through the horde, Domitius would be long gone. He peered down the alley.

There was one other way, though.

Graeson took a deep breath. "I'll take you," he said, loosening his grip.

"Excuse me? I'm not going back to the camp! I will not abandon Frenzia! I will not—"

"Come on," he said, slipping his hand into hers and pulling her behind him.

"Where are we going?" Kallie demanded as they slipped down an alley.

Graeson stopped at a ladder that led to the roof. "To go kill that fucking bastard once and for all."

CHAPTER 86

MYRA

Only Theenah and Gerald were allowed inside Dani's tent. Everyone else, including Sylvia and Moris, waited anxiously outside. Some soldiers patrolled the camp, hoping to keep any unwanted visitors away. Many soldiers brought back injured comrades, keeping the other healers busy.

Myra tried to help the healers, but she found herself constantly returning to the tent, as if Dani's pain called to her. Whenever a loud groan or muffled scream slipped from the tent as another contraction came, Myra winced. For the past twenty-four hours, Myra had been so focused on dulling pain that it was hard not to reach out to Dani's and squash it.

In front of the tent, Sylvia and Moris paced back and forth, their anxiety clouding them. Moris had told Sylvia what had happened to him. Even turned away from the pair, Myra could feel Sylvia throwing invisible daggers at her because of Myra's role in Moris' transformation.

As Theenah left the tent, Myra unconsciously stood, following her to the supplies. "How is she?"

The healer sighed and wiped her brow. "It's too soon to tell. She's not quite nine months. It's early, but if she doesn't calm down…"

Myra twisted her fingers together, her knuckles cracking. She swallowed, but her throat was dry. "I might be able to help."

Theenah eyed her skeptically, hand poised above the bucket, towel still dripping. "Have you ever delivered a baby?"

"No, but—"

"Have you had experience being a nursemaid?"

"No, but—"

Theenah wrung out the soaking towel. "Then unfortunately I don't think you can, my dear."

Myra's hands curled into tight fists. She quickly unclenched them. "You said she needs to calm down, right?"

"Yes, but none of the oils are working. The general is even more stubborn than her father. It's not like I can force her to calm down," the healer said.

There it was—a strand of hope—and Myra latched onto it.

"I can," Myra stated, back straight.

Theenah chuckled. "It's fine—"

Tossing aside manners and formalities, Myra grabbed the healer's wrist, demanding her attention. When Myra poured an ounce of her gift into her, the strain around Theenah's eyes vanished, and her lips parted slightly as her shoulders dropped.

Myra released Theenah and dropped the thread of emotions simultaneously.

Theenah blinked at her. The healer looked around, then pulled Myra to the side, away from prying ears. "You were not on the ships with us. You're not Pontian," she whispered.

Myra rolled her shoulders back, shaking the discomfort from telling someone about her gift. "My parents were. I can help Dani. I promise."

The healer observed Myra more closely, scanning her up and

down. "Fine," she grumbled after a moment. "Grab that bucket. We need to keep her temperature down."

Myra did as she was told and followed the healer. The water sloshed against the sides of the bucket, nearly spilling over the lip. The healer threw the tent flap open and held it for Myra to enter.

"Where is she going?" Sylvia demanded, storming over to the tent.

"Mind your tongue, Larpos," Theenah said, urging Myra to enter. She glanced at Moris, who had followed his friend. "Make sure we are undisturbed."

Moris nodded, but Sylvia was unrelenting.

They blocked Myra's entry, throwing out their arms. "*She* cannot go near Ferrios."

Moris reached for Sylvia. "Sylv, it's—"

Sylvia slapped his hand away. "The commander said to guard Ferrios from any threats. *She* is a threat."

The tent flap fell from Theenah's fingers. Unflinching in the face of Sylvia's wrath, the healer pointed at Myra, who went rigid beside her. "This woman may be Danisinia and that child's saving grace. I have orders from the Queen and the commander to ensure *both* of their safety. Now *move*, Larpos, or I will move you myself."

Moris' hand fell onto Sylvia's shoulder, and he whispered something Myra couldn't hear. But whatever he said, it got Sylvia to take a step back. Although a scowl still curved at their lips.

As Myra passed them, Sylvia hissed, "If you dare hurt either of them, I will slice that pretty little head of yours right off—"

"*Enough*, Larpos," Theenah ordered, pushing Myra inside the tent.

The flap fell behind them, closing out the world. The smell of sweat saturated the small space. Carefully, Myra set the bucket down, afraid to wake Dani, who lay with her hand over her eyes.

Dani's face and neck sparkled with moisture. Beads of sweat rolled down the contours of her brown cheeks and down her collarbone.

"Danisinia," Theenah called out.

Dani groaned.

The healer held out her hand, and Myra handed her the wet rag. "I've brought someone who might be able to help."

Dani peeled her hand away from her eyes an inch and squinted. Her dull eyes flicked around the tent until they landed on Myra. Anger flashed across her face, but pain quickly consumed it before she could act on it.

Theenah waved Myra over. Hesitantly, Myra sat on the other side of Dani. Without Dani's permission, though, she maintained her distant.

"Danisinia," the healer beckoned, sensing Dani's trepidation. She placed the wet rag on Dani's forehead. "I'll be here the whole time."

Agony seeped from Dani's pores and soaked the earth, tainting the ground.

Myra chewed on her bottom lip, nervous. If Dani refused her help, would the healer force her to use her gift anyway?

Myra did not want to violate Dani's wishes, but how long could she maintain this state? If they didn't do something, Myra feared what would happen to Dani and the child.

Dani squinted at Myra, grimacing. But then she plopped her hand down, resting it beside Myra's knee, palm up. "Do it," she whispered, her voice raw.

Myra gingerly took Dani's hand in her own, cradling it. With a deep breath, Myra gently squeezed Dani's hand as the bright pain flooded her senses.

CHAPTER 87
KALLIE

KALLIE PRESSED HER STOMACH AGAINST GRAESON'S SPINE AS HE FLEW over the capital.

For a heartbeat, the clang of clashing metal ceased. Pontian, Tetrian, and Frenzian soldiers gawked at the enormous dragon, dark as midnight, sweeping across the sky. The dragons were supposed to be gone, but today the people would learn the truth.

As Graeson barreled toward the castle, Nyrri was the only one smart enough to keep her distance. The other drakonises and winged soldiers were not as lucky. The force of Graeson's wings sent soldiers tumbling through the sky like a tower of cards. Even those on the ground couldn't withstand his power and were knocked over.

The Tetrian and Pontian forces, who had been smart enough to brace themselves, took the opportunity presented to them and struck. Spears ripped through the air. Steel met steel.

But their advantage was fleeting. The enemy troops recovered quickly, driven by their need to eliminate their foes.

It was as if seeing a dragon was an everyday occurrence for them, which could only mean one thing. Graeson was right. They were under Domitius' control. Nothing else could explain their unwavering resolve.

Kallie's heart sank even further when Graeson flew higher and she finally saw the full extent of the enemy's forces. Soldiers wearing Frenzian steel swarmed the streets, their armor blazing in the golden sunlight like flames across the battlefield.

Even though a section of the allied forces had broken away to flank the enemy, Kallie feared it would be too late. Drakonises continued to ravage the capital, their hunger for blood insatiable.

As Kallie and Graeson reached the castle's gates, the beasts pounced. Graeson roared, and fire poured from his mouth.

Kallie immediately shut her eyes as they flew into the embers. One ember landed on her hand, and she hissed as it singed her skin. But she didn't dare let go, only clenched her jaw and held on tighter.

As if noticing his mistake, Graeson pivoted and soared higher, shielding her from the next wave of sparks.

Kallie opened her eyes when he suddenly dove. Struggling to see against the pounding wind, she squinted. Through her blurry vision, though, she spotted Domitius.

As Graeson's shadow fell over him, Domitius looked back. Although Kallie could not see his expression beneath the mask, she could almost taste his panic. He snapped the reins, pushing his horse to run faster.

Kallie leaned forward, and Graeson flew harder, his wings striking the air.

Kage would not escape this time.

Kallie braced as they approached the castle's stone walls. She briefly wondered if they were as impenetrable as the rumors claimed, or if Graeson could tear them down if necessary. Before she could dwell on it, though, Graeson spun. His paws slammed against the stone steps with a thunderous crash. Rocks crumbled beneath Graeson's feet as his claws dug into the steps.

When the guards stationed at the door surged forward, weapons raised, Graeson whipped his tail out, striking them both with a sickening thud. The nearby horses reared in fright. Several of them sprinted away, their hooves pounding against the ground as they bolted.

Several yards away, Domitius, clinging to his stallion, adjusted his weight and held onto the pommel.

Graeson released a vicious roar, the sound causing the very earth to shake.

Domitius lost his grip and was thrown off his horse. He hit the ground with a painful thud. He rolled over onto his stomach and pushed himself up, shouting at his horse to come back. But the stallion was already darting toward the back of the castle.

Kallie stood. With her dagger in hand and Graeson's blades strapped to her back, Kallie couldn't help but pity the king of Ardentol.

"You were supposed to be dead," she said as she landed on the steps.

A haunting laugh echoed inside the bull helmet as Domitius rose to his feet. His once-clean armor was now dirtied with mud and grass. "I thought I had taught you better," he said, straightening his tilted helmet. "Always confirm the kill, Kalisandre."

Hearing Kage's voice washed away any remaining doubts Kallie had. There was no mistaking it now. He was alive. They had failed.

"I saw your body burn to ash," she spat.

Graeson snarled, echoing Kallie's statement.

"Face it, Kalisandre," Domitius said, his voice hollow. "You cannot kill me. No one can."

Graeson growled. He lowered his head, inching it closer to Kallie as she stood atop the steps of the Frenzian castle.

She lifted her chin, refusing to let Domitius get to her. She wasn't the same girl he had trained. "I might have failed last time, but I won't make the same mistake twice. You taught me that, remember?"

"To be honest, I should thank you for even trying to kill me," Domitius said, as if amused. As if his death wasn't imminent. "I wasn't sure if it would work, but you proved it did."

"If what worked?"

Domitius cocked his head to the side, and Kallie cursed herself. The question had spilled from her mouth before she could stop it.

"Did that handmaiden of yours ever tell you about her brother?"

Kallie's steps faltered at the mention of Myra's brother, Mynhos. Beside her, Graeson snapped his head up, his nostrils flaring. His talons dug into the earth, and he eyed her wearily, their thoughts in tandem.

Myra wasn't the only one in her family who had a gift. Her brother had one, too. One particularly dangerous in the wrong hands.

Was this truly how Domitius survived the fire? Could he have Mynhos' power in addition to Kallie's?

"Ah, so she did," Domitius said when Kallie remained silent. "Good. That saves me some explaining."

Kallie's eyebrows furrowed. Myra had said that her brother had died. She and Laurince had killed him—for better or for worse.

"Mynhos is dead," Kallie said, calling Domitius' bluff.

"That is true. Unfortunately for him, his body could only handle so much. The dagger that had been driven through his heart had been there for too long. When Dr. Thorne's replacement had gotten his hands on him…" Domitius waved a hand dismissively. "Let's just say the young healer can get overzealous in his pursuits. Stone pushed Mynhos' body too far." He shrugged. "No matter. I got what I wanted."

Domitius strolled forward, dragging his sword through the dirt and leaving a trail behind him. "You see, for decades, I had been searching for someone like Mynhos, someone who bore any power resembling his ability. When I discovered him, I was in awe. Not only could he heal a minor wound, but he could regenerate his limbs. And watching it happen with my own eyes? It was as fascinating as it was horrifying."

Kallie blinked, the truth settling in as she reached the bottom of the steps. If Mynhos could grow his limbs back, did that mean Domitius could not be killed?

He was bluffing. He had to be.

Kallie's power surged within her. She let it slip across her tongue, coating her words. "Tell me the truth."

"Fire could not kill me, Kalisandre. What makes you think a measly blade can?"

A low growl sounded, and a puff of smoke twirled around her as Graeson trailed behind her.

"You cannot control me," Domitius said, amusement peppering his voice and sending an unshakable chill down Kallie's spine.

Nearby, iron rattled. Kallie looked at the sky but couldn't pinpoint the source. Her ears buzzed from the sounds of war at the bottom of the hill where their friends and allies were still hanging on. Their screams rang in her ears.

"Even if you somehow killed me, you would still have one problem," Domitius warned.

Kallie's fingers twitched around the hilt of her dagger.

"My army will not stop fighting until your friends die. Killing me will not stop the command."

Kallie snapped her head toward Graeson, who narrowed his molten eyes at Domitius. He snarled, revealing sharp canines as if threatening to swallow Kage whole. But if what Kage said was true, Kallie couldn't let that happen. The soldiers, whether their enemy or not, deserved to be freed.

"Release them," Kallie commanded, her power coursing through her veins.

"And ruin the fun?" Domitius cackled, the sound grating Kallie's bones. "Now, why would I do that?"

Lips parting, Kallie blanched as he evaded her power.

"You have two choices: give up and bend the knee, or burn my men to ash, killing your friends in the process."

Fear rose in Kallie's throat. There had to be another way to end this. She couldn't let Kage win. She hadn't broken free from his control just to fail now.

The clanging noise grew louder, but Kallie stood there frozen, unable to think.

Domitius took a step back and pointed his sword at Graeson. "Let's see if you've learned to heel, shall we?"

Graeson's tail wrapped around Kallie instantly. With a quick flick, he tossed her away from him.

Kallie landed on the ground several yards away. Her back hit the dirt and knocked the air out of her lungs. She inhaled and coughed as she swallowed dirt. Swatting at the debris floating around her, she spotted winged soldiers darting across the field. They closed in around Graeson, swarming him from above and carrying iron chains that gleamed in the harsh sunlight.

Before Graeson could take off, the soldiers dropped one chain after another, crushing his wings to his sides and immobilizing him.

Kallie scrambled to her feet and grabbed her dagger. She charged, a primal scream tearing at her throat.

Graeson roared in defiance, his silver eyes turning pitch-black.

Kallie's power surged through her, the command on the tip of her tongue. Before she could utter a word, someone yanked her back. Hands slipped over her mouth, silencing her.

"Marvelous. Truly marvelous," Domitius said, restraining Kallie against his chest as he watched the guards tightening the chains around Graeson's body.

Kallie bit down on the flesh of his palm, forcing Kage to loosen his grip. Quickly, she reared her hand back. The point of her dagger drove into Domitius' thigh.

Domitius might have claimed he was untouchable, but pain still affected him. He screamed.

A boot slammed into the back of Kallie's knees. Her legs gave out, and she collapsed.

Domitius snatched Kallie's ponytail, yanking her head back. Cold metal scraped against her mouth and jaw. A sharp click sounded at the back of her skull, and the metal pinched her skin.

Kallie clawed at the metal, her fingers scratching at the cold, unyielding surface. A muffled sound escaped her, but the mask swallowed it. She choked. Her mouth wouldn't budge, not even an inch. The mask was too tight, too constricting. Tears welled, burning her eyes. They hung precariously on her lash line before dripping down her cheeks.

"You'll have to do better than that, Kalisandre," Domitius hissed. "Or did you forget I was the one who trained you?"

She tried to scream again but failed.

This couldn't have been happening. She was so close.

He ran a finger along the metal. "Beautiful, isn't it? The most talented metallurgist in Ardentol has been working on this piece for some time. I always hoped I wouldn't have to use it. You were always so well-behaved growing up. But it's clear there is no getting through to you now. They've poisoned you."

Through blurry eyes, Kallie looked at Graeson. The guards tugged on the chains, forcing Graeson to drop to his belly. His massive jaw smacked into the earth and sent up a plume of dust. The iron bit into his flesh, digging into his scales.

Domitius pressed a blade against Kallie's back. "I didn't think the chains would work when Sebastian showed them to me. But he claimed his ancestors used them to bring down the dragons that once graced these lands. For centuries, the Dronias family has housed them in the depths of the dungeons, keeping them in case the dragons ever returned." Domitius hummed in admiration. "I knew the son of a god and seer would be special, but this is superb."

Kallie's fearful gaze locked onto Graeson. But he wasn't done fighting. He screeched, the sound piercing and blood curling. His tail whipped around, knocking several guards over. A stream of fire poured from his mouth. Those in its path went up in flames in an instant, leaving behind only a pile of ash in their wake.

"So, is this how you will stop my army? By burning them to ash?" Domitius laughed. "Yet you think I am the monster?"

Kallie jerked in his hold, but Domitius pressed the tip of the sword between her shoulders. The blade pierced through the leather fabric and pinched her skin. With his other hand, he patted her cheek, and the metal mask bit into Kallie's flesh. "Now, now, Kalisandre. We're just getting started."

CHAPTER 88
MYRA

THE MOANS OF THE DYING, THE QUAKES OF THE EXPLOSIONS, AND THE screeches of the beasts slipped inside the tent. The sounds of war pounded against Myra's ears. As she tried to block them out, Dani's screams and cries pierced her eardrums, flooding her senses.

Myra felt like she was drowning. The creatures of the sea were grabbing her by the ankles and pulling her down, down, *down*.

Myra's palms were slick with sweat, and she struggled to maintain her grip around Dani's hand as the fears crept in.

Was Laurince still alive?

Was Kallie still fighting?

Was the battle almost over?

Would it ever end?

The cries of war shook her to her core. But as Myra looked at Dani's pale face, at the sweat dripping down it and coating her hair, Myra knew she had to keep trying. She pushed the questions and fears away as best as she could. Instead, she rummaged for the good memories that were housed deep within her mind. The sweet memories.

She thought of Laurince and the moments they shared. She

thought of the tavern, of dancing together. The way his dimple showed when he laughed. How he gave away smiles like they were nothing.

She recalled his last words to her and repeated them in her mind like a mantra.

I'll come back to you.

I'll come back to you.

I'll come back to you.

CHAPTER 89

MYRA

Theenah dabbed a cold, wet cloth against Myra's forehead.

"You need to take a break," Theenah whispered.

Myra didn't know how much time had passed since she had sat down beside Dani. Her back and knees ached from kneeling for so long, but she didn't dare voice a complaint. Not when Dani was lying on the ground, her body still covered in sweat as she fought against the encroaching fever.

Myra poured drop after drop of her power into Dani, doing whatever she could to quell her pain. But pain was the hardest emotion to dull, and Dani's was endless.

"I'm fine," Myra said.

"Have you eaten anything? I haven't even seen you drink water. You will be no help to her if you pass out," Theenah warned.

When Myra still didn't move, the healer groaned. "Do not make me drag you out of this tent."

Dropping her shoulders in defeat, Myra uncurled her fingers from around Dani's hand. She had been holding it for so long that her knuckles cracked from the movement. Flexing her fingers, she stood, her knees creaking. Myra wobbled, her legs weak, and the healer quickly caught her by the elbow.

"Come on," Theenah urged. "Let's get you something to eat. Danisinia is resting. You should too."

Despite Myra's protests, they strolled out of the tent. Myra squinted at the sky and held up her hand to block the sun. Several hours had passed, and the sun was now setting, its golden rays blinding.

She scanned the camp and frowned.

Within a few hours, nightfall would soak the land. Yet the battle still persisted.

She returned her attention to the sky, sending a prayer to the gods. As she did, a streak of vibrant color filled the space beyond the trees, as if the sky was on fire.

"What was that?" she asked.

"Shit. This can't be good," Moris said, jumping to his feet. Other soldiers followed suit, their attention fixed on the sky.

A dark shadow swirled above the foliage. Distorted by the foliage, its massive form plunged the camp into darkness.

"Is that a drakonis?" Myra asked, struggling to identify the creature.

"No," Moris said, snatching his sword from the ground.

"Then what was that?"

"A dragon."

"Did those bastards fuck with your head, too?" Sylvia asked, propping a hand on their hip. "Because I swore you just said that *thing* was a dragon."

"I did," Moris confirmed, shoving his sword back into its sheath. He stood and looked around at the confused faces staring back at him. His mouth formed a small O when he realized no one understood what he was saying.

Moris scratched the back of his head. "Right, none of you know. Dragons exist. In fact, Graeson is one."

"I'm sorry. He's *what*?" Myra asked, her jaw hanging open.

Moris exhaled a heavy groan. "Look, I don't have the time to explain," he said, running backward. "Graeson can shift into a dragon. It's how we got here before you all. But that's not Graeson."

"What do you mean that's not Graeson?" Myra shrieked.

"He's too big!" Moris shouted over his shoulder before taking off.

Sylvia ran after him, shouting aimlessly at him. But Moris didn't stop. His wings beat even faster as he wove through the trees and headed toward the capital.

Myra's knees shook beneath her as Moris' words sank in.

Graeson was a dragon.

But if that wasn't Graeson, who was it?

CHAPTER 90
GRAESON

In the seconds in which Domitius placed the mask around Kalisandre's jaw, sealing her mouth shut, Graeson wished he could redo everything.

He regretted not listening to his instincts when he had heard the chains rattling.

He regretted not being strong enough to escape the chains.

But most of all, Graeson regretted leading them to Domitius and falling into his trap.

His gaze flew across the landscape, trying to find a way out. Trying to figure out how they could make it out alive. But all Graeson saw were the encroaching soldiers, their weapons drawn.

He looked at Kalisandre, the woman he cherished above all else. Graeson would have burned down the entire world for her. He would have set it all ablaze if it meant that the two of them could escape alive.

Even from afar, he could see the tears coating Kalisandre's blue eyes, dulling their shine and the fire that had previously burned within them. Her hair was strewn across her face haphazardly, and her soft features were speckled with blood from the gruesome battle in the streets. But it was her muffled screams that made his skin crawl the most, that set every nerve-ending on fire.

Kage thought he could still control her? Kalisandre was *his* soul bond, and Graeson would be damned if he let Domitius take her power away.

Graeson strained against the unyielding chains. The iron dug into his sides, piercing his scales. He scraped his claws against the earth, turning up the soil. He would dig his way out of this if he had to.

A low rumble sounded, and the leaves in the trees trembled, making him pause.

Inhaling, Graeson's nostrils flared. Before he could make sense of the familiar scent, a river of fire sliced across the sky like a lightning bolt.

The guards spun around, searching the sky. The burst of fire was too large for one of the drakonises to have produced. But if one of them hadn't done it, then who had? In preparation for whatever enemy lurked in the shadows of the darkening sky, a soldier nocked an arrow back.

A dark shadow, even larger than Graeson's menacing form, burst through the flames. Two bright orbs blinked, poking holes in the surrounding darkness. A pair of silver eyes as bright as the moon locked onto Graeson. The dragon roared.

A disgrace, Barinthian said, the god's voice filling Graeson's head. *Is this all my son is good for?*

Graeson snarled. *What the fuck are you doing here?*

That's a strange way to say thank you, Barinthian snapped.

Graeson tugged against the chains. *Thank you!? Do you know how many people have died? How many lives have been lost? You could have ended this!*

As could you have. But don't worry. I'll leave a few for you.

Barinthian flattened his wings to his sides and dove. The guards screamed as the massive dragon rushed toward them. Those lucky enough to have wings took off, fleeing. But those on the ground weren't as lucky. Barinthian scorched them, his fire bright-white and merciless.

He flew over Graeson, snatching the chain that lay over Graeson's snout. Barinthian's back claws wrapped around the iron, nicking Graeson's nose. He tugged. Once, twice, three times.

Graeson felt the chain's absence immediately. He snapped at Barinthian's tail, but narrowly missed it.

Next time, don't let a mortal overpower you.

There won't be a next time, Graeson growled back.

A sound akin to a snort came from the god.

Graeson struggled against the remaining chains. Even with his head free, the weight of the iron pressed his body flat against the ground. He tried to use his wings to force them off, but his muscles shook from the strain. He growled in frustration. When he was about to admit defeat and call out to his father, three winged guards charged toward the god.

Behind you! Graeson roared.

Barinthian barely reacted. He swept past the guards, his speed unmatched. As he passed them, Barinthian flicked his tail, striking two of the men in the chest as if they were no more than gnats.

The third guard dodged the attack, dropping beneath the god's tail. The guard dove toward the dragon's belly, finding the softer skin. Sword in hand, the guard went to strike, but Barinthian was quick. In seconds, the god was on him, spinning around faster than he should have been able. Fire spewed from Barinthian's mouth. Ash and embers poured from the sky.

Graeson sighed in relief, but nearly choked when he turned his gaze back to the ground. Domitius was holding his sword to Kalisandre's throat.

CHAPTER 91
KALLIE

Kallie didn't have the time to question where the dragon came from or who it was. Not as Domitius tightened his hold around her and pressed his blade to her throat.

It wasn't long ago when Domitius held another blade to her neck. This time, she didn't think she would be that lucky to escape it. Graeson was chained, and the other dragon was fending off the winged guards that were pouring from every direction, swarming him. Even if he or the second dragon could help her, what would they be able to do? Domitius was too close to her for them to save her.

"Come any closer, and I'll slit her throat," Domitius called out, his voice echoing within his helmet.

Kallie went rigid, and her breathing halted.

Was this how it would end? Kage already had her power. Frenzia was already under his control. He no longer needed Kallie.

Graeson snarled in the king's direction. His eyes darkened with malice, turning pitch black.

Domitius wouldn't kill her. He couldn't. They might not have been blood, but he had raised her. Perhaps first as a weapon, but as a daughter, too.

Still, Domitius increased the pressure, and Kallie sucked in a sharp breath.

Graeson snapped his teeth at the other dragon, who glared at Graeson, his lip curling.

Kallie noted the piles of ash across the field. If this was the result of her being captured, what would Graeson do if Domitius killed her?

Kallie wished she could see Graeson's true form one more time. She wished she had listened to Dani and waited to accept the bond until after the war had passed. Now all it would take was one movement, one slice, and Domitius would kill both of them—one in body and one in spirit. Their bond might have been new, but Graeson had accepted it a long time ago.

"Do it now!" Domitius barked.

A flurry of guards poured from the castle, but Kallie's attention went straight to the young man in the epicenter. She squinted, trying to figure out what he was holding. When he hit the bottom of the steps, the fading sunlight beamed on him, and thin metal sparkled in the light.

Kallie gasped just as Graeson released a heart-wrenching screech. The man was holding a syringe, and she could only guess what was in it.

Her power became a hurricane inside her. It flooded her system and poured down her limbs.

Domitius could take away her memories.

He could take away her voice.

He could even copy her power and steal it for himself.

But Kallie was done letting Kage Domitius hurt the people she loved.

She dug, scouring for her power. With one tug, it flooded her body, flowing into her bloodstream. Her power blossomed inside her like never before. It was stronger, steadier, fiercer. A prickle of sweat dripped down her spine as her senses sharpened. She focused on the pressure of the blade, on Domitius' arm holding her in place. She could hear his heartbeat thundering, its rhythm thrumming across her skin. Kallie latched onto it and poured the command through her body and into his.

She kept pouring it, letting her words seep into his skin.

She was Kalisandre Helene Nadarean, and only she controlled her fate.

With a snap, she released the command.

In a breath that seemed to span time, the metal left her throat, and a soft thump echoed.

But Kallie didn't let herself sit in her relief for long. Grabbing Domitius' arm, she ducked and bent it behind him.

"But you shouldn't be able to—h-how did you—" Domitius sputtered, realizing too late what was happening. "You're too weak!"

Kallie wanted to spit Kage's words back at him. That he was the one who had trained her and made her a force to be reckoned with. But the mask still prohibited her from speaking. Instead, she kicked him in the back, sending him sprawling.

His body went limp on impact, yet his chest still rose and fell. He was still alive.

Kallie grabbed him by the collar and rolled him onto his back.

Her power, a tangible wave of heat, flowed through her skin and spilled into him. With his limbs cemented to the earth, bound by her command, Kallie frantically searched his body.

Quickly locating a key in his chest pocket, she snatched it and fiddled with the metal lock on the back of her mask.

She heard Graeson's panic roar behind her. She had to hurry. She had to help him.

The mask dug into her flesh, pinching her skin. Her chest rose frantically, her panic sending her spiraling and causing sweat to bead on her palms. Frustration tainted her movements as she struggled with the lock.

Graeson's roar continued to ring in her ears.

A pair of calloused hands were suddenly on hers, clamping over the key.

Kallie screamed, the sound mangled beneath the metal.

"I got it."

Kallie nearly sobbed at her brother's voice. Her body collapsed, and she instantly released the key. In her periphery, she saw another figure appear. Through her tear-stained eyes, she recognized Moris immediately as he kneeled behind Domitius' head.

Kallie tried to ask them how they got here so quickly, but she was not free of the mask yet.

As if reading her thoughts, Terin said, "Moris found me as soon as he saw him." He pointed to the dragon that was now ripping a guard near Graeson to shreds with its teeth.

With the nearest guards taken care of, the beast hovered above Graeson's form as he grabbed another chain and yanked it from the posts driven into the ground. The end of the chain sprung, and Kallie flinched. But the second dragon didn't stop there. He grabbed another chain, then another.

"Who the fuck is that anyway?" Moris asked, snapping manacles around Domitius' wrists and ankles.

Graeson's wing sprang free at the same time as the mask fell from Kallie's face. She sucked in a sharp breath, the air cold in her lungs.

"Barinthian," Kallie exhaled. She had never seen Graeson's father, but she knew intrinsically that this was the god Graeson despised.

"His father?" Terin asked.

Kallie nodded. "It has to be."

Graeson's second wing sprang free. He shook, shedding the last of the chains. He leaned back, and Kallie saw his chest rise as he inhaled. The back of his throat lit up as he glared at the guards.

Kallie's heart jumped in her lungs as she saw the fear shining in the soldiers' eyes. She shouted at Graeson to stop.

Graeson swallowed the flame, snapping his attention toward her.

"What is it, Kals?" Terin reached for her, but Kallie stepped away, holding him off.

She closed her eyes, feeling her power running through her veins. The answer had been there the entire time.

It wasn't Moris who had stopped the mob from attacking him. He hadn't prevented their soldiers from killing each other when Rian and the others had arrived last night. She had.

Kallie had barely tapped into her power.

As it flowed through her, she finally understood why Kage had sought her ability. He didn't steal Kallie to just control a few lords, but entire armies.

Perhaps it was because she had accepted the bond, or maybe it was because she had stopped fighting herself. Either way, it didn't matter why. All that mattered was that she could end this.

She could stop the bloodshed, here and now.

She reached for the soldiers and mentally grabbed them. Feeling their hearts beating, she squeezed, bending their will.

Domitius' hold on them snapped like a branch.

As Barinthian was about to exhale, ignoring her request to wait, the soldiers collapsed.

When Kallie looked up, her gaze instantly met Graeson's. For a split second, she thought she would see something akin to fear shining back at her. Instead, there was only adoration. As if he knew she had the power in her all along.

"What just—" Terin gaped at the sight of the fallen soldiers. He turned to her. "Kallie, did you—"

"Let me see that," Kallie said, interrupting him and pointing to the mask.

Still in shock, Terin gave her the mask.

"Take his helmet off," she told Moris.

Moris grabbed the bull helmet by its horns. When Moris pried the helmet off, Kallie's heart dropped to her stomach as Domitius' face showed in the sunlight.

Kage had lied—or at least partially. Domitius had not left the fire in Borgania unscathed.

Along the side of his face, a burn mark trailed around his hairline to the back of his head. The skin was red and raw, healed yet scarred from the flames.

"Lift his head," Kallie said quietly.

With a weary glance in Terin's direction, Moris did as she asked and lifted Domitius' head up.

With shaking hands, Kallie placed the mask around Domitius' mouth and over his jaw. As she snapped the lock in place, his eyes sprang open, and he screamed in fury as he reached for her.

Terin yanked her off him before Domitius could grab her. Yet Kage swatted at the air, enraged. Realizing his screams were muffled, he grabbed his face and felt the mask. He clawed at the metal with a mix of desperation and madness.

Kallie took a step back as the man before her came undone.

She tried to find a trace of the man she once knew. The man she had cared for. But the man lying on the ground was no more than a stranger to her. And not because of the fresh scar, but because she finally saw Domitius for who he was.

"It's over, Kage," Kallie whispered.

Anger flooded his countenance, and beneath it, for the first time, Kallie saw true fear shining within Kage's brown eyes.

"What do you want to do with him?" Terin asked.

"Me?" Kallie asked. "You have more power here."

Terin shook his head. "What happens here is your choice, Kals."

Kallie hesitated. Kage had made her into a weapon, and she wondered if killing him would only prove he was successful. More than anything else, Domitius craved power. He wanted to rule the seven kingdoms. He wanted to steal the powers of the Pontians because he wanted to feel like he was a god. Dying here today would not be the punishment he deserved. He deserved to wallow in his self-destruction. He deserved to know what it was like to lose everything.

Kallie took a step back. "Keep him detained. Death would be a mercy."

She looked over her shoulder, finding Graeson and the other dragon in a stand-off, a cloud of smoke swirling between them.

As if sensing her gaze, Graeson turned away from his father and looked at her. He glanced at the king at her feet, his lip curling in disgust.

The other dragon said something, but Graeson only huffed and headed toward Kallie. When he was close enough, Graeson dropped his head to her height.

Kallie lifted her hand and laid it on his cheek, the scales rough and hot beneath her palm. "Let's end this."

WHEN KALLIE LOOKED DOWN as Graeson hovered above the capital, the streets were teeming with thousands upon thousands of people, the battle still raging. Their friends and allies were still holding their ground.

She spotted Medenia and Ophelia locked in a dance of combat as they fought their opponents, the song never ending. Nearby, Ellie fought valiantly, her hair matted with blood and grime. Dani's father was in the thick of it, his weapon slashing violently. In the air, she spotted a pair of white wings barreling toward a hoard of drakonises with a dark shadow alongside him. Somewhere, Rian tried to end the battle that had ripped his kingdom in half.

But the soldiers who fought against them? They were not their enemies. They were brothers, fathers, sons.

Kallie gripped the dagger Myra had given her years ago, her fingers flexing around the worn hilt. She didn't need the dagger for what she was about to do, but the familiar weight gave her strength, the words etched into the blade empowering her.

She tilted her face toward the sky. With strands of hair that had fallen from her ponytail whipping around her face, she let her power fill her. She gathered it, as though she was taking a deep breath and filling her lungs with air. Then, lifting the dagger high above her head, she released her power, letting it rain down upon the capital.

The war of fires and lies would end today.

CHAPTER 92
GRAESON

As Graeson watched the soldiers collapse all across the capital, he was left in awe of Kalisandre.

If the gods could read Graeson's mind, they would scorn him for what he was thinking. But he did not care.

Part of him wanted to call Kalisandre a goddess, to claim she had been blessed with more of Sabina's blood than anyone could have thought possible.

However, the label didn't sit right on his tongue. Not because she was not worthy enough to be a god, nor because she was less than one, less than the immortals who had granted her the ability she possessed. But because it simply wasn't enough. It didn't encapsulate everything she was and everything she could do.

Kalisandre was more than a warrior, more than a queen, more than a goddess. She was beyond explanations and labels. She was a woman who had finally found herself, who finally trusted herself.

And Graeson, somehow, by the grace of the Fates, was her soul bond, and he had never felt prouder to be anything else.

They both had monstrous parts and pasts that writhed in the shadows of their minds. He knew how nearly impossible it could be to accept that darkness, to conquer it. But Kallie had. She had accepted her darkness. She hadn't let it consume her and bring her to her knees. Instead, she had risen above it.

The bull king had raised Kalisandre to be a monster, to manipulate, seduce, and kill for power. For so long, Kalisandre had thought that she was full of darkness, that she only brought destruction upon those she cared about. But as the clang of metal came to a halt, Graeson realized the truth: she was the kingdom's salvation.

CHAPTER 93

MYRA

Myra sat with her head in her hands, her body heavy with exhaustion. Her hands had only recently stopped shaking after sitting by the fire. But the moment someone began cooking, a knot of nausea twisted in her stomach. How could anyone eat when there was a battle going on?

On shaky legs, she stood. When she teetered, Phaia grabbed her by the elbow.

"Shouldn't you be resting?" Phaia asked, concern tugging her mouth into a frown. "The healer said—"

"I'm fine." Myra shook off Phaia's hand. She was better than those suffering grave injuries from the ongoing battle. Certainly better than Dani, who still hadn't woken up.

Yet Myra would be felled by the smell of roasting meat? Ridiculous.

She made it only two steps before a disturbance erupted at the edge of the camp. A horde of people gathered, their raised voices a loud chorus as mangled cries pierced the air.

"What's going on?" she asked, trying to see over the crowd. When she leaned forward on her toes, her legs shook and she nearly collapsed. Phaia was at her side in an instant, holding her steady.

"I don't know. I—" Phaia swallowed, her trepidation spilling into Myra.

She glanced at Dani's tent. The Pontian healer was still inside, and most of the soldiers guarding the tent had abandoned it. If it wasn't Dani, then who—

The crowd parted, and Graeson emerged, shirtless and bruised. The moment Myra's attention dropped to his arms, she lurched forward on trembling legs. Draped across his arms was Kallie, her arm hanging limp over his.

Phaia hobbled alongside Myra, wrapping her arm around Myra's waist. They hurried over to the other side of the camp, and Myra did her best to tamp down her fears. Soldiers and strangers ran across their path, but Myra kept her gaze on Kallie, afraid that if she looked away, she would lose her—if she hadn't already.

As those who stayed back helped the injured over to the provisional infirmary, Myra locked eyes with Graeson. And though his expression was dreary from the battle, he gave her a small nod in reassurance.

Myra collapsed against Phaia, clinging to her shirt as if it were a lifeline.

"She's alive," Myra croaked.

"How do you know? Are you sure?" Phaia asked, tightening her hold on her.

Kallie shifted in Graeson's arms then. She lifted her arm, tucking it against his chest. Both women sighed in relief.

When they reached Graeson, he said, "She's exhausted and drained, but she will be fine."

"And the war?" Sylvia asked, meeting them.

"It's over."

"Did we…is everyone…" Myra swallowed her question, afraid to know the answer.

Graeson exhaled a heavy sigh. "We will not know the damage until it is done. Terin and Moris are relaying the news now."

"What news?" Sylvia asked.

Overhearing, the people around them halted, the camp going quiet.

Graeson scanned the crowd, his jaw popping. "Sebastian is dead."

Cheers erupted across the camp as the news spread like wildfire. Yet despite the good news, Myra couldn't help but notice Graeson's heavy expression.

"And?" Myra prompted, sliding her hand into Phaia's for support.

"Domitius lives. He…" Graeson swallowed and shook his head.

"He's *alive*? But I thought…I thought you killed him?" Myra stammered.

"So did we. It turns out he didn't steal only from Kallie." He gave Myra a knowing look, but Myra struggled to parse what he was saying.

"He also stole from your brother."

Myra gasped and covered her mouth with a shaking hand. "Is he…?"

Graeson shook his head. "No, I'm sorry."

Myra nodded, tears biting the backs of her eyes. She had grieved her brother's death when she made the laborious journey from Ardentol to Tetria. She wasn't sure if the pain of his death would ever lessen, but for a fleeting moment, she had foolishly hoped Mynhos had made it. That she would get the chance to repair the damage she had helped cause.

Graeson continued as they strolled toward his tent. "Domitius was controlling the army the entire time. He's being detained right now, but we lost many in the fight."

"What about His Majesty?" Phaia asked as Myra asked, "And Laurince?"

"The last I saw them, they were alive, but I cannot say for certain. Once the soldiers return, we'll know," Graeson said, strolling toward the tent.

As Myra leaned against Phaia, Phaia squeezed her hand, a silent reassurance.

Laurince promised, though. He promised he would come back.

"Is that—" Graeson choked on his words as he opened the tent flap.

A tiny cry came from within the tent, and a resounding groan echoed across the camp as the newborn awoke.

As NIGHTFALL APPROACHED, soldiers slowly filed into the camp. A small smile cracked on Myra's mouth as she saw families and friends reunite. Fathers swept their children and wives into tight embraces. Mothers cried. Friends rejoiced.

Yet despite the joy that spread through the camp, Myra's gaze kept wandering to those who waited with bated breaths. Those who were approached by another—a friend or sibling or stranger —and who collapsed upon hearing the news of their loved ones' fates.

They might have ended the war, but at what cost? So many had lost their lives. So many would never come to see another day.

The grief threatened to overtake Myra. She wished she could help soothe their pain and their losses. But she knew that this was something she could not fix. Even if she had anything left to give, the grief would come back, and it would come back tenfold if she were to push it away now. Myra pressed a hand against a nearby tree, letting it ground her. Letting the life within it stabilize her. She took in a deep breath. Crushed leaves, dirt, and iron filled her senses. Her brows bunched together as the hair on her neck stood.

"Hey, Haze."

Myra's legs folded under her as Laurince's voice wrapped around her. Before she could hit the floor, strong hands were on her, spinning her around. Laurince tucked her against his chest. Myra didn't even need to see his face to know it was him. Although she still tried. She blinked through the stream of falling tears.

With the pads of his thumbs, Laurince swiped them away. "I told you I would come back for you. Did you not believe me?"

Myra tried to laugh, but the sound came out garbled, her cries mangling it.

He pressed his palms against the sides of her face, holding her steady and letting her soak him in. Myra grabbed his shirt, curling her fingers into the fabric as though she were afraid he would disappear if she let go.

"I'm so sorry," he cried, pressing his forehead against hers." I'm so sorry that I—"

She tugged him closer and smashed her mouth against his. His tears, a cold contrast to her flushed cheeks, trickled down her face. He palmed the back of her head, his fingers weaving into her hair. Their kiss was messy and clumsy and full of unspoken words. But Myra was tired of leaving things unsaid.

She pulled away from him despite everything in her body telling her to pull him closer. Her lips parted, as did his, and together they said the three words that they should have said the night before. The words that would have haunted Myra if today had ended any other way. But there he was, alive and breathing.

"I love you."

CHAPTER 94
KALLIE

WHILE THE CAPITAL CONTINUED TO SMOLDER DAYS AFTER THE BATTLE, the famed impenetrable Frenzian castle remained standing. Although its stone walls were intact, the front yard was a wasteland, the battle's destruction evident.

The chains that had been used to restrain Graeson sat in an ominous heap beside the castle steps, the metal glowing from the nearby flames. They had tried to burn them at Graeson's request, but the metal wouldn't melt.

Although when Graeson mentioned to Terin, Kallie, and a few others that his father confirmed there were other demi-gods out there, an unspoken exchange passed between them. If there were other dragons out there, who knew if they would all be friendly?

With no other option but to put them back in the dungeon, the chains would stay there for now.

After the smoke had settled, they abandoned the camp outside the capital. When they traversed through the capital before reaching the castle, Kallie could practically see the to-do list in Rian's head growing longer with every step and every destroyed building they passed. Rian nearly combusted when he found the castle steps destroyed. Kallie had intended to leave Graeson's name out of it, but Graeson had other plans, happily admitting to the deed just to piss off Rian. As if the king wasn't already enraged enough after seeing his kingdom nearly razed.

Even now, Rian couldn't help but tally off the items on his ever-growing list: resources that needed to be allocated from other kingdoms, buildings that needed to be rebuilt, interrogating the guards who had fought on Sebastian's side, questioning his mother who had been locked in the castle. He hadn't stopped debating which item should take priority since the battle had ended.

"Perhaps we should save the to-do list for another day?" Laurince suggested, sitting on the bench beside Rian.

Rian's hand fell from his hair and landed on the table with a smack. "If we do not discuss what should be a priority, then we will never—"

Laurince patted him on the back, the force of the smack jerking Rian forward. Rian's mug slipped from his hand and crashed on the ground, shattering into pieces.

"Great! Let's add new dishes to the list as well while we're at it." Rian groaned and pushed himself off the bench. He knelt on the ground and started picking up the broken pieces.

Further down, Ellie leaned forward from her seat, her hair falling over her shoulder. "You know, now that I think of it, I think you're missing something else from that list."

Rian glanced up, a horrified expression widening his eyes. "What else did I forget?"

"A statue."

"Another? Of whom?" he asked, aghast.

"You," Ellie stated with a wicked smirk.

Waving his hand dismissively, Rian returned to his task, plucking the ceramic pieces from the grass. "I don't need another statue of myself."

Amusement wrinkled the corners of Ellie's eyes. "But how else will we remember you on your knees? It's a good look, don't you think?"

Broken shards fell from Rian's hands as his mouth parted. Kallie couldn't tell if he was horrified or embarrassed.

Ellie clapped her hands. "Yes! Just like that! I think it would look lovely as an adornment in the new gardens." She looked around the table. "Don't you all agree?"

As an argument spurred to life between the pair, Kallie rose to her feet and strolled over to the pyre. Her gaze trailed up it, watching the smoke and embers whip around the night sky. With no river nearby for a proper send-off, a pyre had been built in the front yard of the castle. Its flames bounced off the stone walls and lit the faces of those gathered.

There was much to do, but for one night, everyone put those tasks to the side to celebrate their victory and honor the fallen. Those who lost friends and family threw in any belongings they had left to give. A favored clothing item, a piece of armor, a favorite flower.

Kallie looked out toward the table, taking in the group of people who sat around it.

Ellie barked out a laugh, her head tipping toward the night sky, her cheeks glowing in the fire's light. Rian spun on his heel and stormed away, his fists curled in frustration.

Myra sat beside Laurince, her head resting against his shoulder. He wrapped an arm around her and tucked her closer to his side, rubbing warmth into her arm. His wings were spread out behind him as if to shield her from the breeze that beat at their backs.

Across from them, Sylvia and Moris sat, passing a pint of ale back and forth. They held it out to Terin, but he shook his head and returned his attention to the bundle in his arms. Smiling, Terin tucked the blanket tighter around the newborn.

Kallie couldn't help but smile. There was so much loss, pain, and death around them. Yet this small group of people with the new tiny addition was living proof of the light that would come soon.

Someone nudged her in the side, and Kallie already knew who it was before he spoke.

"You know you're allowed to hold her."

Kallie shifted on her feet. "So everyone keeps saying. I'm just..." She peered up at Graeson, knowing he would understand.

"Scared?" Graeson asked.

Kallie nodded, incapable of lying to him.

She wasn't even sure what she was scared of. The child couldn't hurt her. But when she thought of holding the baby, her limbs wouldn't move. Kallie's actions had torn the child's family apart once already. The little girl was too precious, too fragile. What if something happened when the baby was in her arms? What if the moment she was in Kallie's arms, the child cried and thrashed? What if Kallie accidentally dropped her?

Kallie did not know how to take care of a baby. She had never been around many—hardly any, actually.

And in truth, Kallie didn't know if she could handle it if the child rejected her. Because how couldn't she? Kallie was the reason she was fatherless.

Just then, the child started crying, and Terin groaned, tossing his head back.

"I give her to you for less than five minutes, Ter, for a *single* moment of peace. You really can't keep her from crying before I even finish my meal?" Dani said, standing and reaching for the child. A gold necklace hung from her neck, and a dainty ring weighed the chain down.

"I did nothing! I didn't even move!" Terin held up the baby, turning her this way and that as if trying to figure out what was wrong with her.

"Just give her to me," Dani said, reaching for her daughter. "I'll just eat when she can walk, I suppose. For your sake, you better hope Finnley's a fast learner like me and not her father."

Terin handed the bundle over to Dani, who cradled her. She ran her knuckle across Finnley's round cheek. Rocking her, Dani whispered something Kallie couldn't hear.

Graeson leaned toward Kallie. "You can't be any worse than Terin. He hasn't been able to hold her for over five minutes."

A small smile cracked at the corner of Kallie's mouth, but it didn't quite reach her eyes.

"Maybe one day," she said after a moment.

Graeson wrapped an arm around her waist, pulling her against him. Understanding she didn't want to talk about it, Graeson changed the subject. "Have you decided yet about what you want to do?"

Kallie shook her head. She had been avoiding that question since the battle had ended. She wasn't sure what she wanted to do or where she wanted to go. Terin had approached her when the first group of Pontians were leaving and extended the invitation for Kallie to return home with them. Kallie, however, declined. But Terin left the offer open. The rest would head back once Dani was ready. Even with Helena staying behind, Dani still needed time to heal. Her body was sore, but she was slowly regaining her strength.

Kallie's mind drifted to the soldiers returning to Pontia under Dani's father's command with Kage in tow. Terin had proposed imprisoning Kage in Pontia, where they would had the resources to ensure his permanent imprisonment. With no better suggestion, Kallie had agreed. Rian already had his hands full. Frenzia's dungeons were a mess.

Sebastian had wrongfully imprisoned countless people, falsely accusing them of treachery. Some had been injected with a faulty serum. As soon as they were let out, the soldiers rushed them to the infirmary. It turned out Sebastian had rushed the production of the serum when the first battle began. Once the wrongfully accused were transported to the hospital ward, prisoners filled the cells, waiting to be questioned.

"You don't have to choose now," Graeson reminded her.

Kallie turned to look at him. His silver eyes instantly met hers. "Have you decided where you'll go?"

Graeson placed his hand on her face, caressing her cheek. His thumb brushed across her jaw. "I thought we were past the point of asking silly questions like that?"

Pursing her lips, Kallie shrugged. "I don't know. Maybe we are. But I just…I don't know if I'm ready to go back to Pontia yet. I still haven't quite figured things out."

"And like I said, you don't have to choose now. You don't even have to know what you wish to do a week or a month from now. If you decide you want to go to Pontia after they leave, we'll go. If you decide you want to stay here and help Rian rebuild, we'll stay."

"Really?" Kallie asked.

Graeson nodded. "We can go anywhere you want," he said, weaving his fingers into her hair. "Even Ardentol."

Kallie's lips parted.

"You think I don't realize that the people of Ardentol are also on your mind? You've lived there for most of your life. That kingdom is as much of your home as Pontia is."

Kallie stared up at him in shock. "You would really come with me?"

With no hesitation, Graeson nodded.

"But what about your friends and family?"

He lifted her hand in the space between them. In the light of the fire, the gold ring on her finger sparkled as if a fire lived within the metal. He placed a light kiss on the amethyst stone. Laying her hand on his shoulder, he slid his hand behind her back, resting it on her lower back. He stepped closer, leaving only a few inches between them as his gaze darted across her face.

"I'm a dragon, Kal, remember? They're only a flight away." He smiled at her. "Wherever you go, I go. I've waited my entire life for you. I'm not giving you up that easily. When it comes to you, no one else matters."

EPILOGUE
KAGE

PLUNK.

Plunk.

Plunk.

Kage stared at the dark ceiling, watching the condensation drip as he lay on the hard bed. The thin mattress did little to soothe the discomfort from the rods running across the frame.

With a sigh, he pushed himself up and threw his legs over the edge. The soles of his feet hit the ground, and the stone was cold beneath his skin. He padded over to the bucket sitting in the corner and relieved himself. The smell of urine filled the cell, but he barely noticed it. The cell's stench had gone unnoticed to him a while ago.

He mindlessly rubbed the manacles digging into his wrists.

When Kage had woken after the Pontians had transported him here, he hadn't known how much time had passed since the battle. When he commanded the guards to answer him, his demands went unanswered.

That first night, Kage had stared at his hands with utter disbelief. The power that he had spent his whole life searching for was silent. It was gone too soon, but there was nothing he could do. The strange, heavy iron on his wrists prevented his connection to the stolen abilities. If only he had known the manacles existed before. It would have saved him a lot of hassle. And much less blood to clean up.

For a while, Kage counted the days by meals. He quickly lost interest in that futile task, though. After all, what was the point? He knew his fate.

The seer had tried to warn him once. Kage had thought nothing of it when Lysanthia spoke of his future. Maybe he would have been able to change his fate if he had listened.

A small laugh slipped from Kage's lips as he thought of what his father would think if he could see his son. He could almost hear his father's stern voice, the disappointment and anger leaking into every word.

Kage's laughter faded when he heard the light patter of footsteps clapping against the steps. He quirked a brow. The soldiers were early.

He headed back to the bed and plopped onto it. As he waited for the soldiers to deliver his next meal, he ran a hand along the side of his neck, massaging the permanent kink. His pinky brushed the metal mask covering the lower half of his face. At least he would get a reprieve from it soon.

The clatter of keys neared, and he fixed his gaze upon the small window in the metal door. To his surprise, the window didn't creak open. Instead, the door pushed open.

Were they here to clean the cell? They hadn't done so for a while. He supposed it was time.

Anticipating the chain, Kage held out his hands, but the guard standing at the door didn't produce it.

Kage inspected the guard's uniform and noted the emblem on the chest plate. Curious about why the captain was visiting him, Kage patiently waited.

The captain pursed his lips as his gaze swept over the cell, as if Kage was only an adornment inside the room. Satisfied, he stepped to the side and ushered someone inside.

At the sight of the woman, the muscles in Kage's jaw popped. Almost on instinct, he straightened. Even after all these years, he couldn't help himself, it seemed. She still commanded his attention, just like the first time they met.

"Kage," the Queen of Pontia said in greeting.

Kage arched a brow—his only available response, and the only one he wanted to give.

Esmeray stepped inside the cell as she swept her storm-blue eyes across the space, taking it in. Her nose twitched at the scent of urine and filth.

Kage leaned his head against the wall. The mask dug into his skull, but he didn't dare show an ounce of discomfort. Instead, he remained unfazed as he observed Esmeray, and she, him.

The passage of time had transformed Esmeray's features. Her hands, which she held loosely in front of her stomach, were wrinkled. Lines creased the corners of her eyes and mouth as if her years were full of laughter. A different man would have been happy about that, but Kage hadn't felt happiness since the woman in front of him ripped out his heart.

"I would have visited sooner," Esmeray said, the sentiment spoken as if Kage was staying in some vacation home in the country rather than a prison. She tilted her chin up, a flash of emotion passing through her carefully controlled demeanor. "But I wasn't sure if I wanted to see you. If I even could without killing you myself."

Kage scoffed at that. The Esmeray he knew couldn't hurt a fly. The pain she excelled at wasn't visible to the naked eye. Her preferred form of cruelty was a deeper, insidious sort of pain. A parasite that burrowed under one's skin, clawing its way toward one's heart until it could sink its nails into it and rip it to shreds.

Esmeray's gaze turned icy, as if the raging sea within her irises was freezing over. "You took so much from me: my soul bond—"

Kage rolled his eyes at the mention of Markos. Esmeray's late husband was no more than a brute with no respect for others.

"—my daughter, my son." Esmeray stepped closer, the silk fabric of her lilac dress melting over her legs. She pursed her lips as if in disagreement about something.

She sighed and continued. "But Kalisandre believes death would be a mercy. Perhaps she is right." Esmeray grabbed the item hanging from her necklace.

Kage eyed the dainty ring she ran between two fingers. He quickly snapped his gaze away from it.

"Losing someone is strange. The grief never really goes away. We think we will always have our memories of them to hang on to. And to an extent, that is true. Many grand memories will remain. But it is the small moments people often forget that hit the hardest. The sound of one's voice, one's laugh. The way someone's smile would crack at the slightest mishap."

She slid her other hand across the markings on the wall. Her fingers trailed over the ticks etched into the stone. "I thought that with my gift, it would be easier to lose the ones I loved. I could pull on those memories and lessen the weight of their absence. I had hoped that the memories would fill the emptiness." Her hand fell from the markings on the wall. "But it only increased it. Once you're pulled out of the moment and forced to live in the present again, the mourning period restarts all over."

Kage narrowed his gaze, unsure what game she was playing. Because that was the thing with Esmeray: their relationship had always felt like a game, one he wasn't sure he ever received the rule book for. He didn't even know if a rule book existed.

At first, that had been one characteristic that had intrigued him about her, second to her beauty. When Kage had found her in the woods, the young woman's brazen attitude and fiery spirit had shocked him. Esmeray was unlike anyone else he had ever encountered. She was certainly the opposite of the woman whom Kage's father had wanted him to marry. Opposite of Troia in all ways.

He wondered whether that version of Esmeray still existed.

When Kage looked at her, he didn't believe so.

At least, that's what he surmised from the lilac dress she wore. Although the silk fabric fell over her frame and draped her hips elegantly, it made her nearly unrecognizable. The shade of purple, though beautiful on her, was a color she had despised when she was younger. Whenever she had passed lilacs during their time together, she had shaken them from the trees with an angry vigor. An act that made Kage chuckle the first time he had seen her do it. But then she had explained why she hated the seemingly harmless flowers. Lilacs were all over the castle in Pontia. In the spring, they adorned every corner, every vase. The shade alone reminded Esmeray of her future, of the cage she was destined for once she claimed her title.

Now, as queen, she voluntarily wore it.

Esmeray cocked her head to the side. "I'm curious, Kage. Do you remember when we first met?"

When he didn't nod or shake his head, her gaze dropped to his hands, which were now rolled into tight fists on his lap.

"So you do," she mused.

He silently cursed his hands for their betrayal and uncurled his fingers, revealing the deep red grooves marking his skin.

"You see, I wasn't sure if you did," Esmeray said. "Because so many memories have been erased from this world—your wife's name, your past. When I realized I couldn't remember Troia's name years ago, I was confused. I'm fairly good at remembering a name once I hear it, if you recall."

She was now standing within arm's reach of him. Kage could grab her easily and break her neck with a flick of his wrist. He had broken many necks since he was a child. It wasn't that hard. One sharp tug, and then *crack.*

But Kage didn't move.

He didn't react.

Not even when Esmeray reached out a hand, her long elegant fingers worn with time. She scraped her nail across the iron mask. There was a time when he longed for her touch more than anything. But that was a lifetime ago.

The bone-jarring screech caused him to squeeze his eyes shut as a shiver ran down his spine.

Her fingers wrapped around his neck, and his eyes sprang open as she tightened her grip around his throat. Esmeray's face was mere inches from his. A storm thundered within her irises, roaring as violently as a tempest.

"Let's take a trip down memory lane, shall we?"

And before he could stop it, Kage was falling.

EPILOGUE
KALLIE

Some years later

KALLIE TAPPED HER FINGERS ALONG THE ARM OF THE CHERRY-OAK chair. She shifted in the seat, the new velvet cushion still a little too plump to be comfortable. Grabbing the quill, she dipped the tip into the pot of ink, then began scrawling across the blank piece of parchment. Around her, the aimless chatter continued. Those sitting around the table parried fruitless arguments back and forth from one side of the table to the other.

Kallie looked out the window toward the mountains. The sun rested high in the sky, its beams blinding. It was almost high noon. She tapped her nails on the top of her thigh beneath the table.

If she didn't leave soon, she would be late.

"Must we discuss this every meeting, Jordan?" a woman a few chairs down from Kallie asked. She sat with her chin in her hand and her elbow resting on the table. Even she was bored with the conversation.

"I'll stop bringing it up once my sheep stop disappearing!" Jordan turned in his seat. "Your Majesty, can you please tell—"

Kallie lifted her hand, and Jordan snapped his mouth shut as everyone turned toward her.

With a sigh, Kallie scooted closer. Resting one arm on the table, she held up the letter. "I have already written a letter about your grievances, Lord Hare, stressing the importance that King Rian once again get a hold of the drakonises."

"They escape every year!" Jordan whined, pressing his palms against the sides of his head. "How am I supposed to ensure the safety of my sheep if—"

"It will be handled, Jordan," Kallie said, having had her fill of his complaints for one afternoon. Lord Hare meant well, and his patience with the drakonises over the past few years was commendable. But there was only so much Kallie could do. "The crown will provide you with the funds for new sheep."

"*New* sheep? One cannot simply replace my sweet Laia! She was my favorite of the herd."

Kallie lifted a brow. "Do you not wish for the funds, Lord Hare? We're happy to give them to another lord or lady who—"

"No, no," Jordan said, sinking back into his chair with a frown. "Thank you, Your Majesty." He nodded his head in gratitude, although he continued to sulk.

A woman sitting next to him patted him on the shoulder empathetically for his priceless sheep.

"Now, with that settled, I have an agenda to keep to, as I'm sure we all do." Kallie pushed back her chair. "Until next time."

The council members stood and bowed their heads to Kallie as she strolled around the table. When she reached the doors, the guard pushed them open.

Kallie smiled at Penelope, one of her favorite guards. "My apologies that you had to stand through that again, Penelope."

Penelope shrugged. "No apologies necessary, Your Majesty."

Kallie slipped out of the meeting room, leaving the rest of the council members to their goodbyes.

"I thought this one was supposed to be short?" a warm voice asked.

Kallie snorted and said, "It was supposed to be." Although it was annoying that the meeting had gone on longer than expected, she couldn't help but smile when she turned and found Graeson leaning on the wall beside the doors to the council meeting.

With a huff, he bent down and grabbed the bag resting at his feet. As he did, Kallie let herself admire his muscles that strained against the fabric of his shirt.

Cocking a brow, Graeson held out his arm. "Ready?"

Kallie easily took his offer and looped her arm around his. With a squeeze, he brought her closer, their hips bumping into each other and causing Kallic to laugh. He pressed a light kiss on the top of her head, and she hummed, soaking in his warmth.

As they walked, a light breeze, cool against her skin, whisked into the corridor, brushing her cheek and sending a loose strand of hair dancing. On the windowsill, two crimson birds perched, preening their feathers. As Graeson and Kallie passed, the birds took flight, their melodic song drifting in the wind.

When they were far enough away from the council members, Kallie leaned toward Graeson. "You wouldn't know why a flock of sheep has gone missing recently, would you?"

He snorted. "Not me, little mouse. I don't fly hungry."

She eyed him suspiciously. "And Nyrri?"

Graeson gave her a side-eyed glance before turning down the hall to the right. "What Nyrri does when she ventures off the path is her business."

Kallie pursed her lips. "I thought as much."

She would have to speak with the drakonis and remind her of the boundaries. Although Kallie knew it was basically a lost cause.

Where Nyrri went was her business, and no one could stop her. Kallie had tried multiple times, but the drakonis was as stubborn as Graeson, especially when it came to flying.

"Any luck today?" Kallie asked.

Graeson shook his head. "They'll show themselves when they're ready."

Kallie nodded.

Once things had settled after the war, Graeson had started searching for others like him, following any whispers and rumor he heard. So far, he hadn't found any other demi-gods. Kallie had once asked if there was a chance that Barinthian had lied to him, but Graeson didn't believe that was the case.

Maybe he was right. Maybe they would reveal themselves when they were ready.

"Is the council prepared for your absence?" Graeson asked, changing the subject.

Kallie would have been lying if she had said she hated attending the council meetings. Some of them might have been longer than she desired or more tedious, but she enjoyed being a part of the conversations. When the war ended, Kallie was unsure what she wanted to do. Without Kage, she didn't know if she had a place in Ardentol. It was hard at first to decide what she wanted her life to look like. For so long, Kage controlled her desires and wishes. But the moment she stepped into the castle to gather her things, she couldn't leave.

The civilians were scared and on the verge of civil unrest when Graeson and Kallie had arrived. The council was in complete disarray, with too many lords unsurprisingly trying to take charge. Domitius had trained them to compete to gain his attention, money, and support. It was only natural for them to do the same for who would lead in his absence.

Kallie hadn't even realized what she was doing when she

stormed through the castle and demanded a meeting. From there, the shape of the council shifted. New members were added, and old members, who supported Domitius' war, were voted out. The first year was hard, excruciatingly so. But Kallie and Ardentol persevered. Now it was shaping into a kingdom she was proud to call hers. Kallie was not Kage by any means, but she didn't want to be. When the council and the people of Ardentol looked at her, they didn't cower in fear or bow their heads to avert her gaze. They listened, they waited, they smiled.

She loved this kingdom. It was part of her. But all the same, Kallie was looking forward to getting away with Graeson for a little.

For her entire life, she had struggled with the idea of having a home. She had lived in Ardentol most of her life, but it wasn't hers then. When she had learned she was Pontian, she was even more confused. She felt as if she was split in two. It was one of the many reasons she struggled to decide where to go after the war. A part of her wanted to be in Pontia, to spend time with the family that was taken from her. The other part of her longed for the comfort of the Ardentolian mountains.

She looked at Graeson as they walked through the marble halls, their steady steps soft claps against the floors. Her gift stirred within her, reaching out to him.

Over the past few years, Kallie finally realized the true meaning of home.

She shrugged. "I believe they can survive on their own for a little while."

Graeson paused and peered down at her with a rueful smile. "Think we have time for a pit stop?"

Kallie smacked him playfully in the chest with the back of her hand. "Dani will kill us if we're late."

Graeson scoffed as he reached behind him and pushed a door open. "I'd like to see her try to take me down."

"Gray."

Even in Graeson's dragon form, Dani was still a woman to be feared when provoked.

Yet as Graeson's eyes darkened as he stepped backward into the shadows of the room with his hand outstretched, Kallie could do nothing else but grab his hand.

The moment her hand landed in his, he yanked her toward him. Their chests slammed against each other. With a flick, he shut the door, locking it behind them.

"I promise it'll be quick, Your Majesty," he said, his voice tickling the side of her neck as he brushed his jaw across it. He hadn't shaved yet, and his scruff scratched Kallie's neck, sending a chill running down her spine. She arched into him.

"I suppose we can spare a few minutes," she said, her eyes fluttering shut as Graeson pressed soft kisses along the column of her neck, down to her collarbone. "You'll just have to ride harder."

Graeson laughed, and the vibration of it sent goosebumps scattering across her skin. "You'll be the one riding, My Queen."

KALLIE INHALED, and the salt of the sea tickled her nose. Beneath them, the Red Sea glittered the brightest shade of blue she had ever seen.

Her body ached, but she'd rather suffer the post-flight soreness than endure a boat's nauseating rocking motion.

Graeson glanced back at her. At the sparkle of wickedness shining in his molten silver eyes, Kallie's heart fluttered with excitement. Anticipating Graeson's next move, she adjusted her grip on the saddle's pommel, silently thanking Medenia for the early gift. With no other warning, Graeson banked left. Then he dove, and the leather belt dug into Kallie's stomach as she rose from the seat.

The sea's roar grew louder as they plunged toward the water. Right before they hit the waves, Graeson evened out, flying parallel to the water's surface. The waves crashed against his belly. He dipped his wing into the water, slicing a wave in two and causing water to spray up.

A wide smile split across Kallie's face as droplets dampened her cheeks. Laughing, she shook her head. She would get him back later.

Graeson leveled out once more, flying over the water's surface. Up ahead, waves crashed against the familiar cliffs. Kallie's heart pounded as they approached them, her body instinctively bracing for impact despite the number of times they had made this trip. She glanced over her shoulder. Enormous waves chased after them as if Pontanius himself was welcoming them back and ushering them forward.

With her fingers flexing over the pommel, Kallie took a deep breath. When she exhaled, Graeson flew harder.

Right before they met the cliffs, Graeson shot up, soaring through the air and beating the wave up the cliff. As the wind smacked into her, Kallie squeezed her eyes closed, unable to keep them open. She knew when they surpassed the cliffs the moment her weight shifted back and her hair flew into her face.

Opening her eyes, Kallie sat up and took in the sight before her. Graeson glided over the Pontian plains. The lavender field was in full bloom, its floral aroma mixing with the salt and immediately releasing the tension in her shoulders from the long trip. The stone castle peaked over the hill, and her attention flicked to the clearing right before it, where she spotted several small specks. As they approached, those specks took shape, morphing into familiar figures. Graeson tipped his head up and roared, a small streak of fire pouring from his mouth in greeting.

Kallie rolled her eyes at the ostentatious spectacle. But as the smoke cleared and she saw a tiny figure bouncing with excitement, her annoyance melted away.

Graeson spread out his wings, slowing their descent. His feet landed in the center of the clearing, bringing them to a smooth stop.

Kallie held her breath, preparing for the inevitable—

Crash.

Kallie coughed as Nyrri's less than graceful landing kicked up a cloud of sand. As she swatted at the debris, a fit of giggles sounded to her right.

Dani's voice boomed across the field. "Finnley! What did I say about waiting until we gave you the all-clear?"

Kallie chuckled and unclasped the belt. She crawled out of the saddle and carefully stood. Holding out her arms for balance, she gave her legs a moment to adjust before shuffling toward Graeson's tail and hurrying down it. The moment her feet hit the sand, someone swooped her up into a giant hug. The world spun around her.

"It's been too long, sister," Terin said as he placed her back on her toes.

"We were here two months ago," Kallie said, her vision still spinning.

"Yes, but you were only here for a week that time." He ruffled her hair.

Rolling her eyes, she snatched her brother's wrist and dipped under his arm, escaping his torment. She grabbed the bag beside Graeson's foot and tossed it at Terin, who caught it in one hand. "Well, we're here longer this time," she said.

"Thank goodness for that," Dani said, coming up behind Kallie and squeezing her arm with a warm smile. "Finnley hasn't stopped whining since Nyrri left."

A weight knocked into Kallie, and small arms wrapped around her leg, squeezing her tightly.

Beaming, Kallie bent down, untangled Finnley from her leg, and hoisted the child into her arms. "How's my favorite princess?"

Finnley wrapped her arms around Kallie's neck, nearly choking Kallie. Light brunette curls flew into her mouth as Finnley squeezed her. Kallie tried to brush the strands away while maintaining her hold on the child, but failed. Finnley's curls were nearly as uncontrollable as she was.

Finnley leaned back and looked up at Kallie with wide hazel eyes. "Mom said I get to wear a pretty dress!"

Kallie booped her on the tip of her nose. "That's right."

"She also said I get to ride Nyrri down the aisle!"

"Did she now?" Kallie asked, peering at Dani, who rolled her eyes at her child's blatant lie. "And did Grandma Essie approve of this?"

"She said to ask Uncle Gray."

Kallie narrowed her eyes at her niece, whose cheeks turned bright pink. "Did she, Finnie?"

Finnley pursed her lips and slumped against Kallie's chest. "No," she mumbled, disappointed she was caught.

Kallie laughed. Graeson would have given Finnley anything she asked, and the child knew it. But Esmeray would throw a fit if Nyrri was brought inside the castle. There was no way the drakonis would fit down the aisle. Even if she could, Nyrri would not be able to sit still for the entire ceremony. It was a recipe for disaster.

"Where's my little dragon?"

Finnley popped her head back up and squirmed against Kallie until Kallie had to put her down to keep her from falling. The moment her feet hit the ground, Finnley sprinted toward Graeson, who had already shifted and thrown on a pair of trousers.

As Graeson swept Finnley up into his arms, Kallie's attention turned to the rest of the group, who came to welcome them. She smiled and waved at Moris and Sylvia, then finally turned her attention to the woman standing to the side, patiently waiting with her hands folded in front of her lap. When their gazes locked, they strolled towards each other and pulled one another into an embrace.

Kallie sighed into Esmeray's hair, which smelled of lavender and mint. She had missed her mother's hugs.

After the war ended, it took Kallie some time to see Esmeray—more time than her mother probably would have liked. But Kallie had to sort through too many things. Their reunion was awkward at best, and it had taken them a while to familiarize themselves with each other again. Although Kallie understood the sacrifices her mother had to make, it was hard to forgive her. Esmeray, thankfully, understood that and gave Kallie the space she needed.

"Welcome home, darling," Esmeray whispered.

"It's good to be back," Kallie said, pulling back. She gave her mother a shaky smile.

Esmeray grabbed Kallie's hands in hers and squeezed them. "Nervous?"

"More than I thought I would be."

"It's all right to be nervous. I was nervous when I married your father."

"Oh, I almost ran out on Fynn," Dani said, butting into their conversation.

"You did not!" Kallie gasped.

"Oh, she most certainly did," Sylvia said, bumping Dani with their hip. "Fynn had to calm her down."

"Give me a break! It was a big day," Dani said, crossing her arms.

Sylvia snorted. "You were already soul bonds. What's the difference?"

Dani and Kallie exchanged a look, a silent understanding passing between them.

There wasn't a difference between accepting the soul bond and the formal ceremony, but it felt like there was. That was probably why Kallie had been delaying the wedding, finding every excuse possible. The war had already heightened so many things, and she was content with her relationship with Graeson as it was. After accepting the bond, the wedding was just a symbolic ceremony.

Plus, there was the rebuilding of Ardentol and the reconfiguring of the council to consider at the time. She didn't want to be rushed —with any of it—so she kept putting it off.

Kallie wasn't sure who she was after the war, and attaching herself to Graeson would only complicate things further. She wanted to discover who she was first.

It also didn't help that her last wedding had turned into a massive catastrophe. Although she hadn't said as much, she feared weddings were cursed.

Through all this, Graeson was more patient than she deserved. But he was always giving her more than she thought she deserved.

As Graeson chased an unsuspecting Nyrri through the lavender fields with Finnley on his shoulders, Kallie's nerves disappeared on the wind.

Her family surrounded her. Nothing else mattered.

Want to stay updated about upcoming releases, ARC opportunities, and more? Be sure to subscribe to Neena's Newsletter.

Author's Note

Thank you for reading *The Kingdom's Reckoning*, the fourth and final book in the *Of Fire and Lies* series! This series has my whole heart, and now it belongs to you too.

Since fourth grade (and probably even earlier), I've dreamed of being an author. For years, I tucked that dream away, telling myself there would be time "someday." In January 2022, I finally stopped waiting and chose to put my dream first.

Three years, fives books, and countless late nights (and breakdowns) later, I'm here, writing the last pages of this series. To say it feels surreal is an understatement.

When I first started writing the *Of Fire & Lies* series, I knew I wanted to tell the story of a young woman who reclaimed her voice. What I didn't realize was how much writing Kallie's journey would help me reclaim my own. While her story may have ended, she will forever be a part of me.

If you enjoyed this book, I'd be so grateful if you left a review on Amazon or Goodreads. Reviews are so important to authors and help readers find books that are a good fit for them!

And who knows? Maybe we'll see some of these characters again…

Acknowledgments

This book almost knocked me out. Writing a finale is not for the faint of heart, and I wouldn't have been able to do it without my amazing support system.

First and foremost, Nathan—my husband, my best friend, and my anchor. Thank you for listening to my endless rambling about plot lines and character arcs, for being my rock during every hard moment, and for always reminding me to believe in myself.

Jess, thank you for always reading the messy drafts, for going on writing dates that more often than not turned into yap sessions, and for giving me the confidence to finish this story. I am so incredibly lucky to have a friend as talented, kind, and supportive as you.

Gabby, thank you for being my sounding board and for always being up for bookish adventures. You have supported this series from the very beginning, and I am forever grateful for you.

To Liz and Lauren, thank you for the constant support and encouragement.

To my family and friends, thank you for continuing to cheer me on. I love you all deeply.

To the authors, artists, and readers I've been lucky enough to connect with along the way, your kindness, creativity, and generosity inspire me daily. I'm so grateful to be a part of this community.

Thank you to my cover designer, Bianca, for designing a stunning cover that beautifully captures Kallie's journey.

To Millie, thank you for bringing each stage of Kallie's story to life with your breathtaking illustrations.

To Kay, my editor, thank you for always going above and beyond (and for never blinking an eye when I text you random, wild ideas).

And finally, to you, the reader. When I started writing this series over three years ago, I wondered if anyone would pick it up. And now, here you are at the very end. Thank you for believing in this story, for loving these characters (and their flaws), and for giving this series a place in your heart. It means more than I could ever put into words.

With love,
Neena

ABOUT THE AUTHOR

Neena Laskowski lives in Michigan with her husband and their two pets. She earned her master's in Secondary Education and bachelor's in English and Classical Studies from the University of Michigan. When she is not reading or writing about morally grey characters, you can find her camping, painting, or spending time with her family and friends.

For upcoming ARC opportunities and to be among the first to see cover reveals, character art, and more, be sure to join Neena Laskowski's newsletter, found on neenalaskowski.com, or follow Neena on social media.

9 781965 861004